Sweden
Norway
Finland
Helsinki
Oslo
Stockholm
Tallinn
Estonia
Russia
Latvia
Moscow
Riga
Denmark
Lithuania
Copenhagen
Vilnius
Minsk
Poland
Belarus
Berlin
Germany
Warsaw
Kiev
Czech Rep
Prague
Ukraine
Vienna
Slovakia
Austria
Bratislava
Hungary
Vaduz
Chisinau
Liechtenstein
Slovenia
Budapest
Moldova
Ljubljana
Croatia
Venice
Zagreb
Romania
Serbia
Bosnia/
Herzegovina
Belgrade
Bucharest
San Marino
Sarajevo
Kosovo
Sofia
Pristina
Montenegro
Bulgaria
Podgorica
Rome
Skopje
Italy
Tirana
Albania
Greece
Malta
Valletta

THE ROT

THE RAVEN RINGS

SIRI PETTERSEN

THE ROT

Translated by Siân Mackie
and Paul Russell Garrett

ARCTIS

This is a work of fiction. Names, characters, places, and incidents are from the author's imaginations or are used fictitiously.

This translation has been published with the financial support of NORLA, Norwegian Literature Abroad.

W1-Media, Inc.
Imprint Arctis
Stamford, CT, USA

Råta first published in Norway by Gyldendal, 2014
First English-language edition published by W1-Media Inc./Arctis, 2021

Visit our website at www.arctis-books.com
Author website at www.siripettersen.com

1 3 5 7 9 8 6 4 2

Library of Congress Control Number: 2021936135

ISBN 978-1-64690-001-5
eBook ISBN 978-1-64690-601-7

Printed in Germany, European Union

To everyone who loved Odin's Child
and just couldn't shut up about it.

*And to you. The one who is passionate about the planet.
The one fighting alone because the distance between
your dream and our reality is just too great. The one who wants
to leave the world in a better place than it was when you
arrived. The one who has always known we're going
in the wrong direction. This book is for you.*

PROLOGUE

He sat in the tunnel between platforms, a cardboard sign propped against his knees. His face was hidden by greasy hair, but there was no doubt. It was him. And the tube doors were about to shut.

Stefan shoved a teenager aside and elbowed his way through the crowded carriage. He was glad he had earbuds in. They blocked out the chorus of complaints. An old woman's mouth opened and shut like a goldfish, but all he heard was Trent Reznor.

He had to get off the train. Now. He'd lost the bugger twice already, and he wasn't going to lose him a third time. Stefan flung himself toward the closing doors. His arm got caught, but he made it through. He stumbled out onto the platform before the train screeched off.

There were people everywhere. The fluorescent lighting sucked the life out of their faces, making them look like zombies. But none of them were so dead that they wouldn't react if he did what he had to do down here. He had to find another way. Another place.

He walked into the tunnel. The beggar held out his hand without looking up. Stefan grinned.

"Hey, Roast."

Roast raised his head. The recognition barely had time to flash in his eyes before he was on his feet. Quicker than what seemed possible. He took off, running up the tunnel. Dressed in black and disheveled, like a crow. Stefan raced after him. The sound of his shoes pounding against the floor echoed off the tiled walls. He squeezed through a ticket barrier, leaped up the stairs in three bounds, and came out on the street.

Rain pelted his face. It was dark. Roast was almost in his grasp, but then he cut out into the traffic, darting in front of cars that veered away.

Stefan didn't hesitate. Instinct drove him onward. Brakes squealed. He braced himself against the wet hood of a car and resumed his chase. Screeching car horns intermingled with the music.

He cut across Soho Square and gained a few meters. People were watching, but nobody was going to get involved. Not when his prey was a vagrant.

Roast sent people flying as he cut through St Anne's Court, took a left, and continued past Flat White, the coffee bar where they'd first met. Stefan's lungs were burning, but he was willing to bet Roast was faring worse than him.

He was right. The beggar slowed down. Looked around in despair, then stole inside a nightclub.

Stefan pushed past some people and followed him inside. Roast was easy to spot: a scruffy mess among all the tight dresses and plunging necklines.

Roast ran toward an emergency exit. Opened the door and slipped out. Stefan was there before the door managed to shut. He tumbled out into an alley. A dead end. The beggar stood in a corner by the dumpsters, snarling like a caged animal.

"Game over, Roast." Stefan walked toward him.

Roast backed up against the wall, bumping into a drainpipe. Some plaster came loose around the fasteners, sprinkling onto his shoulder. The rain washed it down his faded coat. "I didn't do nothing! I didn't do nothing!" he screamed hysterically.

That wasn't true. He didn't get the nickname Roast by chance, but Stefan couldn't bother pointing that out. It wasn't like there was anything human left to discuss it with.

Stefan was gleefully aware that he had the upper hand. He could keep the Glock by his hip. Save a bullet. Instead he pulled out a pair of pliers.

Roast's eyes widened. He scanned the alley for something to defend himself with. He tore off a metal fastener from the drainpipe, sending the bolts tumbling to the ground. He started to hammer away at his own teeth, splitting his lip. The apparent absence of pain indicated that adrenaline was far from the only drug coursing through his body.

Roast spat into his hand and held out his arm. "Take 'em! Take 'em! You can't touch me. They'll find you if you do! The pigs will find you!" Red mist sprayed from his mouth as he screamed.

Stefan looked at the two white nuggets in Roast's grubby hand. Rain collected around them in a bloody pool.

"Idiot," he replied. "The pigs don't give a shit how you die. Do you think they would waste a penny on you? You're forgotten. Or had you forgotten?"

Stefan didn't wait for a response. He rammed his elbow into the bridge of Roast's nose, sending his head into the wall with a *thump*. He swooped up the teeth before Roast hit the ground. Then he dragged the unconscious body into the corner behind the dumpster, which looked like it was vomiting, the lid straining to contain all the garbage. The smells combined. Rotten food. Blood. And a stench that made it clear Roast no longer took his toilet visits very seriously. Understandable, perhaps, after more than a hundred years.

Stefan tried to snap his neck. But Roast was sturdy. It took two tries before he heard the crack.

He pocketed the teeth and surveyed the scene. No windows. No cameras. No people. He was safe. The pavement glistened. The rain beat against the lid of the dumpster. Stefan ran a hand through his wet hair. He put the pliers back into his bag, straightened his jacket, then cranked up the volume.

THE HOLE

"Peace of mind is all we're asking for," Telja Vanfarinn said, placing her hand over her heart, making the chain looped around her neck jingle.

Rime almost burst out laughing. Anyone, even if they hadn't grown up in Mannfalla, would have seen through that performance. Telja was wearing a black dress with sleeves that brushed the floor. She was playing the part of a widow, even though her husband stood large as life by her side. The grief was nothing more than an act. Put on to ingratiate herself with the Council, after she had shrewdly wormed her way into a meeting with them.

"It's tearing us apart, Rime-fadri. Not knowing. Not understanding Urd's death."

Rime felt his lip start to curl. Urd's name still made him feel ill, and it didn't seem like that was going to change anytime soon. Not as long as his chair remained empty. It was a gaping wound that divided the circle of councillors settled around the table. Perilous. Festering. Impossible to talk about without causing an uproar that could wake half of Slokna.

"You have received our condolences," Rime replied. "I personally visited the head of the Vanfarinn family. She knows what happened. You're … the daughter of her sister?" He looked at Telja, who had approached the council table unbidden.

"Ravenbearer, our mother is old," Telja said, skirting the question.

"Her memory is not what it once was. You have honored us with your visit to her, but … some of the things she says you told her, they're … well …" Telja adjusted her necklace.

"Incredible," Darkdaggar finished. "So incredible that we would expect the family to want confirmation from the man who was actually there when Urd died."

Rime had seen the attack coming, but he hadn't expected it to be so blatant. He looked at the councillor. "Would you have me dragged before the assembly, Darkdaggar?"

"Certainly not, Ravenbearer. The Vanfarinn family simply wants to put an end to the matter." Darkdaggar smiled, but the light cutting across his face made it appear colorless. Lifeless. Drained. A stark contrast to the golden walls behind him, which were divided into twelve panels, detailing each councillor's family tree. They branched up the vaulted ceiling, giving Rime the sense of sitting in a cage. The back of his chair felt like a wall, pinning him to the table.

He was trapped. Chained to a chair that would never feel like his own. It belonged to Ilume. His mother's mother. And he'd sworn never to occupy it. But here he sat. Councillor. Rime-fadri. Ravenbearer. Surrounded by enemies who spent every waking moment plotting his downfall.

"Put an end to the matter?" Sigra Kleiv folded muscular arms across her chest. "Urd was killed at Ravnhov, and as long as those barbarians are not made to answer for it, the matter will never die."

Rime felt himself becoming more and more irritated. It was an effort to stay seated. "This is the last time I'll say this, Sigra. The war has been called off. Accept it. Ravnhov can't be brought before the assembly for something the blind did."

Sigra drew her breath to reply, but Darkdaggar beat her to it.

"Possibly not, but then I don't suppose we can drag the blind before the assembly either, can we?" He sipped some wine as laughter spread around the table.

Rime looked at Telja Vanfarinn. Her cheeks were a fervent red. She could sense the shifting mood in the room. It made her bolder. Her veil of sorrow lifted.

"We might have done, except nobody's ever seen one." She smiled.

Rime stood up. "Nobody?"

Telja's smile withered. She looked at Darkdaggar pleadingly. Rime wasn't surprised. Darkdaggar was the one who had granted her an audience, and Rime expected they'd had many conversations in advance of this meeting. How many points of attack they'd settled on remained to be seen.

"Don't take it personally, Ravenbearer," Darkdaggar said. "Telja is just pointing out what we all know. What's most conspicuous about the deadborn is their complete absence. Who claims to have seen them? A handful of Kolkagga? Is it any wonder people talk of delusions? Of people being poisoned? Or maybe eating something that didn't agree with them? Or being subjected to … sorcery?"

Laughter broke out around the table. Rime clenched his fists and moved closer to Telja. She took a couple of steps back, her dress sweeping the floor. Rime pointed at her.

"The only reason you're standing here is because many in this room remain loyal to the Vanfarinn family. I do not. Calling me and my men liars is not going to help you."

Telja's gaze flickered between Rime and Darkdaggar. "I would never … I didn't say … The mind is a fragile thing, Ravenbearer. It's said that many strong men have seen trolls in the fog, and we—"

"Trolls in the fog?" Rime caught her gaze. Held it. The wrinkles around her eyes revealed that she was older than he had first thought. Maybe that was where her boldness came from. It was now or never for her.

"My sword has tasted blood from what you believe to be a myth. I've driven steel through them and seen the life leave their sightless eyes. Felt their breath. Heard them snarl. And I've smelled the stench of their burning corpses. A smell you'd carry with you to Slokna, Telja."

The laughter died down. Telja swallowed and lowered her gaze.

"In the name of the Seer," Darkdaggar chimed in. "Must we really be so dramatic? All the family asks is for the wound to be healed. They've lost a councillor, Ravenbearer."

Everyone turned to look upon the empty chair. There could be no doubt as to what they believed would heal the wound.

Rime looked at Telja again. "Really? Would this chair give you the answers you require? Would you stop wondering how he died if one of your own sat at this table?"

Telja hesitated but had enough decency to shake her head.

"Of course not," Darkdaggar said. "But at least it would offer assurance that Urd was not done away with in order to free up a seat."

The room fell silent. The accusation was blatant, and to make it in the presence of outsiders? Rime looked at each of them in turn. Men and women three or four times his age. They remained silent. Most of them because they supported Darkdaggar. A few because they didn't want to make matters worse.

Telja Vanfarinn took a step toward Rime. "Ravenbearer, you must forgive us. We're speaking out of grief. All this talk about the blind and stone ways ... For us, this is unfathomable. Nobody has seen proof of—"

"Nonsense!" Jarladin interrupted. "The Rite Hall was full of people when Kolkagga burst through the gateways and the walls crumbled. If you want proof, you can buy a chunk of the red dome down by the harbor!"

Telja seized upon the opportunity lustfully, as if it were up for negotiation. "A rite hall full of people means many stories, Jarladin-fadri. Forgive us, we were not there. We heard only that the building shook. Some say that the walls had been weakened by the dome. Others say it was the earth that shook."

Darkdaggar clasped his hands behind his head. "Such a tragedy that we're unable to reassure you, Telja. That would have made things so much easier. But the truth is that the gateways are as dead today as they have been for the past thousand years. Isn't that right, Ravenbearer?" He looked at Rime, his eyes glinting in triumph.

Rime clenched his teeth. This had gone on for too long. He'd opened the door a crack and now the wolves were squeezing through. Diplomacy was not going to help him anymore.

"People can talk until they rot in Slokna," he said. "Just as they've always done. It changes nothing. I was there. I know what happened. Urd built his own funeral pyre. He was a rabid dog."

Sigra let out an exaggerated gasp. A spark was lit in Telja's eyes. It was all she could do to hold back a smile. She grabbed a black bundle from her husband's arms. Held it up. It was a tunic, which someone had cut into. On the chest, where the mark of the Seer should have been, there was nothing but a gash. A gaping hole above the heart.

"This belonged to an augur, Ravenbearer. An augur who went out on the Ora where the ice was thin. Nobody has seen him since. They say he lost his mind. And that he was not the first. I do accept that Urd was peculiar, Rime-fadri, but he was never crazy. Maybe it was the loss of the Seer that drove him to melancholy. Maybe that was why he acted as he did. And, with that in mind, perhaps it could be said the entire matter was … well …"

Rime could hardly believe his ears. He looked at her. "My fault?"

She bit her lip. Measured him with her gaze.

He stared at the tunic, feeling nauseous. The hole threatened to draw him in. Consume him. A dark void.

He stepped closer to Telja. Her husband held out a protective arm. A pointless reflex. Rime grabbed him by the wrist and forced him back without so much as glancing at him. Telja gathered up her skirts as if preparing to run.

Rime leaned toward her. “Urd killed Ilume right in front of me. My mother’s mother. He broke open the raven rings. Let the dead-born into Ym. Driven to madness by his own blindcraft. No, I didn’t kill him. But I can promise you that if I’d had the chance, I would have done so without batting an eyelid. Take a good look at the chair, Telja, because you’ll never see it again.”

“Enough!” Sigra slammed her fist against the table. Leivlugn Taid gave a start next to her, his double chin quivering. His goblet tipped over. The old man had dozed through most of the meeting and had hardly touched his wine. It spread across the table. Chairs scraped against the floor as everyone scrambled to save their robes.

“This meeting is over,” Rime said. He opened the balcony doors and stepped out onto the bridge, drawing the cold air into his lungs. It was one of the oldest bridges in Eisvaldr, the one he used to cross to get to the Rite Hall. Now it protruded into nothingness, like a frozen tongue. Stone serpents hung out over the edge as if clinging to it. Rime realized he was doing the same, so he let go of the balustrade. The warmth of his hands left an impression in the frost.

On the ground far below was the raven ring. Pale stone pillars witnessing their first winter after a thousand years hidden in the walls. They were dead. No use to anyone. He’d spent entire nights binding the Might in front of them. Drawing upon it until the pressure in his temples was unbearable, but the stone way refused to open for him. He might as well have dreamed that it once had. Darkdaggar had spoken the truth. The gateways had disappeared the moment Hirka passed through them. Taking her away from him.

He heard heavy footsteps behind him. Jarladin came up beside him and stared at the end of the bridge. “If you just keep walking, you'll spare them the bother," he said, the wind toying with his white beard.

Rime chuckled. "I wouldn't give any of them that pleasure. If they want me dead, they'll have to see to it themselves."

Jarladin sighed. "Their patience is wearing thin, Rime. You can't continue being dismissive of them. Not without being brought before the assembly in chains. Darkdaggar crossed the line, but you're not even *trying* to unite them. If you don't set aside your hatred, it's going to be the downfall of you and me both."

Rime was about to say that he didn't hate anyone, but that would have been a lie. He hated them for ruling under a false seer, hated how they bent reality to their will. The intrigue. The lies. The bitter truth was that everyone around that table had no goal other than to keep their chair.

Jarladin thumped Rime on the back, as if that would help matters. "Anyway, they have a point. Several augurs have left us, and that will have consequences."

"Has no one told you that you can't force people to stay?" Rime felt exposed by his own words. He tore his gaze away from the stone circle. Pounded his hands against the balustrade. "This is senseless! They saw it with their own eyes! They saw the walls come down and the stones appear. They know the blind were here. They know the truth as well as I do, but they cast doubt because it serves the Council's interests."

Jarladin looked at him. "Is that what motivates you? Being right? Nonsense. You've never cared about your own position. Had you done so, you would have secured your family's future."

Rime turned away. Jarladin was an ox of a man, and his only friend around the table, but that certainly didn't mean he was any easier to deal with.

"I've said what I'm going to say on the matter. Kolkagga are bound to Kolkagga alone."

"Since when have you cared about rules, Rime? You could plow your way through the entire library without finding a single rule you haven't already broken. At least choose a reason I can believe."

"Do you think I'm an idiot? You and the Council want me to start a family because it would strengthen *you*. Not me."

Jarladin put his hand on the back of Rime's neck and held him firmly, like a father might. "Rime … our interests should be the same."

Rime closed his eyes, listening to the old ox's voice in his ear.

"Listen to me. You cannot let her control everything you do. You're Kolkagga. You're Rime An-Elderin. You're the Ravenbearer, for Seer's sake! You can't let yourself be ruled by a tailless embling that no one is ever going to see again. Use your head, lad! If you want to give people hope and mend this council, then take a wife. Have a feast. Show them that the families are strong. And if you absolutely have to defy them, then choose someone outside the twelve. Take the opportunity to unite north and south. That's what you want. Find a girl from the north. I'm sure Sylja Glimmeråsen wouldn't complain."

Jarladin didn't wait for an answer. He let go of Rime and walked back toward the Council Chamber. "The stones are dead," he shouted. "But we're still alive!" He entered the Council Chamber and shut the door behind him.

Rime remained there, weighed down by reluctance. The cold seeped in through his fingers. He stuck his hand in his pocket and pulled out the raven beak that Hlosnian had found at Bromfjell. Before the fire devoured the stones. It was all that was left of Urd. A beak. Not even the stone whisperer knew its purpose.

There was something sinister about it. Something strange. The color of the bone grew darker toward the tip. Blood was congealed in the scratches.

Rime tested its weight in his hand. Heavier than its size might suggest. It made his skin crawl. But at the same time, it tempted him. The beak was the only thing that felt real. That reassured him that everything had actually happened. And that this was only the beginning.

VIKINGS

"Norway?"

"No."

"Finland?"

"You guessed that already."

"Iceland! It has to be Iceland! You're really good with the *thhh* sound … you know, like the Vikings." Jay touched her tongue to her front teeth and blew. "*Thhh*."

"I don't know the Vikings," Hirka said, pressing down on a knot in Jay's shoulder that made her whole body sag.

"Ow, ow, ow! No, don't stop! Vikings? You've never heard of Vikings?"

Hirka continued massaging Jay's shoulders and didn't reply.

"Norsemen who lived a thousand years ago? Longboats? Pillaging? Berserkers?"

Berserker had a familiar ring to it, but Hirka said nothing. Words often sounded familiar for no reason at all. She'd stopped looking for similarities. She almost always ended up at a dead end, which just left her feeling depressed.

She'd also learned never to be honest. Never to say that she'd come through the stones. And never to try selling tea from another world to people in a café. It turned out that if you did that, the owner called the police and the only escape route was through the toilet window.

"Can you take these out?" Hirka prodded one of Jay's earbuds. She always had them in. Everywhere she went, she looked like she had milk trickling out of her ears. Jay took them out, letting them hang from a clip on her chest.

"You need to stop … what's the word? Hanging? Hanging your back," Hirka said.

"I know. Slouching. I get it from Mum. She says you soon get used to keeping your head down where we're from. You have to, if you want to survive."

"Survive?"

"Survive. Exist. Get by. You know, not die?"

Hirka nodded. She'd heard the word before but had forgotten it.

Jay stretched like a cat. Then she pulled her phone out of a pouch hanging from a glittery cord around her neck. "What are we looking for?"

"Some other time," Hirka said, glancing at the pile of dirty dishes. "We need to tidy up and close."

"No, no, a deal's a deal. You help me, I help you. What am I searching for?"

"See if you can find one with yellow bells. And not many leaves," Hirka said. She rinsed cake crumbs off a plate and put it in the dishwasher.

"Okay. Yellow bells. Coming right up." Jay tapped her phone. Her dark hair fell down into her face. It always did at the end of the day, when her hair clips were losing their grip. Particularly when the café had been busy. Like today.

There were cheers outside. Hirka looked out the window. The couple was standing on the church steps, eyes shining and cheeks aglow. Surrounded by friends and family taking pictures. Pictures that would stay on their phones. Moments, frozen in time.

What Hirka wouldn't give to have pictures from Ym.

Sorrow gripped her heart. She turned to finish loading the dishwasher. There was no point thinking about things or people she was never going to see again.

There was just enough room for the last plate. She closed the door and pressed the button a couple of times. Seeing the little light switch on and off usually cheered her up.

"Here," Jay said, showing Hirka her phone. "Plants with yellow bells. Any of these the one you're looking for?"

Hirka looked at the small pictures. A couple of them were similar, but none of them were yellowbell. She was surprised to feel a stab of disappointment. She thought she'd given up hope.

"It has to be one of them," Jay said. "I've googled all plants with yellow bells, and I'm quite good at searching for things. You should learn, Hirka. You're the only person I know who's never used a phone."

"I don't think I'll ever need one," Hirka replied, painfully aware she had no one to call.

"Blimey, you done already?" Jay got up and brushed off her apron. "All that's left to do is lock up then. You're well efficient."

Hirka smiled. That tended to be the safest option when she didn't quite follow. "We need to wait until they've left, Jay. We're not with them."

She looked at the crowd outside. Men and women with watery eyes and shiny shoes. They filled the square between the café and the church.

The café was a strange annex to the church itself, built in a completely different style. A new wing with space for those who needed it most. Like her. It was somewhere the homeless could get a decent night's sleep. Where the poor could get a bite to eat. It also had a room where they helped the sick, though Hirka had been in there several times and there wasn't a plant in sight.

"We can sort through these while we wait," Hirka said, emptying a bag of clothes on a table. They smelled of dust and sweat, but they looked all right. At first she'd been overwhelmed by what people were willing to give away, but Jay had said it was rubbish that no one wanted. She found that hard to believe.

Hirka put a jumper in a pile of things in need of mending.

"I wouldn't bother," Jay laughed. "You're good, but not even you could fix that."

"The one you're wearing has more holes."

Jay looked down at her own jumper. "Eh, hello, this is different! It's supposed to have holes in it. It's cool."

"So let's cut some more holes in this one and it'll be cool, too."

Jay looked at her with one eyebrow raised. Her eyes were rimmed with black make-up. She shook her head. "I swear it's like you're from another world. Urgh, what is this?"

Hirka grabbed Jay's hand. "Stop!"

She took the shirt from Jay. It had a bloody tear in the sleeve. She folded it and put it in the reject pile. "It might not be safe," she told Jay. "You shouldn't touch blood."

"Christ, you have no idea how much I hate this job!"

Hirka smiled. "You're here almost every day."

"Only because Mum forces me! And it gives her an excuse to be here. So she can make eyes at Father Brody. It's so embarrassing. I mean, a priest? He's not even allowed to get married, and if he ignores her for so much as two minutes, she freaks out. Why do you think she's so cold with you? Because you're here all the time, that's why." Jay leaned closer to Hirka. "She says you shouldn't be living here. That he should report you to child services or something."

Hirka shrugged. It wasn't really any wonder that Jay's mother was fond of Father Brody. Dilipa had lived in the church herself, many years ago. In a room in the basement, just after Jay had been born. Back when they'd been terrified of being sent home. Hirka didn't know where home was, or what they'd run from, but what she did know was that everything was okay now. Jay was the same age as Hirka and had a five-year-old sister.

Where would they send me if they worked out who I was? Where is home?

"It won't last," Jay said with a grimace, watching the couple on the steps.

"You don't think so?"

"Nah. Look at him. He's at least twenty years older than her. She probably just wanted the dress. And the money. As soon as he hits fifty, she'll wake up and realize he's an old man." Jay chucked her apron on a chair. "They're leaving. That's me, then. See you tomorrow, Hirka."

She headed for the door, putting her earbuds back in and nodding along to music that Hirka knew only she could hear. Stored sounds. Just like the pictures.

Hirka wiped the tables and hung both their aprons on a hook. She locked the door and took the back entrance into the church. It wasn't unlike a Seer's hall. A stone building, built to impress.

Father Brody had already left. Hirka walked down the aisle, surrounded by high windows with colorful motifs. Images from stories she didn't know. Gods and humans. No ymlings in any of them. No tails. And no deadborn.

One hundred and fifty-four days. Since Ym. Since Mannfalla.

Since Rime.

She walked around the altar and opened the door to the bell tower, climbing the stairs until she reached the top. She'd been allowed to stay there even though it wasn't a place people usually lived. The priest had said it was like a building site, with no heating or lights. Not that Hirka missed either. He'd wanted to give her a room in the basement. The one Jay and her mother had stayed in. But basements reminded her of the pits in Eisvaldr. She needed to be higher up. As high up as possible. To climb until no one could reach her. So she'd come up here every night until Father Brody had given in. She'd gotten rid of the worst of the dust. And the bat droppings. It was fine now. She just had to make sure she wasn't there when the bells rang.

Hirka looked around at her home in this new world. Most of the space was taken up by the stairs. She could see the bells on the next level when she looked up. It was the same level, really, but someone had put in an extra wooden floor. It was probably supposed to have been temporary, or something to stand on during restoration work, but it had been left in place.

She had a mattress wedged between the stairs and the wall, and a pillow with a deformed swan on it, embroidered by someone she doubted had ever seen a real swan. A narrow dresser with three drawers. The bottom one wouldn't close, so that was where Kuro roosted. A cup that was actually only a half cup, with "You did say half a cup" on the side. Once someone had explained the joke to her, it had made her laugh. She also had a heater that Father Brody had carried up. The heat came through small holes in the wall below and through a long cable all the way up into the tower. Hirka had switched it on and off so many times that it didn't work anymore. But that didn't matter. It wasn't that cold. And besides, she had plenty of candles.

Jay had also given her a book to help with her English. Hirka could just about manage the title. Books were common property here. The sheer volume of *things* was unbelievable. Yet still there were people without homes. And even worse, people like her. People without numbers. Everyone was supposed to have one. Without a number, you didn't exist. Hirka might as well have been a ghost.

She sat on the windowsill and leaned against the frame. Ghost or not, at least she had her own window, with real glass. It curved into a point at the top and had a vent that she almost always left open.

Hirka ran her hands over the cool glass. Glass was good. Stone was good. They were materials she understood. Unlike so many other things here.

She looked out across York, as the city was called. The church was named St Thomas and located close to the city center. The houses were closely packed, like in Mannfalla. The only open space she could see was right outside, in the awful garden where the stones stuck up out of the snow like crooked teeth. There was a body under every stone. They didn't burn people here. They just buried them in the earth and left them to rot. It wasn't right. Only murderers did that sort of thing. But it didn't seem to bother anyone here.

She'd asked whether they ever fed anyone to the ravens, but that was one of many things she wouldn't be asking about again.

Imagine what she could have done with that space if it hadn't been used for their perverse rituals. She could have grown root vegetables, and maybe yellowbell, soldrop, and …

Things they don't have here. Things no one's heard of.

People didn't grow things here. Not even the food they ate.

Hirka poked at one of the plants on the windowsill. Father Brody had driven her to the greenhouse near the school and bought three seedlings for her. They grew slowly, each in their own cardboard cup. She had no idea what kind of plants they were, or what properties they had. She had to learn everything from scratch. Absolutely everything.

She let her eyes wander in search of something comforting to settle on.

There was a man on a bench far below. He'd swept the snow off the part he was sitting on, but not the rest. He looked up, but then straight back down again. Pretending he hadn't seen her. He was wearing a gray hoodie and a leather jacket. She'd seen him before. He'd walked past yesterday. She was sure of it. And she'd noticed him near the shop. What did he want? Why was he here? Was he from the police? Someone who had come to take her away because she was numberless?

The fear came creeping. A chill in her belly.

He got up suddenly. Crossed the churchyard and went out through the wrought iron gate. She watched him until he was out of sight and all she could see were the cars zipping past.

There was no stillness in this world. No matter where you went, you were surrounded by noise. The constant hum of machinery. So much strangeness. So many things to know. So much she could do wrong.

Hirka pressed her palms against her ears until all she could hear was the sound of her own blood being pumped around her body. Faster and faster.

She couldn't get any air into her lungs. She felt like she was suffocating. A sense of unreality washed over her. Her hands started to shake. She tore off her clothes, fumbling with the zip in her trousers. She couldn't get them off fast enough. She emptied her bag, her things spilling across the stone floor. Old things. Familiar things. Her things. Her herbs—or what was left of them. Her green woollen tunic, still just as worn at the seams. She put it on. Her trousers, too. Found her pocketknife. No one carried knives here. It was against the law.

She sank down onto the mattress and hugged her knees. She brought her hand to her chest and felt the pendants. A shell and a wolf's tooth, both with small scratches in them. Each scratch represented something real. Something that had happened. Victories in the endless competition between her and Rime.

Rime ...

She'd gotten used to the sudden bouts of anxiety. Gotten used to being overwhelmed. But she would never get used to the longing. The hole in her chest that had been gnawing away at her for the last hundred and fifty-four days.

Ym was safe. That was her only consolation. Safe from the blind, now that she was gone. Now that the rot wasn't there anymore.

But she still had her memories, and the gifts she'd received.

Her heart stopped racing. It got easier to breathe. She was Hirka. She was real. Her things were real. They just didn't belong here.

So where do we belong?

She shoved her hand in her pocket. Pulled out three blood stones. A gift from Jarladin. The councillor had hidden them in her cloak before she left. In Mannfalla, the stones could have set her up for life, but here there was no way to know. She hadn't seen anywhere that bought and sold stones. No shops wanted them, either.

Then there was the book from Hlosnian. A gift that must have cost the stone whisperer dearly. Rime had given it to her the night she left.

Hirka heard the flutter of wings. Kuro landed on the window ledge and squeezed in through the vent. He swooped down and got settled in his drawer. He hadn't been himself recently. He didn't hop around much anymore. Just walked. She'd even seen him tip over once. It was like he was depressed. Maybe the raven was struggling as much as she was. Struggling to find nourishment in this dead, mightless world.

At least they had each other. She probably wouldn't have coped these past few months without him.

Hirka laid Hlosnian's book in her lap. It was thick, with a brown leather cover and straps to secure it. She'd attached a round object that she'd found in the churchyard to the front. Father Brody said it was an old compass. The needle always pointed north, and it helped to stare at it when the world was making her head spin.

Hirka opened the book. She'd never been good at reading and writing. Only a little better than Father. Still, she'd managed to fill pages and pages with her clumsy words and sketches. Maps of the neighborhood. Drawings of plants. As well as pictures she'd found in the street. And a dead leaf. Foil wrappers. Scraps of cloth.

At first, she'd kept everything. Everything was new and heart-wrenchingly beautiful. She'd also written down things she wanted to tell Rime about, but that had quickly become too painful. Worse and worse with every day that passed. So she'd stopped.

But she still made note of new words. She'd gradually worked out a system. Certain pages for things she was familiar with from before. *Chair. Window. Bread. Rain.* And pages for things she'd never have believed existed. *Telephone. Chocolate. Asphalt. Sunglasses. Washing machine. Petrol.*

She found her pencil and wrote down the new word she'd learned from Jay. *Viking: Someone who lived in a boat a thousand years ago.*

She looked at Kuro. He'd fallen asleep in the drawer. The feathers on his head quivered as he breathed in and out. She lifted the pencil and started writing again.

Survive: Exist. Get by. Not die.

THE STRANGER

You can get away with just about anything so long as you make yourself useful.

People weren't really supposed to live in churches, Hirka had discovered. At least not people like her. They said it was God's house, but in all the time she'd been there, she'd never seen him. She doubted he used it that much. Father Brody could have kicked her out a long time ago. Or called the police. Or—what was it Jay's mum had said?—called child services?

But he hadn't. Not with Hirka doing the laundry, looking after the kids, shoveling the snow, and picking up the groceries. He'd never asked her to do any of those things, she'd just got down to it like she'd done at Lindri's teahouse, and after a few days people had stopped asking where she came from or what she was doing there.

Still, the feeling she'd been longing for failed to materialize. The feeling of being at home. Having a family. It wasn't like that here. There were just too many people, and none of them knew anything about her family. She was a stranger in a strange world.

Whenever things threatened to overwhelm her, she tried to focus on something familiar. The shopping list in her hands, which felt so much like the paper back home. Bare trees in the winter, dotted here and there around the bustling city. Or she thought about things that were new and wonderful. Like the sound of boots on wet snow. Boots were amazing. They never came unstitched and never let any water in. She was wearing a yellow pair that Father Brody had given her.

Yellow boots. What a world.

She took a deep breath and entered the shop. The lights hurt her eyes. Humans had so much light. Along the roads. In windows. Fireless light everywhere you looked.

Hirka went over to the counter and put on her biggest smile for the lady who'd helped her the last time. It was important to appear cheerful. And not to need anything too much. Nothing closed doors quicker than desperation.

The lady smiled back at her. She was plump, wearing a tight belt that made her look like an hourglass. Hirka had the shopping list memorized, but she'd brought it with her just to be on the safe side. The lady helped her find coffee, biscuits, toilet paper, and a few other things they needed at the church. Tea, if you could call it that. Hirka had tried some, and she wouldn't have served it to her worst enemy. Was that what happened to everything in a world devoid of the Might?

The lady stapled the receipt into a book and Hirka picked up the bag of groceries. It was darker now, and the wind had picked up. Snow collected atop the lamp posts. She pulled up the hood on her raincoat. It was almost like a cloak. Not very warm, but it weighed next to nothing and it always kept her dry. And it rolled up so small that it could fit in her mouth. She'd tried, just to see. Nobody back home would have believed it.

She came to a sudden stop. In the café directly in front of her, she spotted a familiar figure. She drew back against the wall and peeked through the window. He hadn't seen her. It was the man from the bench, the one in the leather jacket and gray hoodie. He was sitting with his back to her.

Hirka slipped around the corner and looked through a different window. She could see him better now. He was holding a cup of coffee in one hand and a phone in the other. He was maybe twice her age, with short hair and stubble. He was sitting on a tall stool, his foot bobbing up and down.

Hirka put down the bag and leaned closer. Her breath fogged up the glass.

He turned and looked straight at her. She jumped back from the window. Blood rushed to her cheeks. For a moment she wasn't sure whether to wave or to run. She decided to run.

Her boots sploshed in time with her heartbeat. Was he the only one? Hadn't she seen others? People giving her furtive looks in the street? People hanging around outside the church? Did she really stand out so much that people had reason to stare?

It wasn't until she spotted the church tower that she remembered the bag of groceries. She'd left it back at the café. She stopped. There was something all too familiar about this.

The memory came back to her. Father in his wheeled chair. The cabin. Hirka had made it all the way home before realizing she'd left the basket of herbs by the Alldjup. By the toppled spruce tree. Where Rime had rescued her.

One point to me if I pull you up.

The images were so vivid that she got a lump in her throat. She swallowed. That was another life. Another time. A world she'd never see again.

She turned to walk back to the café. She was careful to avoid looking at anyone, staring at her yellow boots in case she ran into him. The man in the hoodie.

The bag of groceries was right by the window where she'd left it. A thin layer of snow had settled on top. Hirka looked inside the café. Luckily he wasn't there anymore. Relieved, she picked up the bag and headed back toward the church.

Then someone grabbed her. Yanked her back into an alleyway. She tried to scream, but the sound was muffled by a hand over her mouth.

She was thrust up against a wall by a dumpster. The hand tasted of tobacco. Hirka felt paralyzed. Frozen to the spot. Her heart pounded in her throat. She struggled for air. The bag slipped out of her hand and fell to the ground. Biscuits and apples rolled out into the slush. The man from the café stared at her with wild eyes. He said something, but she couldn't make any sense of it. Hirka aimed a kick at him. He moved his hand down to her neck, tightening his grip. She stopped struggling, and strangely, it helped. She could breathe again.

Hirka glanced at the street. They were hidden in some kind of alcove, and people were walking past. They didn't turn to look, didn't know she needed help. Hirka leaned forward and screamed. The man tightened his grip again. A woman in a fur coat gave them a quick glance before scurrying off like she hadn't seen anything. She had. Hirka knew she had. But she'd left all the same. Hope quickly turned to despair.

The man pulled something from his belt and pressed it against her forehead. Something cold. But at least it wasn't a knife. That much was a relief. He barked something at her again. It sounded like a question, but he spoke far too quickly for her to understand.

Hirka swallowed, feeling the muscles in her throat tense against his grip. "I don't understand … I speak badly."

He hesitated for a moment and she noticed a small scar that pulled his lip up at one side. He let go of her neck and brought his thumb to her mouth.

"No!" Hirka wrenched her head to one side, but he forced it back. He was strong. He pulled back her upper lip with his thumb. Stared at her teeth. He seemed more confused now than anything. It was all so strange that for a moment Hirka forgot her terror. She felt like a horse at market.

She put her hand in her pocket and squeezed the bloodstones. She couldn't lose them. She'd have nothing left if she did. Nothing that could be traded for money. Nothing valuable.

The movement attracted his attention, and he tore Hirka's hand out of her pocket. Grabbed the stones before she had a chance to tighten her grip. He didn't waste any time looking at them, just stuck them in his pocket and glanced around like he was in the wrong place.

Finally he let go of her and stepped back. Gave a start when he accidentally stepped on a pack of biscuits and it crunched under his foot.

"It's all right!" Hirka hurried to say. "We've got more."

He looked at her, brow furrowed. He backed out of the alleyway, then turned and disappeared onto the street at the opposite end.

Hirka remained pressed against the wall, trying to catch her breath. A cold terror had seized her and refused to release its grip. She remembered. The pits in Eisvaldr. The man who had tried to take her by force. That time, there had been no doubting his intentions. Now, she didn't have the faintest clue about what just happened, which was somehow worse. She knew nothing. And in a completely different world, anything was possible. Anything at all.

She slumped against the wall and slid down onto the wet pavement. The pack of biscuits in front of her was flattened at one end. A smell of sour milk drifted toward her from the dumpster. All she wanted was to go home. Home to Ym. To Elveroa. To Father.

Father's dead. The cabin's burned to the ground. It's over.

Why had she come here? She didn't belong here. She hated this place. Hated it. The light. The smells. The commotion. So much noise. And yet still so dead.

A place without the Might. A cold world full of terrifying life.

TEMPTATION

They'd been open. The gateways.

Rime had seen the landscape shimmering between the stones. Seen the grass ripple in the pull from someplace unknown. Then he'd been swallowed by the empty space as the world ceased to exist. And re-emerged in the Rite Hall.

In one place, out another. They'd woken the gateways once; it had to be possible to do it again. Just for one brief, harmless moment. For the sake of knowledge. For proof.

For her.

Rime entered the library, intent on finding answers. It seemed that if you wanted to keep the Council's secrets, all you had to do was leave them here. In plain sight. It would take lifetimes to find them.

Conversations here were few and held in hushed tones. The sound of pen on paper drifted from behind a door left ajar. He wondered what was being written, and whether it was the truth.

Rime headed toward the gallery that surrounded the shaft of daylight filtering down from the ceiling. Gray-clad shepherds climbed between floors on ladders that sailed along rails all the way around the library. He hoped one of them could direct him to books about the Might.

Rime was about to ask when he noticed a woman on the lowest level. Her fire-colored skirt drew his eye. She looked around intently, her movements fluid. Graceful. Her eyes met his. There was something familiar about her. Rime realized he was staring, and he turned toward a desk by the balustrade.

On it lay the Book of the Seer, splayed open, baring its lies as if nothing had happened. He felt a stab of disappointment, knowing that people continued to read it. But of course they did.

He ran his fingers over the binding, which was on the verge of falling apart. This book had been here since long before his time. Since long before Ilume. Her only wish had been to see him take her seat on the Council, for him to link the past to the future. But not like this. She had never been keen on change. She'd sooner have disinherited him than see the Seer fall. Than shatter the illusion of divinity that had carried an entire world for a thousand years.

How many false gods had come before the raven? How many more would come after?

The book called to him, as if it might reveal something different than before. Rime remembered every word of it from his childhood.

> *Such was the goodness of He who looked upon them that they were all saved by His grace. Such was His sorrow for the fallen that His tears washed away their transgressions. Innocent, they looked upon their Seer, and He said unto them: "All power from the earth has been given unto me."*

Innocent? What a joke. And there could be no doubt as to who held the power after the war. Rime flipped ahead.

> *And the tree grew straight up into the heavens, blackened and vigorous from the blood of all those who had sacrificed their lives. He wrought it according to His will, according to His desires, to serve the kin of Ym, and He said: "This shall be my throne."*

Rime looked around, feeling scrutinized. An unexpected sense of guilt washed over him. He'd shattered that tree. The Seer's throne. The memory was excruciatingly vivid. Black glass raining down on them. Ilume sinking to the floor. The sound of his heart beating. Urd. And Hirka …

He slammed the book closed. He'd had his fill of lies. Now he needed the truth.

Rime found a shepherd, a gray-haired woman with ink-stained fingers, and asked where he might find books about the Might.

"Two floors up," she said, pointing. "Southwest sector, twelfth set of shelves. I'd be happy to find the books you're looking for."

"Thanks, but I prefer to find them myself," he replied. She smiled warmly, indicating she felt exactly the same way.

Rime went up the stairs. He found the twelfth set of shelves and started to look through the books. They seemed to be mostly poetry. About the Might, about nature, about love. But there were other things, too.

He pulled out a book with a green cover. *The Origin.* His body tingled with anticipation. Hope. The pages were so thin, he worried they might crumble between his fingers. Impatient, he started to read, skipping over words, sections, entire pages.

The Might, the cradle of life … Preceding all else … Arrived with the first. With the forces of creation … The balance.

None of this was new to him. Until …

… Nábyrn's thirst for the Might claimed so many lives that it originated the expression "a body for every raven." But it is my firm belief that the devastation they wrought gave us the strength we needed to fight them. Dead fought dead. The Seer himself is one of the blind and shapes the Might in ways none of Ym's kin are able to. Despite this, blindcraft is feared and despised in every corner of Ym. The Might—as the blind employed it—is regarded

with scorn. It is too strongly linked to them, to decay and destruction. Even to the loss of our souls, if we are to believe those living under the ice in the north.

Rime closed the book.

Blindcraft. The Might as the blind used it.

He'd seen it with his own eyes. How fast they could move. And the waterfall that had turned to sand, spilling over the cliff like an hourglass. What else could it have been, if not blindcraft? Nábyrn trickery. Was blindcraft all that could rouse the stones again? Urd had managed it …

A sudden crash made Rime jump. He turned. It was her—the woman who'd caught his eye. She'd dropped a book. What kind of Kolkagga didn't notice someone approaching?

He picked the book up and handed it to her. She smiled, looking up at him from under heavy eyelids. He knew that look. Self-assured. Inviting. But in her case it didn't seem feigned. It was just who she was. Her lips were uncommonly full, as if demanding to be touched. It was difficult not to stare at them.

"I've seen you before," he said.

She took the book, put it on top of the others she was carrying, and squeezed past. Her arm brushed against his. A floral scent followed in her wake as she headed for the gallery. Her tail swayed with every step, making her jewelry clink. Her hair fell to her waist. Thick and lustrous. Black as coal.

She looked back over her shoulder.

"I've danced for you, Ravenbearer," she said so softly that it could have been the start of a poem.

He followed her, knowing that was exactly what she wanted. She put the books down on a desk. Two were about dancing. He couldn't see the title of the third.

"Nobody's danced for me since I was a boy," he said.

“Have you forgotten your own inauguration, Ravenbearer?” She blinked at him.

Of course. The day he’d become Ravenbearer. The celebrations. The dancers on the steps.

“Rime. Just Rime.”

“Indeed, we have no raven to bear anymore.”

Her words were refreshingly direct. Her hair spilled over her shoulder and she swept it back again with a narrow hand. That small movement was a dance in itself. Everything she did seemed to tell a story. It wasn’t difficult to imagine that men would pay a lot to see her perform.

Her smock was open at the throat, and the material draped over her breasts in a way that was impossible not to notice. She restacked the books to reveal the title he hadn’t seen. *The Art of Pleasure.* The cover depicted a man and a woman in an impossible position.

Rime suddenly felt unsure of himself. Like during a fight, in the moment the advantage was lost. He cleared his throat and turned to leave. She stopped him, her hand resting on his arm.

“I’m Damayanti,” she said. “But you already knew that.”

He looked at her again. “No. Forgive me if I ought to.”

She dragged a finger across her lips like she was going to bite it. “Really? That says a lot about you.”

Her gaze fell on the book in his hand. “But I’ve heard about you, Ravenbearer. What you’re looking for can’t be found in any book. And those with the knowledge you seek don’t dare so much as whisper about it.”

She picked up her books. Hugged them to her chest and turned away from him. “Though there are always exceptions. Come and see me dance sometime, Rime.”

He watched her go. She’d heard about him. Everyone had, but he rarely gave any thought to exactly what they’d heard. Now he felt grudgingly curious. The Council wanted him to start a family, to get married. What would they say if he chose a woman like Damayanti? A dancer?

They'd hate it. They'd be furious. Hurl threats at him. Tear out what little hair they had left.

Rime couldn't help but smile.

VERMIN

The apple was crisp and green. Not so much as a wrinkle. No mold. No rot. And after how many weeks?

Hirka pressed against the peel, but there was no give. Somehow she was holding an apple that looked like it had been picked yesterday, even though the trees in the churchyard were bare.

She put the apple on the windowsill. She didn't care what anyone said, there was no way she was sinking her teeth into something that refused to die. She wasn't stupid. In stories, they were always poisoned.

She heard the scratching of Kuro's claws inside the drawer. He was asleep. That was all he did lately. He wasn't eating much either. Neither of them were. She kneeled on the mattress and gently poked his beak. "You can't just lie there," she said, not sure whether she was talking to herself or the raven. After all, she hadn't ventured outside the church in days. The man in the hoodie was still fresh in her mind. The taste of tobacco on his hand. His brute strength. His voice.

Sure, she'd come out of their encounter in one piece. And she'd been through worse. Far worse. But that was of little comfort now. She wasn't herself in this senseless world. She felt so alone. So defenseless.

Svarteld would have keeled over laughing if he'd seen her in the alleyway. "You call that a kick?" he'd have said. She smiled to herself.

If she ever saw the man in the hoodie again, she was going to introduce his nose to her elbow.

"I know nothing's the same here, but we've got to make the best of it, okay?" Kuro didn't stir. "We've got a roof over our head. Food. Paid work. You know what that means? That means we won't starve." She set her boots down on the floor in front of him. "And just look at these. Look at that color!" Kuro didn't bat an eyelid. She got up and put the boots on. "If you get ill, I'll never forgive you. Just so we're clear on that, you mangy old bird."

Her words grew thick with emotion. There was no point trying to hide her fear anymore. She had to ask Father Brody for help. He was a good man. And he was bound to know someone who was good with ravens.

Hirka descended the stairs of the tower. The stone had crumbled away in several places and been covered over with wooden boards. She liked it. Wood on stone. The way the church was built. It was one of the few things that felt right here. That reminded her of home.

This is home now.

She heard footsteps in the church below and pressed herself flat against the wall. An old habit she hadn't quite managed to shake. She shook her head in frustration, then opened the door and emerged behind the altar. Father Brody smiled at her. He always looked like he needed a wee when he smiled. He had a ruddy complexion and was wearing a dark shirt and trousers but no robe.

"Something's wrong with Kuro," Hirka said.

"Kuro?" He raised an eyebrow. "Ah, yes, the bird."

"He's ill, and I don't have anything to make him better."

"I see. I see."

Hirka knew that he didn't really see, even though he always said that he did.

"Do you?" she asked.

"Do I what?"

"Have something to make him better?" Hirka was trying to hide how worried she was, but talking about it only made it worse.

"No. No, I don't think so. What's wrong with him?"

"He's not moving. Not eating. We have to do something."

Father Brody nodded. His blue eyes somehow seemed younger than the rest of him. "I can ask a veterinarian. An animal doctor. We can call, right after ... I was just about to fetch you. There's someone coming to talk to you."

He made it sound like it was something that happened every day. She was immediately suspicious. Why would anyone want to talk to her? She knew hardly any of the people who came to the church. Apart from Jay.

And her mum, Dilipa. Who'd rather you weren't around.

Hirka nodded. First things first. "Can you call the animal doctor now?"

Father Brody's cheeks turned even redder. For a moment he looked like he was considering saying no, but that wasn't a word that came easily to him. "Of course. Of course."

He pulled out his phone and started tapping at the screen. Hirka bit her lip. There had to be someone who could help. Then a memory flashed before her eyes. The man in the alleyway. The woman in the fur coat who'd seen her in distress and hurried off as if nothing was happening. As if it didn't concern her. It had all happened in a moment, but Hirka knew that vacant look all too well. And the pain of knowing nobody was going to intervene. Or even say anything.

Hirka had wised up now. She could help as many people as she liked, but when push came to shove, she was on her own.

People mean danger.

"Yes, it's a raven. Isn't that right, Hirka?" The sound of her name snapped her back to the present. Father Brody watched her as he spoke into the phone. "Either that or a large crow."

"He's a raven," Hirka said.

"I see. I see." Father Brody nodded to himself. "Is that right? Thank you. No, no, I understand. Thank you all the same." He returned the phone to his pocket.

"What did they say?" Hirka took a step closer.

"She said they don't normally treat vermin."

"Vermin?" That was a new word to her.

"Yes, you know … animals like that. The kind people don't like having around. Animals that are a nuisance."

"So they'll just let him die?"

"They normally put them to sleep. Ravens aren't meant to be kept indoors. It's illegal, so I told her you'd found it outside."

"You lied for me?"

"No, no, no—to the best of my knowledge, that's true!" Father Brody tried to smile again. His I-need-a-wee smile.

Hirka perched on the end of the pew.

Vermin: Animals people don't want around.

They could rot in Slokna, each and every one of them.

The main door creaked open behind them.

"Father Brody?" A woman walked in. She was dark-skinned and wearing a fitted checkered shirt. She had a folder pressed against her chest.

"Ah, yes! Trudy." Father Brody looked at Hirka. "This is Trudy, she just wants to have a little chat. Don't worry, I'd never … It's just that people are starting to ask questions, so we have to—"

"People?" Hirka knew exactly who he meant. Dilipa. Jay's mum. In her mind, Hirka was vermin. Something people didn't want around. Hirka knew that ought to make her feel sad, but that was just the way things were here. She'd learned that now.

The woman in the checkered shirt held out her hand to Hirka. "I'm Trudy. Can we talk for a moment?"

"I'm not good at speaking. Yet," Hirka answered, sliding even closer to the end of the pew so she'd have the option of running if it came down to it.

Trudy said where she was from, but it was just a string of random sounds to Hirka. She sat down and tried again in several different languages. "Don't you know any of these languages, Hirka?" The woman looked at her like she was a child.

Hirka shook her head. "I live here. I speak English."

Trudy gave Father Brody a worried look. He shrugged. "We've tried everything. Nobody's come up with a place she's even heard of. She spoke her own language when she first arrived but hasn't since."

Hirka let her eyes wander, pretending not to understand. There was a good reason she didn't speak her own language anymore. It made everyone ask where she was from, and when she answered truthfully, they thought she was crazy. Or not quite right. Like Vetle. The thought of Vetle brought a flood of memories. Ramoja. Eirik. The sound of the ravens flying above Ravnhov every morning.

She looked outside, but the sky here was devoid of life. Empty. Ravenless.

Father Brody continued. "Someone from Norway came in recently, said he had family in Iceland. Couldn't understand a word of what she was saying, but he did think it sounded similar. We're pretty sure she's suffering from memory loss. Maybe she even made up her own language. That's possible, isn't it?"

Trudy flipped through her papers. "What's the name of the place you're from?"

Hirka clamped her mouth shut. She'd fallen for that one before. But clearly this woman had no intention of giving up without a fight. "How old are you?" Something about her questions unsettled Hirka, but she could no longer pretend she didn't understand.

Father Brody answered for her. "She says she's sixteen."

Trudy looked even more concerned, if that were at all possible, but the smile never left her face. It sent chills down Hirka's spine. "Your parents, Hirka. Where are they?"

At last Hirka could answer honestly. "I thought they'd be here."

Trudy perked up at that. "Did your mum and dad say they were going to be here?"

Hirka shook her head.

"What are your parents' names?"

"I don't know."

Trudy sighed and got up. "Can we have a word in private, Father? I don't know what she's been through, but there's a good chance she's experienced some kind of trauma."

They walked down the aisle as they continued their conversation. Hirka sat motionless, listening to their voices until they reached the annex. When she heard the door shut behind them, she got up and ran toward the tower. She took the stairs three at a time, all the way up to her room. Frantically, she looked around for something to barricade the stairwell with, but then realized how stupid that was. She slumped against the wall.

It was all over. She'd only come to this world because she thought it was where she belonged. Because she was human. One of them. But it was exactly the same here as in Ym. She felt just as hounded. Just as much an outsider. And now this woman was explaining to Father Brody why she couldn't stay, how the police would have to take her away. They'd probably put her to sleep, too. Like she was vermin.

Her bag. Where had she left it? Hirka found it by the dresser and started cramming in her clothes, notebook, pouches of herbs. What else? The half-cup. And the spiral-shaped stone Hlosnian had given her in Elveroa. Before everything had gone to Slokna. Before Father had died. She ran her finger over the grooved surface. The stone whisperer had said it was formed by the Might itself. Long before people. She slipped it inside a pouch. The seedlings on the windowsill would have to stay.

She scooped Kuro up into her arms. He was limp. Warmer than usual. She took a deep breath, trying to stay calm. "You can't get ill now. We can't stay here. Do you understand?"

She gave him a little shake, but all he did was close his eyes. They looked like pale worms against the black of his feathers. She put him back in the drawer and rested her head against the dresser. She'd have to wait until nightfall. She could grab one of the boxes from the café and carry him in that. In the meantime, she'd have to keep up appearances. Convince Father Brody that everything was okay. She shut her eyes and took another deep breath. If she didn't go back down, Father Brody was bound to come up. She had no other option.

She walked back down the stairs. The wind was picking up outside. It sounded like a ghost wailing its way up the tower. But that didn't bother Hirka. She wasn't afraid of ghosts. After all, she was a ghost herself.

Father Brody was sitting on the same pew Hirka had been sitting on earlier. He was staring up at the altar. That usually meant he didn't know what to do. Or that he didn't like what he had to do. Hirka sat down next to him and tucked her feet up under her legs.

"Hmm, hmm," he said, nodding like she'd said something. Then he was silent for a while. The roof groaned with every gust of wind.

"We know so little about you, Hirka," Father Brody said, dragging his hand across his face. A habit that reminded her of Father. Grief lanced through her heart. She suddenly felt like curling up next to Father Brody, but she couldn't give in to her emotions. Anyway, it wouldn't feel right, considering she was planning on running away as soon as night fell.

"About as much as I know about you." Hirka forced a grin. That usually did the trick. If nothing else, she'd have her smile to fall back on. Father Brody's cheeks flushed. He'd been her safe haven for months. He was a good man, and she didn't blame him for what was about to happen.

"You know people aren't supposed to live here," he said. "This is a church. God's house. Do you know what that means, Hirka? Do you know who God is?" He looked almost despondent. Hirka didn't know what to do to comfort him. So she just nodded. She'd seen people pit themselves against gods before. She'd been there when Rime lost his.

His gaze rested on the painting behind the altar. A young man in a red tunic. Half-naked with a wound in his side. Another man crouched next to him with his fingers held to the wound. Was he trying to heal him? Hard to say. A white pigeon soared above them.

Hirka looked at Father Brody. His hands gripped the pew in front as he stared at the painting, waiting for an answer that wouldn't come. She rested her hand on his back.

"Father Brody, I'm pretty sure that's just a perfectly ordinary pigeon."

THE GREENHOUSE

Hirka sat with her back to the wall and stared up at the bells. Black holes, big enough to swallow her if they were to fall. But they'd been there for a long time. Surrounded by pulleys and beams, with ropes hanging all the way down for people to pull on and make a din that would wake all of Slokna—Father included.

She was going to have to leave again. Run. That was what she always ended up doing. It was the only thing she was any good at.

She'd run away from the cabin, the only home she'd known. Run from Lindri's teahouse, sneaking out and stealing across the rooftops of Mannfalla. And then there was the night the Seer's tree had shattered. That fateful night when everything had changed. She still remembered the look on Rime's face when she'd asked him to retrieve her bag. To risk his life rescuing it from the vaults in Eisvaldr.

Her chortle quickly descended into a choked sob. She curled up into a ball and hugged her bag to dull the pain. Her head hurt. But it was like picking a scab. She couldn't help herself.

Rime. That white hair. Those wolf eyes. That kiss.

She'd known there was no going back. That she would never see him again. But *never* had just been a word. Now it was something more. It was hours. Days. Months. *Never* had taken on new meaning.

Rime was the Ravenbearer now. In a world that didn't belong to her. But it was painfully clear that this world didn't belong to her either. That was probably why it felt so unfair. So unsafe.

The man in the hoodie.

It hadn't been some random mugging. He'd been watching her. Waiting for her. And she couldn't shake the feeling that he wasn't the only one. It was dangerous out there. And she had nowhere to go. But still ... she couldn't just sit here until the police took her away. The police were the guardsmen of this world, and she'd fallen into the hands of guardsmen before. Gone against her own instincts and walked straight into the Rite Hall. Straight into the belly of the beast. Never again.

Kuro was gasping for breath now. He lay motionless on a towel in a cardboard box. Something was wrong. She could smell it. Hirka shrugged it off and set about packing the rest of her things. What remained of the money Father Brody had paid her for helping out. What remained of her tea and herbs, which wasn't much. She'd have to ration them. What if she got ill? Not that she could remember ever being properly ill. That was the advantage of growing up with a healer for a father.

Reluctantly, she packed the undying apple as well. It beat starving to death. She pulled on her green tunic. It had been with her through thick and thin, and it looked like it, too. But it helped her remember who she was. She shoved her pocketknife into her woolly sock, pressed firmly against the side of her boot so she could draw it without the sheath coming out with it. She practiced a couple of times to make sure it worked.

Hirka put on her raincoat and pulled up the hood, then shouldered her bag. Then she picked up Kuro's box, took one last look at the beautiful window, and went down the stairs.

It was nighttime, so no one would hear her. All the same, she opened the door at the bottom of the stairs as quietly as she could. The church was a gray void. There was a whispering sound, like an echo from centuries of visitors. Darkness formed black chasms between the pews. The stained glass had dimmed for the night. Switched off its colors. Gone to sleep.

She walked down the aisle. The feeling of being watched didn't leave her until she reached the main door. She opened it, then looked back at the altar. At the painting of the wounded figure and the pigeon she'd thought was Odin. God, in this world. But now she knew it was more complicated than that. Whoever it was, the pigeon remained silent.

"Well, then … it's all yours again," she whispered, and slipped out into the winter night.

The city was almost tolerable at night. Quieter. Without any cars around, the sounds made more sense. Drunkards were drunkards, no matter what world you were in. At least that was something. If she squinted, she could imagine she was walking down the Catgut, on her way to Lindri's teahouse. Until an empty night bus roared past, shattering the illusion.

She put the church behind her and followed the streetlights east, keeping away from all the alleyways. Trying to look relaxed. She was alone. Nobody was out to get her.

Hirka had checked the drawing in her notebook. Her map. She was pretty sure she could find Jay's house. She knew she couldn't stay there, but she had to say goodbye. Jay wasn't as tough as she let on, and Hirka didn't think she had many other friends. She couldn't just disappear without any explanation. Besides, she hoped Jay could give her some tips on where to go. She'd take any help she could get.

The air felt heavy. It would snow soon. She came to a fork in the road and headed up toward the old house leaning into the street. She caught movement out of the corner of her eye and looked up.

What was that? Had she seen someone on the roof? Hirka had always been able to see well in the dark, but her eyes still played tricks on her sometimes. People here didn't putter around on rooftops, as far as she knew. She peered up, but the shadow was gone.

Was it him? The man in the hoodie?

She stopped. Looked down at Kuro. He was hidden under the towel in the box and no help to her at all. Hirka bit her lip. Tried to quell her growing sense of unease. She looked around. Unfamiliar houses and streets. A strange city in a strange world. What was she going to do? She couldn't go to Jay's if someone was following her.

Why would anyone follow you? You're nobody!

Hirka started running down the street. Back the way she'd come. She heard Kuro scrabbling against the cardboard box in distress, but she didn't dare stop. Running had intensified her fear. She glanced up at the rooftops but couldn't see anyone. Still, she kept running. The bell tower came back into view. But any relief quickly faded when she spotted a figure on the other side of the street. He melted into the shadows, but now there was no doubt—she *was* being followed.

This isn't the first time someone's been after you. Use your head!

What she wouldn't have given to have the Might here. Been able to pick her fear apart and use it as a source of strength. Seen it for what it was and found a solution.

She crossed the churchyard, between the stones of the dead, and slipped around the back of the church. If anyone was following her, they'd think she'd gone inside. She hoped.

She pushed Kuro's box up onto the church wall. Grabbed hold of the frost-covered vines and pulled herself up. They creaked, threatening to come loose from the stone wall, but luckily they held. She jumped down on the other side and retrieved the box. She needed to find somewhere safe. Now. She tried to keep quiet, but the air huffed in and out of her lungs. Where? Where could she go?

The garden ...

The place where Father Brody had bought the plants for her. Where they grew herbs. Even in winter. No one lived in those greenhouses. She could go there. She would be safe there—if she could remember where it was.

Hirka hugged the box and started to run again, following the chill down to the icy river. White, skeletal branches reached into the black sky. Would everything have been different if she'd arrived in the spring? While everything was alive, growing and singing?

She followed the path along the riverbank until she reached the bottom of the garden. It was blanketed in snow and ice. Small puddles had frozen into mirrors that crunched under her boots as she walked up to the greenhouse. The glass, which had been clear before, was now all steamed up. But there wasn't a soul to be seen outside. Hopefully there wouldn't be anyone inside, either. She had no choice. She had to hide.

Hirka paused to listen. A siren wailed in the distance. There was something else, too. A humming, but that could have been anything. Everything here hummed or whirred. She followed the glass wall, looking for the door. In the box, Kuro's head was sticking out from under the towel, his beak gaping open. Hopelessness seized her. She couldn't help him. She was running out of herbs, and she wouldn't find any more here. None that she knew anything about. None that could help. And there were no raveners here, either.

"Everything will be okay. I promise," she whispered.

She opened the door and slipped into the warmth. A flagstone path passed between rows of strange plants that had been robbed of their color by the dark. Some of them looked like ones from home, but they were never quite the same. How was she supposed to use any of them? She didn't know whether they'd heal or kill, and figuring out a whole world of new plants would take her the rest of her life.

The thought was unexpectedly comforting. At least it would give her a sense of purpose.

She walked past the plants and into another section at the end that was even warmer. Humid, even. The humming she'd heard was coming from a fan over the door. The windows were steamed up, but she could see the stars through the roof.

Kuro gave a choked screech.

"No! You listen to me!" Hirka put the box down and lifted him out. His head lolled. He writhed as he gasped for breath. She turned him this way and that, checking his warm body for signs of injury, for all the good it did. What did she really know about ravens? Nothing.

"You just need a better place to rest, that's all," she said, her voice thick. She couldn't push down her despair anymore. The raven seemed to grow heavier and heavier in her arms.

She spotted a wooden crate under a workbench. Holding Kuro to her chest with one arm, she pulled it out and flipped it onto its side. Garden tools spilled out, clattering against the flagstones. She no longer cared if anyone heard. If they came, they came.

"Here you go, this is roomier. You can lie here. Until you get better." She arranged the towel in the bottom and gently set Kuro down on top of it. He looked like a heap of feathers—black feathers on a white towel. His head flopped sideways.

"No, Kuro! You can't!" She fell to her knees. Lifted him up again. Shook him. His head was much too limp, like his neck was broken. There had to be something she could do. She had to fix this. That was her job. Fixing things. Healing people. She looked into his eyes and saw every death she'd ever witnessed. Everyone she hadn't been able to help. The people who'd left the cabin, without her or Father being able to do more than delay the inevitable. It wasn't right! It wasn't supposed to be that way!

Crying was making her nose run, so she wiped it with her sleeve. "I'll never forgive you. You hear me?!" Kuro's entire body convulsed.

She lost her grip on him and he fell into the crate with a feeble croak of pain. His wings flapped as if he were trying to right himself, his talons scrabbling for purchase. His beak gaped open, revealing a fleshy red interior. His chest expanded, swelling like a water skin. This was all wrong. This was just utterly and horrifically wrong.

"Kuro …" She tried to reach out to him, but her strength had deserted her.

Then his chest erupted.

Hirka shrieked and backed away. She could see blood. Bone.

Kuro wheezed. Something pale and shrunken pushed its way out of his chest. His tiny body was stretched until it was unrecognizable. Puckered skin became visible between his feathers. Mangled. Torn. Hirka clamped her hand over her mouth but couldn't stop herself from sobbing.

Death had never looked like this before. This was a parasite. Some kind of hideous worm that didn't exist in Ym. Only here. In this heinous world. It had taken her only friend. All she had. Kuro was reduced to nothing more than carrion as the creature flopped out of him. Hirka scrambled even farther back, unable to take her eyes off it, squeezing between the workbenches full of seedlings and pressing herself up against the glass, cold and wet against her back.

The crate exploded. Splinters of wood flew everywhere. Something smacked into the window right next to her cheek. It looked like a bit of intestine. It slid down the glass, leaving a trail of blood in its wake. She hid her face behind her arm. She didn't want to look. She remembered Vetle sitting on the tree trunk over the Alldjup. Face behind his arm, as if that would keep him safe. That was her now. She'd lost all sense of reason.

This is a dream. This isn't happening.

But the pulse thundering in her ears was definitely real. She heard a choking sound. Was that her? Was it Kuro?

She peeked over her arm to see something horrific lying on the flagstones where the crate had been. A pale monster. With feet. Arms.

A man.

A naked man, on the ground. Slick with blood and feathers. His face concealed by black, glistening hair. Gasping for breath.

There was a man on the ground. Not a raven. A man.

Hirka couldn't move. Couldn't even think about moving. She was leaden. Frozen in place. The man tried to prop himself up on one arm. He slipped in the raven blood and collapsed again. Curled up in pain. He reached out. Pulled himself along the ground a bit. Gave up. Stayed where he was, knees drawn up.

Never had she seen … or even heard of …

I have to get out of here!

This mind-boggling creature before her, it could have been anything. Something so foul that the humans hadn't even dared mention it. A raven-killing, man-eating monster.

He hadn't seen her. If she could just squeeze past and slip out …

Hirka forced her limbs to cooperate. She bent forward and started to crawl on all fours, under the workbench. Her raincoat rustled with every movement. She tried to muffle the sound as best she could. Her arms were shaking, elbows threatening to give out on her. She was afraid to even blink. Quiet. Quiet now. She could hear him breathing. Wheezing. She was much too close to him, but the door wasn't far away. She had to get to it. She would get to it. She couldn't die here.

As she reached for the door, he snatched her wrist. A scream lodged in her throat. She wanted to tear herself free, but everything had failed her. Her instincts. Her body. Her mind.

His hand was strong. Pale against her skin. And his fingers were all too familiar. Claws she'd hoped she'd never see again.

He was one of the blind. Nábyrn. Deadborn.

Here. In the human world.

She stopped fighting. Stopped thinking. If she moved, reality would shatter like glass. The fear was like a cold stake through her body. Without it she would have collapsed.

He pushed himself up, barely getting his chest off the ground. He leaned on one arm and stared at her with white, sightless eyes.

"*Kroyo ozá désel?*" It sounded like something straight out of Slokna. A rough voice that was never meant to exist.

"*Kroyo ozá désel?!*" he repeated, and there was no doubt now that he was looking at her, blind or not.

She lifted two shaking fingers to her throat without knowing where the reflex had come from.

He growled like an animal and collapsed back onto the ground.

MERCY

What are you still doing here? Get up! Run!

But Hirka was powerless to act. She stared at the deadborn. He was pure muscle. Like his pale body had been carved from stone. He looked strong and starved at the same time. Every breath caused him obvious pain. His body shook like his muscles were spasming. They extended across his chest to his stomach and down toward … her cheeks flushed. He had no hair down there—but plenty else.

The creature had closed his eyes, probably trying to gather his strength. He was weak. Maybe even dying. She glanced at the door. He wouldn't be able to stop her if she ran. She was free to make a break for it. If she was still there when he recovered, it would be too late. He was a blindling. She'd seen what they were capable of. She pictured the man who had been killed near Ravnhov. His hollow eyes. This creature was death incarnate. A brute. Dangerous. Unpredictable.

Suddenly she realized that the same words had been used about her. Numerous times.

The memories she had tried so hard to suppress forced their way to the front of her mind. Steel gauntlets against her skin. A sword against her back. She had been powerless. Scared to death. Blind, even, with a cover over her eyes. Kneeling on the hard floor. Monster. Child of Odin. The rot.

The similarities made her feel nauseous. Robbed her of the power to move. Stopped her from abandoning him. Abandoning Kuro.

Was this Kuro? No, how could that be possible? There was raven blood smeared all over the flagstones, black in the dark. Kuro had been torn to shreds, having birthed … this. She'd failed him. She, a healer, hadn't been able to save her own raven.

Hirka closed her eyes, exhausted by the realization. She was a healer. And the creature on the floor was dying. She had no choice.

She had a pinch of draggan tea left, the last of her supply from Himlifall. If she gave him that, then she'd only be able to ease people's pain. Would the last life she saved be that of a deadborn who'd tear her to shreds the second he could lift his arm?

He hasn't hurt you yet.

She tried to look at him through new eyes. If only there weren't so … so much of him. His strength was so evident—a raw, dangerous strength. Father would have told her to run. Rime wouldn't have hesitated to kill him. But it was different for them. They'd always been able to choose. To her, life was sacred. Letting him die would be as much the end of her as saving him. She had to help him. It wasn't up to her to decide who lived or died. It never had been.

She was a healer. The rest they could figure out in Slokna.

She found the box in her bag. It was made of bark and fit in the palm of her hand, and contained the most precious thing she owned. She got up and took off her damp raincoat, cramming it into her bag with the box still clenched in her fist.

Where was she going to find hot water? The tea needed heat or it wouldn't help him. There was no hearth, and she could hardly start a fire in a greenhouse. The blindling groaned, convulsing as another spasm ripped through him. He coughed up some blood. He was going to die.

The fan. Fans get hot.

She'd learned *something*, at least.

She filled the cup from her waterskin. Her fingers had stopped shaking. A new sense of purpose had calmed her nerves. She climbed up onto a stool and put the cup on top of the fan, the hum lowering as she did so. She opened the small box of tea while she waited. The leaves were perfectly dried. Not completely black, but a nice dark brown. They would help him. Just like they'd helped countless others.

She sniffed the leaves. The smell of Ym tore at her heart, making her long for home. The feeling she had fought so hard to suppress finally came to the surface. Regret. Foul and unclean. Like a body in a river. So much regret that it hurt. Why had she left? What did she care if the blind killed every last ymling in Mannfalla? She didn't owe them a thing! She'd have given anything to be back in the stone circle with Rime. To feel his arms around her, to tell him she'd never leave. That she'd stay there with him. Forever.

Until you made him yours and he rotted?

The blindling let out a groan. Hirka took the cup down from the fan. Not as hot as she would have liked, but it would have to do. The leaves unfurled as she dropped them into the water. A promise of life. She carried the cup in both hands, afraid she might drop it. She kneeled down next to the deadborn, setting the cup on the ground in case she started trembling again. She slipped her hands under his head. He was cold. His long hair was matted with raven blood.

Kuro ...

He opened his eyes. Hirka shuddered. She searched his milky gaze, trying to find something to focus on, but found nothing. He lifted himself up on his elbows. His jaw tensed, as if he were trying to conceal the effort it took. Like Rime would have done.

He made it halfway up before he fell back into the crook of her arm. She put one hand under his chin and picked up the cup. He craned his neck toward it. He understood. She was afraid to let him hold the cup himself, so she brought it to his blue lips.

"I've only got half a cup," she said, forcing a laugh. He didn't react. She turned the cup around to show him. "Half a cup. Get it?"

No. Actually, it wasn't that funny.

He drank. Hirka kept a firm hold on the cup. He gurgled and spluttered, but quickly recovered and drank until the cup was empty. Then he slumped back, his head in her lap. "More," he mumbled.

Hirka stared at him. It was just one word, but it was a word she knew. He shut his eyes.

"You speak ymish! Hey, Mr. Blindling!" She shook him. He opened his eyes again and she gave a start. Something black had stirred in them. Like ink in milk. But it was gone now.

"Wári," he said through clenched teeth.

"Vari? Vari what? I don't understand—"

"Wári! Might. Give me the Might!" he hissed. But the effort was too much for him. His head slumped to one side and his body went limp.

The Might …

The most beautiful thing she'd heard in months. And it had come from a nábyrn. A deadborn. The lump in her throat grew as she realized she had doubted at times. Doubted that Ym still existed. Doubted that *she* even existed, for that matter. But here he lay, speaking her language, using words she hadn't heard since she'd left. Asking for something she couldn't give him. Not even if the Might existed here would she have been able to help him. She was Hirka. A child of Odin. She couldn't bind.

"You wouldn't believe the things they've got here," she whispered. "You could have asked me for sorcery that lets you talk to people on the other side of the world. Lights that never burn out. And carriages that move on their own, faster than any horse. You could have asked me for hot water that flows indoors. Chocolate. Sound captured in boxes. Any of these things I could have given you. But never the Might, nábyrn."

Her final word made his top lip curl. A sharp canine glistened in the darkness.

FEAR OF DEATH

Graal rested his forehead on the piano and gave his fingers free rein. Chopin's "Ballade No. 4," sullied by his claws on the keys. He tried to play with the tips of his fingers lifted, and he had gotten better at it, but some scratching was inevitable. On good days, a reminder of who he was. On bad days … well, more or less the same. It depended on how comfortable he was feeling in his own skin.

It always ended the same. Growing displeasure fueled by deep frustration until he brought his fists crashing down on the keys, his rage destroying what could have been. Cacophonous violence. Nor could he blame the instrument, a magnificent creation by Fazioli. The problem lay in the execution. The performer. A problem the composer had never had.

He stopped playing and lowered his ear to the keys, listening to the sounds that had faded to nothing. Dead sounds. The greatest beauty was to be found in the incomplete. It was easier to tell himself that than to keep striving for perfection. Especially now, when so much was at stake.

He heard Isac coming down the stairs out in the corridor. His footsteps grew hesitant as he approached, which could only mean he hadn't quite decided how to deliver his news. Not a good sign for either of them. Graal stayed where he was, slumped over the piano.

Isac opened the door and came in. "It's her. No doubt about it," he said with feigned optimism.

Graal surveyed his claws. "Do you know what Chopin told me before he died, Isac?"

Isac walked over to the liquor cabinet. "It's one of those days, is it?" he muttered.

Graal ignored him. "He told me that even with an eternity to practice, I would never be as good a musician as him. Not because of my claws, but because I don't fear death. What do you think, Isac? Is that why my people haven't changed in thousands of years? Do we live too long to create anything of note?"

Isac snorted. "Clearly the opposite is true," he replied. "There's no limit to what's possible when you don't have to worry about time running out on you."

Graal sat up. "Well, you would say that, considering you'd be dead if I hadn't taken you on."

He paused to let his words sink in before continuing. "But you're right. Nothing humans do is about anything other than eternal life. Art as the pursuit of immortality. All that matters is what they get out of it. So what have you accomplished, my friend, that you wouldn't have had you died? How much greater is your existence today? What more have you done?"

Isac filled a glass with gin and topped it off with a modest splash of tonic. "I don't know," he replied, sitting down on the sofa and putting his feet up on the table. "But I've got an eternity to figure it out." He grinned.

Graal looked at him. He'd had Isac for thirty years. Not long in the grand scheme of things, but it felt like ages. Isac wouldn't last. Perhaps he already knew that. Perhaps that was why he was becoming increasingly brazen. An attempt to reinvent himself. To seem interesting. He'd been over fifty when Graal had taken him. A witty and intelligent man. British through and through. But recently he'd started wearing garish shirts with ridiculously long collars. They made him look like a washed-up pop star. His blond hair hung to his ears from a center part, which certainly didn't help his cause.

Maybe midlife crises were genetically encoded in humans. Maybe they had them regardless of whether or not death was coming.

Graal got up. Isac promptly removed his feet from the table.

"It's not your fault," Isac said, as if Graal had anything to apologize for. "It's this place." He gestured around the room, slopping gin on the floor in the process. "Who wouldn't get depressed in here? What sort of a design choice is black stone? Who builds a house sticking out of a mountain, for that matter? Of all your places, this is the worst. Don't get me wrong, it has a certain James Bond villain charm to it, but it's not exactly homey. And that ... thing." He glared at the raven skeleton on the table. "Just because it's hideous doesn't mean it's art."

Graal walked over to the floor-to-ceiling window. The glass was angled out over the edge of the cliff. The mountains sat blue and silent beneath him, stretching as far as the eye could see. He knew Isac always steered clear of the window. It gave him the willies.

"The raven?" Graal asked.

A moment passed before Isac realized what he was asking. "Oh, yeah, the raven. Yes, they saw it. She was carrying it in a box. They're sure it's her."

Graal turned to face him. "What's the bad news?"

Isac lifted his glass to his lips and drank, as if to veil his words. "They haven't seen her in a few days. But it's definitely her! And we know where she is."

Graal sighed. "They've been made, Isac."

"No chance. She's a bloody teenager. Heads in the clouds, the lot of them. And we've got good people on the case. Only the best. Top class." Isac brought the tips of his thumb and index finger together as if talking about a particularly good meal he'd had.

Graal was so furious he could taste it. A metallic prickling on his tongue. His blood boiling. He couldn't afford to make mistakes, yet here he was, surrounded by humans. Humans who didn't have the capacity to understand and never would. They simply didn't live long enough. Humans made mistakes. It was in their nature.

"Come here, Isac."

Isac cowered in his seat. The ice cubes in his glass started to clink. That was the advantage of real power. You never needed to use it. Or demonstrate it. It was always there. Part of you.

Isac got up and walked over to the window. He stopped a few steps away from it, clearly trying to avoid looking out. His eyes were fixed on Graal as if he were a lifeline.

"Isac, have I failed to impress upon you how important this is?"

"No! They know how important it is. They know that to a man." It was just like Isac to deflect.

"But do *you*?"

"Of course I do. The young lady will be here in a few days. Her and the raven. You have my word, Joshua."

Isac's avoidance of Graal's real name was a sure sign of his unease. And his need to convince himself of what he was saying.

"How can you give me your word when you're not even out there, Isac?"

Beads of sweat formed on Isac's forehead, glistening along his hairline. "I-I'll be there! Of course I will. It's in my hands now. Safe as houses."

Graal took Isac's arm and steered him closer to the window. He didn't need to use force. He was what he was, which meant mere suggestion was enough.

"What would happen if we were to fall now?" he asked, nodding at the abyss below.

Isac forced a laugh. "We'd be dashed on the rocks."

"That's right. We'd be dashed on the rocks. Both of us. But do you know the difference between us?"

Isac said nothing. There were probably too many answers to choose from. Too many differences. But he smiled. He had a nervous look in his eyes, but they also shone with love. That was true power. Being able to inspire both fear and love. To tilt the balance between them. An unlikely pair in constant battle for control.

"We'd lie there, both you and I, Isac. Mangled. Broken. Arms and legs shattered by the rocks. You'd remain there. My bones would knit back together again. Heal. Slowly but surely. Eventually I would get up again. But you're the lucky one."

Isac swallowed. "You don't make it sound that way."

Graal looked at him. "Ruin is painful. But it's nothing compared to the pain of healing. It's always easier to break things than to fix them. Believe me, you are the lucky one."

Isac's eyes grew glassy. The corner of his mouth twitched, but Graal was having no part of it.

"Isac, you're making the same mistake many do when they lose sight of death. They think they'll always have another chance. But there are no more chances this time. It's now or never. Another thousand years couldn't help us now. That's why no price is too high. Nothing, absolutely nothing, is more important than this. Do you understand what I'm telling you?"

Isac nodded and lowered his eyes.

"Good. Now leave me in peace. I have things to do."

Visibly relieved, Isac headed for the door.

"And remember," Graal said as he went. "Discretion is key."

He turned his back on Isac and waited until he heard the door close. Then he went over to the raven. It stood upright, frozen in a state midway between cadaver and skeleton. Flesh and feather had long since petrified. Not even he could smell it anymore. He clenched his fist. Dug a claw into his palm and let the blood drip down onto its beak. Blood on bone.

He listened. Waited for sounds of life. Dying sounds were

beautiful, but in truth, they were nothing compared to sounds yet to be born.

The cadaver started to creak. Its neck moved and its beak opened. Moments later, he heard her voice. Soft and simmering with self-assurance.

"Graal, you're going to want to kiss me when you hear my news."

He indulged in a smile. "Good, because right now you're the only one I can rely on, Damayanti."

RAVEN BLOOD

The Seer's tower stood alone. It had always been connected to the Rite Hall by a narrow bridge, but now that both the bridge and the hall were gone, it jutted up in the landscape like a warning from the gods. Last stop before Blindból.

The yellow glass had been removed from the windows to be used in the new Council Chamber. Only a black skeleton remained—a broken lantern atop a cliff.

Rime knew that if he went up there, he'd find fragments of the tree, probably exactly where they'd been since the night he had shattered it. Everything was the same. And nothing was the same.

The gardens to the rear of Eisvaldr were covered in snow. White flowers that had been blindsided by winter poked out on either side of the path. The birdbath before him had frozen over. Icicles gleamed along its edge like wolf teeth.

Rime came to a stop. Hlosnian appeared behind him. This was one of the best places to talk. Even in the larger chambers, words carried a long way, borne by the Might, and this was no conversation for Council ears.

He pulled the ampoule out of his pocket and handed it to Hlosnian. "I should have asked you ages ago, but they've been keeping me busy."

Hlosnian took the ampoule, uncorked it, and took a sniff. "So your plan is to poison them?"

Rime couldn't help but laugh. "It may come to that sooner or later. But that isn't poison, as far as I know. That's the ink they use during the Rite. They mark the children's foreheads with it once they're done. It fades after a couple of days."

Hlosnian re-corked the ampoule and returned it to Rime. "Yes, I have seen a few Rites in my time, young man."

"Well, old man, I'm willing to bet you didn't know that's how they've been suppressing the Might in people."

Hlosnian raised a bushy eyebrow. "The ink? How ... ah ... Raven blood."

Rime nodded. Now all he had to do was keep Hlosnian on-topic. Talking to Hlosnian often felt like having three conversations at once, especially when it concerned something important.

"They say it's a mixture of herbs, ink, and raven blood. I expect you knew that?"

The stone whisperer didn't reply at first. The wind took hold of his red robe, making it dance around his feet.

"Blood, Rime. Isn't that what it always comes down to? We live by it. Die by it. It determines who we are. When we are. They say the Might is born of it. The blood of the earth. And that in turn passes into our blood. And thus the circle is complete."

"You sound like an augur."

The stone whisperer snorted. "Augurs. What do they know of the Might? The Might loves blood. You saw it yourself on Bromfjell. Urd forced the stones. Blood from a raven. Fire from stone. Blood changes people. It changed you."

"Everyone changes, Hlosnian."

"Hm ... Some more than others." Hlosnian swept the snow off the birdbath and pointed at the frozen water. "Look down. Tell me you see the same thing now as you did before her."

Rime looked away. It shouldn't have been difficult to humor the stone whisperer. But still, his legs refused to carry him closer.

"Blood is blindcraft, Rime. I've done as you asked. The guild has talked more about the raven rings in the last few days than it has in ten winters, but you'll not get a definitive answer. There are as many opinions as there are stone whisperers, but if you ask me, that was how the Seer shut the gateways. He drew upon the Might from every man and woman. Dead and alive."

Rime gave a crooked smile. "The Seer? Still a believer, are you, Hlosnian?"

"Question is, are you still a doubter, lad? You saw the tree. You shattered it. You ought to know better."

Rime had lost the thread. He couldn't let Hlosnian go off on a tangent. "What does the tree have to do with any of this?"

"Anything not involving trees isn't really worth talking about."

"Hlosnian—"

"Pay attention when I'm talking! I'm telling it like it is. The tree didn't come out of nothing. It was created by someone. Created by the Might. They say the force it required cleaved the mountains of Blindból asunder. Made the fissure running from Ravnhov all the way to the Alldjup. Do you think something like that comes from nothing?" Hlosnian bashed his fists together to ward off the cold, dislodging snow from his fingerless gloves.

Rime sighed. "You haven't got a clue, have you?"

Hlosnian puffed his chest out like a bellows. "Of course not, but nor does anyone else!"

Rime fought back a smile. The stone whisperer swept the snow off some tall stalks nearby. "Look at these, boy, and imagine that the water they survive on is the Might. What would happen if you drew out every single drop in one fell swoop? They would wither and die. Or what about the opposite, if you forced in more water than they could drink? Just as dead, right? And that's what I'm saying: the gateways died because all of the Might went into the creation of the tree. The flow dried up. The stones fell dormant."

Rime tried to stitch together fragments of memories. He knew what it meant to have too much of a good thing when it came to the Might. Through Hirka, he had been able to draw upon more of the Might than anyone else. What would have happened if the flow had doubled while he was suspended in front of the Council, surrounded by the ravens? Could he have endured it? Or would his body have been torn apart?

Was that what Urd had done to Vetle? Forced more of the Might through his own son than he could bear? Whatever he'd done, it had ruined the boy. Forever confined him to the mind of a child.

Rime shuddered as if Slokna had him in its sights. A raven-black darkness that wouldn't let go.

He looked at Hlosnian. "So if they can draw the Might out of people during the Rite and then mark them with raven blood ..."

Hlosnian tapped his finger against his temple. "Then it follows that they can force the Might in the opposite direction. I think you overestimate the effect, but the flow *can* dry up. Or it can become a deluge. Too much and too little are equally bad."

"And that's what Urd did at Bromfjell? Drew upon the Might using raven blood?"

"Shush! Let me finish," Hlosnian huffed. "It's like tearing down the doors as you open them. It destroys you. Destroys others. Blindcraft, Rime. It's just not done."

"Well, nobody told the Council that," Rime said and looked away. He didn't want the stone whisperer to see his disappointment. Or realize how much opening the raven rings meant to him.

"You say that like they knew what they were doing." Hlosnian smiled.

"Everyone knows what they're doing. The question is whether they can live with it."

Rime put the ampoule back in his pocket. He knew Hlosnian was right. Not even Jarladin could say whether the marks on the forehead had any effect. They'd followed the same formula for centuries, under the pretext of making people less enticing to the blind. And, unbeknownst to anyone, less powerful in the Might.

But it didn't matter whether it worked. It would never happen again. Rime had made sure of that.

Hlosnian stared down at his reflection in the ice. He clearly had something to get off his chest.

"I've taken it myself, Rime."

"Taken what?"

"Raven blood."

Rime stepped closer. The stone whisperer hunched his shoulders like a dog. "I took it, once. And I'm not the only one. They sell it outside the guildhalls. I know it. You know it. There is power in blood. Stone whisperers take it to hear the voices more clearly, but it always ends in misery. Always."

"So what happened? Did you find the source of the Might? The meaning of life?" Rime smiled to temper any judgement in his voice. What some people would do for a brief respite from reality came as no surprise to him.

The stone whisperer looked up at him. "I was never the same again. It's not meant for us."

"Neither is opa, but people still use it," Rime replied.

Hlosnian flapped his arms in an attempt to keep warm, then looked back in the direction he'd come from, like he regretted walking so far. "You're seeing me in a different light now, aren't you?"

Rime was caught off guard. Hlosnian wasn't one to worry about what others thought of him. It was practically a defining trait of the strange old stone whisperer.

"No," Rime replied with a grin. "It's always been obvious that you're a bit crazy."

"Pshaw! Everyone is crazy in their own way, boy." Hlosnian put his hand on Rime's shoulder. "Raven blood opens pathways. In yourself, but not in the stones. It's not traveler's blood," he said. "None of us have that. I don't have it. You don't have it. I doubt any living creature does. So we're not going anywhere. But she had it. Older than sin and more potent than raven blood."

"But that can't be right, Hlosnian. We passed through the gateways, just the same as her. It's not a question of blood."

"It's *always* a question of blood. We traveled from this world to this world. Not far at all, really. We were able to do that because this is where we belong. But she … she makes me wonder about a lot of things."

Rime felt the air grow colder. Had he been looking at it from the wrong angle? Maybe instead of strengthening the Might around the stones, he'd have to strengthen himself.

He looked at the stone whisperer. "You're wrong about one thing, Hlosnian."

"Oh, most things, I would hope. But what are you referring to?"

"If there is such a thing as traveler's blood, she's not the only one with it. The blind also had it."

"You think too much, boy. Can we go now, before my tail freezes off?"

Hlosnian turned and walked away. His robe brushed across the snow, ice crystals glittering along its frayed edge.

Rime looked down into the birdbath. At his own face, frozen in the ice. He was pale as a blindling.

THE OPEN CHURCH

Hirka gave a start. She'd almost fallen asleep.

She blamed the fan over the greenhouse door. Its constant humming had a lulling effect.

She looked over at the blindling, who was resting on a pallet of soil. She'd laid her spare jumper over him. Not because she was worried he'd get cold, but had it been her lying there, she'd have appreciated being covered up.

He was no longer twitching, and his breathing had evened out, thankfully.

Thankfully? He's nábyrn!

She drew her knees up and leaned her head against the wall. She was surrounded by plants with names she didn't know. Green seedlings were stacked on workbenches. Flowers hung from the roof in ceramic pots. It was like being in a forest in the middle of summer. But outside, the world was white. Wet snow lashed at the glass before sliding down into heaps on the ground. She was in two worlds at once. One where things were being born, and one where things were dying. She just wasn't entirely sure which was which.

It was dark, and that was a good thing. That gave her the upper hand, because she could see everything outside but no one could see her well enough to sneak up on her. She swallowed, remembering the man's hands around her neck, the despair she'd felt at not being able to understand him. But he'd gotten what he wanted.

He was probably far away by now. So who was after her now? Seer knows.

The Seer …

Hirka sat up and gazed at the blindling. Everything she'd ever heard about the Seer whirled through her mind. A maelstrom of words and images. He was the blindling who'd turned his back on his own people to save Ym. Who'd taken the form of a raven and become the Seer they'd worshipped for a thousand years. The Seer who didn't exist. Had she just witnessed the exact same thing? Kuro changing form, but from raven to blindling?

Don't be stupid, girl! Does he look like a god?

Hirka crawled over to him. She lifted a finger to poke him, but then decided against it. That would be trying her luck. He wasn't as weak as he had been. She picked up a garden trowel just in case. She could smell the tang of the raven blood in his hair. Several blood vessels had burst along his collarbone, the blood spreading like tendrils of ink under his skin. The imperfection seemed out of place on his muscular body. He had high cheekbones that reminded her of Rime. His mouth was half-open, revealing the only unsettling feature of his otherwise beautiful face: his canines.

He wasn't moving. She reached out to him, resting her thumb on his upper lip before carefully pulling it back. They weren't that long. Not like wolves' teeth. He turned his head, and she tore her arm back.

What was she doing? Hadn't she seen more than enough of the blind? Few knew better than her and Rime what they were capable of. Urd had promised her to these creatures. As a sacrifice. But in exchange for what? Knowledge of blindcraft?

But how could this be one of the blind? This was Kuro. Her raven.

No. Not anymore. She'd gathered the remains of what had been Kuro. A gory soup she'd thrown in a bin outside. Kuro was dead. She'd lost him. All that remained was this creature. Hideously beautiful, more powerfully built than any ymling she'd ever seen. Godlike? Perhaps. But he was young, dead to the world, and smelled of blood and decay. That wasn't very godlike. She also doubted the Seer would smack his lips in his sleep.

Rime would know what to do.

Rime would have woken him up, demanded answers. At the very least he'd have been able to protect them both if the blindling had come to. What could she do? Poke him with the trowel? She tossed it aside, shaking her head at herself. This was surreal. She had to get out of there. No matter who was waiting for her outside, they couldn't be any worse than the creature before her. And it was only a matter of time before someone came. It was Sunday, which meant few humans would be working, but that didn't mean no one would come to the greenhouse.

But where could she go? She didn't have much in the way of money or food, and now she had one of the deadborn to contend with. She closed her eyes in resignation. She would leave soon, but it wouldn't be to run. It would be to help him.

She knew what this world was like, and he wouldn't understand. No one deserved to face it alone. Like she'd done. He needed clothes. And food. And a bath wouldn't hurt, but she had no idea how she'd manage that. The only real option was the church …

Could she risk it? Father Brody didn't even know she'd run away yet. Wouldn't know until daybreak. But it wasn't safe to go now. Someone had been following her. She didn't know who, or why. She needed to wait until morning, so she wouldn't be alone in the streets. No one could get to her if she was surrounded by people.

It was a strange thought considering how she usually felt about crowds. It had been bad at home. Here it was even worse. Even though she was supposedly one of them. A human. Here they were all children of Odin. Emblings. The rot. So why did she feel so out of place?

Hirka got up, picked up a tall plant from the table, and carried it over to the blindling. He was still out for the count. She carried over another plant. And another. Until he was hidden behind a wall of green. She knew it was pointless, really. If anyone came in, they'd still find him. But she had to do *something*.

She could hear cars going past outside. People were starting to go about their day. She shouldered her bag and slipped out of the greenhouse.

The sky was gray, the cold not so biting anymore. She followed the fence to the river. Holes had started to appear in the ice. She rounded the fence and found the road, all the while pushing down the feeling she was doing something stupid. She had to force her feet to keep moving. There were very few people around, but still she glanced down every alley she passed. She wasn't sure how long she had before Father Brody opened the church doors, so she started to run.

What would she say? Would she tell him she'd intended to run away? Or just say she'd been out all night? And what would she say about the blindling?

He would have to be kept secret. Father Brody would call him a demon, and he was scared of demons. Hirka had never met one, but she had a feeling they looked like the deadborn. She could say she'd come across a man. An ordinary man, someone in need of help. Father Brody would give her some of the clothes he'd collected for the poor. She was sure of it.

Hirka stopped outside the church. Gray depressions in the snow told her that Father Brody was already there. Jay and her mum, too. The smaller tracks had to belong to Jay's little sister. But there were others as well. More than there ought to have been. Unease erupted in her chest. Something was wrong. She went up the steps and tried the door. It was open. She slipped into the vestibule. She could hear noises from the main hall. A child crying. Two men arguing.

"Don't you know nothing about kids?"

"Enough to know they talk. That's what kids do. They talk!"

"Christ, she's barely out of nappies! What do you think a kid's gonna say? And just think of the fucking hassle!"

"It's already a fucking hassle, Isac!"

Hirka pressed herself up against the wall. She heard a door open. The voice of a third man rose above the others. "She's not up there, either. But she's definitely been living there."

"Been living?! You said she hadn't been out in days! Would you make that kid shut up?!"

"If the girl's not here, you might as well fucking shoot yourself now. That'd save him the bother of killing you. Because he will, when he finds out you weren't giving her your full attention."

Hirka tried her best to understand what they were saying, but there were too many words she didn't know. The way their voices echoed in the hall didn't make it any easier. But she caught enough to know it was her they were looking for. She kept her ear pressed against the wall. She could hear her blood pumping. Her heart beating. She had to get out of there.

The child ...

The girl was still crying. Sobbing for her mother. The sound was heart-wrenching. Hirka couldn't just abandon her. She had to get her out of there. Her and the others. But where were they? She had to find out. Just a quick peek.

She peered around the wall and into the hall. She stiffened. Knew she should run, but couldn't. Her feet started to move of their own accord. Down the aisle. Toward Jay, who was lying face-down on the floor. Motionless. Her earbuds had fallen out. They were lying in a pool of blood.

Dilipa was lying next to her, head between the pews. Staring up at Hirka with dead eyes. Hirka felt her face go numb. Was this real? Was she in Slokna, having a bad dream? She looked up.

Three men were standing in front of the altar, staring at her like she was a ghost. One of them had Jay's little sister by the scruff of the neck. The girl sobbed. She was practically hanging from the man's hand, her feet having failed her.

Hirka was lost for words. Fury and grief threatened to choke her. She stopped a short distance away from them. Stared at them. They stared back. Time stood still.

Then the tallest of them started to laugh. He had blond hair and was wearing a garish shirt with a zigzag pattern. He gestured around the church. "Maybe there is a God after all!" he said and started toward her. Hirka spotted a figure in black slumped over the altar. Father Brody.

Dogs. Mad dogs. Wild animals. That's what they were. Hirka looked at Jay's little sister. There was only one thing to do. Only one thing would distract them from the girl.

Hirka whirled around and bolted for the door. The men all shouted in unison. Someone grabbed her raincoat, pulling her back. The tall man put his hand over her mouth. There was a bang. Jay's little sister stopped crying. The two men started shouting at each other. The one holding Hirka told them to shut up. He smelled of rotten food.

Then there were two of them holding her. The third stuck his head out the door. Nodded. They pulled her outside. She kicked. Punched. Bit. Tears overwhelmed her. She was dragged through the snow, between the headstones. Into the dark alleyway behind the almshouse.

BLOOD SPILLED

Hirka sat in the back seat, struggling with the car door. It was locked, but she had to get out. Now. Before they drove off. While she could still see the church tower. She knew it didn't make much sense, but it gave her something to focus on. If they took her away from here, it would be over. She'd be completely lost.

Two of the men sat in the front screaming at each other. The car started and lurched forward in the alleyway. The bigger man hit the one who was driving, and the car stopped suddenly. Hirka's head thumped into the back of the seat. She was thrown backward again, but her bag absorbed most of the impact. The door swung open on the other side. Hirka launched herself across the seat to escape but was pushed back by the third man. The man who had grabbed her in the church. The one named Isac.

He sat down on the back seat, feet still outside. "Shut it!" he screamed, holding a hand up to silence the others. It went quiet. Hirka was so scared that her feet were shaking. Then she felt something press against her ankle.

My knife.

She looked down at her yellow boots. Wiggled her foot and felt the sheath slide around in her woolly sock. It was still there. There was still hope. She just had to keep her cool. Wait for the right moment.

The driver was a skittish little man. His mousy face shone with sweat, and he kept muttering the same thing over and over. "Not good, not good." The other man was stocky and kept elbowing him in the ribs, but he seemed equally jumpy. That was a good sign. Nervous men made mistakes. Sooner or later.

Isac pressed a finger to his forehead and sighed. He was calmer than the others. Fearless, almost. Clearly he was the one to worry about.

"Mickey, do us a favor, would you?" he said to the little man, who immediately looked even more petrified. "If I get it into my head to invite you along again, shoot me, would you? Eh? Take pity on me, so I don't have to witness you causing such …" He pounded his fist into the back of the seat to emphasize each word. "Total. Fucking. Chaos."

"He said my name," Mickey muttered. "Now she knows my name! You don't use someone's name in the middle of a job!"

"Lord, give me strength …" Isac turned his eyes heavenward. "This was supposed to be clean, Mickey. No blood. This ain't no film! We ain't going nowhere until you've cleaned up after yourself! You hear me?"

"Cleaned up? What the … we've got her! We're in the clear. I'm not going back in there! Never go back, Isac! First rule in the field. In and out, quick-like, yeah?"

"I'm going to smash his TV," Isac whispered, pinching the bridge of his nose. It went quiet again. The two men stared at the man behind the wheel.

"What? WHAT?! We've got what we came for!"

"The girl, yes, but not the raven. Do you want to be the one to tell him that?" Isac asked.

Mickey swallowed.

"No, I thought not. Then we'd best find us a raven."

"Can't we just grab one of those? Surely it can't—"

"Those are crows, you idiot." Isac looked at Hirka. "It's a wonder his knuckles don't drag along the ground, isn't it?"

Hirka didn't respond. She wanted no part in his attempts at humor. Both men in the front were clearly nervous now. The bigger man cursed, then got out of the car. He lit a cigarette.

"Where's the bird, young miss?" Isac leaned toward her. She didn't understand how someone whose clothes were so clean could smell so rotten. The others didn't seem to notice. Was it just her? It reminded her of Urd. Of the smell that had come from his throat at the stone circle near Ravnhov. His men hadn't seemed disgusted either.

Still, Mickey was the killer among them. And remorseless at that. As though he had the right to just end people's lives. Father Brody. Jay. Dilipa. And a child. A five-year-old … it was monstrous. Hirka had to press her lips together to stop them from quivering.

Isac dragged her out of the car and pinned her against the side. "The raven?"

Hirka shrugged. "He's a bird. They fly where they like," she replied.

Isac leaned in close. She twisted away from his breath, but he followed her movements. His eyes looked almost colorless. Was he sick? If the smell was anything to go by, he was already knocking on death's door. There was something horribly wrong with him, but she refused to let him see how much it scared her.

"So what's the deal with you?" he said. "What's so incredibly special about you that I've had to come all this way? What do you have that we don't, eh?"

He didn't seem to be looking for a reply, but she gave him one anyway. "A soul."

She hadn't expected a reaction, but he gaped at her for a moment. Then he regained his composure. Tossed his blond fringe back. The movement was far too youthful for a man who had to be in his fifties.

"Keeping a raven as a pet, that's most peculiar," he said, tugging on his lapels as though his jacket were ill-fitting. "I'm thinking that means you like him? Shame we have to burn down the church. I wonder …" He gripped her chin and tilted her head back. "Singed feathers, what do you think that smells like?"

The big man chuckled, dropped his cigarette, and stomped it out. He opened the car door and grabbed a container of what she guessed was oil. He started to search for something in his pockets as he walked past them. Toward the church.

Her anger won out over her fear. Had they planned to kill her, they'd have done it by now. But she was alive, and that emboldened her. She glared at Isac.

"One day," she said, "one day you're going to beg me to spare your life."

"Not today," Isac replied and shoved her back into the car.

Mickey rubbed his face in his hands. "Isac, we have to get out of here! We're wasting time!"

"We're not wasting time, we're making time, you ninny! If we run, it'll be all over the news within the hour, thanks to you. So instead of mass murder, we're giving them a fire. If we're lucky, it'll buy us a couple of hours. And if you don't shut your trap, I'm going to use you as kindling."

Hirka reached down toward her boot. Slowly, so nobody would notice. She fumbled under her trouser leg and grabbed the knife.

"He's coming back now," Mickey said, looking out the rear window.

Two bangs came from out of nowhere. Mickey ducked down behind the wheel. Hirka pulled her knife from its sheath and leaped out of the car. The door hit Isac as he keeled over onto the road. He grabbed his chest. Blood oozed from between his fingers, following the pattern of his shirt. He stared up at her in confusion.

Another bang seemed to come from the walls themselves. Impossible to pinpoint. Someone grabbed her and spun her around. It was Mickey. He pulled her close and stared up at the sky. "Who are you? Who the fuck are you?" She spotted a figure coming down a nearby fire escape. He took the last few steps in a single bound. Mickey grabbed something from his inside pocket and pressed it against her head. It was a weapon. She knew that now. And she knew what he'd done in the church. He was going to do it again. She tightened her grip on the knife.

"I'll save you," she said.

Mickey's gaze wavered. Uncomprehending. He lowered the weapon to her jaw, his breath coming in short gasps. It was him or her. Hirka jammed the knife into his chest, right under his ribs, then forced it upward. His eyes grew wide as she leaned close and whispered into his ear. "You don't have to be scared anymore, Mickey." His weapon fell to the ground. Hirka pulled the knife out. The sound made her feel nauseous. He slumped back against the car tire.

The third man.

Hirka turned. The thickset man with the oil container was running back from the church. She would never manage a man his size on her own. But another bang stopped him in his tracks. He fell to his knees. His body swayed. Behind him she saw flames licking at the walls of the church. An alarm blared. Then he toppled onto his side.

Someone ran past her. The figure she'd seen on the fire escape. He kneeled down beside the man on the ground. She heard a crack. For a moment she thought he'd broken the dead man's fingers, but she could see both his hands, so it must have been something else.

Police sirens. Hirka had heard them before. They signaled disaster. The end. She pressed her hands over her ears. She was shaking. Shaking so much she wasn't able to block out the sound. Blood ran down the knife and onto her fingers. Her rescuer got back up and walked toward her. She'd have recognized him anywhere. It was him. The man in the hoodie. She held out the knife and backed away.

He walked straight past her and got in the car. "Come on. Time's really not on our side," he said.

Hirka stared at the flames. Why did everything have to burn? Why did everything she touched turn to ash? All she wanted was to piece things back together. Suddenly she was back in Ym, standing on the ridge, watching the cabin burn. Father was dead. Everyone was dead.

She walked as if in a trance, then climbed into the car with the stranger. He started the car and it lurched forward. She heard a thump and looked back. Mickey had fallen to the ground when the car started moving. Hirka put her hand on the window.

"Don't touch anything!" The man in the hoodie swatted her hand away. The car swerved a little. "They'll find us if you do." What was he talking about? She was touching the seat. So was he. He glanced at her. "The police? Fingerprints?" He rubbed his thumb and index finger together. He was wearing gloves.

"They won't find me," she answered and hugged her bag.

"They find everyone, sooner or later. Why wouldn't they find you?"

"I don't exist," she answered.

He barked out a laugh. "Wishful thinking, girl."

He turned onto a bigger road, into a line of other cars. Then he started to speed up.

OPPOSITION

The swords sang as they came together, and Rime suddenly found himself face to face with Svarteld. The master's gaze was as steady as ever. He gave nothing away when he was fighting. His dark skin made his eyes seem brighter than those of most men. Perhaps that was why it was so difficult to read him. He hadn't even broken a sweat.

But Rime had. Changing tack now would mean losing. His arms were burning, and the master knew it. He thought he could see a hint of a smile in his eyes. Rime gritted his teeth. He was trapped. That made him think of Hirka again.

Rime brought his heel down on Svarteld's toes. The master gave a grunt and jumped back. Rime followed, striking three times until his sword came to rest at Svarteld's throat. The master laughed. His amusement was the only reason Rime had gained the advantage. He could count on one hand the number of times he'd caught Svarteld off guard, and this wasn't one of them.

"To think she taught you more about fighting than I could," Svarteld said with a grin.

Rime let his sword arm drop. "She?" he asked, even though he knew full well who he was referring to.

"You were never impulsive before you met her."

Rime was disappointed that the master wouldn't say her name. Hearing it from others made her real. Like she was somewhere nearby. Somewhere he could get to.

He walked back to the center of the room and lifted his sword again.

Svarteld came toward him. "And there I was thinking you'd get fat and lazy sitting around the table in Eisvaldr. Ravenbearers don't need to sweat. Or is the staff really that heavy to bear?" He started circling Rime, unaware that he'd opened a wound no one could see.

Rime followed his movements. "I've only held the staff once, and that was during the handover ceremony."

"No Seer. No staff. No raven on your forehead. How are you supposed to lead if no one sees you?" Svarteld asked, aiming a blow at Rime's side. Rime turned his sword and parried. He refused to let himself be fazed.

"The most important thing is that they listen to me."

"You're not stupid enough to believe that."

Svarteld unleashed a barrage of blows that forced him back. Rime ducked under the blade and around him. The master rewarded him with a moment to catch his breath.

"Rime, working against them is no help to anyone. The Council must be united. Each and every one of you was born for this task."

"*No one* is born for this task! No one has a god-given right to the chairs!"

Rime opened the folding doors and walked out onto the cliff edge. He'd always thought Blindból gave him a sense of peace, but the truth was he'd never known peace. All he had were moments of oblivion.

Far below him, the fog lay thicker than usual. The snow had settled on the same side of all the mountains. The wind swept it from the peaks, making it appear as though they were crumbling.

He heard Svarteld's footsteps in the snow behind him.

"You'll rue the day you lose to me," Rime said.

"The day I lose to you, it'll be out of love," the master said. The words were unexpected. Spoken completely without warmth, but they were a reminder that Rime had people behind him. Family.

"They're fighting against me, master. Even harder than you with your sword. Every day they do something new in an attempt to silence me. To consign me to oblivion. They'd kill me if they could."

Svarteld stepped up next to him. "Maybe some silence wouldn't hurt."

Rime looked at him. "A submissive ravenbearer? Can you imagine anything more dangerous?"

Svarteld didn't reply. Rime slid his sword into the scabbard on his back. "They want me to pledge myself to someone. Find a wife."

"Well, that would solve a lot of problems."

"That's what I keep saying! Me finding a wife won't solve any—"

"No, I mean it," Svarteld said. "It would solve a lot of problems."

For a moment Rime thought he'd misheard. As Kolkagga's master, Svarteld ought to have been the first to reject the idea of being bound to someone else. Rime clenched his fists. Not even Svarteld was on his side.

"Spending money on a wedding won't put more food on people's tables."

Svarteld chuckled. "How many other excuses do you have?"

"Enough," Rime replied, looking away.

"You're looking at it all wrong, Rime. Think what it could give you, not what it could take away. I've heard mention of a girl from the north. That would certainly bring Ravnhov and the Council closer together, whether they like it or not."

Rime didn't reply. He knew Svarteld was right, but it all still felt ridiculous to him. He had more important things to worry about. Things like the gateways.

Svarteld pointed his sword at the fifty or so Kolkagga scaling the sheer rock face some distance away. On their backs, they carried woven baskets. Fish, birds, winter grass. Even survival was a training exercise in Blindból, and it was often the newest recruits who were tasked with ensuring this. Their black clothes made them indistinguishable from the rock, so much so that it sometimes looked like the baskets were floating up on their own.

"They scale that cliff several times a day," Svarteld said. "To stay alive. To keep *us* alive. Remember?"

Remember? I still have marks on my shoulders from the straps.

"When the day is done, they lie down to sleep. Then they get up the next day and do the same thing all over again. But then comes the winter solstice. They sit around the fire in their huts, drinking wine and fermented tea. They roll up their sleeves and show off their scars. Laugh at each other's mistakes. Give each other things they've made, bought, or stolen. And the following day, they sleep in."

"Sleep in?" Rime raised an eyebrow at the master, who coughed sheepishly.

"Later than on other days, in any case. But my question to you is this: should we deprive them of that evening?"

"Of course not, master."

"Why not?"

"Because the days are hard enough as they are." Rime knew he was walking into a trap, but Svarteld's traps were difficult to avoid. One way or another, you were caught.

"That's true, the days are hard enough as they are. Give a man something to celebrate, and you can torment him for the rest of the year."

"So let's celebrate without bringing wives into it!"

Svarteld looked at him. "You're the Ravenbearer. They can't force you. But if you started a family, the people would celebrate. They'd forget all about the people who died at Ravnhov. Forget the ash that's killing the crops. They'd even forget the Raven. All they'd see was youth, hope, and love. A new generation of An-Elderins. Something constant amid the chaos. And no matter how you look at it, Rime, it is *your* chaos. The worst thing that can happen is you'll have a warm embrace to sink into in the evenings. There are worse things in life, boy."

Rime stared at him.

Svarteld was clearly enjoying himself. "What? Did you think being the Ravenbearer wouldn't come at a price? That you wouldn't have to make sacrifices?"

Rime didn't reply. What was there to say? He'd already sacrificed the only thing that mattered to him. Being bound to someone else felt like a death sentence. It meant accepting that Hirka was lost to him. That she was never coming back.

A black-clad Kolkagga came running from between the trees. "Master Svarteld! A raven!"

He approached them and did his best to hide how short of breath he was. He gave Svarteld a white sleeve bearing the Council seal. The mark of the raven lived, even though the Seer never had.

Svarteld handed the sleeve to Rime. "It's for you."

Rime took it and unrolled the small length of paper. The hairs on his arms stood on end as he read. "It's the last group of soldiers returning from Ravnhov. They're near Mannfalla. They say they've been attacked and that several of them are badly wounded."

Svarteld nodded. "I know. But we sent them all the help we could weeks ago."

"No. They were attacked recently." Rime handed him the letter. "And not by ymlings. They say it was nábyrn."

Svarteld snatched the letter. No one had seen the blind since Bromfjell erupted. That fateful day. The day Urd had died and the Rite Hall had fallen. When Hirka had still been in Ym. She was gone now, and they'd all thought the blind were, too.

Rime squeezed the sleeve in his fist. Svarteld looked at him.

"Be careful what you wish for, Rime An-Elderin. You might just have found your reason to put off the celebrations."

THE HUNTER

I've killed.

The thought was there before she even realized she was awake. Hot blood on her hand as she held the knife. Her murder. Her ruin. "Thou shalt not kill," Father Brody had said. Hirka wished he'd said *Thou shalt not die* instead. Maybe then he'd still be alive.

Her eyes felt puffy, and she remembered crying. It wasn't fair. Waking up was meant to be sacred. Devoid of memory, just for a little while. Until you remembered everything that was wrong. She'd often thought that. In another world. Another time. In the cabin in Elveroa, the gulls shrieking outside, and Father by the hearth, grinding dried soldrop. Back then she'd woken up a normal girl. Until she remembered.

Child of Odin. The rot. What am I now?

As soon as she opened her eyes, everything would be gone. No cabin. No shuttered windows. Not even proper log walls. Just a featureless room in a hotel. A tall inn where nobody knew each other. She could hear the buzz of the city. It was there when she woke up, and there when she fell asleep. It was a wonder people didn't go mad here. Then she remembered what had happened, and realized that they probably *were* mad. Each and every one of them. She should never have come here.

Had she stayed in Ym, they'd still be alive. Father Brody. Jay and her mum and little sister. The pain smoldered in her chest. Layer upon layer of sorrow, for everything and everyone she hadn't been able to keep. She'd been born on the run.

At least she hadn't been entirely alone. She'd had Kuro. A friend who knew she was telling the truth, because they'd come here together. They'd been an *us*. Now it was just her.

And the blindling …

She had to get going. Get back to the greenhouse before anyone found him. Before he woke up and wandered off. Naked. And with as little knowledge of this place as she'd had.

Hirka opened her eyes. A green lamp was humming away on the bedside table. She still had her clothes on, but someone had pulled a duvet over her. It must have been him. The man who'd robbed her. And rescued her. The man in the hoodie.

She smelled smoke and rolled over cautiously. He was sitting in a chair by the window, staring out at the gray sky. He'd lowered his hood. His brown hair stuck out in every direction, like tufts of grass. The tips had been bleached by the sun. He looked like a different person now. Now that she knew he wasn't going to hurt her.

His fingers were drumming on the armrest. A cigarette was glowing between his fingers. Jay had smoked on occasion, though she'd kept it from her mum. Apparently smoking killed. But smoking wasn't what had killed Jay.

The man glanced over and gave a start when he saw that she was awake. He tapped the screen of his phone. "It's four in the afternoon. You've been asleep for hours," he said.

Hirka sat up in the bed. People here were obsessed with time. As though there was never enough of it. All she had to do was look outside. The sky told her how long she'd been asleep. She didn't need time to be divided into smaller chunks than that.

She got up and went over to the window. They were high up. In the distance she saw the church, surrounded by cars and flashing lights. It was impossible to tell how much of it was left, but the tower was still standing. Charred black. People were crowded together outside the gate. Were they still inside? Father Brody and the others?

"Sit down," the man said, pointing at an empty chair. Hirka did as she was told. She'd already annoyed him by insisting they stay in the city. She hadn't even been able to tell him why. But he'd listened to her. For reasons she didn't think either of them understood.

He pulled out his weapon. A black, angular piece of metal that was even uglier now that she knew its purpose. He put it down on the glass table between them.

"You have no idea what this is, do you?" he asked. Hirka said nothing. She knew and she didn't know at the same time.

His feet were tapping nervously. He was wearing blue trousers. The heavy kind, with a name she couldn't remember. A lot of them were donated to the church, usually in better condition than his. There were holes in the knees and the material had worn thin below the pockets. He leaned forward.

"Nobody's that calm when they have a Glock pressed to their temple. Nobody."

He took a drag of his cigarette and put it out in a glass, even though it wasn't finished. "But you were," he said, studying her. He was maybe twice her age. Eyes brown like his hair. Her gaze was once again drawn to the pale mark by his lip. A scar that tugged his mouth up slightly on one side. Almost unnoticeable under his stubble.

"So how does a youngster keep her cool with a muzzle pressed to her head? That's what I keep wondering, right? And you know what, I can only come up with two possible answers." He leaned back. "Either she's been in so many dicey situations she can hide how scared she is, which seems unlikely. Nobody would drag a girl into something like that. The second option is she simply doesn't know what's going on. So this is a Glock 19. A nine-millimeter handgun. A pistol. But you don't know what that is, do you?"

Hirka thought she understood what he was saying, even though half the words were new to her. Glock? Pistol? She looked at the weapon on the table. "It's a weapon. It kills people," she said, then shrugged, trying to make it look like she'd been talking about such things all her life.

"Yes, you know that *now*. But you didn't before, did you?"

Hirka shook her head. There was no point in pretending to know things she didn't. After all, the man had helped her, albeit reluctantly.

"No. And you've never been in an elevator before?"

"Elevator?"

"The hotel elevator. The thing that carried us up here when we arrived."

"Oh … no."

"And you have no idea what these are worth?" He dropped three stones on the table. They were hers. The ones he'd taken.

"Those are mine!" Hirka grabbed them. "They were given to me," she added, giving him an accusing look. He was the thief, not her.

"I'll take that as a no? You have no idea how much they're worth?"

"I do. Just … not here."

"No. And that's the interesting bit. You know how much they're worth somewhere, but not here. Which begs another question." He leaned forward again. "Where the hell are you from?"

Hirka bit her lip. Talking about where she was from never led to anything good.

"Do you have anything to drink?" she asked.

He looked momentarily perplexed. As if he'd never been asked for something so simple before. He got up and went into the bathroom anyway. Hirka glanced at the door. Should she make a run for it? This might be her only chance. She shifted in the chair, but she'd hesitated too long.

He came back and set a glass of water down in front of her. Hirka drank it all. He didn't ask if she wanted more.

"Have you shown them to anyone? The stones?" he asked.

She shook her head.

"Well, I have. And I'd hold on to them if I were you. Such a fucking waste. I could have retired on them and you'd have been none the wiser. I should take them, that's what I should do."

"You did take them."

"Christ ..." He looked out at the flashing lights over by the church. "I thought they belonged to *them*, all right? That you were somehow involved with them. But you don't know who they are, do you? You've never heard of Vardar? Or the forgotten?"

She shook her head. He ran a hand over his face. He looked tired.

"What's your name?" Hirka asked, tucking her feet up under her legs. She felt like climbing something, but there wasn't much to climb here. He gave her a lopsided smile. It made him seem kinder. Nice, almost. It just hadn't been possible to see that when she'd thought he was a threat. Which he perhaps still was. Whatever the case, he certainly wasn't a friend.

"Stefan. My name's Stefan Barone." He seemed surprised by his own answer. She hoped it was because it was true.

"I'm Hirka."

"Strange name, though that doesn't surprise me. So where are you from, Hirka?"

"Where are *you* from?"

He looked her up and down, as if trying to find something to help him decide whether or not to answer truthfully.

"My dad was Swedish, my mum Italian. Home can be a thousand places, as long as there are hotels or familiar faces. I've been to a dozen European countries in the past six months. But that means nothing to you, does it?"

"My father was from Ulvheim. I didn't know my mother. Before I was ten, I'd seen most of Ym from a wagon, and I've traveled through Blindból on foot. But I'm sure that doesn't mean anything to you either."

Stefan laughed and rubbed his neck. He was a grown man, but there was something ... lost about him. Hirka grinned, then realized it had been a long time since she'd smiled properly. The room suddenly felt warmer. She didn't know why, but she felt her shoulders relax a little. Was there that much power in sharing names? Maybe she'd broken the ice enough to get away. Back to the blindling.

And do what? Sit around until more men show up?

"What happened to your lip?" Hirka pointed at her own lip, in case she hadn't used the right words.

"I was born like this. And it's not nice to stare."

"I think it's nice," Hirka said. "Not to stare, I mean. Your mouth."

Stefan laughed and fiddled with his phone again. "So let's see if I've got this right: some nutjobs just tried to kidnap you. You have no idea who they are or what they want. Every single copper in York is working overtime trying to find us. An armed stranger is sitting a meter away from you. And you're talking about my mouth?"

Hirka shrugged and stared at the floor. "I haven't done anything wrong. I don't know why this is happening."

Stefan put his phone down again and got up. He had a chain around his neck that was tucked under his jumper.

"Have you ever met anyone who was truly ill, Hirka?"

Hirka fought back a smile. She doubted Stefan had met as many sick people as she had, but she didn't answer.

"I mean seriously ill. Someone who's at death's door. Imagine you saw them a year later, alive and kicking. Three years later. Thirty years." He looked at Hirka. "Not just alive, but not a year older. What would you think?" Stefan lit another cigarette. Not that he seemed to get any pleasure out of it.

"I'll tell you who those people were, Hirka. One of them was a career criminal nobody needs to worry about anymore. The other, I'm not sure, but it'll come out. The third …" Stefan gave her a pleading look, as though she were making him talk. "Well, he was a man, once. Before he turned into a predator. A blood slave. He's sick."

Isac.

Hirka didn't need to ask. She knew exactly who he was talking about.

"He was infected by something. Something that's been spreading for generations. Those who know about it keep quiet, because it's one of these things we're not supposed to know about. Do you understand? You do what you've got to do, right? I've been hunting them since I was a teenager."

He paced around the room. Picking things up and putting them down again, searching for the right words. "They call themselves Vardar. I followed them here, and they followed you. At first I thought you were one of them, but you're not, are you? Still, they wanted you, and I have no idea why." He spoke too fast for her to follow, using far too many new words.

"What's a blood slave?" she asked.

He stopped and looked at her again. "A person who should have been dead long ago but lives because someone wants them to."

"Who wants them to?"

"I've spent a lifetime trying to find out. If I knew the source, I wouldn't be wasting my time here. The one thing I am sure of is that he isn't human." Stefan sat down again. "And it worries me that you're not laughing now, or looking at me like I escaped from an institution. And what does that say about you? That you're not afraid of such a creature?"

She couldn't help but laugh. He gave her a confused look. It was difficult to find the words to express how backward things were here, but she tried. "I'm used to humans being the ones people fear.

Not being human is a very good thing where I come from. Believe me."

He studied her. "So if what you're saying is true, why haven't you told anyone?"

She shut her eyes. Easy for him to say. He was one of the lucky ones, never having to explain who or what he was. Hirka didn't know whether to laugh or cry.

"You know what? I thought I'd be coming home. I thought that as soon as I got here, everyone would see that I was one of you. A child of Odin. That I'd be welcomed with open arms. That's what I thought."

Hirka knew she should keep quiet, but talking had sparked a fire inside her that wouldn't go out. She couldn't stop. She had to make him understand everything that was wrong with this world. How flawed it was.

"When I first got here, nothing made sense to me. I started walking. I walked for days. And nights. The water tasted bitter, but I drank it anyway. And even though the trees were withered, seeing them made me happy. Because I know what trees are. Something familiar. Something real. And then I saw these …" She was getting stressed now and forgetting her words. "These cars! Racing around, and I … at first, I hid. In dead forests with no animals. There was nothing to live off. So I stood at the side of the road waving my arms, but no one stopped. So I threw a rock. And then one of them stopped. A man got out, and that made me happy, because he saw me. Because now someone knew that I was here. He'll take me to a village, I thought. Somewhere to live. Somewhere like Ravnhov. And there I'll drink tea and tell stories about Ym every night, and …"

Hirka got up. "He grabbed me and shook me. Screamed at me in a language I didn't understand. I bit him in the arm and ran. I came across more people and tried to explain. To tell them that I'd come through the stones, but they didn't understand a word of what I was saying. So I started pointing at things. Asking what they were called. But it was difficult. I … I stole food." She swallowed.

"Father Brody was the first person to actually listen. I noticed all the people going in to see him, and I thought it was some kind of seer's hall. I followed them. Lay down on a … chair. What's it called? A pew. And Father Brody didn't chase me off. I was allowed to stay. He asked me the same questions every day until I started to understand. He knew a lot of people, and I told them who I was, but do you know what? It meant nothing to them! They said I didn't even know what I was saying. That I was making things up. Some of them looked at me like I'd been hit in the head by a rock. An old lady told me straight out you can't go around saying you're from another world." Hirka was talking faster and faster, gasping for breath. "I'm not stupid. And I'm not crazy. So yes, I've told people who I am. Any more bright ideas?"

She picked up her bag. "Anyway, it doesn't matter what I say. I'm an outsider all the same. It means nothing to them that we're the same. That I'm human, too."

Stefan grabbed her arm. "So you come from some Disney dreamworld, do you? A place where no one kills, steals, or lies? Is that what it's like? Everyone's equal where you're from?"

She tore her arm away. "No! But where I come from, everyone knows that's the way it is. No one pretends it's better than it is. We have murderers and healers. Poor and rich. Here you all think you have what you need to survive, but you don't. You're blind, all of you. Blind …" Her voice faltered. "But at least that makes it easier to be invisible."

He got up and Hirka took a step back. Stefan was broad and more than a head taller than her. He grabbed a lock of her hair and pulled it through his fingers.

"If invisible is what you were going for, maybe you should have picked a different color."

"I didn't pick it. That's just the way it is."

"Really? You were born with hair that red?"

"You were born with that lip. See the problem? Well, I'm leaving now. I can't stay here. I have things to do. Can I borrow these?" Hirka pointed at a packet of cookies on the table. She was getting restless now. Feeling vulnerable. Exposed. Like the deadborn who was waiting for her.

"Be my guest. I hope you get a chance to eat them before they come after you again." Stefan hooked his thumbs into his pockets, confident his words would make her stay.

"Let them come. Besides, you came after me first." She shoved the cookies into her bag.

He sighed. "Yeah, sorry about that. I've said more than I should, but I had to be sure you weren't one of those sick creatures. Now I know you're not, but they are hunting you. They're not like other people. The sickness does things to them. To their heads. It's an infection. The body tries to fight it off, but it always loses. Sooner or later. You're not safe, Hirka."

"I never have been. Anyway, they're dead now."

"More will come."

"Then I'd better keep moving. I'm pretty good at that."

Hirka put her boots on. Her knife was lying on the floor. She hesitated for a moment before shoving it back down into her woolly sock. She tried not to think about what she'd used it for.

"Where's my raincoat?"

"It's hanging in the shower," he said. "I'd burn it if I were you. There was blood on it. That's how they get you, you know."

She clenched her teeth and fought down the feeling of guilt. It was what it was. She was alive because she'd killed.

She fetched the raincoat and put it on. Opened the door. It was heavier than she'd expected. Nothing was keeping her here anymore. Apart from Stefan. He clearly wasn't without his danger, but even so, she believed him. He wasn't out to hurt her. He hunted down people who were infected. But whereas she tried to heal, he chose to kill.

In any case, she couldn't stay. Wherever she went, blood followed. Both in Ym and now here. Staying with Stefan would be as good as killing him.

"Thanks for your help," she said.

"Not that it matters to me, but you're walking to your death, girl. Do you want me to force you to stay? I can if I have to."

"You won't do that."

"Why not?"

"Because you have no time for anyone else, Stefan Barone," she said and left.

UMPIRI

Please be all right, please let him be all right.

Hirka had run all the way from the hotel. The woman behind the front desk had merely waved as she'd sped past. Hadn't asked questions. Hadn't come after her. Hirka kept running anyway.

It was starting to get dark. She'd gotten stuck in the snow once already. One of her boots had come off and now it was all wet inside, but she couldn't stop. And she couldn't go straight to the greenhouse, either. First she had to be certain that no one was following her.

She crossed the park, where the snow lay untouched. Then she circled around so she ended up back where she'd started. On the same corner. Her own tracks were the only ones she could see. Good. That meant Stefan hadn't followed her. And no one else had either.

She ran toward the greenhouse, taking the shortest route. She was in too much of a hurry to follow the river, so she climbed over the gate and jumped down on the other side. The snow around the greenhouses was untouched as well. Fortunately. The blindling hadn't left. And no one had found him. But someone was bound to stumble upon him sooner or later. They had to find somewhere else before morning.

Hirka slipped into the greenhouse, past all the plants, and into the section at the end.

He wasn't there.

The raven blood had dried on the flagstones, but the blindling was nowhere to be seen. Her stomach churned. She started dragging bags of soil aside, as if he might be underneath them. Looking around, she suddenly became aware of his presence. She glanced up.

There he was. Perched on a rafter with his knees pointing in opposite directions and his arms in front of him. He cocked his head. Blinked his white eyes. Hirka set her bag down.

"Feeling better, I see," she said dryly, not expecting a response. She felt stupid for worrying about him.

He lifted his feet up toward the roof until he was doing a handstand. There was barely an ounce of fat on his body, and she could see every single muscle at work, including some she was sure she'd never seen before. Not in ymlings or humans, in any case. The lean ones along his spine. The folds around his shoulder blades. He spun around. Slowly, as if to demonstrate that he could. Then he dropped to the ground and smiled at her.

She took a step back. He was scarily close. And there was nothing weak about him anymore. He was more nábyrn than she remembered.

She opened her bag and gave him the apple and the cookies. "You can't walk around like that," she said, nodding in the direction of his crotch. "Normal people don't walk around naked." It was good to speak her own language again, even if she wasn't sure how much he understood. He took the food and she quickly snatched her hand away from his vile claws. She hadn't forgotten the grip he'd had on her wrist.

He circled around her. For a moment she considered running, but then he settled onto the bags of soil and stuck his claws into the apple. The peel started to shrivel. To cave inward. Rotting before her very eyes. Hirka felt her jaw drop.

"You eat with your claws ..." she whispered, then closed her mouth again so she wouldn't look like an idiot.

"You would too, had evolution been kinder to you."

Hirka clapped a hand over her mouth and backed away. His voice was deep and rough, but his ymish was more eloquent than hers.

"You see?" he said. "This is exactly what I mean. No control over your own body whatsoever. It's a miracle you're alive." He shook what remained of the apple off his hand. "Do you have anything more nourishing?"

It was starting to dawn on her that no thanks or praise would be forthcoming. Not that she'd been expecting any. She hadn't even expected to be standing here having a conversation. She'd been prepared to run for her life.

She walked toward him. He was incredible. "You're one of the blind. Nábyrn."

Something stirred in his eyes again. He got up. Loomed over her with his canines bared. His long hair brushed her face. She was rooted to the spot. Caught between fascination and fear. He hissed.

"Nábyrn? You call me deadborn? I am Naiell. I am Dreyri. I am Umpiri, blood of the first. I've lived through three millennia. You are born in droves, birthed by mothers who are dying before you are expelled from their bodies, and you call *us* deadborn? Tomorrow you'll all be gone. What are you, if not walking corpses?"

Hirka stumbled back and ended up sitting on the flagstones. "Three millennia …"

He straightened up and surveyed his claws. "The world suddenly looks a bit different, doesn't it? And as far as my vision is concerned, I can assure you I see better than you ever have or ever will. Blind are those who cannot see that we see."

"Three millennia …" She gaped at him. How could that be possible?

He spread his arms wide, as if to confirm everything he'd said. Or perhaps just to let her stare her fill. It was all she could do. Stare. It felt like all the wind had been knocked out of her. So much death.

Jay. Jay's little sister, who had hardly lived at all. Gone now. And here he stood, claiming … three millennia …

She'd laughed at her musings on who he could be. The blindling who'd taken the form of a raven.

But it *was* him. He was exactly who she'd thought he was. The raven who couldn't die, and here he stood. Right in front of her.

She'd run away to Ravnhov, snuck around in Mannfalla, all to elude the Raven. The Seer. And he'd been there the whole time! She'd fed him honey bread! She'd … she'd denied his existence.

She was suddenly overwhelmed with shame.

"We didn't think … we told them you didn't exist! You weren't there! Why weren't you there? The Seer doesn't exist!"

He crouched down in front of her and cocked his head.

"Check again."

Hirka knew she was gaping again. She lifted her hand to touch him, but then pulled it back to her chest again. Her heart started pounding. Full of anticipation. She had to do something. And soon. This changed everything.

Rime! I need to talk to Rime!

Everything they'd done, everything that had happened … And here she was, in the human world, the history of Ym standing before her. The Seer they'd thought was a lie. Images fought for space in her head. The Rite. The marks on the councillors' robes. The sculptures. The coins. Everything.

He got up and continued hoarsely: "Of course, the problem is I'm not the only one. The raven rings have lain dormant for a thousand years, and then you come along, little Sulni, and everything changes. Umpiri have come to Ym again, and that's a situation we cannot have. And the stones let you pass as if you were an old friend. Not exactly a good sign, you might say. The question is why you're here, and what you intend to do," he said, making it sound like anything but a question.

"What? I …" Hirka didn't know what to say. What to think. She understood every word, but even so, he wasn't making sense. Did he think she wanted to be here? Kuro had shown her the way through the stones. To an unknown place she'd hoped to call home. Because ravens always know.

"I followed *you*!" she replied.

"Hmm. Yes. People do have a tendency to do that, don't they?" He smiled, flashing his canines. She suppressed the urge to shield her throat.

"You're here, Sulni, because someone out there wants you to be. You're a stone wanderer, made to break down doors that were never meant to be opened. Is he a friend of yours?"

"What? Who?"

"The man sneaking around outside."

Stefan!

Hirka got up, making a concentrated effort so as not to fall again. What could she do? What could she say? Stefan would never understand. And the blindling … He'd … She looked at him.

"I don't know. I don't know whether he's a friend or not. He might be. What should we do?"

"We can kill him or we can invite him in. What do you think would be best, Sulni?"

"I think … my name's not Sulni. It's Hirka."

"I'm Naiell. And I know who you are. Shall we invite him in, do you think?" He seemed amused, though he wasn't laughing.

Naiell. The Seer's name is Naiell.

The name made her hair stand on end. It was strange yet familiar all at once. Like something she'd heard before, even though she knew she hadn't. Hirka walked through the greenhouse to the door. She opened it but couldn't see anyone.

"Stefan?"

Stefan was suddenly right in front of her, cheeks flushed.

"He says I should invite you in."

"He?"

Hirka went back in and heard Stefan follow. "Just to warn you," she whispered. "He's naked. And he's a bit … much."

Stefan followed her through the greenhouse to where Naiell was waiting. He drew his gun the moment he laid eyes on him. Hirka shouted, but it was too late. Naiell was on him. Hirka heard a snap, and the weapon fell to the ground. Stefan screamed. He collapsed against the wall, cradling his elbow. Hirka darted over to him.

Stefan looked at her. Confused and disappointed in equal measure. "And to think I spared you the worst of it! I didn't think telling you would do any good, and now … Christ! If I'd known …"

He stared at Naiell. "There's a scourge out there. A man who can bind people to him. Kill and heal all at once. I've been hunting him for fifteen fucking years and I've often doubted his existence. But it's you, isn't it? You're the source."

Stefan glanced at the gun on the ground. Hirka picked it up so he wouldn't do anything stupid. "I promise you, he's not the one you're looking for," she said. "Naiell came here with me. Not even a year ago. We're both new to this world."

"Naiell?" Stefan repeated the name as if he couldn't believe he had one. Hirka knew how he felt.

"Like that matters," Stefan said. "I don't know what the fuck they are, but they're the same." Stefan tried to bend his elbow and grimaced.

Naiell looked at her. "What's he saying?"

He hadn't understood a word of their conversation. Hirka took a moment to enjoy the feeling of having the upper hand before translating what Stefan had said into ymish.

Naiell snarled. "The embling is mistaken. We're nothing alike."

Hirka translated what he'd said for Stefan. "He says they're nothing alike. Him and the man you're looking for."

“How the hell does he know that if he’s only just arrived?”

She looked at Naiell again. “How do you know?”

Naiell bared his teeth. “*Sí wai umkhadari dósal.*”

Hirka and Stefan looked at each other. The words belonged to a language neither of them understood. Naiell looked at Hirka and repeated what he’d said in ymish:

“He’s my brother.”

FAREWELL

Hospitals. The last bastion of humankind. A gateway to death, veiled in just enough superstition that people weren't afraid to go there. A practical place. A technical place. But to the dying, a temple. All reason was abandoned at the door. And once inside, all that was left was prayer. A futile hope that someone in a white coat might be able to offer salvation.

As Graal walked through the corridors, he took in the smell of life coming to an end. Even the healthy ones were dying. Humans were all dying, though they denied it with a vehemence that bordered on the comical. Had they known who he was and the power he had in his blood, they'd have trampled each other to death to get to him. No price was too high when time was running out.

He walked into what they called an isolation ward. An optimistic name for an area that, at best, closed its doors a little more frequently. No one made any attempt to stop him or ask him what he was doing there. Not that he'd expected anyone to.

Isac lay in a drab room surrounded by machines and tubes. Technology that told the humans what they couldn't see for themselves. His head was wrapped in bandages, and from the smell of him, Graal knew they'd gone to great lengths to save him. Such a shame. He didn't like effort going to waste. Hard work should pay off.

He shut the door and went over to the bed. Isac turned his head. Slowly, like a marionette. It seemed to cause him great pain. His eyes lit up when he saw Graal. It would have been touching, had his love not been tainted by desperation.

"Graal ..." Isac fumbled for his hand. "You came."

"Yes, I came, Isac."

Then, the inevitable excuses. The stories about everything that had gone wrong. Everything that wasn't Isac's fault. Details. A study in human weakness. A plea to the most forgiving god of all: the god of unpredictability.

Isac had never understood the importance of his assignment. That was all too clear now. But it was a problem lacking a solution. How could anyone with a mere eighty years to live ever understand what was important?

The strange part was it was becoming more and more difficult. For the first couple of centuries, explaining to people what was important had been easier. Despite the fact that their lives were only half as long back then.

Graal tuned out Isac's voice. He sat down on a chair by the bed and switched on the TV using a greasy remote. A distressingly overlooked source of infection. He flicked through the channels until he found the news. A woman with a microphone stood outside a church. Blue lights were flashing in the background. He put it on mute. Couldn't bear to listen.

Isac stopped talking. He knew what was coming. His blond hair was plastered to his temple. He had green circles under his eyes.

"Isac, what was the last thing I said to you before you left?"

"I tried to stop him, but it was—"

"The one word I used, Isac? What was it?

Isac swallowed. "Discreet."

Graal closed his eyes. Listened to the beeping of the machines. The wheezing of Isac's lungs. The stench of damaged flesh and disinfectant was unrelenting.

"I tried, Graal. I tried to stop him, but it was too late! Mickey was a rotten choice." He huffed out the sentences. "We never meant—it wasn't supp—"

Graal brought a finger to Isac's lips. Isac grabbed his hand and breathed in his smell as though he would get more benefit from that than from the drip hanging by the bed. Which he would, to be fair.

"Discreet, Isac. Discreet!" Graal stood up. He rarely got angry. He'd been around far too long for that. But he was furious now. He pointed at the TV. "Discreet! A priest! A priest, a mother, and her two daughters! A small child! Left bleeding in a church, in the middle of town! A massacre! A midwinter sacrifice!"

"There … there's still time, we can …"

Graal sat back down. He stared at the floor. Smooth, lime-green linoleum. "I like children. Have I ever mentioned that, Isac? Children are the future, as they like to say here. But they don't understand what that means. I understand. And I like them. Should I have mentioned that, Isac?"

Isac flinched every time he heard his name. Graal squeezed the arm of the chair. The wood splintered. "I like children. And you don't have the girl. You don't know where she is. That upsets me, Isac."

"A drop, Graal. A single drop and you'll have her in no time, I promise!" Isac strained toward him. The tube going into his hand pulled taut, and that was enough to make him give up. Graal took off his gloves and pulled a piece of paper out of his pocket. He unfolded it.

"Sometimes I write to myself," he said. "On good days. So that on not so good days, I remember that everything is not as bad as it feels. Do you know what I wrote here? I wrote that it's human nature to fail. That I have to forgive and be patient."

Isac grimaced. Graal recognized it as an attempt at his usual charm offensive. Considering he was lying there, pale and thin in a hospital gown, it was a horribly misplaced effort. At least they'd gotten rid of that god-awful shirt.

"I wrote that on a good day," Graal said, returning the piece of paper to his inside pocket. "Today is not a good day."

Isac's hand was shaking at his side. Graal fiddled with the machines. They'd be of no help to him.

"Say what you like about humans, but at least they're able to extract bullets, I see. You've had a long life, Isac. You're over eighty years old now, but you don't look a day over fifty. You've had more than most."

"Graal, don't—"

"You've nothing to fear. Nobody here knows who you are. And the doctors have no idea what's wrong with you, so I expect you'll be here for some time. At least until they've run every test in the book. It's just as well, under the circumstances. Their ignorance will keep the police away."

Isac's eyes glistened. No trace of his arrogance remained. He was no longer Vardar. All that was left was a shell. A human.

Graal went over to Isac's jacket, which was hanging from a hook on the wall. He tucked a letter into one of the pockets. "Everything you need to know is written on that. Where to collect your things. Where to withdraw money. You'll not want for anything. Not until the pain sets in. Try to get them to prescribe hydromorphone. It's a morphine derivative. It will help."

He walked back toward the door. Isac began to sob quietly, like a little boy. It was annoying to listen to, but there was nothing more Graal could do. He'd already extended this man's life by half. From now on Isac would have to manage on his own. Some managed for a century, maybe longer, surviving on secondary blood. Not Isac. He was too dependent. Five years, if Graal had to guess. No more.

"Graal ... I love you."

Graal looked at the human in the bed. “No, Isac, you love what I do for you,” he said, and left the room.

Isac’s scream was lost in a gurgling cough.

DEATH BY BLINDLING

Rime followed the twalif through the throng of exhausted men. It wasn't a high rank, being a twalif, with eleven soldiers to command, but there was no one with a higher rank left alive.

The last of the soldiers had returned home to Mannfalla after the attack on Ravnhov. Back after months of making and breaking camp. Marching through ash and snow. And through contradictory orders from a council in two minds, until Rime had stepped in and put an end to it.

But they were far from jubilant. They were subdued and tired. Worn down by toil and illness, but also by the knowledge that the war had been for nothing. The Seer was gone. Ravnhov remained free. On Rime's orders.

He wouldn't blame them if they hated him.

The soldiers bowed as he passed. Mumbled "Rime-fadri" and threw stolen glances after him. The rumors of his spectacle in the Rite Hall had spread far and wide. But the fear in their eyes had nothing to do with him.

"Here they are, Rime-fadri."

The twalif stopped in front of a small group of men resting on stretchers. The soldiers around him were taking off leather and steel, but these men were covered by nothing more than their shirts and blankets. The wounded.

Rime had seen more than enough wounded men in his life. These would pull through—all apart from one. The only one no longer shivering.

He was lying on his back, his eyes half-open, but he said nothing. Reacted to no one. Sweat had frozen in his hairline. His lips had lost all color. He wouldn't survive the night.

"That's Karn," the twalif said, nodding at the man, who wasn't much older than Rime. Barely twenty winters. Rime pulled the blanket back and lifted the boy's bloodied shirt. His chest had been torn open. Three deep cuts, but not made by steel. These were claw marks. A single swipe, with bear-like strength. Stretching from one shoulder toward his armpit on the opposite side. The wounds were starting to fester. The smell of death hung in the air.

"The men were calling him Klawn Karn, but … they've stopped now," the twalif said, taking his helmet off.

Rime gritted his teeth. "Why hasn't anyone seen to his wounds? Dressed them?"

"We're out of supplies, Rime-fadri. We could have sent for more, but by the time the message got there, we'd have been halfway home."

"Mannfalla's not without its means, twalif. There's enough armor for everyone! No man should die because he's ill-equipped."

The twalif dropped his helmet and opened a supply basket nearby. He pulled out a set of leather armor and held it up in front of Rime. "I can promise you, Rime-fadri, no man goes naked here."

The leather he was holding up was hanging together by a thread. Torn to shreds across the chest. Rime grabbed the armor and threw it back in the basket. But he knew the others had seen it. And probably long before he arrived. There was no point trying to hide it from them.

Rime stepped closer to the twalif. "Did you see them?"

"No, Rime-fadri, a party of twelve went out alone. Karn here was the only one who came back."

"Where? Where did this happen?" Rime tried to keep his voice steady. The men glanced at them. They were slow to take off their armor, hoping to catch some of what was being said. Some had found other excuses to listen in. Sorting tent poles, blankets, and pots into piles.

What was he to tell them? That this wasn't what they thought? That everything would be okay?

Give them strength. That's your job. Give them hope.

"Twalif, where? Give me a location!"

"Two days north of here, on the eastern side of Lake Stilla."

Rime closed his eyes. Two days. The blind, two days from Mannfalla.

"Get your men home, twalif. I'll take Kolkagga and set out at once. And get someone to see to Karn."

"Yes, Rime-fadri."

Rime left them. Men whispered as he went, and he found himself wishing it were about women and ale, not him.

Nine black shadows ran silently through the forest. They kept to the outskirts of Blindból, where the wind blew in from Midtyms. They ran without stopping, until darkness fell. Then they slept in shifts for a short while before continuing. They made do without fire, using the Might to keep warm instead.

Rime's feet felt heavy. Fear of what they might find was holding him back. His instincts told him it was the deadborn, but he hoped he was wrong. Hirka had left Ym because of the blind. Because both she and Hlosnian believed she was the reason the blind were there. And they'd been right. The dead stones bore witness to that.

Perhaps these were just stragglers. Deadborn who had been

trapped here. But it seemed unlikely that they'd have kept to themselves for six months only to start killing again.

No. If they were here, they had to have come through the stones recently. Meaning Hirka had left for no reason. The thought was like poison in Rime's veins, impairing his judgement. At least he could see Svarteld from the corner of his eye. Having the master along increased the odds of everyone coming back from Lake Stilla alive.

They stayed together the entire way, approaching the area from the south. The view was the same in every direction, with silver birch trees sticking straight up out of the snow. It made it seem like they weren't making any progress whatsoever.

Up ahead, Rime saw one of the others raise his hand. He'd spotted something.

They all dropped down and crawled across the snow between the trees, heading for a ledge jutting out over the water. The lake lay black beneath them, sickle-shaped and covered with a thin layer of ice. Eleven bodies lay lifeless nearby. The wind swept snow over them, across the ice, and between the trees, where it settled in drifts.

The bodies were out in the open. Exposed. The other soldiers hadn't even looked for them. They'd taken one look at Karn and gotten out of there. No army wanted to fight the blind.

Svarteld signaled that they should spread out. They swept the area. But there was no one else there. They were alone with the dead. Rime got up and made his way down the slope. A line of silent shadows followed him.

He pulled down his mask and stopped next to the body of a thickset man lying on his side. His hair had frozen in waves down his chest. Rime turned him onto his back. He was cold, but not frozen solid. None of the others were either. There were no traces of blood on the ground. And none of them seemed to have sustained mortal wounds. What had happened here?

Two of them were women. Archers. They still had their bows on their backs. Only one of the dead had drawn his sword. Rime felt the cold seep under his skin. Whatever had happened, these soldiers had been taken completely by surprise.

He heard someone whisper behind him. "What killed them?"

"Fear," another said.

Rime turned toward them. "Fear doesn't kill anyone."

The others didn't reply. Rime looked at the dead. They'd had no idea what they were up against. They might as well have been fighting with their eyes closed. Was that the fate of Mannfalla? To die in ignorance? Laboring under a delusion?

No!

Rime was overcome by a desperate need for knowledge. He had to find out what he was dealing with. No matter the cost. If it could bleed, it could die.

He lifted his sword. Brought the blade down on the dead man's leg. Through the thigh, just above the knee. The foot tipped sideways. Away from the rest of the body. Svarteld whispered his name, but Rime didn't reply. He stared at the sword. It was clean. Dry and unbloodied. A pale red dust trickled from the stump. The wind caught it, drew it out of dead veins, and carried it across the ice.

She left for no reason.

Rime heard himself laugh. Quietly at first. Then louder. Joylessly, as if ridiculing anyone who had ever laughed.

Svarteld laid a hand on his shoulder. Black-clad warriors stared at him. Only their eyes could be seen behind their masks, but he could tell what they were thinking. They thought he'd lost his mind. But they didn't understand.

The blind were back. She'd left for no reason. For good.

Rime gnashed his teeth and plunged his sword into the ice, cracking it in two. The sound rippled out across the frozen crust. Water welled up from underneath. Two sheets of ice. Two emotions.

Grief, because she was gone.

But also hope, depraved as it was. Hope because this proved the gateways were still open. The raven rings were alive.

THE KEY

Hirka sat in the doorway between the bathroom and the bedroom, trying not to look at the creature standing in the shower. She focused on Stefan instead, who was cramming his things into a brown satchel. It was square, with pockets on the sides. The corners were almost worn through.

He looked over at her. "What? It does the job, all right?"

Hirka had no idea what he was talking about, so she kept quiet.

"I've had it for over ten years, and it puts up with just about anything. Real leather, see? They don't make bags like this anymore, that's all it is. I don't have a sentimental bone in my body, if that's what you're thinking."

"Sentimental?"

"Nostalgic. Romantic. Soppy," he said and continued packing as if he hated his clothes. "And it's practical. Lots of pockets."

"For all of your dark things," she replied, looking at the glass table. His gun was lying there. And a folding knife. His phone, and some other things she didn't recognize.

"Hey! Those dark things are the reason you're still alive, so thank your lucky stars you're not questioning my morals from the depths of hell."

"Morals?"

"Right and wrong. That's what you're talking about, right?"

She pointed at his things. "I'm talking about color."

"Oh … you mean black." He dragged his hand over his face. Halfway through he winced and grabbed his elbow in pain. He kept forgetting about his injury.

He checked his phone again. "Christ, every second we stay here brings us one step closer to a prison cell," he muttered. "You did say we're in a hurry, right? Or did you fluff the translation and tell him to move in to the shower?"

She shook her head. He was so tense she was afraid he might crack. And he wasn't the only one. If anyone were to come in at that moment, they'd take one look at them, turn tail, and run. Hirka wished she could run.

Stefan was a hunter. He'd spent his entire life hunting something he wasn't sure existed, the source of a sickness he despised … and now it was in the shower washing raven blood out of its hair.

Naiell had refused to close the door. The blindling wanted to be able to see her the whole time. So there she sat, in the doorway. Caught between two men who both claimed they wanted what was best for her, but who wouldn't let her be alone with the other. It was anything but reassuring.

"I've seen a lot of monsters in my time. But him? I've never seen anything like him," Stefan said, looking at her. "Do you understand what I'm saying? A monster?"

"An outsider?"

"No, not an outsider. Well …" Stefan sighed. "Talking to you is pointless. You don't have a clue what I'm saying."

Hirka knew how he felt. She'd been where he was now. In a position where some things simply weren't meant to exist. She'd also had to contend with her own incredulity the first time she saw one of the blind. It did something to you. Stefan had just discovered the difference between believing and knowing, and it changed everything.

At first she'd thought he'd take off. Run. From the blindling. From her. But Stefan had been hunting for too long to quit now. So there they were: three outsiders, brought together by circumstance. And perhaps by a number of other things she preferred not to think about.

It was dark outside. Out the window she saw the lights of the city. They were scattered everywhere, as if the stars had fallen from the sky. They'd smuggled Naiell through the streets in her raincoat, which had just about covered the most important bits. They'd kept to the alleyways to avoid people, but the lady at the front desk of the hotel had taken a good hard look at his bare legs.

"He's not *that* different," Hirka said. She could hear the doubt in her own voice. "He'll look like everyone else if we get him some normal clothes. We can buy him some in the shop. They sell clothes everywhere here."

"Oh, perfect. So you're going out tomorrow, are you? To do a little shopping?" Stefan laughed. "You don't get it, do you? How long do you think we have before they hear about the redhead who was living in the church? The girl who, oddly enough, is suddenly nowhere to be found? They'll find a picture of you. And if they find you, they find me."

Hirka pushed her feet against the doorframe. Wedged herself in the opening and crossed her arms over her chest. "You can leave whenever you like. I didn't ask you to come with us. We'll manage on our own."

Stefan looked at her, on the verge of hysterics. "How can you trust him?! Have you *looked* at him? He's not human, Hirka, don't you get that?"

"So humans are the only ones who can be trusted?"

"You know what, I have no idea what's going on in that head of yours, girl." He shoved the gun into his belt. He kept it in a sheath. Like the one in her sock, the one she kept her knife in. It was a scary thought. She didn't want to be anything like him.

"Then why don't you leave?" she asked defiantly.

"Because he knows who I'm hunting. He knows where that bastard comes from. That wretched creature he calls Graal. It has a name. I mean, fuck me, it's even got a family. They're brothers, if you can believe a word he says. Brothers, can you imagine? I've never been this close. And even if I *wanted* to leave, do you really think he, or it—" he nodded in the direction of the bathroom "—would let me?"

Hirka didn't answer. He was right. She hadn't tried, but she was pretty sure Naiell wouldn't simply let her up and leave. He wouldn't even leave her alone with Stefan.

Suddenly Naiell was next to her. She gave a start. She tried to move, but then just sat there, staring up at his pale, dripping body. A puddle was forming on the white floor tiles. His claws were hanging right by her face.

Stefan unleashed a volley of words she was sure weren't very nice. "Put some clothes on, for Christ's sake! Here!" He chucked a bundle of clothes at the blindling. Naiell caught them and looked at Hirka. He smiled, and she felt a shiver run down her spine. "He doesn't like seeing me naked, this human," he said smugly.

Hirka got up. "You don't walk around naked in front of strangers. Not here, at least."

Stefan secured the straps on his bag. "Tell him to put some clothes on. We have to get going. We can talk in the car."

"What car?"

Stefan didn't answer. Hirka was pretty sure that no matter what car he was talking about, it wasn't his.

Stefan was driving way too fast. In a car he claimed they were just borrowing. There was a child's mitten on the floor. Hirka had the feeling it was never going to see its owner again.

The snow flew at them in the dark, before being swept away by two sticks swinging back and forth across the glass. Hirka wasn't feeling well. Stefan wiped the fog off the front window. She caught his eye in the mirror again. It was like he constantly had to check she and Naiell were still there. That he hadn't simply imagined them. She knew the feeling. Nothing felt real here. At times she'd wondered whether she was dead. Whether she was in Slokna, dreaming. Being punished for all the things she'd done wrong. Ym was real, but this place was ... she didn't know.

Naiell was sitting next to her on the back seat. If he was scared of being in a car for the first time, he didn't let on. But she was pretty sure he wasn't. She wasn't even sure whether the blind felt fear.

He was wearing the clothes he'd borrowed from Stefan. A white shirt that was too tight across his shoulders and too loose across his stomach. In his hands he held a pair of gloves and dark glasses that Stefan had bought at an all-night shop along the way. One of those places where they filled cars with petrol.

Gloves and glasses. That was all they had to conceal a deadborn if they were stopped. It was pathetic, really. A flimsy veil between what was real and what wasn't. But sitting there next to her, Naiell was real enough. He had a familiar smell that set her at ease for some inexplicable reason. Which probably meant she could get used to just about anything.

Stefan held his phone to his ear. After a moment he started talking to someone. The words all slid together, so she didn't understand much. Having been born here, he knew this world better than either of them, so the fact that he was nervous made her nervous.

"Is he damaged?" Naiell asked. She gave a start. Getting used to that voice wasn't easy.

"Well, you nearly broke his arm."

"No, I mean *damaged*." Naiell tapped two fingers against his forehead.

"Oh—no, he's talking on … it's a telephone. He's trying to get a hold of someone who can help us."

Naiell made no attempt to hide his skepticism. "You're sure this man is my brother's enemy?"

Hirka looked at Stefan. Every time they were caught in the lights of another car, he stiffened. She didn't know this man, but he was clearly taking a risk. Apparently for her sake. "Yes," she replied. "He says he's been hunting him for a long time. His entire life."

"So not that long," Naiell replied.

He enjoyed reminding her what he was. A proud deadborn. She felt a stab of jealousy. How had she reacted when she found out she was a child of Odin? She'd hidden in shame. Fled. Believed everything that was said about her. That she was something horrific.

And here she was, still being hunted. Why? What did they want with her? She had so many burning questions, but her fear of what the blindling might say left them smoldering on her tongue.

Instead, she asked somewhat timidly, "So who is he, your brother?" The black in Naiell's eyes spread until it engulfed the white. Had she been able to, she'd have jumped out of the car.

"What do you fear more than anything, Sulni?" he said.

"That's not—"

"That's what I'm calling you. So what do you fear?"

She caught Stefan looking at her in the mirror again. He didn't understand ymish, so she could speak freely. Finally. She could actually speak to someone in her own language and be understood. Someone else was on the outside now. Left to wonder. The feeling made it easier to find her words.

"People. I fear people. Men who take. Men who kill. Who think …" She hesitated, remembering her time in the pits of Eisvaldr. The weight of a man who intended to take her by force, pressing down on her. The darkness when she'd kneeled, blindfolded, before the Council. Her woollen tunic, soaked in her own blood. And Urd.

Her futile attempts to reason with them had only led to one thing. Pain.

"I'm afraid of screaming at people who refuse to listen. People who lash out blindly. Wild animals who can't be reasoned with. Full of hatred. Hatred is poison."

Naiell leaned closer. "That's Graal. That's my brother."

Hirka regretted asking. Nothing had turned out the way it was supposed to. There wasn't supposed to be blindlings here with the humans.

"Why did he have to come *here* of all places?" she mumbled.

"Do you like it here? Do you think this is a nice place?"

Hirka looked at the floor. "No."

"The ymlings didn't think so either, so they sent him here. This is his punishment."

"For what?"

He looked at her. "Have you been living under a rock? Have you never heard a story in your life? He was punished when he lost the war."

"So it's true? That the Seer saved Ym from the bl—from you? From your people?"

"You're welcome," he replied, linking his hands behind his neck. "I've had so many uneventful days in my life, but that was not one of them, let me tell you."

She felt like hitting him. She'd have given anything for an uneventful day, but she'd never had that option.

"But what does he want? Why is Graal sending people after me? I'm nobody, I've nothing to give him!"

"It must be nice to think that, but you're mistaken. You can give him the one thing he desires."

"What's that? What does he want?"

Naiell looked at her. "Ym."

The car suddenly felt too small. She leaned her head against the window. The cold seeped into her forehead. She stared outside, trying to fight down the nausea. But Naiell's words had made it worse. He continued.

"Graal has done what they said could never be done. The stones were dead. In a thousand years, I haven't seen so much as a fly pass through them. Until one day I recognized the scent of my own. Blood of the first, in Ym. And then suddenly *you* show up ..."

Hirka shuddered, but she had to look at him. She was drawn toward the inevitable. Toward the truths he could offer her. The words that encompassed all that she was.

Tell me who I am.

He answered her silent plea. "Nothing passes through the raven rings without the Might, Sulni. Yet here you are. He's done something to you. Given you traveler's blood. You woke the raven rings, and now he needs you in order to use them."

"He's safe, then," she whispered.

"He?"

"Them—I mean them. The people of Ym. If I'm here, they're safe, right?"

The answer hung in the air between them, louder than if it had been spoken.

Safe. Until he finds me.

She swallowed. "What will happen if he gets his hands on me?"

"Well, he suffered a crushing defeat instead of what should have been his greatest triumph, so after a thousand years of shame and banishment, it's reasonable to assume that he's a little upset." Naiell smiled, exposing his canines.

"So what are you going to do now? Are you going to save this world, too? From him?"

A snarling laugh escaped his throat. "This world is dying. A mightless place is powerless against my brother's poison. It might take ten years, or a thousand, but there's nothing anyone can do for this world."

Hirka knew it was true. She'd known it from the moment she'd set foot in the human world. The water was disgusting. The soil contaminated. Nothing smelled the way it should. She'd come to a dying world.

An echo of Rime's words came to her.

Everything dies. As sure as you're alive right now. Nothing changes, Hirka. We're torn apart and put back together, as something new. You're the sky, you're the earth, water, and fire. Living and dead. We're all dead. Already dead.

She worried at her lip. It was all so much harder when she remembered the details. The creaking of his leather armor. His voice in her ear when he held her. So vivid it was eating away at her.

"Don't let it bother you," Naiell said. "There are far more important things than this world. The most important thing is to stop my brother's poison. Stop the rot."

There it was. The word she hadn't heard in such a long time. It sounded uglier coming from the mouth of a deadborn.

"Does he get the humans to spread the rot?"

"The rot is not something they can give, it's something they get. That is how much power lies in the blood of Umpiri."

Hirka closed her eyes again. Sifted through her thoughts, without finding anything of much use. "But … I know that humans spread the rot! That's what everyone says. That's what the stories say. The song." She grabbed him and started to hum. The girl and the rot. The lump in her throat grew, cutting the melody short.

He laughed again. "Do they still sing that song? How droll. It was born of fear, nothing more. I promise you, not a single human has existed with the power to spread the rot, Hirka."

She noticed him use her name, but right then it meant nothing to her. Nothing at all. She felt her mouth pull into a grimace. She'd left Rime. He'd kissed her and she'd stopped him. For no reason. She wasn't the rot. She never had been. And now it was too late.

She was nothing more than a weapon. Hunted by an ancient, deadborn warlord who wanted to destroy everything she loved.

Something inside her snapped. She pounded Naiell's arm with her fist. He lifted it with a growl, but she hit him again. She tasted tears on her lips and hit him again and again. Deep down she knew it was senseless, and anyway, she was hitting like a child. At least that's what Svarteld would have said.

Naiell grabbed her wrist and squeezed until she screamed. Stefan shouted. The car swerved and came to a sudden stop. She was flung against the seat in front.

"What the hell do you two think you're doing?!" Stefan jumped out of the car and yanked open the back door. He dragged her outside. She fell onto the road. She tried to get up but slipped in the slush. Stefan held her back. She screamed at the blindling.

"Where were you?! Where in Slokna were you when we needed you?" Naiell's blindling eyes were all she could see in the dark car. "Answer me! If you're so om-fucking-niscient! If you're the Seer, then answer me! Where were you when Kolkagga nearly killed Eirik? Where were you during the Rite? When they said that I was the rot? When they threw me in the pits? WHERE WERE YOU?!"

She gasped for air as she remembered how alone she'd been. In the dark, peering up at the grating. The guardsman who had locked the shutter so Kuro wouldn't …

He was there. Kuro was there.

Stefan dragged her to her feet. "Listen, girl! This is neither the time nor the place! We have to keep moving, and we have to stay out of sight. And you're doing a really bad job of that right now. Do you understand?"

Hirka tried to catch her breath. Her throat was raw from all the screaming. She heard another car approaching. Stefan shoved her into the back seat. He slammed the door and climbed into the front.

The lights of the oncoming car rounded the bend. She held her breath. The car passed and disappeared into the darkness.

Stefan drove on. Hirka's rage dissolved into sorrow. She felt empty inside. Her wrist was smarting where Naiell had grabbed her. It was going to leave a mark.

This was the Seer. A blindling. Powerful. Dangerous. And conceited. But maybe he had been with her, in the only way that he could—as a raven. Maybe he hadn't abandoned her. He was here, with her, despite everything. And he was all that stood between her and his brother.

"He's never going to stop hunting me, is he?" she whispered, not daring to look at Naiell.

"No."

"And he's never going to die?"

"Umpiri don't kill their own, but I'm willing to make an exception where my brother is concerned."

"You can do that? Kill him?"

"I can. The question is whether I will."

"Why wouldn't you?" She was shocked at how easily the words came to her. She'd already killed. Out of necessity, not hatred. But now she felt hatred. She was becoming what she feared most.

"He's discovered something that allowed him to open the gateways again. And if we don't get our hands on it, then annoying as it is, he's the only one who can get us back home. Until then, we're stuck here."

Stefan looked at them in the mirror. "What's he saying?" The car swerved a little and he straightened up again. "Tell me what he's saying."

Hirka hugged her knees and curled into a ball.

"He says I should have stayed in Ym."

SKYNROK

Rime rearranged the books stacked around him. Everything he'd been able to find about the blind—and it had all been a waste of time. Children's stories. Songs. Interspersed with boundless praise for a Seer he now knew didn't exist. He coaxed a history book out of one of the piles and opened it on the desk.

This was the last place he ought to be. He ought to be in the forests with Kolkagga. Out finding the deadborn, not reading about them. But Svarteld had said no. To him! As if there were anyone in Ym who could refuse him anything at all.

He closed his eyes for a moment. Centered himself again. There were enough men to choose from, and besides, Svarteld had said they needed knowledge more than they needed swords. He was right, but he had clearly never set foot in this library. Finding the blind in the forests was easier than finding them in here. Unless he was to believe what he'd read so far. And if he was, then Ym was threatened by blind, half-rotten gods with canines to their knees. Deadborn who never died, who could assume different forms, who switched out babies for their own, and who ate souls, much to the despair of the denizens of Slokna.

He stared down at the book. He knew what he was going to find. The same story he'd found everywhere else. An embellished tale of the Twelve who had ridden into Blindból. One of them his own ancestor. Stories about how they'd met the only deadborn who could see the beauty of Ym, and who had turned against his own to save it. The Seer. In the form of a raven. How the twelve families had formed the Council and united the kingdoms. If he was really unlucky, there would be chapters devoted solely to the honor of these families. About how strong they were, how wise and merciful. The same empty words that had been repeated for centuries until they were accepted as the truth.

Rime tossed the book aside. If there was one thing he'd learned from being on the Council, it was that nothing was perceived so uniformly by so many. He could take two men to the river and they wouldn't even agree on what direction it was flowing in. If too many people agreed on the same thing, something was wrong.

Footsteps approached behind him. He turned. It was a bare-headed shepherd, one of the gray-clad people who worked in the library. He stopped and folded his thin arms across his tunic, looking at Rime.

"Can I help you?" Rime asked, expecting the shepherd to disappear between the shelves again like the specter he was.

He didn't. He came closer. "It's usually the other way around," he replied. "Can I help *you*, Rime-fadri?"

Rime glanced down at the empty space in front of him. No wonder he looked like he needed help. The shepherd came over to him and rested a hand on the balustrade. "Another man stood here some six months ago," he said, his eyes wandering along the shelves and down the levels. "He stood right where you're sitting now. With the same piles of books around him." He looked at Rime. "And with the same frown. He couldn't find what he was looking for either. He tore a drawing from a book and took it with him. To a Council meeting, I think. Do you know who I'm speaking of?"

Urd. Urd was here.

"Yes, I know who you're speaking of. He was looking for power. I'm looking for salvation." Rime wasn't sure why he suddenly felt the need to defend himself.

The shepherd smiled. He had a gentle countenance. An enviable calm. “Forgive me, Rime-fadri, but I believe he too was looking for salvation. Many who come here are. It’s difficult to find elsewhere at the moment, but I’m sure you know that already.” Rime didn’t know what to say. It was hard to make sense of the shepherd. He seemed remarkably indifferent to the magnitude of the matter at hand.

“What’s your name?” Rime asked.

“Northree, fadri.”

“Northree? What kind of a name is that?”

The shepherd pointed at the other side of the room. “I’m in charge of the north side there. On level three. Northree.”

Rime smiled. “So there’s a Norfour, too?”

“Well, most of the others use their own names. They rotate, you see. I don’t. I’ve been in charge of the north side of this level for almost twenty years. That said, we do have a Norfour, and a Soufive, but I wouldn’t ask her for help unless I knew what I was looking for.” He winked.

Rime sighed. “I know what I’m looking for, Northree. I need to understand the blind. I need to know what we’re up against.”

“Up against? You say that like it isn’t over.”

“Haven’t you heard?”

“Oh, I know it isn’t over. Most people know that,” Northree said, looking at him. “But few say it aloud. Few who come in here, anyway. Those who can read come from families that have taught them what one does and doesn’t speak of.”

“I used to be better at that,” Rime replied.

It was true. He’d spent years furious at what wasn’t being said. But then he’d become just like them. Just as tight-lipped. Right up until the Seer had fallen. Until he’d met Eirik in Ravnhov. And Hirka.

“We do have books referencing the deadborn, but in truth, we know very little, Rime-fadri.”

"How can it be that there are creatures out there that no one understands? Even a thousand years ago we clearly knew enough to fight them. We knew what we needed to know back then, about them and the stone doors. How can we not know now?"

Rime couldn't hide his anger. The sheer lack of knowledge was unforgivable. How was he to keep people alive when no one knew what they were facing?

"There was knowledge of the nábyrn, fadri. And of the raven rings. Of course there was, but nothing survived skynrok."

"Skynrok?" The word sounded familiar, but Rime couldn't place it.

"The death of knowledge. The end of all wisdom. Almost all the stone circles were torn down. And the books were burned. There's not a single shepherd who doesn't know the story. It's said that they burned as many books as there are in the library. Though having said that, they mostly used scrolls back then."

"And no one stopped them?" The shepherd didn't reply. Rime realized his stupidity the moment the question was out of his mouth. Of course not. Fear was fear. He knew that better than most.

So what was he to do? Resign himself to the fact that he had an enemy stronger and faster than any ymling? That turned blood to dust in people's veins? That was as difficult to kill as a shadow? As Kolkagga?

The dancer had been right. She'd looked at his books and come straight out with it:

You won't find what you want to know in any book.

There had been something about her. She didn't strike him as the type of person who usually spent time in a place like this. She must have been looking for something more than harmless flirting. She had something to tell him. Rime stopped and looked at the shepherd.

"Forgive me, Northree, but I think I know where to look. I just realized knowledge comes in many forms."

“I could have told you that,” Northree replied, though he didn’t seem affronted.

Rime thanked him for his help and left the library. He walked as fast as he could without running. He had a dancer to see—a far more appealing prospect than a Council meeting.

AS THE RAVEN FLIES

The harbor was deserted. Normal people were asleep at such an ungodly hour. But not Hirka. She was curled up on the back seat, but she didn't want to close her eyes. Stefan had stopped the car right by the quay. He drummed his fingers on the wheel, pausing every now and then to shift in his seat.

"Where are we going?" she asked.

"Nowhere you've heard of," Stefan answered, ducking his head to check outside, again. "How long's he been gone? He's been gone a while, right? He'd better be here by the time Nils arrives, that's all I'm saying."

"He'll be here. He just needed to eat something," Hirka answered.

Stefan hadn't wanted to let Naiell out of his sight. Not that he could have stopped him. The Seer was taller and stronger than he was, not to mention deadborn. But the three of them knew they needed each other. Knew they had a common enemy. All the same, it felt like the balance of power could shift at any moment.

"Eat what, though? That's the question. He doesn't have an ounce of fat on his body! He must run on something, that's for sure. He didn't touch the sandwiches, and he didn't even give the crisps a sniff, so what the hell does someone like him eat? Raw meat?" Stefan laughed, though it didn't sound like he found it all that funny. Hirka decided not to mention that she hadn't eaten either. Things out of bags smelled sweaty. And tasted of either poison or dust. She couldn't bring herself to choke it down.

The snow at the end of the quay had melted. The same two boats were still moored there. The sea was black, but whitecaps frothed farther out. She didn't know much about this world, but some things were the same, no matter which world you were in.

"I wouldn't put out to sea in weather like this," she mumbled.

Stefan didn't respond. He pressed one of the buttons, and low music began to play. He pressed the button again and it changed. As if there were someone behind the buttons playing whatever came into his mind. He pressed it a few more times. The sounds cut short and intermingled. One final press, and it went quiet again.

Hirka was always astonished by how unfazed humans were that such things were possible. How they took such incredible things for granted.

"Nils should have been here by now," Stefan said. Mostly to himself, by the sound of it. "I said it was urgent. Extremely urgent."

"You should never say that," she said, curling up into a ball. He turned and looked at her. His leather jacket creaked. It reminded her of Rime.

"Never say what?"

"You should never say you're ... what's the word? When you really need help?"

"Desperate?"

"Yes. You should never say you're desperate. No one will help you then."

"So what should you say when you're desperate?"

"Depends. I'd say I have something they need."

"Well, I said that, too." Stefan turned around again but caught her eye in the mirror. "How old are you?" he asked. She was about to say fifteen but then remembered how much time had passed. "Sixteen winters."

"How many summers, then?"

He was trying to be funny. And she got it. Even though she had a poor grasp of the language. They were from two different worlds, but they could still share a joke. She was surprised by how much it affected her. She smiled and swallowed back her tears. He smiled in return. "So how long have you been here?"

"Nearly six months now. Not that I'm counting ..."

"Well, in any case, you've learned something it takes most people a lifetime to figure out."

He rested his head against the steering wheel. He'd asked her about what Naiell had said, and she'd told him. But Stefan hadn't said a word about her outburst. It was as if it had never happened, and she was grateful to him for that. It was pretty decent of him.

She drew a circle on the fogged-up window. What did it take to break through a stone circle? What had Graal done to her? A thought was gnawing at her. Something Urd had once said. She couldn't put her finger on it, but it made her feel like she was holding something dangerous. A box containing an unknown poison. All she knew was that she couldn't let anyone see what was in the box. Especially not Naiell.

Stefan prodded his elbow. "He's really fucked up my arm. This isn't normal. Here, does that feel normal?" He held out his arm. She gave it a feel. He managed not to wince, she had to give him that. "It's perfectly fine," she answered.

"Really? Is that your diagnosis, Dr. Sixteen-Winters? Don't you feel that dent? Maybe a bit of bone's broken off. What if it gets into my bloodstream?" He sounded genuinely worried.

Hirka had to laugh. "You're perfectly fine, Stefan."

"Right. I'll ask again when my heart explodes. Is that all right with you?"

Hirka heard a faint rumbling. "I think someone's coming."

Stefan got out of the car. Hirka put on her raincoat and followed. After a while she saw something coming toward the quayside. It was unlike any boat she'd ever seen.

"It's him. It's Nils! Shit, where is that creature?" Stefan ran up toward the trees. Scanned for Naiell. "What did I say? I said there was no time, and still he had to … Christ, we have to find that damned beast!"

He turned and jumped. Naiell had been standing right behind him.

"You're lucky he doesn't understand a word you're saying," Hirka said, grabbing her bag from the car.

Stefan spat on the ground. Then he started to open all the car windows. "Come on, we have to get this in the water. They'll find us otherwise, won't they?" He walked around to the back of the car and started to push. Hirka joined in and the car started to inch forward. "Is he always this helpful?" Stefan asked, nodding at Naiell, who made no move to assist.

"Naiell, he says we have to get this in the water so no one finds us," she said in ymish, before adding, "and he doesn't think we're strong enough to do it alone."

Naiell came over, put one hand on the back of the car, and gave it a little push. Hirka nearly fell over as the car lurched forward. A moment later, it plunged over the edge. They went to inspect their handiwork. The car gurgled as it took its last breath. The last thing she saw was the sign with the numbers. Then it was gone.

Stefan looked at the blindling. "Christ, he's … he's …" Hirka nodded.

Something came floating up from the deep. The mitten. It bobbed and swayed in the waves.

"Come on," Stefan said.

The boat that had come to get them was white and had wings. It drifted in toward the quayside. A door opened and Stefan clambered in. Hirka followed. It didn't feel safe, the way it was rocking. She dreaded to think how it was going to cope on the open sea.

"Wait, wait, wait! Stefan, what the hell?!" a man's voice boomed from up front. He was swarthy and was wearing cups of some kind over his ears. Stefan pretended not to hear. He pointed out seats for Hirka and Naiell, but Hirka stayed where she was. She didn't think there was much point in getting comfortable.

Stefan leaned toward the man. "Nils, I promise, this will be worth your while."

"Worth my while? This isn't a bloody taxi!"

Hirka stared at all the instruments in the front. Buttons, switches, dials, sticks … more than she'd seen in any car.

Nils shook his fists. "Stefan, this is the last time, you hear me? Never again. I've barely enough fuel as it is, and then you come bounding in with a girl and a …" He glanced back at Naiell. "A metalhead! His hair alone's going to cost us another ten liters! And the longer the trip, the greater the risk. Hell, you'd think you were a … Am I just supposed to let anyone on board and take your word for it that it'll be fine? I mean, hell …"

Stefan flung his bag onto a seat, acting like Nils's rant didn't bother him. Hirka leaned forward to touch one of the glowing buttons.

"Hey, hey, hey!" Nils swatted her hand away. "Don't touch! What the hell, kid!" He stared at her and Stefan in turns, speechless. Hirka put her hands behind her back. It was like she'd just spat on an icon, but she tried to smile all the same.

Nils found his words again. He started slowly, as if she had a hard time understanding. "This is not a game. This is a Lake Buccaneer. *My* Lake Buccaneer. Don't touch the instruments. Don't touch … anything!"

Hirka nodded. *Don't touch.* She understood that.

Stefan steered her into a seat and strapped her in. He slipped something over her head. Small cushions that covered her ears. Everything went quiet. Muffled, like she had a cold. Nils started pressing buttons as he mumbled to himself. She heard his voice in her ear like he was standing right next to her. Hirka didn't understand what he was saying, but she was sure it wasn't anything nice. She was glad he hadn't taken a closer look at Naiell.

Stefan sat down across from her, and they started to glide over the waves.

"Five hours, and we've got some thinking to do on the way," Nils said. "What would you do if I didn't have connections? Eh? Just asking."

"So I take it she's not happy?" Stefan answered without looking at Nils.

"That'd be putting it mildly."

Stefan looked out the window. "It'll be worth it."

They started picking up speed, and suddenly they were in the air. Hirka gripped the armrests. A plane! She was in a plane! She'd seen them in the sky above the city. Father Brody had told her about them. Hirka leaned toward the window and saw the coastline disappear behind them.

I'm flying. Like the ravens.

But without the Might. Maybe they had something similar here? Something that worked in the same way? In any case, it wasn't unlike how she'd felt when she and Rime had soared above Mannfalla. That had been the middle of the night, too. She'd been weightless. Dizzy. Enveloped by Rime. And in that moment she'd realized she loved him, more than she'd ever dared admit.

It hurt just thinking about it.

"You don't scare easily, do you?" Stefan looked at her. "I mean, you'd never seen an elevator before. And if you are who you say you are, being on a plane ought to scare the red out of your hair."

She knew all too well what he was doing. He was looking for signs that she was lying. Searching for an explanation other than the actual one. One that was easier to accept. Hirka expected he'd be doing it for the foreseeable future. She had to give him the time he needed. She'd needed time, too.

Hirka shrugged. "I've had worse experiences."

"And him?" Stefan nodded at Naiell, whose head was tipped back like he was sleeping. Hirka smiled. Naiell had been flying for centuries.

"Yeah, him as well."

The droning of the plane reverberated through her body.

"Where are we going, Stefan?"

"We're going to see the tooth fairy."

"Okay," she said and gave him a thumbs-up. You could never go wrong with that, Father Brody used to say. Stefan looked at her as if she were the strangest creature he'd ever seen. Despite the fact that there was a deadborn sleeping in the seat in front of him. Or maybe he wasn't sleeping. Maybe he was just saving his strength. She should probably do the same. She had a feeling they were going to need it.

KARASU

"Has it occurred to you that you might be overestimating your own allure?" Graal asked. He smiled at the raven skeleton in front of him. The beak opened again.

"I'm yet to have that experience," Damayanti replied, clearly affronted.

"There's a first time for everything. So has he sought you out?"

"Not yet," she replied, before quickly adding, "But he will. Trust me."

"I trusted Urd. Not my finest hour, was it?"

The beak hung open as she hesitated. The silence was tedious. He surveyed his claws, giving her the time she needed to come up with a good response—which she usually did. Damayanti was a clever woman. Passionate yet unsentimental. She had a knack for understanding people's motivations. He couldn't have found a better contact in Mannfalla. Why she wanted nothing more for herself than to dance was beyond him.

"The boy's no fool," she finally said. "No power-crazed idiot crippled by fear. He's the Ravenbearer. He's not even seen twenty winters and he's more of a man than Urd could ever have dreamed of becoming. He can serve you as no one else can. And he's seen me. Trust me, Rime will come to me."

"And it doesn't worry you that he's toppled a council, refuted a faith, and put an end to a war?" He was taunting her now.

"It doesn't take much to bring down a monolith. He's mine," she replied.

Graal laughed and she purred with satisfaction. He knew she felt every word he said in her body. But she wasn't like Urd—that was for sure. He'd been able to control the councillor with pain. Damayanti had to be controlled with pleasure. But at that particular moment, he didn't have time.

"You'll be hearing from me, Damayanti. In the meantime, I've got an appointment with a needle."

He closed the raven's beak. The sense of endless space dissipated. He was alone once more. He locked the fossilized bird back in its box. Rumors could start anywhere, even in hotels of this price range, where one was generally given carte blanche. There were other options, of course, but he had a soft spot for the Shangri-La suite. The elegance. The terrace. The location, right next to the floodlit Eiffel Tower. The palace had retained the charm he remembered from long evenings spent with Prince Bonaparte, discussing developments in various fields. Botany, music, philosophy … 1898? Had it been that long?

Graal glanced at the clock. One of the things he'd spent a human lifetime getting used to. He'd been born with all the time in the world. He'd always had time. Human lives were fleeting, whereas his went on and on. Through generations. Through epochs. Right up until Hirka had arrived. Since then, he'd been rushed off his feet. Pressed for time for almost seventeen years.

He looked in the mirror to check that he hadn't forgotten anything. It had happened before. He'd gone out without his contact lenses and scared the life out of the man at the newsstand. It wouldn't have mattered as much in the past. This world had been easy to live in, once. Until technology had exploded. Far more effort was required to move unseen among people now. The only planes he could take were his own. He'd been forced to establish a network of companies just to do something as simple as spend his own money. Companies that did nothing more than move numbers from one place to another. Not exactly a gentlemanly pursuit.

He did up his top button. Pulled on his coat and leather gloves. Dark glasses completed the ensemble.

He was ready for a meeting with the needle.

The studio was above the Chinese tea salon on Premier Rue Saint-Médard, within walking distance of Notre-Dame. It was a nice neighborhood, but the area didn't really matter. The key was always the artist, and he'd searched a long time to find her.

Graal pressed the buzzer. The lock clicked straight away. He opened the door and went up the stairs. The door stood ajar on the second floor. He went in.

The room was dimly lit. The evening light squeezed in through the blinds, landing in strips across shelves full of books, boxes, and pictures. It was a classic artist's loft, but clean. Her previous work was displayed on the walls. The usual dragons and koi carp, but a lot of abstract patterns as well. She worked exclusively in black, and she was extremely talented—for a human.

The table stood in the middle of the room on a concrete floor. An altar to beauty and pain.

The artist was sitting on a stool at the counter, cleaning her needles. She was Japanese. Petite with black hair pulled back into a ponytail. Gray T-shirt. She got up and walked over to him. "I'm Mei."

He took her hand. "Joshua Alexander Cain."

She had an unassuming countenance, but beneath that he could smell passion and strength. That boded well, because they would be spending many evenings together, and sooner or later she'd realize he wasn't human. They almost always did, and he'd lost count of the number of tattoo artists he'd had over the years.

He knew what was coming. It was always the same. Like some kind of dance. Graal draped his coat over a chair by the door. First she would say something about the technique they both preferred.

"Not many people ask for work by hand," she said, as if on cue. "Tebori is both more time-consuming and more painful."

He smiled. "Call me a traditionalist."

Soon she would ask him to undress and lie on the table. She'd say it might get warm and that he could take his gloves off.

Mei gestured to the table. "Please. Would you like a glass of water?"

She surprised him. Considerate. Attentive. A good sign. This could be fun.

"Yes, please."

She filled a glass and put it on a smaller table next to the one he would be lying on. "You won't need your gloves."

He took them off. Over the years he'd developed a singular ability to keep his fingertips hidden until he wanted them to be seen. He also took off his sunglasses and set them aside. It was dark enough in the room that she wouldn't wonder about his eyes. The contact lenses did the job, except in daylight, when they were too lifeless.

He unbuttoned his shirt, all the while waiting for her to say something about continuing the work of others.

Mei looked at him. Stared for a moment, like they all did. It was a blessing bestowed on the first, a body that couldn't help but impress. Inspire fear. Simple enough to achieve when you could ingest the sustenance you needed and discard the rest.

She lowered her eyes again and readied the ink. "I rarely continue the work of others. Can I see?"

He lay down on his stomach and tucked his hands under his head. Let her look at his back. Moments passed before she said anything.

"I've never seen anything like it. This must have taken—"

"Yes, it's taken some time. Can you make sense of the pattern?"

"Yes," she said hesitantly before rallying again. "Yes, I understand. From the center outward. This is … these lines? They look like Horiyasu's work."

"Horiyasu the first. You have a good eye."

"The third, you mean. Horiyasu the first died over half a century ago."

Graal smiled. He didn't bother correcting her. "I need fifty new marks. No more, no less. Understand? And get some paper so you can keep count."

"Why?"

"Because you'll forget. Trust me."

He heard her do as bidden. Find a pen and paper. Then he felt her hands on his skin. This was the moment of truth. Some people asked whether he'd been a bodybuilder, or had implants, but most wouldn't let themselves notice how different he was. Humans had an unparalleled ability to ignore what they couldn't explain.

It was quiet in the room. Mei ran her fingers along his spine as she considered where to make the marks. She reached the strange muscles. The folds around his shoulder blades. The smell of the room changed as her emotions shifted.

She grew more uncertain. Tense. Then he felt the needles in his back. Pain that made his blood start pumping. His skin was pierced, prick by prick. He listened to the rhythmic sound, the needles being removed. After a while, he started to smell sweat. And fear.

She knows.

Mei's fingers had started to shake. The needles were pushed in slower and slower. Then he felt something drip onto his skin. He turned his head to look. A tear ran down her cheek. It hung from her chin for a moment before letting go. Interesting.

Graal sat up, which put them eye to eye. "You're hesitating."

She didn't reply. The stinging in his skin started to ease.

"Why?" he asked.

She lowered her gaze. "Karasu ..."

It was only a whisper, but the word sounded familiar. "Crow?" he asked, more gently this time. This was clearly one of his good days. He wanted to draw out the passion he smelled in the artist.

"A legend," she said. "An urban myth among those of us who work with ink. Karasu. A demon with wings. He only comes to the best. Karasu always asks for something simple. He is beautiful and pays well, they say. But those who agree to work on him are taken to the kingdom of the dead once the job is done."

Graal smiled. He rested his fingers on her chin. Let her feel his claws. "So being one of the best makes you sad?"

Her face was a sight to behold. A study in change. First, utter shock. Then disgust and desire, a heady combination that would result in her either kissing him or stabbing him. Sometimes they even did both.

"Fear and prejudice give rise to many legends, Mei. This job will take years. Will you help me?"

Her gaze faltered. She wanted to. He knew she wanted to. But she was struggling to accept it. He liked her. Still waters that ran deep. So much untapped energy. He wanted to go deeper. And he wanted to get there without laying a hand on her.

"I think only the best of you," he said. "You needn't think the worst of me." He got up. Tilted her chin. A tiny movement. It only took her a fraction of a second to come to him. Her lips found his throat, and she grabbed hold of his belt. Fumbled with the buckle and tore at the buttons on his pants. She pushed her hand down toward his groin. He let her. She'd find nothing.

She soon realized. Her hand groped around, looking for something long gone. She froze. Gave him a questioning look.

"I haven't had one in a thousand years," he said. "It was one of the things they took, but I'm pleased you wanted to."

Her eyes brimmed with tears. More disconsolate now than when she'd thought death had come for her.

THE TOOTH FAIRY

The morning was gray, with domes and towers partially effaced by fog. Hirka dangled her feet between the bars of the railing, looking out over the new city. It made her feel heavy with longing. It was as if someone had heard of Mannfalla and tried to replicate it. And if she squinted, it almost looked like they'd managed, though Venice was a mere shadow of it.

Hirka hadn't heard a single car since they'd arrived, which made her feel even more at home. Cars couldn't drive here because the streets were made of water. There were boats, but she didn't mind them as much. Boats she understood. She could imagine Lindri's teahouse just up ahead, where the canal branched off. Jutting out into the river, with a view of the fishermen's isle and the houses on the opposite shore. Maybe he was sitting there now, sipping tea. Lindri. Did he ever think of her? Or had they all forgotten her?

Rime. Has he forgotten me?

She wrapped her arms around herself. It was chilly. Though not nearly as chilly as inside, where Stefan and Naiell watched each other's every move, waiting for *her* to call. The tooth fairy. The woman Stefan claimed could help. Hirka was too tired to doubt him.

After they'd gotten off Nils's plane, she'd slept nearly the entire day. Then she'd snuck out for an evening stroll. Along canals, over bridges, until she wasn't sure where she was anymore. She knew she ought to be careful, but it seemed pointless. What did getting lost in a city matter when you'd already gotten lost in a world?

People had walked past in the rain without paying her any mind. It was a lovely feeling. Eventually she found her way back, where a furiously pacing Stefan told her she was lucky to be alive, the way she used her head.

Hirka's bum was cold. She got up and went back inside. They were staying on the top floor of a house right next to the canal. The house belonged to the lady, who clearly hadn't called yet, if the restless tapping of Stefan's feet was anything to go by.

He looked out of place, sitting there in his worn old trousers on a pink velvet sofa. He got up. Brushed some imaginary dust from where he'd been sitting. Stared at the phone on the table.

The remains of Naiell's dinner were on the table. A bowl of sludge and bone that had once been a whole chicken. No matter what he sunk his claws into, he always left behind something unidentifiable. Hirka had asked whether he missed the taste of food, and he'd asked whether she missed not smelling like spoiled meat.

Stefan's phone rang. He gave a start and grabbed it. Got up and paced around the room while he talked.

Naiell came in from the kitchen. The black of his eyes was becoming more and more pronounced, but it was still impossible to tell whether he was looking at her or not. There was something odd about seeing him in Stefan's clothes. Not just because they didn't fit, but because it was clear he wasn't made for them. Something about the way he held himself. He was straight-backed and strong, like Rime. Striking. Made to wear armor. But if anyone asked, he'd probably say he was made to go around naked.

Stefan put the phone in his pocket. "She wants us to come now." He looked at both of them as if at a loss.

"Should we be worried?" Hirka asked.

"You would be worried if you had any sense, girl."

Naiell looked like he was ready, but then he always did. He leaned closer to Hirka. "This woman … she knows something about my brother? What's he waiting for?"

"I think he's scared of her," Hirka answered, glad Stefan didn't speak ymish.

Stefan put on his jacket. She knew he hated it when he couldn't understand what they were saying. "Come on," he said. "And for God's sake, get him to put his sunglasses on."

They went downstairs and came out onto the street. The ground was wet. The water in the canal was high, and the boats were sloshing it everywhere. Stefan put his hands in his pockets and kept glancing behind them. The street jutted out onto the canal, where a group of people were getting on a boat. They hurried to join them.

Hirka sat as far away from the other people as she could. Naiell remained standing, until Stefan pulled him down. Then they started to move. The boat made stops in a few places, but they didn't get off. They chugged past a row of wooden boats. Open, with snow on their gunwales.

Hirka poked Stefan and pointed. "Why don't we take one of those?"

"They're for tourists. Overpriced and overhyped."

"I'm a tourist," she tried. She knew that word. A visitor. Someone who didn't belong.

"You're not a tourist, you're devil bait."

Stefan was clearly not having a good day.

The boat stopped again and they stepped out onto the pier. They followed a smaller canal past a row of white and orange houses. They were freshly painted with tidy balconies and light shining from all the lamps. A sure sign of wealth.

Stefan stopped outside one of the houses and pressed a brass button. "Just do as I say," he said. "Don't start chattering, okay? And …"

He looked at Naiell. "Don't rile him up. No nonsense. Do you understand what I'm saying?"

The door opened. A small, dark-haired lady let them in and said something Hirka didn't understand. Stefan took off his shoes, so she and Naiell did the same. Her yellow boots looked out of place next to the other shoes. The lady gestured for them to follow, still speaking an incomprehensible language. The words rolled off her tongue as she pointed up a staircase.

Stefan nodded, and they went up. The staircase had a burgundy runner down the middle and an ornate banister. A chandelier that was probably taller than Hirka hung from the high ceiling.

She found herself wishing she had other clothes. Maybe a dress. Father had bought her a dress once.

Stupid girl. You made it through the Rite in this tunic.

She followed Stefan into a room with tall windows along one wall. At the end, a blonde woman sat at a polished wooden desk. Behind her on the wall hung something that looked like a carved horn or animal tooth. But it couldn't be. Its curve was longer than a man was tall. Bigger than any animal Hirka had ever seen.

"Wait here," Stefan whispered.

Hirka stopped, but Naiell kept walking. "My brother? Where is he?"

His rough voice made the woman look up from what she was doing. Hirka went up to them. "Naiell, he'll ask. You need to wait." She quickly realized that was the wrong choice of words. Naiell was not one for waiting. He snarled like a wild animal and took off his dark glasses. Removed his gloves. He stood in front of the desk and glowered at the woman.

She got up unsteadily. Said something to Stefan. They started talking in that same rolling tongue. Hirka closed her eyes for a moment. It was hopeless. There was nothing Stefan could say that would explain what was standing before the strange woman. But it didn't stop him from trying. He always spoke quickly, but now he was stumbling over his words.

The woman raised a hand to silence Stefan. He obeyed. The woman came around the desk and stopped in front of Naiell. Curious. Fearless. Hirka felt a flash of admiration. It had taken her much longer to work up the courage to approach him, and she'd seen the blind before. This woman hadn't.

She was tall and slim. Approaching fifty, maybe, even though she'd initially seemed younger. The lines on her neck and around her eyes gave her away. Her fair hair was pulled back and held in place with a decorative pin. She was wearing gray trousers and a silk blouse that shone in the light. Her earrings provided the only splash of color. Heavy stones. Blue, like her eyes.

She raised a hand to her chin and stroked her fingers along her lower lip. Sized Naiell up with unabashed awe. Naiell didn't move. Hirka smiled at Stefan, hoping to set him at ease. It didn't help. His hand was dangerously close to the sheath on his belt where he kept his gun. He was ready for everything to go wrong.

The tooth fairy circled Naiell, scrutinizing him as if he were a statue. A work of art. She stepped back to take him all in. Naiell's lips curled up into a crooked smile. He was arrogant, and he was enjoying this.

"You're exceptional," the woman said. "But obviously you know that already."

Hirka sucked in some air. She'd forgotten to breathe for a moment.

"He doesn't understand English," Stefan said. "He doesn't speak any language I've heard before. She's the only one who understands." He nodded at Hirka, and the woman looked at her.

"You speak his language?"

"He speaks mine," Hirka said, crossing her arms.

"He's exceptional. Tell him that. Tell him he's exceptional." The woman rested her hand on Naiell's cheek. Ran her thumb over his skin. An enormous stone glittered on her finger.

"I don't think that's necessary," Hirka said dryly.

"Tell him," the woman said, with a voice that left no room for objection.

Hirka sighed. "She says you're … good," she translated into ymish.

Naiell turned his head in her direction. A black tempest raged in his eyes.

"Exceptional," she corrected herself. "She says you're exceptional. Don't let it go to your head."

Naiell pulled off his shirt and let it fall to the floor. He held out his arms demonstratively and grinned. Curled his clawed fingers. The woman let out what sounded like a gasp and brought a hand to her chest. Then she leaned closer. Pulled back his upper lip to reveal one of his canines. Hirka was ashamed to remember that she'd done the same.

Naiell grabbed her wrist. The woman showed no sign of fear or pain. She half-closed her eyes, like a contented cat. Hirka had had about as much as she could take. "Naiell!"

He let go of the woman. It seemed to surprise her. She tore her eyes away from the impossible creature standing before her and turned her attention to Hirka.

"So what are you, my dear? A monster tamer?"

"You'll have to excuse him," Hirka replied. "It's been a while since he was a god. He's clearly making up for lost time."

"So it is him. It truly is him?"

Stefan broke in. "No, it's not him. That's what I'm trying to tell you, Ms. Sanuto."

The woman put her hand on Stefan's arm. "Call me Allegra, Stefan. We've known each other long enough." Stefan blinked, as though he'd misheard.

"So who is he?" Allegra asked, shamelessly admiring Naiell's physique.

"He says he's his brother," Stefan laughed. An almost hysterical attempt to make light of the bizarre situation. "Hirka says they came here together. They're not from here."

"Clearly," Allegra smiled, leaning against the desk. She flicked her thumbnail against her other nails as she thought. Then she straightened up again. Her gaze hardened until her eyes were like the stones dangling from her ears.

"And yet you've brought them here, Stefan. Into my home? Without stopping to consider the consequences?"

"Who else was I sup—"

"You find yourself in a sticky situation, on the run from the English police. You ring Nils in the middle of the night and ask for an unsanctioned five-hour flight across Europe. Then you come here with what you claim is the brother of a creature no one can prove exists. Not even those who have dedicated their lives to finding him. And now I have a new creator … a new source. Here. In my home. What do you think the consequences of that will be? Did you at any point consider that this makes both of us targets? Do you think you're the only hunter on the planet?"

Stefan walked in circles, running his hand over his face. Nervous. Tired. Taken aback.

"And the stones?" Allegra asked.

Stefan stopped. He nodded at Hirka. "They belong to her."

"Goodness me …" Allegra seemed to be enjoying herself all of a sudden. "Are you becoming a better man, Stefan?"

Stefan tensed his jaw.

Hirka felt bad for him. Allegra clearly knew how to make him feel small, but enough was enough. Hirka picked the shirt up from the floor and chucked it at Naiell. "Leave Stefan alone. It's not his fault, it's ours," she said to Allegra. "Our story goes back a long way, as does the story of the one you're hunting. That's why we're here. So do you know who he is or not?" She tried to remember the word. "Do you know where we can find the devil?"

Allegra Sanuto studied her. Long enough to make her feel uncomfortable. Then she put her arm around Hirka's shoulders and led her toward the door. "Stefan, I expect you to be gone by the time I return," she said over her shoulder. "Go back to the apartment. Don't let this creature parade around. And don't talk to anyone. You can leave the goods on my desk."

"Where are you going?" Stefan asked tamely.

Allegra squeezed Hirka's shoulder like they were old friends.

"I think it's about time someone took this young lady out to lunch."

PREDATORS

Hirka couldn't remember the last time she'd felt so self-conscious. She was sitting at a window table with a view of the canal, in a suffocating room decorated in shades of gold and cinnamon. The curtains were heavy and lifeless. Huge paintings were displayed in frames that had to weigh more than the wall.

Other diners sat around an open fireplace near the kitchen, conversing in both English and Italian. Words she knew interweaving with words she'd never heard. She'd moved her chair so her back wasn't to them. Not that it mattered. Everyone was tailless here, but old habits died hard.

Hirka reached for the breadbasket before changing her mind and taking her hand back. As soon as she dropped a crumb, the man with the beaklike nose would come back to brush off the tablecloth again.

Her clothes wouldn't sit properly either. A gray skirt and a light-colored blouse that Allegra said wouldn't clash with her hair. Hirka glanced longingly at the paper bag from the store. Her old clothes were in there. The ones she could wear without thinking about it. She hadn't wanted new clothes. Didn't need them. But Allegra Sanuto clearly wasn't the kind of woman people said no to. She was a bit like Svarteld. She expected things to be done her way. And she'd made it very clear that she couldn't take Hirka out to eat in the clothes she had on.

Hirka didn't like owing her anything, but she'd been assured she was the one doing Allegra a favor, not the other way around. Judging by how painful the boots were, she was inclined to agree. But it was a small price to pay for looking like she owned Venice—at least according to the much-older woman sitting across from her going on about how much they had in common.

Like what? Are we both being hunted by the devil?

"The tartare is to die for. Won't you try it? It's raw veal. Oh, I suppose you young people don't eat that sort of thing. Perhaps something simpler?"

Hirka looked at the stiff menu in her hand. The words meant nothing to her, so she wasn't sure how to respond. She felt ashamed, without being sure why. It was really irritating. She felt like standing up and shouting that she wasn't actually from here. That she hadn't learned all the languages and wasn't familiar with all the customs yet. She wasn't sure why she felt the need to defend herself. After all, it meant little in the grand scheme of things. They were only there to eat. There were far more important things to think about than what she was wearing and whether she was doing anything wrong or not.

I had the Council wrapped around my little finger. Why should I be afraid of anyone?

All the same, she stiffened when the man with the beak suddenly reappeared. Allegra intervened, letting loose a stream of Italian that sent him on his way. Hirka put her menu down.

"Don't worry, darling. They know only the best will do. That's just how it is when you have a name like mine."

"Allegra?"

"No, sweetie," she said, laughing. "Sanuto. As in Beauty by Sanuto."

Hirka nodded, wishing she was back with Stefan and Naiell. She had more in common with a man-hunter and a deadborn than this woman. Allegra raised a sculpted eyebrow. "Really? You haven't heard of it? The creams? The make-up?"

Hirka couldn't take any more. No one acted this nonchalant unless they were desperate. "Why are we here?" she asked.

Allegra leaned back in her chair. She tilted her wrist, touching her thumb and ring finger together in a particularly feminine gesture. She surveyed her nails for a moment before meeting Hirka's gaze again.

"Is it because of the stones?" Hirka asked.

"Spare me the judgemental tone, sweetie. I've more than enough precious stones in my life. I need neither them nor the money. I'd have thought that was fairly obvious." She leaned over the table again. "But I'd love to see them, if you don't mind. Stefan sent me a picture, and I'd like to know whether I was right. Call it a hobby."

Hirka fished around in the bag until she found the leather pouch. She put it on the table. It was one of the few things she had from home. Every time she saw it somewhere new, it was like two worlds colliding. The old world she loved and the new world she hated. What she understood and what she would probably never understand. A brown leather pouch tied with a cord, on a white tablecloth unsullied by crumbs.

"How charming," Allegra said. "Is that Sámi work? Something like that could really take off here at the moment."

Hirka opened the pouch and put the three blood stones on the table. Allegra lifted one of them up so that it caught the light, though not high enough for anyone to notice. She had a talent for discretion. Allegra turned it over in her hand and put it back with the others.

"You don't know what they are, do you?"

"I know exactly what they are. They're blood stones."

"And they're common where you're from?"

Hirka's blood ran cold. The question threatened to lift the lid on the dangerous box in her mind. The one containing the unknown poison. For the first time, she was glad it was impossible for her to get back to Ym. Because if she could, others could too.

"No. They're rare. They were a gift," she replied.

"In that case, I'd like right of first refusal."

"Right of first what?"

Allegra reached out and tucked Hirka's hair behind her ear. Hirka wasn't sure how to respond. There was something affectionate about the gesture, but no one had ever done it before. She didn't usually tuck her hair behind her ears. Much to her relief, it fell back into its usual place straight away.

"You've quite the head of hair, Hirka. It's a bit unruly, but that's easily fixed." Hirka didn't reply. "Listen, sweetie, I get it. You don't want anyone cheating you. But I'm sure you could use the money. That's why I'm happy to give you some, so long as you promise you'll sell to me, if you ever do decide to sell. Of course, you don't *have* to sell them. You can keep them for the rest of your life, if that's what you want. But I'm willing to pay to make sure you don't sell them to anyone else. Understand?"

Allegra didn't wait for a reply. "You need money to survive. And if I understand you and Stefan correctly, you have no passport, no papers, no bank account. You don't exist. And believe me, my dear, the world is a cruel place for those who don't exist. That means you can't buy or sell anything in the normal way. I'm offering to make it easier for you, and you don't have to give me anything in return. And you needn't worry about the price. I'll pay you well. I can give you a life without care."

"I'll have to ask Stefan," Hirka said, taking a sip of water. She hoped it would put an end to the discussion.

Allegra laughed. "You want to ask a hunter for advice? A man who's little more than a primitive weapon?" She folded her arms across her chest. "I realize it's difficult to know who to trust, so let me help you. It can be our little secret. It's all about give and take, right? Watch your step around Stefan. You realize he was probably planning to put an end to you? It's just as well he tends to make a mess of things."

Hirka fumbled with her glass. She caught it before it tipped over completely and wiped the tablecloth with her sleeve. No sooner had she done so than Allegra lifted her arm and laid a napkin underneath.

She's lying!

But Hirka remembered Stefan threatening her in the alleyway all too well. Holding the weapon to her head. Why? He hadn't known about the stones back then. Why had he been planning to kill her … and why hadn't he gone through with it?

"Don't look so shocked, sweetie. You've fallen into a viper's nest, so just be careful who you trust. I might be wrong, but I doubt it. It's not an uneducated guess."

Hirka didn't bother asking about the words she didn't understand. "How do you know he was planning to kill me?"

Allegra pursed her lips. *Kill* clearly wasn't a word you were supposed to say, even if that was undoubtedly what you were talking about. "Because he is what he is. He hunts *them*. The forgotten. And Stefan knows they're hunting you. What no one knows is why. But I can promise you that once the wounded king has noticed you, you're not safe anywhere."

Hirka studied Allegra Sanuto. She exhibited none of the sympathy that ought to have accompanied such words. She might as well have been talking about the weather.

"Wounded king?"

Allegra glanced at the other diners before replying in a low voice.

"They say he was marked by a war. That he ruled long before countries had names, if we're to believe a somewhat doubtful theory once posited at a lecture I attended. A lecture given by an academic who's been studying the lore of this creature for many years. Academics are harmless because they seek only knowledge, not gain. You won't have to deal with the likes of them. You'll have to deal with predators."

Hirka felt less sure of herself with every word this woman said. She was like a fist wrapped in silk.

"You need protection. And, quite simply, someone to care for you," Allegra continued. "I'll take some cash out for you. That's what you need most. Your companions have no concept of what a young woman needs, but I'm here now. I'll introduce you to people who can help. You needn't thank me, just promise you'll listen to me. And keep a low profile, okay? I'll contact Stefan and we can go out to eat again tomorrow. Maybe do something about your hair."

Hirka was flabbergasted. She had no words. What was she supposed to do now? Go back to Stefan and Naiell and pretend that nothing had happened? Run away again? To yet another strange town? With those strange people, the forgotten, still after her?

"But don't worry about that now, sweetie. That's not why we're here," Allegra said airily.

"Then why are we here?"

The man with the beak was suddenly back. He set a patty of raw meat down in front of Allegra, and a salad down in front of Hirka. Allegra waited until he'd gone again before replying. "Because of your beautiful friend."

Hirka picked at the green leaves in front of her. She wasn't going to eat anything. The food here was tasteless. Lifeless. Despite the bright colors. And didn't they know raw meat could make you ill? They were all out of their minds.

"He's nowhere near as beautiful as he thinks he is," Hirka replied, and she meant it. Naiell was beautiful, in a scary way. The way the blind were. But she didn't really see the appeal.

Allegra mixed raw egg yolk into the bloody patty before looking at Hirka. "Your restraint is inhuman, my dear."

Rime. His name is Rime.

But Hirka said nothing.

"Eat up," Allegra said. "There's someone I want you to meet when we're done."

BOUND BY BLOOD

The room was far too cluttered. But with things Hirka recognized. Things she understood. Dark bookcases. Swords fixed to the wall in the shape of a fan. A full suit of armor, with a metal helmet, gloves, and boots. The first she'd seen since leaving Ym. Hirka ran her fingers across the metal, suddenly feeling like the victim of some big joke. She'd never be allowed to forget. Every time her homesickness eased a little, the gods put something familiar in front of her. Rubbed salt in the wound.

Allegra put her hand on Hirka's back and steered her toward some chairs in front of the fire. "Silvio, we have a guest," she said.

The man sat in one of the chairs, squinting at a book. He looked up. He looked to be around seventy, with white hair and a fastidiously trimmed beard. Smart clothes, brown shoes. He and Allegra both wore shoes indoors—probably because they didn't have to clean the house themselves.

"This is my husband, Silvio," Allegra said.

"Hirka." Hirka held out her hand. He got up and shook it but was unable to hide his uncertainty. He hadn't been expecting anyone. His eyes shifted between her and Allegra. "I … I was …" He turned and walked over to the window. Rested his palms on the sill. He seemed confused. As if he were looking for something that used to be there. "I was trying to find something," he said at last.

"Your dictionary," Allegra said. "You were trying to find your dictionary."

He nodded and returned to his chair. The book was open on the seat. He looked up at Allegra and she nodded in approval. He picked it up and sat back down. Hirka furrowed her brow. She knew what this was. He was suffering from memory loss.

Behind him, a door stood ajar. Through the opening she could see a wall covered in pictures and drawings. She had a feeling she was looking at something important, without knowing what. Allegra followed her gaze and quickly went to shut the door.

"That's his study. You must forgive him, it's in a terrible state," she said. "It's because—well, it may not seem like it, but he's ill. I realized some months ago."

Hirka stared at Allegra in astonishment. "Haven't you given him ylir root?"

"Oh, sweetie, I've given him everything money can buy. No one and nothing can help him."

Hirka gaped at her. She suddenly felt unsteady. They didn't know. They actually didn't know. She'd stopped memory loss before. It wasn't complicated. Right enough, you lost a lot of weight, and you couldn't eat much of what you used to without feeling nauseous, but that was a small price to pay when the alternative was slowly forgetting yourself and the people you loved.

I haven't seen ylir root since I got here.

The room started to spin. The game the gods were playing seemed to grow before her eyes. The big joke. There were things in Ym that could save people here. And things here that could save people in Ym. Two worlds. An ocean of problems. And no trace of the Might. No way of getting through. The only one who could open the gateways between worlds was the one who wanted to destroy them.

Hirka collapsed onto a foot stool. Allegra crouched down next to her. "I know, sweetie. It's horrible. There are no words." She brushed Hirka's hair behind her ear again. "But you can help us."

Hirka shook her head. She didn't have so much as a tea leaf left. Nothing. She was powerless to heal. "There's nothing I can do," she said. The words came out as a croak.

Allegra got up. "You can talk to him. You speak his language. And you can save Silvio."

Hirka closed her eyes. Stefan's stories raced through her mind. Graal, who spread the rot. The sickness. Kept people alive past their time. If he could keep people alive, then so could his brother. Naiell.

Allegra wanted to turn her husband into a blood slave.

Hirka stared up at her. "You hunt them, yet you want to turn the person you love into one of them?"

Allegra twisted the ring on her finger, as if it had suddenly gotten too heavy. "I don't hunt them. Stefan hunts them. He's always hunted them. That's what I'm trying to tell you. He's a simple man. He doesn't understand that the source can also save lives, not just take them."

Hirka shook her head. She'd come up against the forgotten. Seen what blood of the blind did to people. "They rot … they smell …"

"They don't smell! They live! They remember! And they're stronger and better than any normal person could ever be! Stefan has already manipulated you. He doesn't see the possibilities. His past has blinded him. He'll never be able to do more than hate them. He'll never be able to give you a clear picture."

Hirka looked at Silvio. He was leafing through the book, faster than he could possibly read. He didn't know what he was doing. Just turning pages. He was nothing more than a shell that would get emptier and emptier with every passing day.

Allegra held out her hand. "Hirka … my dear. What would you do? If it was someone you loved? Would you save him?"

A thousand times if I had to.

But she didn't say that. She took Allegra's hand and pulled herself up. Allegra led her out onto the balcony. It had started to rain again. "I understand your hesitation. He's painted a picture of the devil. But Stefan doesn't see clearly. And he must never know. I understand them better than he does."

"Understand them?"

"There's a family legend concerning one of my ancestors. An artist. A respected painter who simply vanished in his youth. Some said he went off and drank himself to death. Or took his own life. But pictures that could only have been painted by him kept turning up, even after what would have been his one hundred and fiftieth birthday. In his diary, he tells of a man he encountered. A man who had seen all that the world had to offer. Who had razed cities then built them anew. Venice was one of them. His new friend was a founder, destroyer, doctor, scientist, adventurer ... This man enthralled him so much that he abandoned everything to follow him. Neither wife, child, nor fortune could make him stay. His powerful new friend had teeth like a predator. Sanuto. Fang. That's my family name."

Hirka rested her hands on the wet railing. Looked at the houses huddled together along the canal. The rain formed rings in the water, rippling the reflection of the city. Nothing seemed solid anymore.

"I know," Allegra said. "It's a story that would make any vampire lover swoon, right? But it's not like in the stories. Of all the forgotten I've encountered in my life, none of them has had the teeth of a predator. Or sucked blood. They're like you and I."

"So why do they go crazy? Why do they kill?"

"That's the tragic part. I believe the forgotten are those who were once close to him. Friends. They live for as long as they're useful to him. After that they have to manage on their own, and they rarely manage long at all. I think them randomly attacking people is simply the result of withdrawal."

"I don't know what that is."

"Withdrawal? It's what happens to your body when you don't get something you're addicted to. Do they not have stimulants where you're from?"

Hirka ignored the more difficult words. She knew what she was getting at. Father had sold opa. She'd hated it. Yes, it had its uses, but many people were unable to control their need for it.

The rain was leaving dark patches on Allegra's silk blouse, but she didn't seem to notice. "Or maybe it isn't the blood alone that makes them sick. Maybe it's just longing. Maybe missing him is what makes them sick. I've never been a slave to any man. Never really been in love. So I wouldn't have thought it possible. That is until I laid eyes on him today. Your beautiful friend. He's not like other men." Allegra smiled. "Do you think it's possible? To be sick with longing?"

Hirka had to turn away. The memories came thick and fast. Rime. His white hair, heavy with rain. He'd pulled her close and pressed his lips to hers. She'd caught fire. Burned. Forgotten the world. Forgotten everything. Apart from the rot.

She'd left him because she believed in something that didn't exist. She'd had proof. Urd's throat. He'd said it himself. That he'd gotten the rot from her father.

Hirka stiffened. Her mind stopped racing, her thoughts all converging on one in particular. The box of poison opened, and the poison flowed through her. Ice-cold. Merciless.

She knew.

Child of Odin? Human?

No. She might have looked human, but she wasn't one of them. Never had been. Urd had gotten the rot from her father.

The rot. From her father.

And who spread the rot here? Among the humans?

Graal.

Allegra seized Hirka's arms. "Sweetie, don't look so terrified! You've nothing to fear! The wounded king might as well be a legend. Nobody can get to him, but we don't need to. We have a new source now, and he's very real. His actual brother. I need his blood. Just a little. Nobody will know. You have the power to save a life, Hirka. There's no wrong in it. No shame. There is no god or devil here. No magic. It's just chemistry."

Hirka had no idea what chemistry was. Or magic, for that matter. But she had a feeling they were exactly the same thing. Either way, they couldn't help her now. Nothing could.

She looked up at Allegra. "Could I have a glass of water?" she whispered.

DESIRE

A lone flute played. It was all that could be heard, even though hundreds of men were crowded in front of the stage, all gaping mouths and stupid smiles. Spellbound by Damayanti's dance.

Rime knew he shouldn't be there. If he'd let them put the mark of the Council on his forehead, he wouldn't have been able to set foot there. Or walk alone through the streets of Mannfalla. The symbol that was meant to give him all the power in the world would have become a prison.

And now it had lost all meaning.

The Seer didn't exist, but people had other altars to worship at.

He followed Damayanti's movements. Fluid enough to impress even Kolkagga. She was naked. Completely naked. Her body was painted in orange and red. Flames licked their way across her breasts and up her sides. The colors grew darker and darker the lower they plunged, fading to black at the junction of her thighs.

She fell backward as if her back had been broken. The melody from the flute stopped. Men gasped. An illusion. A game intended to make people think that something had gone wrong. The flute started to play again. Damayanti twisted around until she was standing on her forearms with her feet stretching toward the ceiling. Her back blazed orange. Then she lowered her feet. Slowly, slowly, until her toes touched the back of her head.

The men around him hollered and applauded. Sweaty faces

glistened in the darkness, likely because of the paler seam now visible in the black between her thighs.

Rime lowered his eyes. What was he doing here? Did he really think this dancer had anything to tell him that he couldn't find out for himself? Or was it something else that had drawn him here?

It was hard to argue with the warmth he felt in his body. He'd never been with a woman. As a son of the Council, an An-Elderin, he'd led a sheltered existence until he was fifteen. He was the successor. The child everyone had been waiting for. After the Rite he'd fought tooth and nail to be Kolkagga, and as far as he knew, there were only a handful of female Kolkagga among thousands of men, none of whom were in his camp. His training and his disdain for the Council had kept that fire at bay. He hadn't craved female company. Or so he'd thought.

Is the rot the only thing you choose to believe in, Hirka?

His words. Back in Blindból. After the fall of the Seer. After the death of Ilume. Halfway up a mountain with the rain pelting down around them. She'd sat close to him. Held his face in her hands so all he could see was red hair and green eyes. Until the senselessness of it all had stopped hurting. And he'd kissed her. Deeply. He'd known then. She was ready. There was no doubt in his mind that she wanted him just as much as he wanted her. But she wasn't an ymling. She didn't belong in this world, and her fear of the consequences had been too great.

He was suddenly overcome by the feeling of being in the wrong place. There was nothing for him here. He pulled his hood down over his face. Squeezed past a row of men to get to the door. Then he felt a hand on his arm.

"She'll be pleased to see you."

The girl was much too young to be in a place like this. She was barely Rite-ready. Her fair hair had been pulled into a ponytail that curled at the end. She looked up at him. She was blind in one eye. It was milky and colorless. “You can wait upstairs. Follow me,” she said, slipping between some tall men.

Rime followed her up the stairs and into a pleasantly quiet room. The smell of sweat was replaced by perfume. The girl pointed at a low chair and left him. Rime looked around. The stifling room was lavishly decorated. Shiny tiles covered the pillars. Red and gold fabrics shimmered on the ceiling and hung in folds down the walls. A lamp made of colored glass hung over the table, smoke puffing out of small holes. A smaller table with a mirror stood against one wall.

An opening led into another room. It was too dark to see anything, and a curtain of thousands of small stones hung across it. They rattled discreetly in a draft from an unknown source.

Rime raised his hand to his breast pocket to check that the beak was still there. It felt strangely heavy. As did his head. Maybe it was the smoke.

Whoops from outside told him that Damayanti was done. Men whistled and hollered. Music started to play. Rime looked at the door, but no one came. He ought to leave while he still had the chance.

No. He needed to talk to her. The dancer knew something. Something she thought he should know as well. He was sure of it.

The curtain rattled, and Damayanti entered. The painted flames seemed to flicker as she walked. Many would have considered it highly indecent. But it was a nakedness that was difficult to object to. Her nipples were nothing more than bumps amid the flames. And the paint between her thighs was so dark that you'd have to look twice before you realized she was naked as the day she was born. Even the tip of her tail was smooth.

The last time they'd met, she had kept her eyes averted, only occasionally glancing up at him. A temptress, but a coy one. There was nothing coy about her now. The woman before him was a snake, blazing passion on two feet, and she was smiling at him. Inviting his gaze.

Two young girls entered the room. One of them was the girl who had shown him in. The other was a dark-haired beauty, a few years older. They set down basins of water and kneeled on either side of the dancer. Damayanti lifted her arms and the girls started to wash the paint off. Rime turned away. He could sense her smiling. A while later he heard the girls disappear through the curtain.

"You're not like the men out there, are you?" Damayanti said, right behind him now. Closer than he'd thought. He glanced over his shoulder. She'd put on a short top that pushed her breasts together, and a skirt with small rings that jingled as she walked.

Her hand slid across his back before she crawled onto the sofa opposite him. He sat down, getting the distinct impression that she'd done this many times before.

"I'm not here to see you dance," Rime replied. "Although it is impressive," he hastened to add.

"I know what it is, Rime An-Elderin. Would you like something to drink?"

"No, thank you," he replied, immediately regretting it. His throat felt dry.

"That's fine. We don't always know what we want, Ravenbearer."

"We don't always give in to what we want," Rime replied. A shadow of disappointment passed over her face.

He pulled the raven beak out of his pocket. It had been scrubbed clean but still felt dirty in his hand. A rough surface with rust-colored blood in the scratches. He put it on the table. Her eyes widened. She leaned forward to pick it up. He did the same. Her hand ended up on top of his. She had reacted instinctively, and he could tell she regretted it. There could no longer be any doubt that she knew what it was.

She devoured him with her eyes. Her lips parted. Full. Moist. She dragged her thumbnail across his palm. Rime held his breath. It would be so simple. And he already knew she would never tell anyone. But what would that make him?

He shook his head and she withdrew her hand, smiling as if to say it was worth a try. But she wouldn't sway him. Or make him forget what she'd just revealed.

Damayanti got up. Her muscles formed a line down her stomach, as defined as a spine. Her skirt jingled on her hips as she walked over to a gleaming cabinet and pulled out a decanter and two glasses, which she filled. She handed him one. It smelled sweet and fermented. He took it, but didn't drink. He set it down next to the beak, which lay half-open on the table.

"Do I come across as a strong woman to you, Ravenbearer?"

"Strong in your own way, certainly."

She sat down again and crossed her legs.

"I know what you're thinking, Rime. You're thinking that I've underestimated you. That I've tried to beguile you with my feminine wiles. The truth is a good deal simpler: this is me. This is who I am. But a lot of men have thought the same. My strength lies in seeing the difference between them. But what you don't see, Ravenbearer, is that I have no choice."

He hoped she wouldn't come to her senses and let him speak. If she did, she'd soon realize how little he really knew. So he listened.

"I have no choice because men need to believe I'm strong. I'm alive because they all think different things. Some think I'm a temptress and, for that reason, leave me in peace. Others think I'm as strong as I am soft. There are even some who think I prefer women and leave me be because of that. My strength is knowing what kind of man I'm dealing with so I can do what I have to in order to survive. I want to dance without fear of rape. Without ending up face-down in the Ora. So yes, I'm a strong woman. But you know better than most that strength is not the same as fearlessness. I've had to do all kinds of things to save my own skin."

He looked at her. Had she been lying, she'd have tried to appear more pitiful. To disappear into the pile of cushions on the sofa. But she sat straight-backed, one hand resting on the back of the sofa and the other playing with her glass. She was telling the truth.

He laughed. "So now you're going to tell me about all the things you've been forced to do?" he asked, hoping to put an end to her performance. Conversations were always so much easier once the masks had been put aside.

She lowered her chin and looked up at him. Her eyes were rimmed with dark make-up. She nodded at the beak. "Yes, I know what that is. And yes, I thought it had disappeared along with Urd."

The hairs on the back of Rime's neck stood on end. His instincts had brought him here. A remote possibility. But he was going to get so much more. He didn't dare speak in case she brought her guard back up.

"What you need to remember, Rime-fadri, is that Urd was a powerful man. He knew I'd grown up among wise women and disreputable men. That I'd learned things as a child. Things he could greatly benefit from. So I was left with a choice: share those things with him or die. And it would be such a shame to deprive the world of this body, so I went with option one. But you're not like him. So tell me, why should I share something with you if it might cost me my life? Why should I admit to anything and give you what you need to have me set alight and thrown from Askeberg?"

Rime stared at the beak. She was right. Urd *had* practiced blindcraft. The forbidden Might. The knowledge Rime had thought was lost and forgotten. Had the Council found out what Urd had been up to, he'd have been stopped long before he'd been able to do any harm. Damayanti knew that, too. And she had every reason to fear the Council. He had to assure her that they would never find out.

He looked at her again. "You have my word."

"You say that like it means something. And it actually does to you, doesn't it?"

He could see that she was surprised.

She bit her lip. "Blood is life. Blood rouses the raven. And the raven is a talkative creature. I've been hearing that since long before I was old enough to understand. Give the beak a body to speak from, and you can talk to whomever you like."

"Blindcraft."

The word made her gaze falter. "No one who uses that word today knows what it means, Rime-fadri. The Council once used the Might the way the deadborn did. That's how it was before. Before the books were burned. Back when men were slaves or bled to death on the battlefield."

"People still serve and bleed."

"You're just as bullheaded as Urd was. He once sat where you are now. He too considered it a show of strength to contradict me."

Urd again. I'm following in the footsteps of a madman.

Rime was desperate to get out of there. His head felt heavy and he was no longer certain of what he wanted. If this woman was truly familiar with blindcraft, and could use the Might like the blind once did, then … so what? What use was that to him?

She could destroy us.

He took the beak and got up. "Urd was Urd. I'm Rime An-Elderin. I'm Kolkagga, and Ravenbearer to the eleven kingdoms. I've shown more than enough strength for one lifetime. When I say people still serve and bleed, it's because it's the truth."

She looked at the beak in his hand. "Don't you want to know how it works?"

He didn't reply. She got up as well. "You think what you hold in your hand is evil. You think it's an instrument of death. Nábyrn sorcery. But the Might is neither good nor evil. It is what it is. It can give you everything you want, or take from you everything you have. Refusing to use or master it is madness, but you know that already. You thirst for control. So what if I were to tell you that the voice of the raven knows no boundaries, Rime? That it can carry across mountains, across countries?"

She gripped his belt and moved closer. Whispered in his ear. "What if I were to tell you that the raven can carry a voice across any boundary, even between worlds?"

He closed his fist around the beak. Pulled away without looking at her. He couldn't let her see the effect of what she'd said.

Hirka. He could reach Hirka. Hear her voice, even though impossible boundaries separated them.

"At what cost?" he asked, remembering Urd being dragged screaming between the stones in the hands of the blind.

"Urd's capacity to overestimate himself was unparalleled," she replied, as if she'd read his mind. "He was a weak man with a big mouth. You're not like him, Rime An-Elderin."

How did we get here? Why are we discussing this?

It had all happened so fast. From one moment to the next. He'd put a raven beak on the table and now they were talking about blindcraft. About something abhorrent that could cost them their lives. Though nobody would take her side over his.

He couldn't help but admire her courage. All she'd had to do was feign ignorance. Say she'd never seen the beak before. That she didn't know any more about the Might than anyone else. But she'd opened up. Just as vulnerable and exposed as she was onstage. To the head of the Council. To the Ravenbearer.

"Take all the time you need, Rime An-Elderin. It doesn't happen overnight. To understand the Might you need to understand our history. Understand the war."

"I was weaned on the history of the war," he replied.

"Really? So what was the most important thing that happened?"

She leaned closer. Her breasts heaved as they were squeezed between her arms.

"We won," he replied dryly.

"Ah, but what you have to realize, Ravenbearer, is that the most important thing isn't who won. The most important thing is who lost."

A CHOICE

Leaning houses huddled together along the canal. The evening had enveloped the city in fog. Hirka didn't mind. She was more than happy to remain unseen. Allegra had accompanied her on the boat, dropping her off right outside the house they were staying in. The moment she was out of sight, Hirka yanked off the torturous shoes and put her yellow boots back on.

She knew she shouldn't be out on her own, but the fog made her feel safe. And she needed time to think. To figure out what was true. But the line between truth and lie had blurred. What was right and what was wrong seemed to change depending on what certain people wanted. The only thing she had to hold on to was the fact that no one knew who she was. And nobody could be allowed to know. Especially not Naiell.

A foul stench was drifting up from one of the canals. Nobody else seemed to be troubled by it. Hirka had a horrible feeling she was smelling something that hadn't happened yet. Allegra had told her to enjoy the city while it was still there. Before it sank. Apparently nothing human was meant to last. Not Venice. Not the world.

She stopped outside the door. What was she going to do? Go inside to Stefan, the man Allegra claimed had been planning to kill her? Inside to the blindling who said she was an instrument for the destruction of Ym? Or should she just keep walking in the hope she'd never see any of them again?

Hirka wasn't afraid of being alone. She was used to that. What was weighing on her was the feeling of never having anyone to trust. Being surrounded by hidden motives. Riddles. Like Naiell. He held secrets from a world she didn't know. He'd lived for so many years it was unfathomable. He was a blindling. And he was all that stood between her and his brother, who was desperate for revenge.

Him and Stefan.

She needed Stefan. Without him she'd never find her way in this world. She might just as well be a dog slinking around in alleys, begging for food. There was too much at stake now. She had to stop running.

She walked up the stairs and knocked. Stefan was nothing like Rime. Rime would have heard her coming before she got to the door. Stefan was more likely to jump out of his skin and riddle the door with holes. And her along with it. Maybe Allegra had been telling the truth. Stefan would sooner kill her than feel unsafe. Fear made people dangerous.

"Naiell?" she heard from inside.

"Have you lost Naiell?' Hirka tried to open the door but was stopped by a chain. Stefan closed the door again and took the chain off. He let her in, securing the door again before looking her up and down. He seemed angry and confused. She'd forgotten she was wearing new clothes. She tugged at the skirt.

"Allegra?" he asked tersely. She nodded.

He kept staring. "You look—"

"—like I own Venice? Where's Naiell?" She scanned the room and spotted Stefan's weapon on the table. Bent into the shape of a hook.

"He needed some air," Stefan snapped.

"And you tried to stop him?"

Stefan grabbed the weapon. Held it up for her to inspect, as though it were her fault that it was destroyed. "This had a custom silencer! Do you have any idea how much they cost?" He roared and chucked it against the wall. It fell to the floor, leaving a tear in the red wallpaper. He slumped against the wall and dragged his hands over his face.

"What did she say?" he asked, revealing the fear behind his rage.

Hirka set down the bag with her old clothes. "She said the skirt showed off my legs, and that the blouse wouldn't clash with my hair."

He looked at her, momentarily confused. Then he laughed glumly. "I don't know how I ended up here, Hirka. I've dug myself into a hole so deep I can't get out."

Hirka grabbed his hand. It was warm and rough against hers. "Come," she said, pulling him out onto the balcony. She pushed one of the wrought-iron chairs against the wall of the building and clambered onto it. Then she stepped up onto the window ledge, where she could reach the ladder on the wall. She started climbing, then paused to look down at Stefan, who stood staring at her. "Come on, chicken."

She pulled herself up onto the roof and found somewhere dry to sit. The city was like a dream. Devoid of color. Blurred. Was she starting to wake up?

She heard Stefan making his way up. It felt safer up here. She could be herself. Hirka, the girl who liked to climb. She could cope with anything up here, no matter who Stefan was. He sat down next to her.

"You're not very bright. You know that, don't you?"

"On the contrary," she replied. "I'm brighter than you think. For example, I know we have a choice to make."

"Choice?"

She hesitated for a moment. Searched for the words.

"You're hunting the source of a sickness. That rot. And he's hunting me. So either you're with me because you think I might lead you to him, or you're planning to sell me to someone who can help you find him. That means I have a choice to make. Do we stick together or not? That's my choice."

At first he looked dumbfounded. Then he turned away. He knew what was coming.

"You work for Allegra," she continued, "in some way or another. Whether I trust you or not is my choice. Allegra claims to be looking out for me. She's trying to get close to me and Naiell. Whether I let her or not is also my choice. I may be wearing clothes she bought for me, but I already know she can't be trusted. She says you were going to kill me. And that might have been true. Until Naiell turned up and everything changed for you. But she *said* that. And that means none of us can trust her. So what choice are we going to make, then?"

She turned to Stefan. He was sitting with his legs apart, his elbows resting on his knees. Fiddling with a loose roof tile. "Do you believe her?"

"That's not important."

"Of course it's important! If you think I was going to kill you, then what's the fucking point in us talking, girl?"

In that moment she knew it was true. That had been his plan. Had it been a lie, he wouldn't have gotten so worked up.

His eyes looked painfully tired. Yet brown and full of warmth. That's what had stopped him. The warmth. Stefan may have been a hunter, but he would never think of himself as a murderer.

"I can rest easy knowing I'm still alive," she said. "That should be good enough for you, too." The words left a bitter taste in her mouth. She was lying. More than anything, she wanted to show all of them. All the killers. All those who took what they wanted by force. Who hunted. She wanted to crush them. Destroy them. Tear them to pieces. So they'd know how it felt.

But she'd already done that. Killed. And it hadn't helped.

Stefan's head drooped. His eyes glazed over. A grown man, at least twice her age. But in that moment, she was dealing with a child.

"I feel like I can't breathe, you know?" he mumbled. "We left behind a hell of a mess in England. They might have surveillance footage from the alleyway. I might already be done for. And now Allegra's gone and stabbed me in the back. For you. To get you to do what she wants."

"No, not for me. For Naiell. It's all about Naiell and what he's capable of. Him and ... Graal."

His name sounded different now. Now that she knew. No longer just an empty sound. It was raw. Harsh. Laced with meaning. Burning her tongue. Was she right? Was that a name for a father? She pushed the thought aside. There was no time for it. Or space. Even up here on the roof. That's how bad it was.

Stefan tossed the red roof tile aside. "Jeez, you say that like it's normal."

"It is. Where they're from." Hirka grinned.

Stefan looked at her. "Who are you, girl? And like hell you're sixteen."

It sounded like he was saying something nice, so she didn't question it.

"Stefan, there's a reason Allegra is trying to come between us. She doesn't think she needs you anymore. She wants to control me. Control Naiell. Because she knows a lot more than she's letting on, and we need to find out what."

Stefan snorted. "If she hasn't told you by now, she's not going to."

Hirka lay back and looked up at the colorless sky. "Well, she says plenty without knowing it. For example, she's gone to hear people explain their theories about Graal. Why would she do that? And what does she want with a hunter like you? Someone who's also looking for him? And why is it so important to keep us here? I know the reason, and she's going to tell us whether she likes it or not. I have a plan, Stefan."

"*You* have a plan?"

"I have a plan."

He pressed his hand to his chest. "I'm the one who comes up with the plans here, girl."

"In that case, it's your plan, too."

"What, then? What's my plan, Your Highness?"

Hirka got up. "We're going to break into Allegra's."

THE INNOCENTS

Rime pulled his tunic over his woollen undershirt and tied it at the side. The cord was concealed. There weren't any loops, pockets, or fastenings. Nothing that might impede movement. Nothing that might get caught on a sword. He was back in black. Kolkagga black.

Svarteld stood before him with his arms folded over his chest. "So this is how you think you serve us best?" he asked. "In black? At war and in danger?"

Rime pulled his hood up and slid his mask over his face. It concealed almost everything, apart from his eyes. "Better like this than in the chair."

He sheathed his swords behind his back. Svarteld could think what he wanted, but Rime knew who the greatest threat to Ym was. And they weren't sitting around a table, whining. They were out there, with claws and twisted minds, a threat to ordinary people. And it was out there they had to be fought.

"And when you die, who will sit in your chair then, An-Elderin?"

"Am I not Kolkagga? A black shadow? Already dead?" Rime tightened the leather around his wrist.

Svarteld started toward him. He didn't stop until they were face to face. "You can't govern the world from Slokna, boy! You're the Ravenbearer. You took the Seer from them. You've made yourself the beginning and the end. And you're going to use that power to offer yourself up as blind bait in the wilderness? Contempt of death has its place among Kolkagga. Not on the Council. You've more than just yourself to think about now."

Rime tried to step around him but was stopped by a firm hand on his shoulder. Svarteld's skin was almost as dark as his clothes. There wasn't really any point in him wrapping his tail in black before missions, but he always did. He led by example. It annoyed Rime that he still feared the man who had taught him fearlessness.

"You think I don't know that? I was born for them. I live for them. And I risk my life for them. And for everyone else." Rime tore himself free, making for the door.

"No," Svarteld said from behind him. "It has nothing to do with anyone else."

Rime stopped, just for a moment. This was a wound he didn't want to poke at. He glanced at Lindri, who was standing behind the counter drying teacups, pretending not to listen. Everything in this place reminded Rime of Hirka. They'd sat there together the evening she'd left. Him furious and inflamed with the Might. Her sensible and level-headed, like only someone who's about to leave can be.

Rime went out the back door and walked along the platform that stuck out across the Ora like a jetty. The river was black and silent in the dark. Lights from the fishing camp flickered in the distance. He could hear the wind chime tinkling mournfully inside the teahouse. The door opening. The others had arrived.

Twelve Kolkagga were heading out that night. Few enemies had ever faced so many shadows at once, but this was different. This was more than just an attack. One of the deadborn had been captured—at least according to the survivors in Reikavik.

Svarteld and the others came out onto the platform. Kolkagga. In plain sight. Rime knew it was after closing time, and there was no one else in the teahouse, but just last winter it would have been unthinkable to meet there. The Council had denied the existence of Kolkagga for generations. But after the Seer had fallen, there had been no going back. The black shadows had swarmed Mannfalla, reining in a city out of control.

The boats bobbed alongside the platform, having broken through a thin layer of ice to moor. Kolkagga split into two groups, six men in each boat. Then they started to row. The boats were built for speed, and in no time at all they put the lights of Mannfalla behind them. Rime reckoned they'd be there by dawn. Hopefully they wouldn't start burning the dead before they arrived.

The first thing they saw was the pyres. Five unlit structures that would carry the dead to Slokna. Some of them on logs so fresh that they wouldn't burn. They were arranged in a row in front of similar structures laden with fish.

One row for drying fish, one row for burning the dead.

It was early, but Rime could see a woman out on the jetty. She stood immobile, almost as if asleep, dressed in clothes the same gray as the sky. Then she saw them coming and ran up toward the houses, shouting. A handful of other people appeared. Rime looked at Svarteld, who shook his head, exasperated. So much for taking any deadborn lurking in the nearby woods by surprise.

They brought the boats ashore with a couple of powerful strokes and hopped out. The water had frozen between the rocks. The people quieted down again, as if only now realizing who had come. If their expressions were anything to go by, they were wondering whether dealing with the blind might be preferable.

"Who speaks for you?" Svarteld asked. Rime and the others fanned out behind him. The people looked at each other. Tired and frightened faces peered out from under fur-lined hoods. The woman who had been waiting on the jetty stepped forward.

"My name is Melda, fadri. Ordinarily my brother speaks for us, but he's dead."

"Where?"

She pointed at one of the houses. Her hands were tinged blue from the cold.

"Where is the blindling?"

"Fadri, we've—"

"I'm no councillor," Svarteld said.

Melda bowed. "I-I don't know what to call you."

"Nothing. We're nameless. Where is the blindling?"

"In the cellar, fa—in the cellar. The dead are in the room above. He's below. We've weighed the cellar doors down with rocks. At first we thought he'd break out, but—"

Svarteld turned on his heel and went up toward the house. Kolkagga followed him. The woman put a hand on Rime's arm. "We wanted to burn the dead, so they wouldn't rise, but no one dared go in and get them."

"Rise?" Rime looked down at her. She had fair hair and dark circles under her eyes. He suspected he did, too. She didn't reply. Just looked back at the crowd of people. Rime tensed his jaw. "Dead is dead, and you can tell them that! No one escapes Slokna, whether blindling or ymling."

He drew his sword and followed the others up toward the houses. Svarteld signaled for one group to go around the back and for the others to spread out to the neighboring houses. Rime found the cellar doors. It couldn't be that deep. This was rocky terrain. Near the river.

He leaned forward. He couldn't hear anything. He heaved a couple of the rocks aside. Then he heard something. Scratching. Just for a moment.

"I'll bet my tail it's a dog," one of the others whispered. Rime raised a hand to silence him. They were nervous, and he couldn't blame them. Rime had fought the blind before, but these men had never even seen them.

Rime ran around the corner of the house and found Svarteld at the front door. He opened it and they went in. The dead lay on the floor, and in the only bed in the room. Five of them. A family. Rime stepped over their waxen bodies. Some of them had gaping wounds in their chests and stomachs. Shreds of clothing were plastered to them with blood. Brown trails on the floor showed where one of them had tried to get away. Rime cloaked himself in the cold he needed to survive.

All death is senseless. Not just these.

"Rime."

Svarteld was pointing at one of the bodies. One so small that he hadn't noticed it when they'd come in. A boy. No more than two winters. He was sitting against the wall with his head resting on a washtub. His lifeless eyes stared into thin air from under copper-colored hair. His shirt was bloodied around a stab wound in his chest. No heavy blows or open wounds, like the others. Just that stab wound, from a knife. Had the deadborn ever been known to use knives? Not as far as Rime knew. Something wasn't right. Nothing about this was right.

Rime crouched down and closed the boy's eyes. Eyelashes tickled his palm. A certainty bored its way into Rime's chest. Sharp as steel. His icy shield cracked. He got up. "This wasn't them."

"Clearly," Svarteld replied.

Rime opened the door and went out. He heard Svarteld shout behind him but didn't stop. The villagers had come closer now, emboldened by the protection the black-clad men offered. Rime swept over to them, sword in hand. They gasped in unison, recoiling like a multi-headed serpent.

"The boy," he shouted. "Who killed the boy?"

They said nothing. Stood motionless. Only their breath in the cold air indicated they were alive at all.

"ANSWER ME!" He tightened his grip on his sword.

"He was one of them!" a voice shouted from the crowd. "They swap our children for their own," another said. "The boy was the only one they didn't kill. And he had that red hair. We all know what that means."

Rime raised his sword. The Might engulfed him. What remained of his icy shield melted away. He had nothing to hide behind. No distance. Only fury. "Tell me who killed the boy or die!"

Svarteld was suddenly right next to him. "You're the Ravenbearer, boy!" Rime stared into his dark eyes. Ravenbearer. What did that even mean? What raven? There was no raven to bear. And who would they have him bear it for? These ymlings who killed their own children?

Svarteld gripped his arm. "Calm yourself!"

Rime heard himself laugh, a macabre imitation of what laughter was supposed to be. He tore free of Svarteld's grasp and yelled at the mindless puppets before him. "Why should we fear them when *we* are the ones doing the killing? Well?! You are responsible for the most heinous of these deaths. Not even that blindling would have killed a child. But you did!"

He lowered his voice along with his sword. "You did ..."

He turned his back on them, pushing past the other Kolkagga and heading back up to the house. He lifted the rocks from the cellar doors and drew the bolt. Kolkagga fanned out behind him, ready to face whatever might emerge. The doors opened with a screech of the hinges. He stared into the darkness. Into nothing.

Someone called for a lamp, but Rime was already on his way down the steps. Something snarled. Something big. He felt it coming, felt the force of a blow before it landed. Early enough to duck. He swept his sword around him. It met with resistance. There was a roar. Saliva spattered his face. Something crashed to the ground in front of him. Something so big that it seemed to take up the entire room. The other Kolkagga arrived, carrying swords and lamps. They ran past on either side. Light flooded the cellar, revealing rough stone walls. Broken bottles and jam jars. A sack that had been torn to pieces. Root vegetables strewn across the floor. And a dead brown bear.

"A bear …" he heard behind him. "Blackest Blindból, it's a bear!"

"In the middle of winter?" Svarteld's voice. The others started to examine the dead animal. There was blood on its claws. One of them pulled something out of its body and held it up. A broken arrow.

Rime closed his eyes. A starving bear driven mad by pain. Someone had killed the boy because of a bear. No blindlings. No deadborn. Just fear.

The walls were closing in. He needed to get out. His body felt numb. He sheathed his sword and forced himself up the steps. He emerged through the doors and drew air into his lungs. "It's a bear," he said, voice cracking. The villagers came closer. Wide-eyed. Gaping. There were maybe fifty of them.

"Is he dead, the blindling?" asked the woman they'd spoken to first.

"It's a bear!" he shouted. "A bear! A wounded, starving bear!" The echo fled down toward the riverbank, as if it were running away with the horrifying truth. Downriver toward the sea. Away, so no one would ever have to hear it again.

A woman started to cry. She tried to hide it with a hand over her mouth. Rime surveyed their faces, leveling a hard stare at anyone carrying a knife.

There. Him. He could see the death in his eyes. The man twitched but stayed where he was. Rime stalked toward him.

"You killed the boy."

The man lowered his eyes. Quivered. Rime drew his sword again. "You have a choice. You can languish in the pits in Mannfalla until the assembly sends you to Askeberg to be burned or beheaded. Or you can die here. Now. For murdering a child."

The man looked up at him. His gaze was empty. No anger. No grief. A woman took a couple of steps toward them. "He thought he was doing what had to be done! You've no right!"

Rime tore his hood off to reveal his face. "I am Rime An-Elderin, Ravenbearer of Ym. If anyone has that right, I do."

The man's knees gave out on him, dropping him in the hoarfrost. "Now," he croaked.

Rime nodded. "Then in the name of the Seer, in the name of the Council, and for a crime that will hound you into Slokna, prepare to die."

Rime raised his sword. The blood surged through his veins. The Might hungered for more. For something to destroy. For someone to pay for everything that was wrong with the world. He prepared to strike. To avenge the red-haired boy. Red hair. *Hirka ...*

The murderer looked up at him. Black hair. Flushed skin. A grimace of fear. Rime could feel the weight of the sword in his hand, but it wouldn't fall. He'd killed for the Seer before. Who was he killing for now? The boy? Himself?

You've made yourself the beginning and the end.

The man suddenly jerked as a sword was plunged through him. He let out a strangled noise and keeled over. Svarteld pulled the sword out again with a squelch. He wiped the blade on the man's cloak and looked at Rime. "Don't start something you can't finish," he said, sheathing his sword again. "You can't sentence a man and not follow through, An-Elderin. Haven't I taught you to do what's necessary?"

Svarteld walked past him and down toward the boats. Rime turned. The other Kolkagga were still standing there. Ten silent, black-clad figures waiting for him.

He'd hesitated. Failed. And it was going to cost him.

The Might whispered to him. Burrowed into his thoughts and uncovered another truth. He'd have failed no matter what he'd done. Whether he'd killed or not.

Rime shut out the sound of crying and followed his master down toward the boats. The ice between the stones crunched under his feet, and he remembered what he'd said when they'd found the bodies on the banks of Lake Stilla.

Fear doesn't kill anyone.

He'd never been more wrong.

INTERCONNECTED

The boat glided along the canal. Hirka stood at the front, watching the prow slice through the water. It was nighttime in Venice. Quiet. There were only two other people on board, two girls who'd had a little too much to drink. They were speaking a language she didn't understand and trying to fold a map.

The boat pulled up alongside the jetty and the girls stumbled ashore. Stefan pushed Hirka after them. "Hurry up, before I come to my senses."

"Why are we getting off already?" Hirka watched the boat glide away.

Stefan lit a cigarette. "Oh, real sneaky," he replied sarcastically. "Take the boat right up to the house you want to snoop around, with us as the only passengers. Maybe we could even get the boat to wait until you're done."

Hirka didn't respond. Stray snowflakes danced around the streetlamps, melting as soon as they hit the ground. Stefan took a drag of the cigarette and tossed it in the canal. "I don't know why I listen to you. If we get caught, best-case scenario is I have to find a new job. And I'm too old to be flipping burgers. You know what I'm saying, girl? Worst case, I get a bullet in the back of the head."

Hirka started walking, but Stefan kept grumbling. "And what are you going to do if your friend wakes up? Something tells me he's not exactly housetrained. Not well enough to be left home alone, that's for sure."

"He'll cope. Naiell's used to being alone. Or are you starting to miss him?" Hirka smiled, but he didn't smile back.

They followed the row of houses along the canal, toward Allegra's. Stefan looked over his shoulder. "We're *not* going in. Do you understand? You can look in through the window, but don't—"

A young couple came walking toward them. Stefan kept his head down until they'd passed. Hirka looked at him. "If you stop talking every time someone walks past, you'll only draw more attention to us."

Stefan stopped. "Do you know what your problem is? You act like you always have a way out. As if the rules here don't apply to you. But let me tell you something: you have nowhere to go! You're stuck here, same as the rest of us, and if you're not careful, you'll be locked up until your hair falls out. Either that or you'll be found face-down in the canal. You have no idea who you're dealing with. Do you think anyone gets that rich by being a good person?"

"Go back, then!" she answered. "Why are you here if you're so afraid?" Hirka kept walking. No matter who Allegra was, breaking into Eisvaldr—into the Seer's tower, no less—had been far more dangerous. If she'd managed that, she could manage this. Though that time she'd had Rime. Now she only had Stefan, and he was a chicken.

Hirka heard him follow. He sidled up next to her. "Only an idiot wouldn't be afraid," he muttered. She smiled to herself. When all was said and done, Stefan was as curious as she was. Allegra had been trying to hide something from her, that much was obvious. They just had to find out what.

They stopped outside Allegra's house. Or houses, actually. Two buildings side by side. Both painted the same sandy color, with white moldings. Unless she was mistaken, Silvio's study was in the closest of the two. Hirka looked up at the second-floor window. Getting up would be simple enough. She climbed onto a ledge that ran the length of the wall.

"What are you doing?" Stefan grabbed her foot. "You won't get in. Not without smashing a window, and you can forget about that."

"We won't have to smash anything. Follow me."

"Follow you?! Dammit, girl."

Hirka found a drainpipe to hold on to so she could pull herself up. "I asked her for a glass of water," she whispered over her shoulder. "And while she was out of the room, I opened the window a crack." Hirka pulled herself up onto the balcony. From there, she could reach across to the second-floor window. It was in two parts, one sticking out a little farther than the other. Open. Exactly as she'd left it.

She grinned down at Stefan. "Don't worry about getting caught. We can always buy our freedom with Naiell's blood." She didn't wait for a reply, mostly because she was worried it would make her change her mind.

She pried the window open and climbed in. She gave a start when she saw the outline of a person in the dark. The armor. It was just the suit of armor. She breathed out and waited for Stefan. He climbed in the window, out of breath. Hirka motioned for him to follow her over to the door that Allegra had closed. Then she opened it and stepped into Silvio Sanuto's study.

The room was in such a state of chaos that they could have charged people to see it. Hirka had never seen anything like it. It spanned two floors. A floorboard intersecting the room marked where there used to be a wall, as if several rooms had been combined.

Hirka went down a spiral staircase to the floor below. Quietly, so as not to wake anyone. Books. Books from floor to ceiling. Stacked on windowsills, and in towers that propped each other up. Precarious piles of binders and papers. In the few places there were no books, the walls were covered in pictures, words, and drawings. People and symbols overlapping. The room smelled like a casket that had just been opened after centuries.

There were tiny scraps of paper everywhere, some of them spread across a blackboard with circles and arrows drawn in chalk. A figure had been erased and redrawn multiple times. At the bottom of the board, bits of chalk rested on a shelf that was too narrow to protect the floor, so it looked like it had snowed on the cardboard boxes below.

But the most remarkable thing was the white threads stretching across the room in every direction. They crisscrossed at various heights. Hirka stared up at them as she walked around. They looked like some kind of stringed instrument. Or a broken web. A few of the threads were red and had bits of paper attached to them.

Stefan used his phone to light up the walls as he looked around. "Wow," he whispered. "The man must be obsessed with how things interconnect."

"Interconnect? What kind of word is that?" Hirka followed one of the threads with her hand. At one end it was attached to a picture of a golden cup. At the other, a newspaper clipping.

"When things link together," Stefan answered. "Networks, you know? Looks like the overindulgence has finally caught up with someone, if you ask me. This is mad."

Hirka looked at the chaos of papers and pictures and suddenly realized what all this was. "No," she answered. "He has to do this, because he's started to forget." She touched a large ball with a map painted on it. She jumped back when it started to spin. Stefan smiled. "Careful. Globes can be sneaky like that."

The room made her think of Father and of the mess of boxes and chests she'd had to leave behind. One day somebody would have to clear this place out as well. Remove all traces of Silvio Sanuto. Hirka felt heavy. She sank down onto the stairs.

Stefan held up his phone and took a picture of a drawing on the wall. A fang. "This is crazy. What a mash of superstitions. Relics, stone circles, codes … what's this?"

He pulled the picture of the golden cup off the wall and stared at it. Then he turned to Hirka and huffed out a laugh. "Do you see this? The holy grail? The wounded king. It's him! It's Graal! Fucking hell, she's been searching for him longer than I have!"

Stefan seemed to have completely forgotten about being afraid. He put the picture down on the desk, mumbling as he started to follow one of the threads. "Graal … the Grail. Eternal life, yeah? Jesus." He found the end of the thread. A picture of something Hirka knew all too well. Vengethorn. It was vengethorn!

She got up, almost tripping on the stairs in her excitement. "Where is this from? Where can I find this?"

"It's just a drawing," Stefan answered. "A drawing of a plant."

Hirka stared at the drawing. There was no doubt in her mind. Sharp, bluish-black leaves on a stalk that curved into a spiral at the top. She knew she'd seen something through the open door. Something important.

"It's vengethorn! It's poisonous, but it can stop blood … bleed …" She was getting too excited. Forgetting her words again. "Bleeding! It stops bleeding. And cleans wounds. I need to know where it grows!"

Stefan looked at her. "It doesn't grow anywhere. It's a made-up plant."

"Made-up?! This isn't made-up, I've been using this plant all my life!" Stefan put a hand over her mouth. Held a finger to his lips and pointed at the other pictures overlapping the one of the vengethorn. "See that? That's from the Voynich manuscript. A centuries-old riddle collecting dust in a museum. That plant doesn't exist. And these don't either."

Hirka let her eyes wander over the other plants. She'd never seen any of them before. Only the one. Only vengethorn. She felt like grabbing Stefan and shaking him. Telling him what this meant, but he'd never understand. This was the first drawing she'd seen in this world to suggest that someone knew. That someone had seen a plant from her world.

She couldn't begin to explain how important this was. She wasn't alone. No matter how old this document was, others had used the raven rings. She wasn't mad. She wasn't suffering from memory loss, like Silvio Sanuto.

Hirka was suddenly struck by how warped reality was. How warped it had been ever since she arrived in this world. She'd doubted herself. In the worst moments she'd even doubted her own story. But it was true. And this was the proof. She ran her fingers over the paper. It was lifeless. An insult to the longing that burned inside her. She pulled the drawing down from the wall.

Stefan started lifting the overlapping pictures on the wall. "These other things … these books … the images all came from the same website. They're all in the same place." He looked at Hirka. "You understand? In a collection."

"With Graal?"

"No, in a museum." He squinted at the tiny letters at the bottom of the page. "Rún Museum of Art. Never heard of it, but if they didn't have something to do with Graal, they wouldn't be here, right?"

He was right. Hirka stared at the pictures as if they might come to life and tell her what they were. Vengethorn. Pictures of strange things. From strange books. All kept in one place. Why? And what could they possibly have to do with Graal, unless …

The gateways.

"Naiell was right," she whispered. "Graal's found a way to open the gateways. Maybe he's—"

"Written it down and left it in a museum?" Stefan laughed. "Sorry, but he's no idiot."

Hirka didn't reply. The walls felt like they were closing in. Soon the room would only be big enough to hold one thought. Graal had found something. And it could be something as simple as a book. Something she could read. Learn from. Something she could use to get home. She'd been writing things down since she got here. Why wouldn't he have done the same? The thought drew her like a moth to a flame. Like a door left ajar. A chance to run away from this world, back to the one she knew. Back to being menskr. A child of Odin. Nothing more.

"Maybe he's looking for them, too," Stefan suggested, though he didn't sound convinced. He ran his fingers over his stubble. The rasping was joined by the sound of footsteps. Someone was coming!

Stefan's eyes widened. Hirka stuffed the drawing in her pocket and spun around. A man stood in the doorway. Silvio. Silvio Sanuto. Wearing striped pajamas and holding a glass of milk.

Stefan's hand moved instinctively to his belt. To his gun. Hirka grabbed his arm. "Wait!"

The old man's gaze shifted between them and the glass of milk. Like he was trying to find a connection. Hirka tightened her grip on Stefan's arm. She could feel his pulse thumping against her palm. "He doesn't remember," she whispered. Astonishment mixed with horror. "He doesn't know we're not supposed to be here."

She smiled at Silvio. He nodded back. Turned and left, his bare feet shuffling across the wooden floor.

She stood there for a long time before she dared take a breath. Stefan slipped over to the door. Closed and locked it. Hirka felt relief wash through her, but then she was gripped by a strange sensation. A change in the air. Something was headed their way. Something dangerous. Something familiar.

Naiell ...

The window exploded.

Glass flew everywhere. Stefan shouted. A man skidded across the floor, as if he'd been thrown inside. A stack of books collapsed on top of him. He groaned and tried to move, but quickly gave up. Someone jumped down from the windowsill. Naiell. He crouched down, teeth bared and claws out. A pool of blood spread from under the man on the floor. He was badly injured. Hirka ran to him and tried to turn him over, but he lashed out at her. Pain spread through her stomach. She fell back.

A knife! He has a knife!

Someone pulled her to her feet. She tore herself free. The man on the floor tried to get up. She stomped on his elbow, but he wouldn't let go of the knife. Panic. The taste of blood. Hirka reached for her own knife.

The man tried to grab her. She stuck him with her knife and he screamed. She was pretty sure she did, too. She let go of the knife and stepped back. It was lodged in his chest. Stefan stared at her. Naiell picked the man up off the floor like he weighed nothing and flung him at the staircase. He slid down a few steps and ended up sitting with his head slumped to one side like a puppet. A dying puppet, broken on the ornate wrought-iron staircase. He tried to pull the knife out of his chest but gave up, leaving one hand resting on the hilt. Giving the sickening impression that he'd stabbed himself.

Hirka felt a damp warmth on her stomach. She was bleeding. She'd only wanted to help. What had he done? What had *she* done?

Dreyri. I am Dreyri.

The thought was free of doubt. Fortified by blood.

Then came the smell. Sweet and rotten. A nauseating smell no human would recognize. She knew that now. The man on the floor was one of *them*. The ones Stefan called Vardar. He belonged to Graal.

A dog was barking somewhere. An alarm blaring. Hirka crawled toward the rot-infected wretch. Stefan got there first. He lifted the man's chin. His eyes rolled back. He didn't have much time left.

"Where is my brother? Ask him!" Naiell shouted.

Why? So you can run away from him?

Hirka wouldn't let herself be fooled any longer. Naiell's fear of his brother was so intense that she could smell it. But still she nodded. "Stefan, we need to know where he is."

The man was fading fast. "Too late. It's too late. He knows. He'll always know." His body spasmed and his head thumped back against one of the stairs. He whispered Graal's name. Then his body went limp and slumped forward.

Stefan pressed his hand to the man's forehead to hold him in place. Then he pulled something out of his jacket pocket. Something that looked suspiciously like pliers. He held the man's jaw with one hand, forced his mouth open, and yanked out his canines.

The dead man's head bounced as Stefan tugged. Bone splintered. A sickening sound. Blood ran from his mouth and onto his shoulder.

Hirka stared at both of them. She had no words. Couldn't make a sound.

Stefan wiped the bloody teeth on the dead man's jacket. Then he pulled out the chain he kept hidden under his jumper. There was a small glass bottle hanging from it. He dropped the teeth inside and slipped the chain back under his jumper.

The tooth fairy. He sells them. He sells the teeth of the forgotten.

Stefan looked at her. "What?! Mind your own business, girl! It's no worse than what you've got hanging around your neck!" He pointed at her pendant. The wolf tooth. A sharp pain shot through her stomach. Bile rose in her throat, leaving a bitter taste in her mouth. Disgust. Fear.

He knows. Graal knows. He's on his way.

Sirens. A door slammed somewhere in the house. Stefan pulled her knife out of the dead man with a squelch. He crouched down and held it out to her.

I don't want it!

But she took it anyway.

"Tell Naiell to get rid of the body," Stefan said. "We have to get out of here." His voice was steady. Mechanical. But she could see that he was just as scared as she was.

COUNCIL FEVER

Rime was still wearing his Kolkagga blacks. They were like a shield, protecting him from everything he'd done. His swords felt heavy on his back. As long as he was Kolkagga, he was free to use them. No questions asked. No need for remorse. Without his Kolkagga garb, the world was more difficult.

The sky blazed red behind the mountains. The others had gone back to camp to rest. Rime could find no rest. No peace. Nor would he ever. He was standing in the center of the stone circle where Hirka had left him. Trapped. Torn between Mannfalla and some unknown place he couldn't get to.

The stones cast long shadows across the planks that had been put down to protect the old floor from the elements. The Might was in him. Around him. But it offered no warmth. And he knew that no matter how much he tried, he'd never be strong enough to open the gateways. Not without her.

But what if he could? What if he had what Hlosnian called traveler's blood? Would he just leave? Would he cast himself into the unknown, in the hope that he could put the known behind him? Everything he'd done, and everything he *hadn't* done?

Jarladin was right. Jarladin was always right. Rime knew he was driven by anger. By his fury at the way things had been. The actions of the Council. The power of Mannfalla. Now he was one of them. What choice did he have but to rage against himself?

He felt for the bear he'd put down in Reikavik, and that unsettled him. A wild animal that had attacked people. Driven mad by pain, desperate for food. For relief. So wild that people had thought it was a blindling. The times were so uncertain that fear was driving people to kill children.

Such a waste. He'd been shown no mercy. Rime couldn't get the image out of his head. The red hair. The chin resting on a pale chest. The small fingers ...

Rime had been ready. He'd had his sword raised, only one strike away from killing everything he hated. Until his thoughts had turned to Hirka. Until he'd caught a glimpse of himself. Ravenbearer. Judge. Monster. So he'd hesitated, and Svarteld had stepped in.

Don't start something you can't finish.

He heard someone coming. Someone light on their feet. A woman. He knew who it was before she said a word.

"I heard what happened."

Sylja Glimmeråsen. The girl they wanted him to marry. The girl who could give the people something else to think about, unite north and south. And they were right. He was wasting time and energy on things he could never change. Someone he could never get back.

"I doubt that," he replied. He didn't know what she'd heard, but the likelihood of it being the whole truth was practically non-existent. After all, this was Mannfalla.

She stepped up beside him. She was wearing a deep blue winter dress. A white fur cloak over her shoulders. Garments fit for a councillor. She laid a hand on his arm and looked up at him. "It's good it wasn't them, though, right?"

"Yes. It's good it wasn't them."

If she'd heard about the execution, she hid it well. Or maybe she wasn't even thinking about that. What would Hirka have said? That violence only leads to more violence? No. Hirka wouldn't have said anything. She'd just have shot daggers at him, making her disappointment perfectly clear before turning her back on him and leaving.

Sylja came closer. "It's so awful, what happened to that boy."

He looked at her. She was a beautiful girl. Fair hair and blue eyes. Would it be so unbearable? He didn't doubt she'd make his days easier. And she'd be preferable to all the other suggestions that had been made. Someone he'd known for years and who had a sense of him. She would be a barrier between him and the Council. His young and eager representative at all the parties he'd rather avoid. People would love her. She was, in every way, the right choice.

He put an arm around her, and she leaned her head against his chest. He was too tired to consider whether she was really sad about it or whether it was another way of getting close to him. It didn't matter, because what she had said was true. Awful was the only word for it. People were awful. Himself included, but Sylja didn't judge him. She saw a son of the Council. An An-Elderin with god-given power. She saw no wrong, and she never would. Sylja would make it easier for him to lead. Easier to live with himself.

She looked up at him. Her lips parted and she pressed them to his throat. They were warm. Full of purpose. Of forgiveness. He didn't move. She pulled back and smiled. "Don't let them see you this way, Ravenbearer. Get changed and come with me to The Snake Mirror. They have a nice big fireplace, mulled wine, and Jarladin's grandson plays the flute like a god. Until he gets too drunk, that is."

Rime couldn't help but be impressed. Once upon a time in Elveroa she'd begged him to take her with him, to help her through the Rite and into the schools here. Sylja loved Mannfalla. Even the things he hated. And now she was rubbing elbows with sons of the Council.

"Have you been home to Elveroa at all since the Rite?" he asked.

She laughed and led him out of the stone circle. "Turns out not even the blind can scare Mother back to staring at herring barrels on the quayside."

She used her mother as a shield. Kaisa was domineering, but Sylja had never seemed to mind. Rime smiled. "They call it Council fever."

She tightened her grip on his elbow. "Really? It has a name? How funny!" She laughed again. "But I know what you mean. There are people living in squalor along the river who think their lives are better for just being here. Once you've seen something powerful, you can't let go. It's probably just the way we ymlings are made."

Rime stopped.

She was right. Those who had tasted power wanted to cling to it, no matter the cost. Just as those who had seen knowledge would never accept ignorance.

The books. The library.

The knowledge he'd searched for in vain. For the shepherds, books were power. Life itself. They had been for generation upon generation. Hadn't he himself seen the shepherds cling to the books as if they were a last meal? They loved them. Lived for them.

So how could they burn them? No matter who ordered it, how could anyone who devoted their life to preserving knowledge, destroy it?

The answer was simple.

They wouldn't.

STITCHES

Hirka leaned on Stefan as she climbed aboard the boat. She was unable to suppress a gasp of pain as it rocked in the waves. He helped her down a ladder to a room below deck. Naiell followed. Nils stayed on deck, shouting. "A doctor, Stefan! You have to get her to a doctor!"

Stefan ignored him and threw her bag onto a cream leather sofa. "Shit, shit, shit," he whispered, looking around like a lost puppy.

Supporting herself on the back of the sofa, Hirka made her way over to a low berth with a bed and nothing more. She eased herself onto it. Nils bounded down the ladder. He was so tall, he had to stoop. "Stefan! Stefan! A doctor! Are you listening to me? We can't leave the harbor with her on board. She's going to bleed to death! And for Christ's sake, put something down on the bed!"

Hirka pulled off her raincoat and tried to tuck it under her so she wouldn't get blood on anything. Stefan collapsed onto the sofa and lit a cigarette. Nils tore it from his mouth and crumpled it in his fist. He cursed as it burned his fingers.

"What the hell are you playing at?! You can't run away from this. You hear me? It's over. The girl needs a doctor."

Stefan tried to interject but couldn't get a word in edgewise. Finally, he grabbed his friend's arm. "Nils! Listen to me. We can't. It's impossible, do you understand? I'll pay you more than this fucking boat cost, no matter how fucking much, but we can't stay here."

Nils clenched his jaw. He was younger and skinnier than Stefan, but in that moment, he was the stronger of the two. "That's the problem with you, Stefan. You think everything's about money." He glanced at Naiell, who was sitting with his eyes closed on a bench by the stairs.

Hirka wished they would both shut their traps, but she couldn't find the strength to open her own. She pressed her hand against her side and let out a groan. Nils started rummaging in a green box. He tore open a bag and handed her a wet napkin with a smell that stung her nostrils.

"Here. Hold this to the wound. I have to get us out of the harbor before the police show up. You've gotten yourself mixed up with the wrong people, girl. I hope one of you knows how to sew."

Sew! Hirka started to laugh but was stopped by a wave of pain. None of them were in any position to be sewing. Least of all a wound.

Stefan's eyes grew moist. He pounded the empty seat beside him with his fist. Stared at the table. His hands were shaking and he could barely sit up straight. And Naiell … well, he was a deadborn.

So am I. I'm deadborn. Half-blindling.

The certainty of it no longer had such sharp edges. It was almost soft now compared to the fear that she might be running out of time. Hirka lifted up her tunic to look at the wound. She quickly tugged it back down. Felt the blood drain from her face. Reminded herself that it was normal to be scared. It was okay. She was in shock, that was all. She just had to take a moment and breathe.

She thought of Rime, the time he'd pulled her up from the Alldjup. When he'd seen her bleeding hand and said she'd better get Father to look at it. What had she said?

I've been patching people up since I was seven!

It was true. It was what she was good at, who she was. She patched people up. Fixed things. Mended people when they were broken. As best she could. And in any case, she'd seen far worse than this. It was her this time, but it was the same. Exactly the same. The more she repeated the words, the less she believed them.

Nils disappeared above deck. Hirka hoped the boat wasn't stolen. She didn't think Nils was the type to do that sort of thing. He probably just liked having things that went fast.

There was a rumbling and the boat started to move. They picked up speed and soon they were practically flying across the waves. Hirka pressed down on the wet napkin. She'd have to wait until they were in calmer waters, until the vibrations stopped. It was just a little cut. Nothing serious. Not to someone who had been weaned on such things.

But weaned by who?

She laughed and the pain tore at her again. This time in her stomach and in her heart. She was half-blindling. Graal's child. Offspring of a blindling who was thousands of years old, and who was hunting them. Urd had told her as much. That he'd gotten the rot from her father. A father who had power over Urd and power over the blind. Who wanted to sacrifice her to them. Who else could it be?

But she was also a child of Odin. A human. So who was her mother? Had she ever needed to be weaned? Blood was the first thing she could remember tasting. Would it also be the last?

Naiell was convinced that her parents were dead. But sooner or later he would realize that she wasn't like other people. That she was family. What would he do then? Snap her neck, killing one of his own kin?

There could be another explanation.

She clung to that hope, pretending she believed it. But deep down she knew. If there was one thing she'd learned, it was what made her different.

After a while the boat slowed down. The water wasn't as choppy. She breathed a sigh of relief, but then came the guilt. She'd survived.

Had she been less fortunate, she'd have been the one at the bottom of a canal in Venice. Two teeth worse off. Forgotten. Stabbed to death.

Think of something else!

She gave Naiell an imploring look. He got up and came over. "Can you pass me my bag?" she asked. He picked it up and dropped it on the floor in front of her. He sat on the edge of the bed. She liked to think that she could read his eyes now. But maybe that was just wishful thinking. Although, if it had been wishful thinking, surely she'd have seen some hint of sympathy in them.

He cocked his head. The way he used to do when he was a raven. When he was Kuro. "I can't help you without the Might," he said.

"As if the Might could make any difference to a gaping hole in my body," she answered.

That seemed to amuse him. "The things you don't know could fill Maknamorr, Sulni."

Hirka had no room in her head for insults or new words. She had to cling to reality as best she could. Reality was here. Far out to sea. In a roaring boat. With a deadborn. And a wound that stretched halfway across her stomach.

She pulled up her tunic and squeezed the napkin. Liquid dripped onto the wound. She flinched. Clenched her teeth. It stung like Slokna.

That means it's working!

How many times had she said that to people? It wasn't true, but she'd told them all the same. She'd just never thought she'd have to tell herself.

"I can ease your pain," Naiell said.

"You can leave me alone," she answered. "I don't need an audience."

He leaned closer. She stared into his eyes as they flooded with black. "A thousand years," he said hoarsely. "A thousand years, and you still have no clue what you're doing. You stand face-to-face with salvation and choose damnation. I withdrew into the raven and I remained there. So I wouldn't have to wonder why I decided to give up everything I had to save your people."

She moved the napkin over the wound and winced. "'Your people'?" It hurt to talk, but it had to be said. "You forget I'm not one of them. I'm not an ymling."

They looked at each other. He had no pupils, no irises, nothing, but still she stared. Eyes fixed on the center of the glassy blackness. She could hear her pulse thrumming in her ears. She was the child of this creature's enemy. This blindling sitting next to her, too close for comfort. Naiell. Kuro. Her raven. Her protector. As long as he didn't know …

"Not an ymling," he whispered from somewhere deep inside. "But humans also feel pain. More so than the cows." It took her a moment to figure out what he meant. Cows. Ymlings. People with tails. She couldn't blame him. After all, it was no worse than *deadborn*.

He held two fingers to his throat. She'd seen the blind do that. She'd done it herself, at Bromfjell, without knowing why. And now she was afraid to ask.

"I am Dreyri," he said. "I have blood of the first. My brother is the only one of our kind in this world, yet still he has managed to become a legend. People seek him out, follow him, kill and die for him. All for this blood. For a chance to slowly rot and see the sun rise a few more times. And you think fixing a hole in your fragile shell is a challenge for me?"

A sudden and involuntary hope filled her. A longing for him to be right. For him to be the Seer everyone had believed in. Omniscient. Eternal. Someone who could save her. Fix what she couldn't fix herself. What would it take? A drop of his blood? Would that be enough to keep her from Slokna?

Her willingness scared her. It was easy to let yourself be taken in when you were bleeding to death.

"I thought you were helpless without the Might," she said, immediately regretting her choice of words.

The black in his eyes receded. Ink turned to milk. He ran his hand over her stomach, his touch cold and abrupt. She tried to protect the wound with her arm, but he moved it aside. Brought his index finger toward the opening. A prick. His claw sank into her skin. She let out a gasp.

Her skin started to tingle. The pain flowed out of her body. Her fear that he would realize who she was went along with it, until only a wonderful numbness remained.

"Might or no Might, I can always halt your blood."

She smiled lazily. "You're walking around with drugs in your fingertips? That's ..." No words in her own language could express how she felt. Then she remembered what Jay used to say. "That's cool."

She looked down at the wound. A red gash in her right side, the length of her hand. But it had stopped bleeding. She couldn't feel anything now. That would make it easier. She could pretend it was someone else.

Hirka pulled her bag closer and opened it with her left hand so she wouldn't have to turn her upper body. She fumbled around until she found what she was looking for. Her sewing things. Naiell got up to give her room to stretch out.

She cocked her head the way he used to, staring at him until he got the message. He shrugged and slunk through to where Stefan was. She unrolled the sewing kit and pulled out a needle and thread. She wiped them on the wet napkin, hoping it would kill the germs. She didn't know what Nils had put on it. Humans knew nothing about plants, but they had to know something, seeing as they weren't dropping like flies.

Stefan kept glancing over at her, but she pretended not to notice. He'd have to deal with his demons on his own. But clearly he wasn't ready for that. He got up and came over to her.

He looked at the wound in her side and blanched. He slid down onto the floor beneath a round window. A black hole out toward the sea. He wrapped his arms around his knees and sat rocking back and forth against the wall. His fear was catching. Her mouth went dry. Her lips felt swollen. She almost wished she hadn't sent Naiell away. About the only thing he felt was superiority. And he feared nothing—apart from his own brother.

Stefan was undeniably strong, but he felt too much. He feared everything that could happen, and probably a lot of what had happened. How could a man like that make a living from selling the teeth of dead men? How had it come to that?

She was overcome by a sense of hopelessness. Standing on the precipice. About to fall.

So what's it gonna be? Live or die?

She had to keep her spirits up or she wouldn't be able to do what she needed to. She threaded the needle. "For a hunter, you're a real wuss," she said.

He stopped rocking. "Can I help?"

She laughed. Braced herself for the pain, but none came. She was numb. Freed by Naiell's poison. Blindcraft. "Have you seen the state of your trousers, Stefan?"

Stefan looked down at the holes in his knees. Gave a tired smile. The spark came back into his eyes. He'd be handsome if it weren't for the stubble.

"Hirka ..."

He was finally ready, bursting with things to tell her, but she didn't have time for that. Not now. She propped herself up until she was half-sitting so she could see what she was doing. Pulled the edges of the wound together and held the needle to her skin. Her hand was shaking. There was only one way to do this. Fast and firm. She pushed the needle in and through to the other side. The thread tugged at her skin, but she felt no pain.

Don't think. Just sew.

If only she still had some salve. All she could do now was cross her fingers and hope it was clean. She was at the mercy of fate, something so much bigger than her.

She made sixteen stitches. One for every year of her life. She was about to cut the thread, but then added one more. Seventeen. In case some higher power decided to take her at her word.

Crones' talk.

She tied a knot and cut the thread. Then she rolled up her sewing kit and let her body go limp. The boat skipped over a wave and the wall slammed into her back. Stefan crawled over and positioned an extra pillow behind her. Then he rifled through Nils's green box, pulled out a strip of something and placed it over the wound.

"Don't. It needs to breathe," she said.

"It's a bandage. Bandages breathe, right? Nearly as impressive as elevators and guns, aren't they?"

She let him stick the bandage over the wound. She could always take it off later. His fingers trembled against her skin. Then he grabbed her hand. It was unexpected but nice. "I've never met anyone like you, girl." He stroked her hair. "Never. Do they all have hearts of wolves where you come from? Are they all like you?"

Hirka would have been touched had Stefan not been in such a daze. He was just trying to get close to someone so he didn't have to be alone with his fear.

"I wish," she whispered. "If everyone were like me, I wouldn't have had to come here."

"Then I'm happy they're not."

She looked into his eyes. Everything about him was so warm. His skin. His eyes. His brown hair with light tips. He was the exact opposite of Rime.

"You're too old for me," she said.

He made a despondent sound that might have been a laugh. "Not too old to save you, am I?"

She smiled. Stefan Barone. Her knight in shining armor. The man clinging to her as if he were drowning. And this was supposed to be his world. She closed her eyes. She wanted to go to sleep and not wake up until she was old.

"I do it because I have to," he said.

She forced her eyes open to watch him defend himself.

"Because I have to. Not because I—She gives me shitloads of money for them, you know? I don't know why, but it pays the bills. Sure, sometimes I have to travel halfway around the world in the middle of the night, but needs must. She was a chemist when she was younger. There's something in them. Something she uses."

The teeth. He was talking about the teeth.

The image of him yanking them out of the forgotten's mouth flashed before her eyes. His body still warm. Her knife in his chest. She'd pushed it all the way to the hilt, but it hadn't killed him. Not straight away. He'd still been able to do damage.

"What are you thinking?" Stefan asked. His eyes begged for forgiveness. He could have been one of Father Brody's lost souls. Kneeling before the altar.

"I'm thinking ..." Hirka stopped fighting and closed her eyes. "I'm thinking I need a longer knife."

GUARDIANS

Rime walked past the first rows of shelves. The ceiling was low by the entrance to the library. The room didn't open up until you made it to the middle, where all the levels came into view.

Once he reached the middle, he could hear the wind outside. A whisper between stone blocks and wooden beams, mixed with the sound of ladders sailing along shelves. A woman approached on one of the ladders, stopping just above him.

Rime asked after Northree, the shepherd he'd spoken to during his last visit. Although Northree may not have been in charge, he was clearly among those with the most knowledge. The woman directed Rime farther into the library before climbing higher up, out of sight.

Rime found Northree halfway up a wooden ladder, where he stood browsing a drawer full of small cards. He smiled when he saw Rime, stuck a wooden peg in the drawer to mark his place, and climbed down with an almost feminine grace. Though in here everyone seemed sexless. Equally gray, equally gentle, and equally content in their work.

"How can I help you, Rime-fadri?"

Rime grabbed him by the arms and steered him toward the center of the room. "This is an impressive tower, Northree, isn't it?"

"It's the biggest in all of Ym, Ravenbearer. Not the tallest, but certainly the most spacious. It has no equal."

"I'm counting on that. How long do you think it would take to pull it apart?"

The shepherd blinked a couple of times. "I don't understand ..."

"Let's say I decided to find the books we both know are here but that you say were burned. How long do you think it would take to pull apart the entire tower if I were to get every guardsman in Mannfalla to help?"

The shepherd took an unsteady step back. "Pull apart ..."

The shock tactics had worked. Northree was shaken and surprised. But that wasn't enough. He had to be afraid. He had to fear for his life. Rime stepped up close to him and tightened his grip on a thin arm before whispering, "Shepherd, yesterday we plunged a sword through the heart of a man trying to hide something he'd only just done. What do you think I'd do to a man who's been hiding something for a lifetime?"

The shepherd closed his eyes. For a moment Rime thought he'd won. "I swear, Rime-fadri, there's no knowledge of use to anyone here that you've not already seen. What you're looking for was destroyed over eight hundred years ago."

"Of use or not, I intend to find it. You can either give it to me now or you can accept your punishment when we do find it."

The shepherd shrugged sadly. "There's nothing I can do."

It clearly wasn't enough to make the shepherd fear for his life. Rime could threaten him with everything under the sun and it wouldn't help. Something more was needed. Something bigger. Northree had to believe that Rime would prevail. That he would never give up.

"I'm the Ravenbearer," Rime snarled. "Nothing can stop me. There's no secret that doesn't belong to me. I'll be back at sunrise with every able-bodied guardsman, and I promise we'll find it. Even if I have to tear down every wall and rip up every floor. Until then, shepherd."

He turned and left without looking back. That final megalomaniacal flourish ought to have done it. Now there was only one thing left to do.

Wait.

Even in the middle of the night, there were always lights to be seen in Mannfalla. Lamps burned around the clock along the main streets. Hundreds of them, particularly here on the north side, where Eisvaldr was situated. The city at the end of the city. No longer the home of the Seer, but still the home of the Council. Still home to those few who had more than they would ever need. And a library with more books than they would ever read.

Rime jumped down onto the library balcony and found the nearest window. It was a sturdy thing, tall and reinforced with glazing bars. Had Hirka been here, he could have drawn enough of the Might through his body to melt them. Like they'd done when they'd broken into the Seer's tower. He hadn't been able to do it again since, and the greatest minds in Ym couldn't explain why. Would he ever find out?

He drew his knife and wedged it between the window and the frame. Slid it up until it met with resistance. Then he whacked the hilt of the knife with the back of his hand. Heard the hasp open inside. He did the same to the one above and opened the window. It creaked. Definitely not a window that was opened every day. Rime sheathed his knife, climbed inside, and closed the window behind him.

The books slept in the pitch darkness, as they'd done for generations. Endless rows of text. But nothing that would contradict what the Council had established as the truth over the centuries. Doubt had no place here. Other voices had been weeded out, so mercilessly and over such a long period of time that it no longer occurred to anyone to ask about them. All things considered, could it even be called knowledge?

Rime moved in toward the middle of the room. The open shaft swallowed what little light there was. It was impossible to see anything on the levels below. It was quiet.

He started to bind. Drew the Might through his body and listened. Sounds made themselves known. Sounds only the Might could carry. The wooden shelves creaking. The frost permeating the walls. The echo of pen on paper, even though there was no one here. The Might remembered. After a while, he could hear footsteps as well. Someone whispering. A key in a door. They were here.

Rime smiled. This was the sound of victory. He had been right. The shepherds were panicking. They had secrets, and he'd threatened them. The Might tingled in his body. Riled by the possibilities. He'd been seeking the truth for as long as he could remember. Would he finally find it?

The glow from a lamp stole across the floor far below him. The light flickered and was lifted higher, as if someone was trying to see the levels above. Rime's clothes hid him, but he pulled back toward one of the rows of shelves all the same.

There were three people down there, walking close together. One of them whispered and another shushed them. Their gray robes fluttered before they disappeared out of sight beneath him. Rime leaped over the balustrade. He let the Might absorb the impact, landing without a sound.

The light danced farther ahead, like a firefly. He followed it between the shelves, past the archive room, and down the steps to the repository. He'd been here before, he remembered. When he was little.

Familiar outlines hove into view. Walls of small drawers that he knew contained stones of all shapes and colors from all over Ym.

Shelves of skeletons and fossilized animal tracks. A growing monument to a longing for understanding. An illusion of control.

The lamp stilled. They'd stopped. Rime pressed himself against the wall, well away from the light surrounding the shepherds. One of them was Northree. Rime didn't know the two women. They were pulling a cart.

They were standing in the middle of the room, next to a skeleton on a stone plinth. A bird-like creature that could have swallowed them all. Its ribs cast macabre shadows across the ceiling.

"Help me," Northree whispered. He stood on his toes and started feeling around for something on top of the plinth.

"This is madness," one of the women whispered. "We're just making it easier for them. Let them look!" But she still helped him. A metallic whine cut through the silence in the room. The sound of bolts. A dark gap appeared in the plinth. The shepherds stood listening for a moment, in case someone had heard.

"Gretel, I looked into his eyes, and I swear, he won't stop until he finds what he's looking for."

"He's not yet twenty winters! Who among us wasn't zealous when we were that young? And with the power he has? No wonder it's gone to his head. It doesn't mean anything. He'll probably have forgotten all about it tomorrow."

"He won't have," Northree replied, disappearing into the plinth. The other two followed. Rime darted closer. Let the Might carry him. Muffle the sound of his feet. He listened.

"Has it occurred to you that this might be a trap? That you might be doing exactly what he wants you to do?" It was the other woman. The echo made her lower her voice as she spoke.

"Do you see him anywhere?" Northree asked irritably.

"He's an An-Elderin," Gretel replied. "Ilume-madra's grandson. Can you really see him tearing down the entire tower to find something he's not sure exists? I refuse to believe it. It was an empty threat, Northree. An-Elderins aren't destroyers, they're preservers."

"What about the Rite Hall? What about the Seer? Rime An-Elderin has torn down more in six months than has been torn down in the past five hundred years combined. I think we can safely say that the will to preserve died with Ilume-madra. In any case, it's not our place to judge. It's our place to protect what we can. Do you want us to be the generation that failed?"

Rime leaned against the stone plinth. The cold soaked into his back. As if infecting him with their contempt. What did they know about destruction? They sat here in a tower of dead paper and thought everything that was, was meant to be. That all destruction was a curse. He'd have liked to have seen them in the claws of a deadborn and given them the choice. Destroy or preserve?

He peered in. Northree and Gretel had wedged a crowbar between two flagstones in the floor and were struggling to lift them. They were so big that all three of them had to pitch in to move them aside. Northree kneeled on the floor and brushed away the sand where they had been lying. Then he lifted a door. A trapdoor, hidden under the floor. How long had it been there?

One by one they disappeared through it. Gretel brought up the rear with the cart. In silence, they must have thought, but it was ridiculously easy to hear them. Their footsteps. The lamp swinging from its handle. The creaking cart.

Rime felt his body tingle. The Might was starting to beg. His heart was racing. He had to rein in his excitement. He was getting close. He was going to find the Council's darkest secrets. About what? About the raven rings? The blind? Everything he needed to know?

From the trapdoor, a narrow passageway sloped straight down into the rock. Eventually it opened up, and the air became less stale. When it leveled out, he saw the three shepherds. They'd stopped up ahead. It was exhilarating to know that he couldn't be seen in the darkness. That he could stand close enough to hear them breathing without any of them realizing.

The passage was so narrow that the cart had to be pulled lengthwise. The light from the lamp flickered over a row of shelves on both sides. A cold draft came from the darkness at the other end of the passage. The shepherds whispered among themselves. Not that they had to, because who would hear them? There was no sign of life down here.

"There are too many. Far too many. How are we supposed—"

"We need to choose, Gretel."

"But that's impossible! Using what criteria?"

"Your own. That's all we have! Take what you think has to survive."

"I don't think *we're* going to survive," Gretel mumbled.

Rime walked over to them and stopped in the circle of light.

The shepherds froze. They stood like gray statues, staring at him. Northree with three books in his arms. Gretel with her hand on the spine of another. He watched the blood drain from her face. One of Northree's books fell to the wooden floor with a thud. Rime had never thought he'd see the day shepherds ignored something like that.

He pulled his mask away from his face. "Really? All these books? In that little cart?"

The third shepherd threw herself at the cart and grabbed the crowbar. Nothing a warrior would use. Just a perfectly ordinary crowbar. She clung to it and stared at Rime with wild eyes. She had close-cut hair and was younger than the others. Thirty, maybe. He doubted she'd ever hurt a soul.

Rime had to stop himself from laughing. "That's a good way to break an arm," he said, taking a step closer. The woman raised the crowbar over her head.

"Yours, not mine!" Sweat beaded on her forehead. She started toward him. The Might surged through him, showing him how it would all unfold. He wouldn't need to draw his sword. Just lock her left arm. Elbow. Knee. Then she'd be on the ground, unharmed.

But that wasn't what happened. Northree grabbed her robe. "Berglin—he's Kolkagga."

Berglin looked at Rime. The courage left her eyes, clattering to the floor along with the crowbar. "But …" she whispered despondently. "But …"

He couldn't blame her. After all, their lives were on the line now.

He looked around. "So this is it? This is everything the Council's hidden?"

Northree put the books in the cart. "No, Rime-fadri. This is what *we* have hidden from the Council."

Rime went over to him. Forced him to look him in the eye. "Are you lying to me, Northree?"

Northree shook his head. "Why would I lie? Would I not have more to gain from you thinking we work for the Council?"

Rime didn't reply. He hated the thought of being one of *them*. He ran a hand along the shelves, pulling out one book after another. Books about the war. About the old gods. Diaries from long deceased noblemen. Books about the Might. Books in a language he didn't understand.

Rime smiled at Northree. "So if I were to bring them here now, they'd be just as surprised as I am, is that what you're telling me?"

Northree took a deep breath and closed his eyes before replying. "More so, I should think." He opened his eyes again, and Rime recognized the calm in them. Northree was binding the Might. He was prepared to die to defend their secret. Rime realized he would have to explain. Before he was forced to hurt someone.

"How long have you known?"

"We've always known. We were all chosen by someone before us. And we've already chosen those who will follow. Someone must always know. Three. Never more."

"So now we're four," Rime said, holding out his hand. Northree glanced at the others. "Just four," Rime said again. "I'm not here on behalf of the Council. Let them live in ignorance, just as they always have."

Berglin gasped. Rime took no notice. He'd said far worse before and wasn't going to hold back now. "You're shepherds. You're known for using your heads, so don't disappoint me now. You can try to stop me and throw your lives away. Or you can help me."

"Help you do what?" Northree asked. "Learn about blindcraft? Increase your capacity to bind? Sell your soul for power?" There was no venom behind his words. He was saying what he felt he had to.

"If that's what's needed to stop the deadborn, then so be it," Rime said. "But hopefully nothing that drastic will be required."

Northree hesitated for a moment. Then he took Rime's hand. The two women looked at each other. "But you're the Ravenbearer!" Gretel exclaimed, somewhere between incredulity and protestation.

"There's no raven to bear anymore," Rime replied, picking up a book from the cart. What was this language? He'd never seen anything like it.

"But … you're not just part of the Council. You *are* the Council. You can't keep this from them!"

"To Slokna with the Council! I'm not the Ravenbearer for them. I'm the Ravenbearer for every single soul in Ym. I refuse to let the eleven kingdoms die out of ignorance! So do what you were always meant to do. Use your heads. Tell me who they are!"

Northree picked up the lamp and led Rime farther along the passage. A cold draft engulfed him.

"We've only guarded these books, Rime. Not studied them. I'm afraid all we can do is point you in the right direction."

As they approached the end of the passage, Rime realized that there wasn't any wall there. Just a gaping, black hole. They stopped. Northree lifted the lamp. The light was swallowed by an infinite void. A shaft in the mountain with no beginning and no end. Just darkness. If Rime had taken one more step, he'd have fallen. Seemingly into nothingness.

"But there is one thing I can tell you about the blind," Northree said, staring out into the darkness. The walls were black and smooth as glass. The passage they were standing in was only one of a thousand. Silent, black openings. Rime's blood ran cold. It was like nothing he'd ever seen.

Northree's voice suddenly seemed distant.

"They were here long before us."

AWAKE

Raised voices. Stefan. And a woman. Allegra.

Hirka opened her eyes. She was alone. For a moment she didn't know where she was. Then she heard the boats in the canal and remembered. Venice. A sinking city in a sinking world.

The memories came flooding back. Allegra's house. The boat. Stefan dumping the body of the forgotten. She remembered Nils and Stefan arguing. About her. And she remembered them turning back when Stefan had felt sure the police weren't after them. Then his respect for Allegra had kicked in. The woman he couldn't run from. What were they talking about now?

Hirka propped herself up in the bed. The pain she expected didn't come. She lifted up her white shirt, peeled off the bandage, and looked at the wound. It had healed absurdly fast, but she'd always been quick to heal. Now she knew why.

She pressed her thumb against the stitches. Still tender, but it smelled clean. How many days had she been drifting in and out? Four? Five? Had Naiell helped her again, numbing the pain with his claws? She knew so little about him. About herself. About the one hunting her.

But there was one thing she did know—she'd had enough. She was sick of always waking up afraid. Sick of her life always being in the hands of others. Before the Rite, she'd feared Kolkagga. The black shadows. And the Council. Everything had been up to them.

Then there was Urd. And after the Rite she'd lost what little control she'd had over her own life. Helpless in the pits. At the mercy of others.

She had to smarten up. Be the master of her own fate.

She reached for her trousers, which were in a tangle at the end of the bed. She shoved her hand in the pocket and pulled out the drawing she'd taken from Silvio's study. Smoothed out the creases. Vengethorn. Made-up to Stefan. Real to her. More than real. This gave her hope.

There was something out there that could give her back control. Give her the upper hand. Or even better—something that could get her home again. Whatever it was, it was in a museum. What had Stefan called it? Rún Museum of Art? Hirka didn't know much about museums, but she did know that anyone could visit them. Even her. But how would she talk Stefan into taking her?

She put the picture back in the pocket and threw the trousers on the floor. Then she spotted her knife. She felt drawn to it. Attracted and repulsed. Was that just the way it was? Was it impossible to control your own life without hurting others? Hirka leaned over the edge of the bed and grabbed the knife. Then she lay back and fiddled with the blade. The metal was gleaming, but she thought she could smell something on it. How it had been lodged inside two men. Both of whom were now dead.

They'd taken a part of her with them. The part that had always believed there were only two types of ymlings in the world: those who lived peacefully and those who killed. Good and evil. Was she evil now? Had she been driven from one side to the other out of fear? Out of necessity?

It made her think of Kolgrim. Back in Elveroa. The time she'd goaded him into hitting her, just so she could hit him back. She'd known it was wrong. But he was such an idiot! He'd lured Vetle out onto the fallen spruce. He could have killed him. What had been going through her mind back then? That it was okay, because she was human? A child of Odin? If only she'd known. This was far worse. She was half-human and half-deadborn.

A new fear was creeping in. Stefan had said the forgotten always go mad. Every single one of them. Sooner or later. Something in Graal's blood destroyed them. The rot. Humans couldn't handle it. Hirka had that same blood. Would she also go mad? Had it already happened?

No. She'd lived her entire life with mixed blood, and she hadn't rotted or gone mad. Well, she hadn't rotted, at least.

She put the knife down and looked around. The room was a pale pink color, with a carved border around the ceiling. There was a large bouquet of bloodred lilies on the table by the bed, accompanied by a gold card. Probably from Allegra. It was either a death sentence or something nauseatingly pleasant. Like an invitation to lunch.

There was also an empty glass. And a lamp. A shiny brass one that she'd never have realized was a lamp if she'd come here straight from Ym. Differences that had threatened to overwhelm her before had become more manageable.

She pressed the switch. The light came on. She pressed it again. Off. She did it a few more times. On, off. On, off. She kept doing it until it wouldn't come on again.

Stefan and Allegra's voices were getting louder. They were speaking Italian. That rolling language she didn't understand. How much was he telling her? Did she know they'd broken into her house? A door slammed and the house went quiet.

Hirka got up, put her trousers on, and went into the living room. Stefan was standing by the door clutching a fistful of money notes, which he stuffed into his pocket before looking at her.

"I broke the lamp," she said, walking past him and into the kitchen. She drank some water and refilled the glass.

"I just told her you couldn't walk yet," he replied, his voice a bit higher than usual. He was embarrassed about something, but she didn't know what. Maybe it was the teeth he'd just sold. Maybe it was the affection he'd shown her on the boat. Or maybe he was just scared, as was so often the case with him.

"Where's Naiell?" Hirka took her glass of water out onto the balcony. It was a chilly evening.

Stefan followed her and lit a cigarette. "Out. She's not happy."

"Allegra?"

He took a drag and blew the smoke out of the corner of his mouth. Away from her. "She wants me to keep him under control. Keep him indoors."

Hirka smiled. "Pfft, I'd like to see her try to control him."

"That's exactly what I said."

They laughed. It felt good. It was always easier when Naiell wasn't around. Then she didn't have to worry about him figuring out who she was. And sometimes she could even pretend that he didn't exist.

But unfortunately that wasn't the case. He did exist. And worse still, he had a brother.

A wooden boat sailed past below. Waves sloshed against the side of the house. Hirka noticed a stone face carved into the wall under the balcony. Half man, half monster. Angry eyes, worn by the elements.

"So what did you say?" she asked.

"As little as possible," Stefan answered. He was quiet for a moment before continuing. "I said one of the Vardar was heading her way, so we followed him. And I said Naiell threw him through the window. We cleaned up and got out. I said we probably saved her life."

Hirka couldn't help but be impressed. "Smart. Very smart."

"You could at least try to sound a little less surprised."

She smiled at him. "So what were you arguing about? With a story like that, she should be thanking you."

Stefan tapped ash into the canal. "That's not really her style. Thanking people, I mean. But we were in Silvio's study, so everything's a bit weird now. She knows we know something. And we know we're looking for the same thing, but ..."

Hirka understood. "Being after the same thing doesn't make us allies."

He didn't answer. His silence gave her the opportunity she needed. "We've been running long enough, Stefan. Allegra and Silvio found something. Before he lost his memory. Something that belongs to Graal. Or something he needs. We don't know what, but that doesn't matter. It could be what we need to get the upper hand. To stay alive. We have to find the books, Stefan."

He nodded. She'd thought it would take more to convince him. It was encouraging and alarming at the same time. "We'll rent a car as soon as Naiell gets back," he said.

"He's coming. I think he's just out trying to find his courage."

Stefan snorted. "He doesn't seem to be lacking in that department."

"That's what I thought, too. I thought he was hunting his brother. But all this talk of finding Graal ... I think it's mostly about knowing where he is. So he doesn't just run into him. I think he's scared."

Stefan laughed. "*He's* scared? Girl, I get the shivers just looking at him. Those eyes ... the claws. He's un-fucking-real! What does he have to be scared of?"

They stood with their hands on the railing, the two of them, and she knew they were thinking the same thing. Whatever Naiell was afraid of, now *that* was something to fear.

Stefan dragged his hand over his face. She could see the determination he'd had moments earlier starting to fade. She pulled the drawing out of her pocket and handed it to him.

"Stefan, you've been hunting Vardar your entire life. Hunting the source of this sickness. And if you get what Graal wants, you'll find him. It's that simple. We have to go after those books. It's our only lead! And if he's after them too, then we just have to find them first. Easy as pie."

"And what if he's there? Have you considered that, Wonder Woman?"

"In a museum? Full of people? Why would he be there? He doesn't know we know. And maybe there's nothing to know! Maybe it's a coincidence the books are all in one place, but I don't think so. We can't ignore a clue like this. This is bigger than both of us. This is about my world—and yours. If Naiell is right, whatever it is, it can be used to open the gateways. I have to know. I have to stop Graal. Even if that means I have to destroy what we find."

Stefan gave her the drawing back. "As if you'd destroy anything. You can't even part with a picture."

Hirka crumpled up the drawing and threw it in the canal. She regretted it straight away, and as a show of her capacity for destruction, it was pretty pathetic. "I can destroy something if I have to," she muttered.

"Is that right?" Stefan looked at her. "Even if it means you have no way of getting home?"

Hirka felt warmth blossom in her chest. It was the first thing he'd said to suggest he actually believed her. She fought back an urge to hug him, settling for a nod instead. "If I can't get to Ym, he can't either. At least that's something ..." She took a sip of water. It tasted unnatural. She tipped the rest out. It rained down over the canal.

Stefan pulled his phone out of his back pocket. "Well, I poked around a little while you were snoring away. The book collection was donated by a company." He continued as though she understood what he was talking about. "It was purchased a few years ago, by a developer. Investors, you know? There's one partner I can't find a picture of. Joshua Alexander Cain."

"What does that matter?"

"I don't know. It might not. But ... Cain, I mean, talk about sibling rivalries. It doesn't get any more epic than that. Bit too much of a coincidence, if you ask me."

The name *Cain* sounded vaguely familiar to Hirka. Maybe something Father Brody had talked about. "You're afraid it's him? That he's already been there?"

Stefan shrugged. "It probably doesn't matter. We don't even know what we're looking for."

"Something that doesn't belong here."

He flicked his cigarette in the canal and went back in. She followed him and sat down next to him on the pink sofa. His gun was on the table. A strange object that gave far too much power to someone like Stefan. To anyone, for that matter. He fiddled with his phone and a small hatch opened. A white chip appeared, and he swapped it for another. "Anyway, we've got bigger problems than Allegra," he said and snapped the old chip in half with his teeth.

"What are you doing?" she asked.

He held up the phone. "That's how they get you, isn't it? If anyone is stupid enough to steal this, it takes me thirty seconds to find it. If *I* can find it, what the hell do you think *they* can do? Think about it." He rubbed the back of his neck. The fear had returned to his eyes, so she changed the subject.

"What do you mean, bigger problems than Allegra?"

He looked at her. "Your priest has woken up."

"My priest?"

"I saw it in the news. Two of them survived. The priest has been in a coma until now."

"Father Brody? He's alive?!" The glass almost slipped out of her hands.

"It isn't good news, Hirka. Don't you get it? He's going to tell them about you. If they weren't looking for you before, they will be now."

Hirka knew what he was saying, but it didn't matter. Father Brody wasn't dead. "He's alive ..."

"Barely. Comas are pretty serious. You're asleep, but you can't wake up, you know? I guess you don't have those where you're from."

"I know what it is. It's when a small part of you is in Slokna and won't leave." She put the glass down and grabbed his arm. "You said two. Who's the other one? Is it Jay?" It had to be Jay. It had to be. She could picture her so clearly, like she'd just walked out of the café. Buds in her ears and her ripped jumper fluttering in the wind.

"A man," Stefan answered. "The older one. They don't know who he is."

Hirka knew. Her heart sank. Jay had never hurt anyone, and now she was dead. While *he* had survived. Isac. The man with the zig-zag shirt. The man who had smelled like a festering wound. Rotten. Sickly sweet.

Stefan smirked. "They don't know what's wrong with him either. They're at the same hospital. Sounds like fun, don't you think?"

Hirka didn't think so.

She leaned over and picked up his gun. Stefan had already told her not to fiddle with it. It felt cold in her hand and made her feel clumsy. He looked at her.

"Careful, girl. You don't want to go down that road. It's bad enough one of us has messed up their life, don't you think? Anyway, you barely know what it is you're holding."

"I know what it is," Hirka said. "It's a longer knife."

The corners of his mouth twitched. There was a pained look in his eyes. He took the gun and wrapped his arm around her, pulling her close. "They'd have made me king where you're from," he said, patting her on the shoulder. It was an awkward gesture, but it still felt nice.

THE THAW

Damayanti sat alone at the table. Rime guessed she'd arrived early to make sure he would be the one coming to her, not the other way around.

There were few others in Lindri's teahouse. Fewer and fewer every time he visited. Two women—merchants on the wrong side of town—sat at a window table, their age obscured by jewelry and make-up. Maybe they were there to see how fortunate they really were.

A lone drudge with a backpack sat in the corner, a wooden puppet on the table in front of him. The strings were tangled around the puppet's neck. Its head lolled as if it had been strangled.

Rime sat down on the bench across from Damayanti. For a brief moment her eyes betrayed how happy she was to see him, but then she caught herself and gave him her usual beguiling smile.

Rime dropped two heavy books on the table. The other women glanced at them but continued their conversation.

"Stories?" Damayanti asked, leaning forward so that her bangles clinked against the table. Rime caught a whiff of her perfume.

"I used to think so, but it's not that simple, is it?" Rime nodded at Lindri, who shuffled toward them carrying a fully laden tray. Lindri was old, but he'd never looked older than he did now. He put the tray down on the table. One of the cups was chipped, a small triangle missing from the rough ceramic.

"It's good to see you again, Lindri."

"You honor me, Rav—Rime-fadri. It'll be ready once you've forgotten it."

"Sorry?"

"The tea. It'll be finished steeping once you've forgotten about it." The tea merchant's smile tugged at all his wrinkles. He hesitated for a moment, as if he wanted to say something else, but then he left them to it.

Damayanti lifted the lid from the pot and inhaled. "Mmm, you should bring me here more often," she said, looking up at Rime from under heavy eyelids. "Clearly only a select few are treated to the good stuff."

"Clearly," Rime replied. "But you get to choose what you want, unlike me."

"Because he always gives you the best. You make that sound like a bad thing."

"Try going a year without the freedom to choose and get back to me."

She raised an eyebrow and Rime realized he knew too little about her to assume anything at all. She swept her hair forward, her ponytail brushing her collarbone.

"The women by the window know who I am," she said without lowering her voice. "They're pretending not to, but they've heard about me. They're talking about me. And they've already decided what kind of woman I am. To them I'm a whore. I'll never be anything else. I'm free to go where I like, but I'll never be free from people's assumptions. I'm the dancer. That means that all of Mannfalla thinks they know me."

"I'm Rime An-Elderin."

The smug look was wiped from her face. She blushed. Something he'd never thought he'd see. He did her the favor of changing the topic. It was time they got down to business.

"Graal lost the war."

She glanced around. She knew the name. Rime rested a hand on the books. "What are you scared of, Damayanti? No one here knows that name. No one in this teahouse, no one in Mannfalla, no one in all of Ym. Who here cares about a war that ended a thousand years ago? And a name that's been buried for just as long? It's not in the book of the Seer. It's not in the war chronicle. So how is it that you know a name no one else does?"

She ran her fingers through her hair. "One hears things ..."

"Damayanti, if I wanted to see you rotting in the pits, you'd be there already. I'm not here to punish you for what you've heard or what you know." She gave him a suggestive smile and he felt his irritation grow. "No, I'm not here for *that* either. I'm here because you're going to help me fight the blind. I'm no fool, Damayanti. You sought me out. You invited me. You said I had to understand the war to understand the blind. So tell me why."

"You still think the Seer doesn't exist?"

"I *know* he doesn't exist." Rime didn't sound as sure as he wanted to. He'd read too much of late to be sure of anything.

"In that case, what you know is worthless, Rime An-Elderin. They were brothers."

Rime knew that. He'd found the books. He knew more than she realized, and it was time she understood that. Rime leaned toward her.

"There's a story of two brothers. Graal and Naiell. Deadborn, blindling brothers. Nábyrn. Idolized by their people. They led the war against the ymlings. Until Naiell took the form of the raven and saw the beauty of Ym. He turned his back on his own and became the Seer. Fact and fiction intertwined. A soup of history and lies we've been served ever since. But the brothers did exist, didn't they?"

Damayanti nodded. She wasn't able to conceal her surprise. Rime continued.

"Losing a war is a costly affair. Graal's punishment was a study in cruelty. He was betrayed, maimed, and exiled, while his brother was worshipped like a god. An eternity has passed since then, and none of it should matter anymore. But it does, doesn't it? Because that's why the blind are back."

Damayanti shifted on her bench. Rubbed the back of her neck and stared at the ceiling, considering what she should and shouldn't say. But when she looked at him again, he could tell she'd made a decision. She had come down on the right side—she was going to tell him what she knew.

"It matters because they don't die."

"Keep your superstition to yourself. I've killed them with my own two hands. Sure as Slokna they die."

She leaned toward him. "Everything can be killed, Rime. But what does that mean? A thousand years is nothing to them. Nothing." Her eyes were burning. "Not even half a lifetime for a blindling." He suddenly had the feeling he was seeing her clearly for the first time, and it unsettled him.

He'd thought he had the upper hand, but the conversation was going in a direction he hadn't foreseen. He tried to fight off his doubt. She'd known Urd, but still … She was wrong. She had to be wrong. Nothing could live forever.

"Think about it," she said, like she was reading his mind. "How did he become the Seer? What made us worship one of the dead-born for a thousand years? And why would people lie awake at night, terrified of something they barely knew anything about? How are myths created, Rime?"

"You're telling me the Seer exists? That he's alive?"

"I'm telling you they're both alive." She leaned back against the wall again.

"You can't know that."

"I can."

"How?"

"Graal and Urd talked," she said, shrugging as if she were talking about the weather.

Rime stared down at the table, his thoughts scrambling to find the right hooks to hang on. They all converged on one. "The beak ..." He looked up at her. "It's the beak, isn't it?"

She nodded. "Urd took the beak."

"Took?"

"That's what they call it. *Taking the beak.*"

Rime knew he was entering dangerous territory. He'd been focusing on all the wrong things. He'd wondered how any of this was possible. The gateways. The Might. Blindcraft. He of all people ought to have known better. The how wasn't important. He gripped her hand.

"Why? Why did he take the beak?"

"Because he really wanted to talk to Graal, but Graal isn't in our world. He was exiled, remember?"

Rime let go of her hand. The sudden certainty was unstoppable, making his pulse race. He closed his eyes. "To the children of Odin," he heard himself say. "He was sent to the humans."

Damayanti got up. She leaned over and whispered in his ear. "And from there he can orchestrate another war. He has the means now, and I think you know why."

Hirka ...

Rime remembered Hlosnian telling him that Hirka was the reason the gateways were open. She didn't belong here. There was something about her. Something that influenced the Might. She had traveler's blood, and now there was someone who needed it. She was alone. Alone in an unknown world. Alone with an ancient evil that wanted to reclaim Ym.

He'd sent her to her death.

"You've forgotten the tea," Damayanti said, then left.

Rime stared at the pot. The tea had stopped steaming. He felt cold as well. He got up and surveyed the other patrons. The women tittered. The man with the puppet was still sitting in the corner, nursing the same cup. Lindri was filling small boxes with tea. All of them going about their lives, unaware that there were monsters that could live forever. Deadborn a thousand years old. None of them even suspected …

Suddenly there was a loud crack. For a moment Rime thought it had come from him, but it had come from outside. It was the ice. The ice along the riverbank was starting to melt.

Rime put a stack of coins on the table and headed for the door.

"Ravenbearer?" the man with the puppet asked tentatively. Rime looked at him but said nothing. "It's you, isn't it? Rime-fadri?"

Rime nodded.

"If you hadn't taken your seat on the Council, I probably wouldn't be sitting here right now. I feel I ought to thank you."

Rime moved closer. "What do you mean?"

"They said I was lucky for making friends with the rot while I was in the pits. She was the one who demanded they let me out."

"Hirka?"

He nodded. "People say you know her. Would you thank her for me? If it isn't true that she's dead, that is."

"She's alive." Rime barely suppressed the urge to grit his teeth.

"Good. Tell her not to drink the water. They forget to change it. She'll know what I mean." He laughed awkwardly. His eyes only met Rime's very occasionally. He mostly looked at the puppet. A king, dressed in blue with a copper crown.

Rime turned to leave, but a niggling thought made him stop.

When? When would Hirka have demanded that the Council release people from the pits?

"When did they let you out?" He turned back toward the man.

"Just before the handover ceremony, Rime-fadri. I got to see you take the staff. The youngest ever. They say everything will be different now, but I'm not so sure. In any case, I'm out. Poor but free, and that's good enough for me. I wanted to thank her, but … They say she's not here anymore."

Rime was no longer listening. If the man was right, it could only mean one thing. Hirka had met with the Council before the handover ceremony. Under what circumstances would she have been able to demand anything from the Council? And have those demands met?

They made a deal. Forced her to leave.

Rime had said as much to Hirka the night she'd left. That had been his first instinct, that the Council had forced her to leave Ym. What had she said? Had she denied it? Or just brushed him off?

He opened the floodgates for the Might. Rage. Fear. It surged through his veins, forcing them open. The man in front of him pulled back into the corner, staring.

Rime grabbed his swords at the door and started running up toward Eisvaldr.

They forced her to leave. And now she's in danger.

He was going to wring their necks with his own two hands.

RUIN

One by one they came puttering in, as if they had all the time in the world. Led by Noldhe Saurpassarid, who at the age of eighty ought to have been the slowest, but the eldest among them still respected Council meetings. She pulled her chair out from the table.

"No need to sit down," Rime said coolly.

She looked at the others. They said nothing, so she pushed the chair back in and remained standing. Sigra Kleiv folded her arms over her chest and smothered Rime with her gaze. Few things bothered the leaders of the eleven kingdoms more than being frog-marched to an unscheduled meeting. The fact that Rime was behind it only added insult to injury. A pup, Ilume had called him. A nineteen-year-old pup. The Ravenbearer for a council where hardly anyone was under fifty.

They gathered at the other end of the table. As far away from him as they could get. Every movement they made tested his nerves. Shrugs. Eye-rolls. Smiles hidden behind wrinkled hands. How long would he hold out? Was he going mad?

No—if he were going mad, he wouldn't be aware of it. Wasn't that how it worked? He clung to that thought.

Garm was yet to arrive. Rime let them wait. He wouldn't say a word until they were all there. Sigra Kleiv opened her mouth just as Garm Darkdaggar entered.

The Council was assembled. Eleven men and women. There

should have been twelve, but Rime still hadn't filled Urd's place. Ravnhov would have that chair, no matter the cost. It was time to do what was necessary. Like Svarteld had said.

Don't start something you can't finish.

Rime turned away. If he had to look at them, he wouldn't be able to control his fury. He stared out the window, at the ruin of the bridge. The ice had started to melt. Water trickled down the carvings and collected in one big droplet at the end of a serpent's tongue. He began.

"Anyone who tries to deny their actions will never set foot in this chamber again. I haven't called you here to ask. Or to explain. I know. I'm here to tell you what is going to happen."

He heard someone approach. "Rime ..."

Jarladin. The big-hearted ox. A man he'd respected since he was a child. He was the only one of these wretched relics he could bear to listen to. But not now. The time for listening was over. Rime shut him out and continued.

"I know you asked her to leave."

He heard them mumbling. They weren't even sure what he was talking about. Hirka was insignificant to them. Forgotten. Sent away. As far as they were concerned, she might as well have never existed. The drop of water on the serpent's tongue fell. Rime felt like he was doing the same. Dropping down toward the stone circle below, to be dashed on the ground.

He turned to face them. "What did you promise her? What did you have to offer her that was enough to make her leave? Answer me!"

The silence roared in his ears.

"Don't make me draw my swords ..."

Noldhe gasped as if she were only a girl. They huddled together. Mumbled to each other. Leivlugn Taid put a hand behind his ear. "What's that he said? Did he say swords?"

Garm Darkdaggar swept his cloak over his shoulder and walked toward the door with determined strides. Rime knew exactly what would stop him. "Leave and you'll never set foot in here again, Garm!"

Darkdaggar stopped. He was a practical man. They were all practical. They were loyal followers of the path of least resistance. He hated them in that moment. More than ever.

"Things are going to be different," Rime said, ignoring the tremor in his voice. "Tomorrow I'm traveling to Ravnhov to meet with Eirik. And on behalf of all of us, I'm inviting him to take Urd's chair."

Sigra snorted. "We've already discussed this to death! What about the heirs? You can't—"

"Heirs? Heirs no longer exist. No one is going to inherit a chair. Never again. The eleven kingdoms will choose who sits in the chairs, and the families will cease to dominate this council. I am the last heir the world will see."

"You'll be the ruin of us all," Freid whispered, face haggard. She was a Vangard, and their family had never had a ravenbearer. Now they never would. It was over. It was all over. He'd reduce Eisvaldr to ashes if he had to.

"Ruin? You wouldn't recognize ruin if it slapped you in the face! You have no idea what you've done! You've sent her to her death. And her death will lead to your own. Another war. A thousand-year war. Our fate won't be decided here. Not in Ym. It will be decided where she is, and you haven't even stopped to ask how she got here. Or why. You know nothing! You understand nothing! She cracked open the gateways and now ... now we're ..."

Rime couldn't find the words. He looked at them. They looked at each other, and he could tell they thought he was insane. After all, what did they know about the deadborn? About Graal? They'd never known the Might the way he had. They weren't seeing the big picture. Their own downfall.

"You gave her away ..." he heard himself say. "You gave the key to our enemies. Traveler's blood."

He felt Jarladin's hand on his shoulder. "Enough, Rime."

Rime swept toward them. Only Sigra stood her ground. "What did you promise her? Answer me! What did you give her to make her leave?!"

Jarladin grabbed him and held him back. "Rime, I'll explain. You have my word. But let them go. They don't know what you know." Jarladin nodded at the others. They left the room, one by one, the same way they'd come in. Garm and Sigra could barely conceal their smiles. He knew the reason. They thought he'd lost his mind, and that would make him easier to get rid of.

Rime glared at them until they were gone. Then he turned to Jarladin. "What have you done?"

"It was Eir, Garm, and me. The others did nothing."

"What did you do?"

"We went to meet Hirka in Blindból. After ..." He didn't need to say more. After the Rite Hall fell. After the world was turned upside down.

Jarladin pulled out two chairs, but Rime remained standing. The ox sat down and rested his elbows on the table. His well-groomed beard quivered on one side. Rime stared at him. He'd never seen him look so small.

"You have to understand, Rime. The Council all knew that she couldn't stay. You know that, too. You've said it yourself: she led the blind here. And what sort of peace do you think we'd have managed with a child of Odin walking around Eisvaldr? The girl didn't belong here. So yes. We asked her to leave. No coercion. No threats. We asked. And she accepted our offer."

"Liar!" Rime seethed. "Hirka can't be bought. Not for any price. There's nothing in the world you could have given her."

Jarladin's face was racked with sorrow. His eyes were laid bare.

He was telling the truth. Rime swallowed. "What? What was the price?"

"You."

Rime braced his hands on the table and stared at him. "Me?"

Jarladin nodded. "She understood more than you do. She understood that this chair is the most dangerous place in the eleven kingdoms, so she only asked for one thing—my word. She left in exchange for my promise that I'd keep you alive, as leader. A promise you're making increasingly difficult to keep, boy."

Rime collapsed onto the chair. Jarladin kept talking. Saying that Hirka would manage. That she hadn't left empty-handed. That Rime had to forget about her. Let go. His words ran together into a meaningless jumble. About repairing the damage. About assuaging the others. Then it was quiet, and Rime realized that Jarladin had left.

He raised his hand to his chest. Felt for the pendant, but it wasn't there. He'd given it to her when she left. All the points they'd competed for as children. It was as if it had never happened. How many points would she have gotten for this? For leaving him, in exchange for Jarladin's loyalty?

All that was good in Ym had left with her. And he hadn't stopped her. He'd let her leave. And to face what? A bloodthirsty deadborn who'd been trapped in the human world for more years than anyone could fathom. Rime's thoughts circled relentlessly around the questions he'd been trying to avoid. What would become of her? What would she be used for? To open the gateways even wider? To start another war?

Fallacy! Myths and lies!

It was hopeless. Deep down he knew that everything he'd read and heard was true. And he couldn't find her. Or warn her. Maybe he could force the gateways open the way Urd had done?

No. That would destroy them, and then he'd never get her back.

Rime stared at the table. His family name stared back. *An-Elderin.* Set in stone. Trapped. For generations. He was what he was. Ilume's blood. Council blood. Was he doomed to be like all those before him? Unable to act? Unable to change anything?

He rested his head on the table. Felt the cold stone against his forehead. His pulse throbbed in his ears with the echo of Freid's words.

You'll be the ruin of us all.

GRAAL

Rún Museum of Art in Copenhagen was a marvel. Taller than a Seer's hall, with entire walls and roofs made of crystal-clear glass. Hirka kept bumping into other visitors because she couldn't stop looking up at the sky, even though she was indoors. It was a bit like the greenhouse, but much, much bigger.

Glass doors. Glass windows. Glass cubes in the middle of rooms with nothing inside them other than carved wooden figures. When she squinted, it was as if the entire building disappeared. A dream. A fantasy. A fragile palace that existed and didn't exist at the same time.

"Hello!" she shouted, just to hear the echo bounce off the walls. A group of elderly visitors in padded clothes turned to look at her. She raised a hand in greeting, but they pretended they hadn't seen her, like she was as transparent as the building itself.

Stefan dragged her up an impressive curved staircase with floating wooden steps. "I didn't drive all day and night just for you to get us thrown out," he whispered, tugging at his leather jacket as if it wasn't sitting properly. She felt as uncomfortable as he looked. She'd reluctantly agreed to wear the clothes that Allegra had given her, in what Stefan had called a futile attempt to blend in.

"Why would they throw us out?"

"Do we look like the type of people who hang out in museums?" Stefan glanced back at Naiell. The blindling was the only one in the museum wearing sunglasses. He was carrying his jacket over his arm. His white shirt was pulled taut across his chest, and it was plain to see that he wasn't like anyone else. But that was because she knew what he was.

"Here it is." Stefan pointed at a gray sign she couldn't read. She shifted her bag on her back and followed him along the railing and farther into the room. She stopped in front of a huge hole in the floor. Stefan kept walking but didn't fall. She gaped. More glass. Glass you could walk on.

Stefan made it to the other side in one piece without seeming to notice what he was doing. Hirka couldn't bring herself to follow him. She wanted to, but her entire body screamed no. She walked around instead. Naiell strode straight across like he'd been walking on glass his entire life. Maybe he thought he could still fly.

They found the books, volume after volume arranged in locked cabinets on the walls. Nine of them had their own display cases. They sat in a row, protected by glass.

"This one?" Stefan stopped in front of one of the display cases. Hirka looked down. The thick book lay open, its pages full of red and blue patterns.

"What is it?"

He leaned over to read a small sign on the glass. "Music, I think. Old sheet music."

"Wrong section. We need to find the gateway room."

"Find the *what*?"

"The gateway room," she said. "And then the recipe shelf."

"Do you mean instructions?"

"Instructions, yes."

"You think you're hilarious, don't you?"

"I do," she said, grinning, mostly to conceal her frustration. She was surrounded by books and pictures she couldn't even begin to understand. Colorful and illustrated and important-looking. What did she have to go on? Pictures stuck to a wall by a forgetful old man. What had she really seen? Vengethorn, or just some straw?

Stefan had probably been right all along. Why would anyone leave something valuable in a place like this? In the open, where everyone could see it? If instructions for the raven rings really existed, surely Graal would have taken them a long time ago.

"We're on a wild goose chase," Stefan said.

"I was thinking exactly the same thing," she replied, unexpectedly relieved. What would she have done if there had been something here? Destroyed it? Stolen it? And kept running for the rest of her life with some treasure that a millennia-old blindling would kill to sink his claws into?

It was probably just as well there was nothing here. She breathed out, feeling lighter than she had in weeks. Almost free. Although she'd always feared crowds, she suddenly felt safer with people around her. Humans. Children of Odin, all of them. Ambling between the displays. Chatting and admiring the exhibits. It was all so normal to them. Maybe one day it could be normal to her as well.

She smiled and walked along the row of books. One of them caught her eye. It lay open, like the others. Balanced on a stand that cradled its spine. It was an entirely ordinary book, bound in black leather. The binding was thin and bendy, making it look like a crow in flight, hovering under the glass. No decoration. No color. Compared to the others, it was boring. Unremarkable in every way.

The strange thing about it was that there was nothing written in it. One page was completely blank, and the other only had three small circles, drawn in black ink. Rays emanated from them, reminding Hirka of the way Vetle used to draw the sun. They were positioned seemingly at random on the page, and apart from them, there was nothing else. Not a single letter. Not a single symbol.

"Art," Stefan snorted behind her. "That crap probably costs as much as a Jaguar. Like I've always said: completely pointless. I need a smoke."

Hirka crouched down so she could study the cover. Two diagonal lines had been stamped into the leather. The symbol seemed familiar, for all its simplicity. She couldn't put her finger on what it was. But it gave her chills.

Chills?

Hirka straightened up again. Something was wrong. The air seemed to thicken around her. It was charged. Waiting. Like before lightning strikes.

She wasn't alone.

The certainty made her blood run cold. She looked at Naiell. He took off his glasses and lifted his chin, as if scenting the air. He could feel it, too. He threw his jacket on the floor and backed away.

"Naiell?" Hirka reached out to him, but he paid her no heed. His eyes darted around as he turned in a circle like a madman.

"What is it?" Stefan asked. "What's wrong with him?"

Hirka knew. Her entire body knew.

"He's here ..."

Stefan gave her a confused look before catching on. Then he reacted. Reached for his gun. Hirka grabbed his arm, and he seemed to realize his foolishness. Weapons were madness, particularly in a place like this.

Hirka looked around at the humans. Ordinary people. Or was *that* him? The bald man leaning over the first book they'd looked at? No ... his fingers were completely normal. Was it that other man? The one with the little girl? No, normal eyes. Completely normal.

Hirka felt all her hair stand on end. She knew he was here. She could feel it. Smell it. There was no other explanation for the certainty that had gripped her.

He's here. Graal is here.

She ran over to the railing and looked down at the level below. There were far too many people milling about down there. Smiling. Unsuspecting. Some alone. Some in groups. Hirka wanted to scream, to yell at them to get out, but she couldn't find the words. What would she say? She didn't even know what the danger was. All she knew was that Naiell was terrified. The Seer. Deathly pale and pressed up against the wall of books. Held fast by an unseen danger.

A man came up the stairs. He was nicely dressed in a brown leather coat, gloves, and dark glasses. His hair was short and black. He ran two fingers along the railing as he climbed. Slow. Deliberate. Step by step. It was like time was standing still.

The man looked up. Hirka somehow knew he was watching her, despite the glasses. He reached the top of the stairs and walked around the edge of the room, as if circling in on them.

Stefan ...

Hirka looked around for him. He was moving toward her, as was Naiell. Probably the worst place to be at that moment. She knew she ought to do something, but her head felt frozen. Bloodless. The man stopped a short distance from her. His coat was open. He slipped his hands in his pockets and stood looking at her.

He was a bit shorter than Naiell. Narrower in the face. And he carried himself differently. Calm. Unafraid. With the ghost of a smile tugging at the corner of his mouth. That was the scariest part. Hirka swallowed, her throat dry as sand. All that stood between them was two display cases with books in them. A couple of long strides and he'd have her.

She suddenly remembered what Rime had said in Blindból, the time Slokna had almost claimed him. When Kolkagga had been closing in on them in the mountains. He'd asked her to stay behind him, to make sure he was always between her and Kolkagga.

But Rime wasn't here. She was on her own. Stefan and Naiell were still some distance away. She was alone before the man who was planning her downfall. Everyone's downfall.

Graal took off his glasses. Folded them up and put them in his vest pocket. His eyes were black as ink. He pulled off his gloves as he looked at Naiell.

"You look tired, brother," he said in ymish.

Naiell bared his teeth and arched his back like a cat. Hirka hadn't really grasped the intensity of his hatred until now. What the war between the brothers meant. Fear and fury controlled every muscle in Naiell's body.

A young couple came up the stairs. Hirka wasn't sure whether to scream for help or tell them to run. They quickly realized that something was wrong. They whispered to each other, turned around, and went in another direction.

Graal took a step closer to her. Naiell did the same, as if they were pieces in a game. Stefan's eyes darted between them, panicked. He had one hand by his belt, and she knew he was going to draw his gun. She had to do something.

The book. He mustn't get the book.

Slowly, she started edging closer to the display case. Graal gave her a broad and brilliant smile. A powerful smile. Hirka tasted blood and realized she'd bitten her lip.

"You are mine. What does he say to that?" Graal asked.

His voice was deep. Rough and guttural, like Naiell's, yet somehow more real. And he had revealed the truth. The secret she'd been desperate to keep from Naiell was out. There was no going back now.

"I haven't told him yet," Hirka replied, inching even closer to the book.

Graal threw his head back and laughed. "Told him? Blood of my blood, he knows very well who you are. We know when our own are near. How else do you think he found you?"

Hirka hesitated. Locked eyes with Naiell. He slowly shook his head. She knew what he was trying to say. That she shouldn't listen to this monster.

Graal nodded at Naiell. "He's awfully serious, isn't he? Have you ever seen him laugh at himself?" Hirka didn't reply. "No, I didn't think so. Still the same. It's shameful, not changing at all in a thousand years, don't you think? So what else hasn't he told you, blood of my blood?"

"He's told me enough," Hirka said. She was standing right next to the book now. But she knew that as soon as she lifted the glass, everything would happen at once. Stefan and Naiell were standing a couple of steps away from her. In the middle of the glass floor. A desperate plan started to form. She glanced down at the book.

"Now, now. What do you want with that? You don't even know what it is," Graal said, killing what little hope she had of surprising him.

"I know it can help you open the gateways," Hirka said. "And that's enough."

He laughed again and took a step toward Naiell. "The raven rings are already wide open. To anyone with the Might. Our people are free to enter Ym every single day, and there is nothing you can do to stop them." He looked at Hirka again. "He knows that, too. That's why he's here. What do you think our people would do if they got hold of him? The man who betrayed them all?"

"Enough!" Naiell screamed. People turned to look at them. Someone came running from behind the counter by the entrance. This wasn't going to end well.

So do you want to live or die?

Hirka pushed the display case over. The lid shattered in front of Graal. She grabbed the book before it hit the floor. Graal moved toward her. She flung herself at Stefan, grabbing his gun. He shouted her name. She pointed the gun at the glass floor and pulled the trigger. There was a bang. Several bangs. Her arm jerked. People screamed. The floor fell out from under her. Shattered. She was in free fall. An alarm blared. She hit the floor and rolled.

For a moment she couldn't move, uncertain as to whether she was even alive. But she was. Alive and in one piece.

Stefan!

Stefan came crawling on all fours, his hand leaving a trail of blood in its wake. The glass crunched. She was kneeling in a sea of glittering ice. Naiell was already on his feet and heading for the exit. Hirka hugged the book to her chest and looked up at Graal, who stood looking back, broken glass jutting out like teeth around him. Hirka crawled toward Stefan, between the legs of people screaming and running for their lives. Stefan leaped to his feet and grabbed her, pulling her through the crowd toward the doors.

Hirka threw a glance over her shoulder. Graal had jumped down through the hole in the ceiling. He stood motionless in a sea of people, watching her. Wild black hair. Black eyes. Her father. Her death.

She could have sworn he looked proud.

NEW BLOOD

They had driven across the sea. Over a bridge that never ended. Driven into a blue nothingness, with no destination in sight. North. Always north. Toward Stockholm. They kept to the backroads. Argued about where to go. Argued about what had happened. Whether or not they were on what Stefan called "the radar." They'd had cameras at the museum, he said. Making pictures of them. The whole world was going to know who they were. What they'd done.

Hirka didn't really care. And she had no idea what the radar was. They could have all the cameras in the world, for all it mattered to her. Those realities belonged to this world. Not hers. She wasn't one of them. Didn't belong here.

"Aren't you supposed to tell me to take it easy?" Stefan said over his shoulder as he drove. "And you're supposed to patch me up. Isn't that what you do? Patch things up? I'm bleeding here!" He took his hand off the wheel and showed her his palm. She didn't respond.

"And what about you?" he continued, looking at Naiell in the mirror. "Where the hell were you? Christ, a rat would have been more help than you!" Naiell didn't respond either, but he certainly would have, had he understood what was being said. "Tell him what I said! You hear me?" Stefan had reached breaking point.

"Stop," Hirka said, but he didn't hear her. Two lights came toward them on the road, and he veered away.

"Shit, shit, shit!"

"Stop!"

"We can't stop! We can never stop again! You've fucking ruined me, girl! Ruined everything."

He swore again and took a sudden left turn. The road narrowed and disappeared into the trees. Hirka suddenly smelled something strange. Something foul. Stefan stopped the car in front of a wire fence. He sat staring at his hand. "Dammit, I'm never going to get these bits of glass out!"

Hirka tore open the car door and jumped out. She tucked the book under her arm and ran toward the fence. She found a gap where one of the posts had fallen over and squeezed through. She heard Stefan shouting at Naiell. Shouting that he should stop her. That they couldn't stay there.

She looked back. Naiell tore up one of the fence posts and came after her. She wasn't scared of him anymore. If he'd wanted to kill her, he'd have done it in the car. She just wanted to get away. Away from him. Away from all the things he hadn't told her. Things that now threatened to overwhelm her. He'd known. He'd known all along. Who she was. And that the blind were still in Ym.

With Rime.

She'd left for no reason. Left him. Left Ym. Left everything she loved. For nothing.

She stumbled and fell forward. Crawled up a mound and stopped when she realized what it was. Garbage. A mountain of garbage. Several of them. Filling the landscape. It stunk. Scraps of food. Boxes. Bags. Broken toys. Newspapers. Things she couldn't begin to describe. Crows and ravens hopped around, pecking at all manner of things. What was this? Where was she? And who did all these things belong to?

The rot. It's the rot. The world is dying.

She got up and backed away. Straight into Naiell. He spun her around and wrapped his pale hands around her face. His claws were sharp against the back of her head. She stared up at the beautiful blindling and knew she would have given anything for him to be someone else. To be Rime. No one else was allowed so close to her. No one.

"You lied to me," she snarled.

"No. I didn't lie to you. I refrained from telling you something I knew would destroy you." She tried to squirm free, but it was useless. "Listen to me, Hirka! If I'd told you who you were, would that have made things simpler? Well? Would being stuck here have been any easier, knowing you were my brother's child?"

She nodded. "Everything's easier when you know! Everything! But what do you know about that? What do the deadborn actually know?"

He growled at the word. His hair fell in long, black tangles over his chest. One of the buttons on his shirt had popped. "We know more than humans and ymlings combined. We are Dreyri! We have blood of the first. And you'd do well to remember you're one of us."

Hirka swallowed. She was one of them. One of those now laying waste to Ym. One of those—her chain of thought ground to a halt. She realized she knew nothing more about them.

Naiell pulled her closer. Black ink danced in his eyes, converging in a pulsating ring. "And who lied to whom? You figured it out, but you didn't say anything to me about it either, did you?"

"You would have killed me!"

"Are you not still alive, Sulni?" he hissed.

"I am. But what about Rime? What about Ym? Or have you razed everything?"

"I'm not them!"

"But you knew! You knew the blind are still there! You knew that I came here for no reason, and you said nothing! You didn't say a word, you brute!"

He tightened his hold on her and gave her a shake. "And now you know! Does that make it any easier? Well? Answer me that. Is it easier being here, knowing who you are? Knowing you can't help them?"

She wanted to cry, but her body felt drained. Dry. Dead. "That's how you found me," she heard herself say. "You knew. Even before we left. As a raven. You found me at the Alldjup as Kuro, because you knew ..."

"We smell our own blood, and you were an impossibility."

It wasn't fair. She'd been an impossibility in Ym, but everything was supposed to be different here. She wasn't supposed to be impossible here. Not with the humans.

He let go of her. Her feet fell out from under her and she crumpled, landing on a black garbage bag made of that loathsome material that never went away. It would lie here long after she died. Maybe even long after the world died. Lie here smelling rotten.

She saw Stefan by the fence. He was running toward them. The car was behind him, with the doors wide open. The crows shrieked under heavy clouds.

"I'm not impossible, Naiell. I've never been impossible. I'm here, aren't I?"

He sat down next to her. Not the way Stefan would have done. Or the way Father used to. Naiell wasn't there to comfort her. He wasn't the type. Maybe blindlings weren't the type.

Am I the type? Haven't I been comforting people my entire life?

"I knew you were my brother's child. I just didn't understand how that could be."

Stefan stopped in front of them, out of breath. He rested his hands on his thighs. "So, what could you two possibly be talking about? About how you're sitting on a mountain of garbage, waiting for the cops? Is that what you're talking about? What the hell is wrong with you two? It's like reality doesn't apply to you! What do you think is going to happen when they find us?" He straightened up. Ran a hand through his hair. His gaze wavered. He didn't know the answer to his own question.

Naiell leaned back and rested on the garbage. He didn't seem bothered by it. Maybe it was like the food he ate with his fingers. Just parts of a bigger whole. Nothing was moldy or fresh. Everything was made of small, small parts. Too small to see, but still of use.

Hirka looked up at Stefan. "He knew who I was, Stefan. But he didn't say anything."

"You knew it too, and you didn't say a word to me! And I'm human. What the hell is *he*? You can't seriously be shocked that he can't be trusted?"

She suddenly felt so stupid. He was right, of course. Could anything so different be trusted? Hirka stared up at the sky. It had grown darker. The first stars were out. Stars. Like they had back home in Elveroa. Were they the same stars that shone every night, fading every morning as the gulls screeched at the fishermen returning with the catch?

Naiell sat up. "Graal shouldn't have been able to continue his line. They chopped off his manhood before he was sent here."

It took a moment for Hirka to realize what he meant. *Manhood* was such an old-fashioned word.

"You're joking."

He didn't answer.

"You castrated him?"

"They stopped the bloodline," he snapped. "That was his punishment."

"For what? For losing a war?"

A war he lost because of you. The Seer …

She didn't dare say it. She looked at Stefan. "He says Graal is … that he can't become a father. That he has no …" She glanced down at his crotch.

Stefan dug a cigarette out of his pocket and lit it. His fingers were shaking. "So he's dickless? The guy we just ran into?"

Hirka wasn't sure what the word meant, but she nodded anyway.

"Nice work, then," he said, taking a drag before he went on. "Having you, I mean."

"That's what Naiell says, too. He didn't think it was possible. I didn't either."

Stefan shrugged. "You can become a father without … as long as you have … as long as everything's still functioning on the inside. You know? People have kids without sleeping together all the time. Test-tube babies. Surrogate mothers. Things like that."

Hirka blinked. Tried to make sense of the words. Stefan blew out some smoke and threw away the cigarette he'd only just lit. Maybe he was trying to quit?

"I mean, as far as making babies is concerned, it's what's on the inside that matters. People have children all the time without being able to … How old are you again?"

"Old enough," she answered dryly. She didn't know whether to be relieved or annoyed that he was uncomfortable discussing this with her. She turned to Naiell. "Stefan says it doesn't matter. You can become a father without sleeping with anyone. He says they do it all the time. Test-children. I don't know …"

Naiell got up and jumped down from the mountain of garbage. He started pacing back and forth in front of them. It was the first time she remembered saying something that interested him. "So he's found a way to open the bloodline. A way to be a father, without being with a woman? Surely he needs a woman?"

"I'd think so."

"Ask him!"

Hirka asked. Stefan looked at them like they were both out of their minds. "Yes, Jesus, obviously you need a woman."

My mother. I had a mother. A human. Half-human, half-blindling.

Naiell tapped his claws against his chin. "But why? He still won't be able to use the gateways," he said, mostly to himself.

"I thought that's what he wanted?"

"Of course that's what he wants, but it shouldn't be possible! They scorched his blood to trap him here. Forever. If he uses the gateways, he'll die. Every drop of blood in his veins will ignite, and he knows that."

Hirka shuddered. The darkness felt like it was creeping ever closer. The ravens screeched above them. This was blindcraft. *Scorched blood. Castration.* What kind of world was it, really? How dark was it, the land of the blind? The thought was so horrifying that she couldn't even bring herself to tell him off for keeping yet another secret from her.

"So if he can't use the gateways, how is he going to do what you say he's going to do?"

Naiell's lips pulled back, baring his canines. "I don't know!" he hissed. "We could spend days sitting around speculating. Maybe he'll send an army from here to Ym. Maybe he's found other gateways. Gateways he can use without his blood catching fire. Or maybe he's found someone who can fix him, however unlikely that may sound. Or maybe he's content to stay here and just needs you as a slave with blood powerful enough to run errands between worlds. Take your pick, Sulni, but we have no way of knowing!"

Hirka pulled away a little. Whether because of his anger or his theories, she didn't know. Both were equally horrendous.

But he was right. They knew nothing. The book that was meant to help them made no sense.

Stefan was getting impatient again, so Hirka translated. "He says Graal can't use the gateways himself. They … they did something to him. After he came here. They ruined his blood. Burned it, he says. Poisoned it. I don't know."

"Seriously? That's what he's going to use you for?"

"What do you mean?"

"New blood? If you're his child, then he can use yours, right?"

Hirka stared at him. Had he finally cracked? "You can't use other people's blood, Stefan."

Stefan wiped his bloody hand on his trousers, then cursed when he realized what he'd done. "Listen. I don't know what kind of world you're from. But I'm starting to think it's in the stone age or something. Do you have hospitals? Do you even have medicine? Of course people can have kids without sleeping together! And of course you can use other people's blood! Christ, girl, they swap out people's blood all the time. Cancer patients, for example. Out with the bad, in with the good. Blood transfusions? What do you use? Leeches?" He sounded like he was on the verge of hysterics.

Hirka was stunned. What little energy she still had left drained out of her. She looked at Naiell. "He says ..." She swallowed, then tried again. "He says they can swap out people's blood. At hospitals."

Naiell cocked his head. "All of it? Really?"

This was the first time she'd seen him accept anything anyone had to tell him, but she derived no pleasure from it. "Really," she whispered.

Stefan looked at her and Naiell in turn. He hunched his shoulders. "What? What did I say?"

Neither of them responded. Hirka stared down at a rotten apple core. Broken glass. A newspaper page with a picture of a skull half-buried in the ground. Death. Death and decay. Then Stefan started to laugh. "That's it, isn't it? That's what this is all about?" He laughed even louder. A despondent noise that cut right through her. "You're a blood bag!"

She knew exactly what he meant even though she'd never heard of it before. Some things transcended language. It had to be the most horrible thing she'd ever heard. *Blood bag.* She was a blood bag.

New blood for old evil.

TO SLOKNA

"Sneaking in the back way, eh, councillor?" Eirik boomed from somewhere above Rime. "Were you afraid we wouldn't let you in?" The chieftain's laughter echoed across Blindból, setting his companion off as well. Rime looked up at them as he continued to climb. After several days traveling through Blindból, it was good to hear people's voices.

The rock face was bare and somewhat lacking in hand and footholds. Rime made his way up toward the fissure where the men were standing. A gap in the rock, dark as the space left by a missing tooth. He pulled himself up over the edge and stood next to the hairy giant of a man that Ravnhov called chieftain. Eirik's beard had gotten longer. A wiry tangle streaked with gray that probably hadn't seen a comb since the Rite.

Rime mopped his brow and looked out across Blindból, at the black mountains sticking up like fingers from the forest floor far below. He'd stood here before. Right here, with Hirka. Before the mountains had turned white and the trees had frozen. They'd traveled through Blindból together after that fateful night in the Seer's tower.

He'd kissed her that night. Halfway up a mountain, while the heavens raged. Her lips. His fingers in her wet hair. His body quickened at the memory and he immediately forced it out of his mind. In any case, she'd pushed him away. Afraid of the rot. Terrified because she was a child of Odin and he was an ymling.

Eirik's blue eyes twinkled at him, seeing right through his melancholy. "Come!" the chieftain rumbled. He threw his arm around Rime's shoulders and they started walking. "What did I tell you, Ynge? You owe me a silver."

"Don't I always?" Ynge replied.

"You were betting on my life?" Rime asked. "Is it any wonder Mannfalla calls you wild men?"

Eirik patted his shoulder. "We bet on whether you would take the main road or come through Blindból. I won because I know you're a wild man at heart, Rime An-Elderin."

Ynge snorted. "A ravenbearer, traveling alone through Blindból in the winter? Without guardsmen? Without a carriage? You have to admit, the odds were in my favor …"

Rime decided not to comment.

They climbed up the stone steps and came out on the plateau. A yellow bridge lay across the ravine—the way into the chieftain's household.

"Ynge, tell them Mannfalla's here," Eirik said, shooing Ynge away like a dog. "And remember the silver!" Ynge made a hand gesture that was anything but polite. Rime followed Eirik past the tree in the yard, an ancient spruce that towered over the great hall. That was where Rime had fought Tein, the chieftain's son. He'd let Tein win, to save face. For the sake of peace. For Hirka.

Ravnhov had been transformed. Icicles hung from steep turfed roofs on houses that huddled together on the slope. Beneath them, the road meandered its way down toward the town. Rime could see more people on the wall than before. They were heavily armed. Blue banners with yellow crowns fluttered in the wind. A burned-out cart sat half-buried in the snow by the gate. Broken shields were piled in front of one of the houses. Remnants of war.

People stared at him as they crossed the frost-covered courtyard. Two girls came toward them carrying a brace of dead rabbits. They whispered together and smiled at him from under snow-dusted hoods.

"Do they still hate me?" Rime asked.

The chieftain chuckled. "No, I don't think so. From what we've heard, you're doing a better job of toppling Mannfalla than we could do ourselves. Come on. The messages you sent with the ravens were a bit light on details, but I think we've got what you're looking for."

Rime followed him around the back of the great hall and up into the mountains. The same way they'd gone when Eirik had shown him the dead blindling in the ice, but that wasn't where they were going this time. Instead, Eirik ushered Rime into a crevice in the mountainside. It opened into a snow-covered space, circular with sheer rock walls. An idol stood in its center, a shapely woman astride a two-headed raven.

Rime had heard about this place. It must have been from Hirka. Once she got talking, she never stopped.

Who does she talk to now?

"These are our books," Eirik said, pointing at the rock wall. It was decorated with images. Carved into the stone and painted, all the way around. "A far cry from the library in Mannfalla, though."

"Maybe," Rime replied. "But I doubt what you have here can be found in the books of Mannfalla."

Eirik's beard lifted, betraying a smile. They looked at each other. The chieftain and the Ravenbearer. Ravnhov and Mannfalla.

"Bleakest Blindból, Rime, it's good to see you," Eirik said. The warmth was unexpected, but appreciated. Rime's respect for him had grown since they'd last seen each other, and he had the feeling it was mutual. But they both knew that the world was bigger than them. Whatever they thought of each other, it paled in comparison to the will of the people. They were still enemies, fresh from battle—and with fewer men than before. Memories wrought in blood weren't quick to fade.

They followed a path along the wall, where the snow had been trodden down. Even with gloves on, Rime's hands were frozen stiff, but he wanted answers and he needed Eirik on his side.

"I've asked quite a few people about your concerns, Rime, and I've been given just as many answers. They might live forever, the blind. Some say they're already dead. But we've killed them together, you and I. So we know they can die. That's what counts. Whether they live ten years or a thousand years is beside the point." Eirik stopped. "Here. The victory."

Rime lifted a hand to the wall and brushed snow away from the carving. It depicted a group of ymlings. A man kneeled before them, hollow-eyed and holding his hands in front of his groin. A blindling. A tall woman with upturned palms stood next to him, a sword floating over one of her hands, a flower over the other. She might have been a goddess, or a councillor. It was difficult to say. The one thing Rime was sure of was the figure hovering above the others. His arms were outstretched, his fingers splayed like feathers. Wings. He was the Seer. The victor. God.

"Do you know who this is?" Rime pointed at the kneeling blindling. Red lines crossed his back.

"The learned say he represents the blind," Eirik replied. "That we shouldn't think of him as a specific individual."

"They're wrong, Eirik. He existed. He was their leader."

"The elders agree. Those old enough to sneer at the learned." Eirik chuckled and crossed his arms over his chest. His jacket was in danger of splitting across his shoulders. "Listen, we're not stupid, Rime. I know you're angry, that you think the girl left for no reason. But we knew that already, didn't we? Her leaving was never a guarantee that we wouldn't see the deadborn again, no matter what that old sot of a stone whisperer says. Let them rattle on about sorcery and blindcraft until they rot. It's of little help to us. Hirka's not here. The blind are. We need to deal with the problem at hand. War is war."

The chieftain's words rang true, but Rime could hear the concern behind them. Not about the nábyrn, not about the war, but for Rime.

"You don't have to tell me that, Eirik. That's why I'm here. War is war. But it doesn't matter what we do. The deadborn will keep coming. We can fight for our survival, but the war can't be won here. Not in Ym. It can only be won where she is."

The chieftain's eyes softened. "Rime, the elders say the stones have been devouring people since the circles were built, sending them straight to Slokna. What makes you think she's still alive?"

"She's alive."

The chieftain rubbed his bad shoulder. It was easy to read the doubt in his eyes. Rime grabbed hold of him. "She's alive, Eirik, and like I said, she can do what none of us can! She can open the gateways. Hlosnian calls it traveler's blood. You need to listen to what I'm saying. She's alive, and she's the key to the war we both know is coming."

Rime could hear the chaos of his words. How they were coming out in the wrong order and making no sense. He sounded like a madman. He needed to think like Kolkagga. He needed to set his feelings aside. He needed to be a councillor. Ravenbearer.

"Eirik, the nábyrn live for a long time. The deadborn coming for us now are the same ones that came a thousand years ago. The Seer saved us from his own people. And he closed the raven rings so they would never come back."

Eirik chuckled again. "The men got a real kick out of your letter. The Seer you said doesn't exist, does exist after all. Is that what you're saying, An-Elderin?"

Rime slammed his palm against the image carved into the rock, dislodging more snow. "He's alive! And the man kneeling before him is alive. They're not just symbols or legends. They have names. Graal and Naiell. They were brothers—deadborn brothers who fought side by side."

"Listen," Eirik replied, pulling Rime into the middle of the hollow, over to the idol. "We still make sacrifices here, just as our ancestors did, and their ancestors before them. Slokna is full of people who have sacrificed their own blood and the blood of others to the stones. So maybe you're right. A lot of the people I've talked to think that's how it started. People gave blood to the stones to open them, to let people—and who knows what else—in and out. I'd have said it was nonsense if I hadn't seen what I've seen. But we can't fight something we can't see. Or get to."

"We can get to them! Urd talked to Graal, and I can do the same. I can stop him." Rime was chilled by his own words. Maybe he hadn't realized until just then how far he was willing to go.

"Rime, call me crazy, but if these stories are true, I'd say you're worrying about the wrong man. It's not the enemy who's lost the most you should fear—it's the one who still has something to lose."

Rime frowned. Eirik's words challenged everything he'd believed. He wanted to argue. Graal had lost all that he was. All that he had. He'd been betrayed. Punished, tortured, humiliated—and exiled. What kind of anger would emerge from such seeds? And what would it be like now, after a thousand years? But still …

Eirik kept talking like they were still just discussing stories. Not matters of life and death. "If the blindling turned on his own people to gain absolute power over the eleven kingdoms, I'd bet they're hardly singing his praises. In which case, he has every reason to be pissing himself now that the blind are returning—whether he's here or not."

"He's where she is."

"The Seer?"

"The Seer is where she is."

Eirik raised a bushy eyebrow. "So what you're saying is that the one with the greatest incentive to keep the gateways closed is with the girl who can open them?"

Rime closed his eyes. The chieftain's words were sharp as knives. He said it as it was, more plainly than Rime had dared say it himself. He nodded.

"Hmm … So let's hope you've lost your mind and that all this is nonsense, Ravenbearer! If not, it's bad news for the girl. And gods help me, but I liked her. She had real backbone, solid as a rock."

Eirik patted Rime's shoulder and led him back through the chasm. "Mannfalla's taken its toll on you, Rime. You're pale as a blindling. Luckily that's nothing that can't be cured with ale and a good night's sleep. Everything will seem better tomorrow."

Eirik's words reminded Rime of his other errand. He fell into step beside the chieftain. "Eirik, I'm here on behalf of Eisvaldr, to offer you a place on the Council." Rime had repeated the words to himself several times, but now they just sounded hollow. Eirik stopped.

"On behalf of Eisvaldr, you say? They sent you?"

"I'm the Ravenbearer. I don't need to be sent."

"No, I suppose not. And I know you mean well. So thanks, but no thanks. I have enough chairs here. I don't need another one in Mannfalla."

Rime had been prepared for him to say that. "Do you remember the last time I was here, Eirik? I fought Tein. Your son. Do you remember what you said to me afterward?"

"I remember." Eirik looked embarrassed but continued. "I said that if you were Mannfalla, I'd follow you."

Rime stepped closer and looked the chieftain square in his bright blue eyes. "Now I am Mannfalla, Eirik. I need you there. The eleven kingdoms need you there. That's why you'll say yes tomorrow."

Eirik laughed, but he didn't protest.

A black cloud appeared above them. A croaking chorus on wings. The ravens were coming home, as they did every evening. As they'd done since the world was born. And as they'd probably continue to do long after everyone was dead. Some of them danced in pairs, as was their wont in mid-Helfmona. Spring would soon be upon them, and with it, the celebration of Egga, of egg-laying and new ravens. Life went on.

But not for Rime.

Somewhere, on the other side of the stones, Hirka was surrounded by traitors. Deadborn monsters. He needed to find her. He'd promised he would, and Rime was Kolkagga. He kept his promises. And Damayanti was going to help him.

Rime slept fitfully, drifting in and out of dreams. Hirka lured him up a bare tree, asking him to come to her. He wanted to, but the trunk was slippery and cold as glass. It grew as he tried to climb, cutting his hands. She got smaller and smaller, disappearing up into the gray sky. The smell of death hung in the air. Smoke. Ash.

It started to rain. The water washed the dirt from his face. Made the tree trunk even more slippery. He slid down. Blood poured from his hands. The rain turned to sand. Black sand, like in an hourglass. It poured and poured, thundering against the ground. An intolerable noise. Hirka was standing high up in the tree, arms outstretched. She was going to jump.

No! Don't do it! He reached out to stop her, but no matter how he tried he couldn't reach her. She smiled. Then she fell backward and plunged deep into the sea of mud and sand.

Rime jerked awake. He reached back and gripped the hilt of his sword, which was sticking out from under his pillow. He'd heard something. He kept his breathing deep and even so as not to tip off the intruder. He stared into the darkness. There was movement behind the door.

Amateurs. They haven't even made it inside.

He got up without a sound and arranged his bedding so it would look like he was still lying there. Then he pulled himself up onto a rafter, just as the door cracked open. A black figure entered. Even a rock would have heard him coming. One thing was for certain—he wasn't Kolkagga.

The figure was wearing a frost-encrusted fur jacket that creaked with every movement. He padded uncertainly toward the bed holding a knife out in front of him. Clumsy. Wide open to attack. Was this the standard of assassins in Ravnhov? Rime caught himself hoping his services hadn't cost much. Would the man even get up the nerve to attack? Or was he here to rob him?

He didn't have to wait long to find out. The figure threw himself at the bed, knife-first, and barely suppressed a gasp when he realized no one was there. Rime drew on the Might, jumped down, and slammed the door shut. He wasn't going to let his assassin escape.

The stranger whirled around, his eyes shining with terror in the darkness. Rime's anger swelled with the Might. If they were going to kill him, the least they could do was put some effort into it.

Rime moved his arms to his sides, exposing his bare chest to give the man a false sense of security. "What have they promised you in return for killing the Ravenbearer?" The man swallowed in response. Rime waited. Realization would soon dawn in the stranger's eyes. The certainty that only one of them would leave the room alive. The man's gaze faltered.

There. He understands.

The man raised the knife and came at him. Rime intercepted him and sent him careening into the wall. He dropped like a stone, knocking over a stool and flailing on the floor. Rime could have killed him in an instant, but he needed to know who had sent him.

The man let out a groan but was back on his feet surprisingly fast. Fuelled by panic. Rime could hear the blood roaring in his ears. This was what he was trained for.

The man came at him again, knife held far out in front of him. Still completely open to attack. Rime swung his sword into the man's side. He screamed and fell onto the bed. Rime flung his sword aside and jumped on top of him. He wrested the knife from the man and clamped a hand over his mouth, muffling his screams.

They lay face to face in the bed, like man and wife. Rime felt hot blood against his skin and smiled in the knowledge that it wasn't his own. He plunged the knife into the side of the man beneath him. Screams and spittle forced their way between his fingers. The man wrenched his head back but couldn't break free.

"Shhh ..." Rime whispered in his ear, holding him tight. The man quieted down, only the occasional muffled sob pushing past his hand now.

"I'll give you a choice," Rime said quietly. "Death has come for you. You can either rest in Slokna, or face an eternal nightmare. It's up to you." The man stared at him, his eyes wet and disbelieving. Terrified.

"Tell me, who sent you?" Rime waited a moment for an answer. None was forthcoming. He twisted the knife deeper into the wound. The man tensed beneath him like a lover. "Who?" he asked again.

"Dark ..." Rime lifted his hand just enough for him to get the word out. "Darkdaggar."

As he'd suspected. The Council.

"Are you alone? Are there more of you?"

The man shook his head frantically. His breath was making Rime's hand clammy.

"Sleep it is, then." Rime pulled the knife out and plunged it into the man's heart before he could so much as groan. He died instantly. Blood pumped out between Rime's fingers. Death. Not politics. He was no ravenbearer. No councillor. This was what he was. An assassin. He wasn't made to sit at a table playing war games. He was Kolkagga. A destroyer.

Rime dragged the man's body outside and into the courtyard. His head thudded down the stone steps. People had been woken up. Two night watchmen came running. Shouting. A woman appeared with a lamp. She put a hand over her mouth. Eirik moved past her, walking at first, but then he started to run.

The chieftain stopped in front of the body, his breath dancing in the air around his mouth. The realization of what had happened was written in his eyes. Eirik lifted both hands, as if to ward off a catastrophe. "Rime, he's not one of us. No one here would …"

Rime had only seen the chieftain afraid once before. When he had fought his son, Tein, right where they were standing now. Back then, Hirka had stopped him from dealing the death blow. But she wasn't here now.

"I know," Rime replied. He could hear the ice in his own voice. The coldness keeping him alive. The Might wouldn't release its hold on him. It filled him, defined him—made him feel as if he were born of the frost.

"So who is he? Who wants to kill you?"

"The Council." Rime shook the blood from the knife.

"They want to kill you? Here, in Ravnhov?"

Rime smiled coldly. "Where better? That way Ravnhov gets the blame."

Eirik stared at him as if looking into the abyss that was Mannfalla for the very first time. He put a hand on Rime's shoulder. It burned against his skin.

"You said it yourself, Eirik. The enemy with the most to lose is the one to fear."

The chieftain's household was well and truly awake. People thronged together in the dark. Blue figures in a blue night, with lamps and shawls. As the chieftain's wife wrapped a blanket around Rime, he belatedly realized he was naked. And covered in blood. But it didn't matter. It was high time Ravnhov saw Mannfalla disrobed.

Rime raised his voice. "Eirik Viljarsón, I have an empty chair at the council table in Eisvaldr. It's the most dangerous chair in the eleven kingdoms, and it belongs to you. It belongs to Ravnhov. Will you take it?"

People looked at each other. Whispered among themselves. Someone shouted "yes!" Rime spotted someone he knew among them. Tein. The chieftain's son came forward and stood next to his father. "We'll take it," he said.

Eirik sighed. Ravnhov had spoken. He looked at Rime. "So what are you going to do?"

Rime put the knife back in the dead man's sheath, where it belonged.

"What I do best," he replied.

HALF-BLINDLING

Stars filled the night sky. Hirka almost lost her balance as she wrapped the blanket around herself. She grabbed on to the trunk to stop herself from falling. What kind of idiot climbed a tree in the middle of the night? With a blanket? In the winter?

A half-blindling—half-human, half-deadborn.

She tried to get comfortable in the small hollow where the trunk forked. She had her bag next to her, though she wasn't sure why. She wasn't planning on going anywhere. Still, it was reassuring to know she could run. If she had to.

Sometimes being with Stefan and Naiell all got a bit much. They were both so strange, but in very different ways. They weren't three people who would ordinarily mix. The only reason they were there at all was because of her.

She pulled out her notebook and found her most recent entries. Where to start? There was no way she could remember all the words she'd learned. Maybe that was a good sign. Maybe it meant she could speak so well now that she didn't need to write everything down. But there was one thing she remembered.

Blood bag.

She wrote it down. It looked so ugly on paper. Even the shape of the letters made it look horrible—a promise of impending pain. How was she to describe it? A container? A waterskin? An expendable life, created for the benefit of someone else?

Those were the words they'd used. Stefan and Naiell. Easy for them to say. At least they were still able to sleep. She looked over at the hotel. It was in the center of Stockholm, so she'd had to cross the road to reach the park. Wrapped in her blanket. Cars had whistled at her, and she'd kicked at them as they roared off.

She could see her footsteps in the snow. They were reassuring, in a way. They were proof she existed. She flipped back in her notebook. Found some old drawings of plants she'd seen back when she'd been staying in the church.

Rosemary. Herb. No one knows what it does.

Tomato. Used for sauces. Meant to be healthy, but no one knows what it does.

Lilac. Decorative tree. No one knows what it does.

Nobody she'd asked had been able to tell her anything about plants. How could it be possible to live in a world you didn't know? Eat food without having any idea where it came from? She knew far from everything about Ym, but at least she knew how to survive. And what the plants did.

She continued flipping through the notebook and came across a map she'd drawn. There was the church, with small crosses marking the churchyard. The route to the shop. To the greenhouse. A desperate attempt to find her footing. To make sense of the world around her. Of where she was.

She closed the notebook. If she kept going, she'd reach her early entries. Words and experiences she'd wanted to share with Rime. But that would never happen now.

She'd left him. Come here, to this nightmare straight out of Slokna, to make sure he'd be safe. To make sure she'd be safe. But there was no safety here or in any world. Not as long as she was a blood bag. A living breathing threat who was meant to die so that others could break their chains and bring Ym to its knees.

She pulled the blanket tighter. How would he do it? Would she be hung upside down like a slaughtered animal, while the life drained out of her veins and into someone else? Blindcraft!

And what would Graal do then? Was anyone back home safe? Would Mannfalla burn? Ravnhov?

No! She had the book. It was clear that he needed it, even though it made no sense to her. Even though the three of them didn't know what the uniform lines were meant to depict. It wasn't any kind of language. There were no sentences. Just page after page of randomly placed circles and lines. But at least they had it. Not Graal.

Graal? Father? No. She had only one father, and she remembered him sitting in his wheeled chair by the hearth. Back home in Elveroa. Where every day she woke up and fell asleep to the sound of the sea. Here there was only noise. Father knew what it meant to be an outsider. So much so that he'd taken his own life, for her. It hurt to think about it. It would always hurt.

She ran her tongue along her teeth, remembering the morning after she'd found out who she was. She'd leaned over the river's edge and looked at her own reflection. She'd thought that her canines looked a little sharp. As if she'd turned into a wild animal overnight.

They *were* a little sharp, though. Was it her blindling blood? She thought about her sense of smell. About how well she could see in the dark. All the little things she'd thought she just did a bit differently than other people. Signs that she was a deadborn. Nábyrn. What else didn't she know about herself?

I'm not scared!

She stared down at the compass attached to the front of her notebook. The needle pointed north. It always would. Even if she was spun around until she was dizzy. Even if the cars whizzed past and blinded her with their lights.

The strange thing was, she preferred being a blood bag to just being a child of Odin. Of course it made her hair stand on end just thinking about it, but at least now there was a good reason for it.

Being hunted simply because she didn't belong—that was so senseless. So impossible to fight. Now she had something. Something of value, something others needed. Something they hunted and killed for. She had to remember that.

Anyway, being half-blindling wasn't a death sentence. At least she was *someone*. She was descended from the blindling who had shaped the entire history of Ym. That made her far from a nobody.

And this from the girl who'd always envied Rime's roots. His family tree, which could be traced back to the first An-Elderin, the warrior who had marched into Blindból. A family tree of a thousand measly years wasn't much, was it? She had a father who was nearly three thousand years old! Sure, a monstrous one who thirsted for blood and revenge, but she wasn't a nobody. She was Hirka. She could fix this. At least now she knew what he was after. Why he needed her.

Naiell had said Graal's blood was ruined. Scorched. So he could never escape this world. His prison. She'd seized on that, protesting that she would have inherited the same ruined blood.

The moment she'd said it, she realized that she'd long since disproved that claim. She was here. She'd already traveled through the gateways. And survived.

Whatever sort of blindcraft they'd subjected him to, it hadn't been passed down. And right now that made her as attractive to Graal as water to someone lost in the desert. That was how Stefan put it, but he could be wrong. He'd also said that people had been to the moon, so clearly his judgement wasn't exactly reliable.

Knowing that Graal needed her gave her power. She couldn't control what he or the forgotten did, but she could control what she did. She had power over her own life. Would she be prepared to do what Father had done? Sacrifice her life to prevent Graal from reaching Ym? From reaching Rime?

She felt a lump growing in her throat. Her hands were like ice.

No! I won't let that happen!

It would never come to that. Graal had found a way of getting her through the gateways as an infant, a newborn. And alone. Who knew, maybe it wasn't as hard to send a child through. In any case, there had to be a way of doing it again. She didn't need to sit here rotting in a dying world, a world she neither understood nor liked, while the blind took over the only world she could call home. Ym needed her. She had to find a way back. And she knew someone who could help.

Hirka jumped down from the tree. Rolled up the blanket and flung it over her shoulder along with her bag. Tomorrow she'd talk to Stefan, explain to him what they had to do. He wouldn't like it, but that couldn't be helped. The forgotten were the only ones who knew where Graal could be found. They knew his weaknesses. And they were no longer his friends. He'd discarded them.

And if they refused to help, she could compel them. Now that she had something they needed. Now that she knew she had the same blood as Graal.

THE CHALLENGE

The front door to the Darkdaggar family home was clad with rusted steel, perforated with small crosses through which the underlying wood could be seen. Rime had been there as a boy, for a gathering he barely remembered. The Darkdaggars were experts on the law—cold, calculating bureaucrats—but then, the same could be said of everyone in Eisvaldr.

Rime rapped the door knocker three times, all the while reminding himself to think with his head and not with his heart. Anger would have to wait. This was bigger than him.

He adjusted his grip on the heavy stone slab tucked under his arm.

A servant opened the door. He was young, but he recognized Rime straight away. He bowed. "Rime-fadri. Ravenbearer. Welcome." Rime thanked him and stepped inside. The boy seemed unsure of what to do next. He started to lead the way but then clearly decided it was wrong of him to be walking ahead of the Ravenbearer. He dropped back to Rime's side and gestured up a staircase. "Would you like to speak to Garm-fadri? Or is it …" He looked down at the stone slab Rime was carrying. "Would you … could I take that for you?"

"No, thank you. Where can I find Garm?"

The boy started to sweat. Rime understood his dilemma. He couldn't ask a ravenbearer to wait, but he also couldn't send him upstairs without notifying his master. Rime didn't wait for a reply. He started up the stairs with the boy at his heels.

On the second floor, a door stood ajar. Rime pushed it open and went in. Garm looked up from a sloping desk. Rime hadn't told anyone that he was back from Ravnhov—least of all Garm Darkdaggar. He'd hoped to see him lose his composure when he came in, but if Garm was surprised, he hid it well. Presumably he'd expected to hear from the assassin a long time ago. No news was bad news. Garm had known that Rime was still alive.

The servant came in behind him. "Garm-fadri. Rime-fadri is here. The Ravenbearer."

"Thank you, I can see that," Garm replied dryly. The servant nodded and withdrew.

The room was rectangular and well lit. The long wall behind Garm was fitted with tall windows grouped in threes. The walls were covered in maps from all of Ym—towns, regions, rivers.

Garm got up, putting down his pen. It rolled down the sloped desk and clattered to the floor. He let it lie.

"So how was Ravnhov?" he asked coolly.

"Enlightening," Rime replied. He didn't have time for intrigues, for this game. He'd never had time for it.

He threw down the stone slab. It thudded onto the floor. Garm stared at his own name. *Darkdaggar.* Golden letters engraved in stone. He closed his eyes for a moment. Rime smiled. The mask had slipped. Garm had lost, and he knew it. The lines running from either side of his nose to the corners of his mouth seemed to deepen as Rime looked on. His short, blond hair was almost indistinguishable from his scalp, and had it not been for that, Rime could have sworn it would have turned white in that moment.

"What have you done?" Garm whispered.

"Not me. Two stonecutters. It left an ugly scar in the Council table, but better a scar than your name."

"You can't … for centuries it—"

"I can, and I have," Rime interrupted.

"No one will accept this. No one will let you do this. You have no grounds, boy."

Rime drew his sword. Garm backed into his desk and gaped.

"Are we really going to play this game, Garm? Are you going to deny it? To say it wasn't you so I can say it was, over and over until someone separates us as if we were squabbling children?" Rime prodded the embroidery on the councillor's chest with the tip of his sword.

Garm collected himself. "What will people think? Someone tried to kill you in Ravnhov, yet you're blaming your own? You have no proof. People will think you've lost your mind—and they wouldn't be wrong."

"So live and let live? Carry on like nothing has happened? Sit together at the table until you find another opportunity to kill me? You know, I think we all have more to gain from me killing you first." Rime jabbed Garm with the blade and he fell to the floor, where he started dragging himself back toward the window.

"Get up," Rime said. "Get up and find a sword to defend yourself."

"Sword?" Garm sounded confused, like he'd never owned such a thing in his life. "Think about what you're doing, Rime! I'm not the only person you've threatened. You're a threat to the entire Council. They'll make sure you're punished if you do this, if you kill me in cold blood. You'll lose your chair. There will be an uproar! Even *we* can't kill each other without punishment. And you're Kolkagga! What chance do you think I stand?"

"You should have considered that before," Rime replied. But he knew Garm had a point. If they were going to do this, it couldn't be done behind closed doors. The Council had done far too much behind closed doors. If they were going to do this, it had to be done where everyone could see and hear. Rime loomed over Garm.

"I'll give you a choice: die here and now, or find someone to die for you. I'll fight whatever and whoever. The result will be the same regardless. When I win, you'll admit your guilt and take your punishment like a man. All of Mannfalla will bear witness. No secrets. Everyone will see."

Garm clambered to his feet and brushed the dust from his robes. "So we're regressing to the time of the berserkers? The first duel in living memory?"

Rime smiled. "The first? I was challenged to a duel in Ravnhov less than a year ago, by Tein, the chieftain's son. Hirka stopped me from killing him so no one would win and peace could be preserved."

"Clever girl. You should try listening to her."

Rime leaned closer to Garm, so close that he could smell the sweat on his brow.

"But she's not here anymore, is she?" he said through clenched teeth.

Garm swallowed. "What's worse? Someone wanting to kill you, or not having her here to stop you from killing?"

Rime didn't reply. He turned and headed for the door, stepping demonstratively over the stone slab.

Garm shouted after him. "And what if you don't win? What then, boy? How am I to defend myself against an enraged crowd? What if you die?"

Rime turned toward him again. "That won't happen. I'm not the dying type. I'd have thought you'd noticed that by now."

He sheathed his sword and left the councillor with his maps of the world and a name that would nevermore hold sway over it.

THE ALLIANCE

Graal dropped down from the roof, landing on the balcony. He looked into the bathroom. There was marble everywhere, with gold accents. Expensive. Classic. Right down to the claw-foot tub, which was as ridiculous now as the first time he'd seen one. That had to be over two hundred years ago.

Allegra stood over the sink, washing her hands with liquid soap. He caught the smell of lemon through the open door. Subtle, not overpowering, as soaps so often were. Not to mention sanitary wipes. Small chemical bombs for everyday use. Humans had yet to learn about correlations.

She was a slender woman of about fifty. Dressed in gray high-waisted trousers and a white silk blouse. Another classic look. For a moment he recognized himself in this woman. He'd also learned the rules of the game once upon a time. Presentation. Power. She piqued his curiosity, and that pleased him. What would he have done if they didn't still arouse his curiosity?

Her hands were covered in fine lines, like they'd shrunk a little and forgotten to take the skin with them. Watching people age was fascinating. They were so impotent. So ignorant. They raged against nature's onslaught, despite their lives being twice as long now as when he'd first arrived. And they did look better, there was no denying that.

Allegra dried her hands and opened a small box. It was filled with crushed ice. He knew what else it contained before she picked them up. Teeth. Two of them. She held them up to the light. Then she leaned toward the mirror and studied her face.

Graal cocked his head and smiled. He wondered what she was thinking about. Maybe her hair, which no one could call blond anymore. It was gray. She could have dyed it, but something told him she'd consider that an even greater defeat.

She pulled a pair of pliers from a drawer, a vulgar tool in her hands, and clamped them around one of the teeth. Graal heard a crack as the tooth split over the lid of the box. Clearly she was afraid of wasting something.

He pushed open the door. It didn't make a sound. She was fiddling with the tooth and still hadn't seen him. The wind caught the curtains. They danced in front of him like veils. An unpredictable beauty. He stepped inside.

Allegra looked up at the mirror. Saw him. Spun around with a gasp. Her hands fumbled for the counter and gripped the pliers. He remained where he was, giving her time to overcome her panic and realize that she didn't stand a chance. It didn't take long.

She let go of the pliers. They fell to the floor as if in slow motion, striking a tile and chipping its corner. More incidental beauty. Mathematical perfection. Circumstantial symphony.

She glanced at the mirror, as if to check that she could still see him there. Myths. Layer upon layer of stories that influenced people's behavior, without them realizing how deep the roots went.

He stepped closer. "Did you know that during the Renaissance, women would apply that directly to their skin?"

She gave a start at the sound of his voice. The corner of her mouth was quivering. He continued as he looked around the room. "It kept them young, and pale. Until the skin flaked off, of course. A few hundred years later, they discovered that putting it in cream helped. A little."

Her eyes settled on the broken tooth in the lid.

He stopped in front of her. "But you don't use it for that, do you?" Her eyes searched for somewhere to land. He did her the favor of taking off his sunglasses. He folded them up and put them in his vest pocket. "Do I have to take out the contacts as well, or can we consider ourselves introduced?" He smiled. So that she understood. He hadn't been sure how much she actually knew. It was difficult to be sure with humans. They could know things without knowing them. Hear without listening.

He picked up one half of the tooth from the lid. Her hand twitched. Fear couldn't suppress the instinct. She would protect what she owned.

"You don't need to be scared, Allegra. Yes, I am the origin, but I'm not one of ... what is it you call them? The forgotten? A rather hurtful term, I must admit. It makes it sound as if the responsibility for their choices rests on my shoulders. But I can live with that. For a long time." He looked at her to see whether she got the joke, but she gave no reaction.

"This tooth belonged to a human who was once my friend," he said, turning it in his fingers. It looked malformed due to a small abscess that had grown near the root. He couldn't be sure who it belonged to. It could have been anyone. One acquired quite a few friends over the course of a thousand years. Luckily, few of them were still alive. Most of them succumbed as soon as they were cut off from him. To madness. Longing. Rot. Or they were taken out by hunters, as was the case with the owner of this tooth. It belonged to someone he'd once shared his blood with. Blood of the first. Dreyri.

Blood like that couldn't be repressed. It wreaked havoc on the human body. Kept it going when it would otherwise have given up. Kept it alive. *Sorcery*, people used to call it. *Witchcraft. Magic.* But it was so much simpler than that. And so much more compelling. It was nature.

The blood triggered a dormant process in humans. It forced new blood forth, into the gums. Vessels forced their way into the canines and started to grow. You could tell from the tooth how much time had passed since the rebirth. This abscess was still small. No more than thirty years had passed. Had the forgotten lived longer, it would have continued growing. After fifty years the old teeth would crack and new ones would grow out. That was usually when the trouble started.

But until then, the old tooth was full of life. Potency. Unbridled power.

He looked at Allegra. Her eyes were shining, but she'd raised her chin in a show of strength. He put the tooth back on the lid. "Had it not been so young, it could have been a relative of yours. Someone I once knew. But neither you nor your parents were born then."

"Sanuto ..." she whispered.

It was the first word she'd said since he'd come in.

"Yes. Poetic choice of name, I must say." He leaned closer. She stood transfixed. Her face had already softened like a young girl's. A lover's. He got such immense joy out of this process. Of seeing the change in their eyes. Love. Humanity's greatest strength. And weakness.

He looked past her at his own reflection. His black hair was less untamed than usual. His eyes were turned down at the corners, and he'd heard it made him look sad. Humans thought he was beautiful. He had no opinion on the matter. He didn't see beauty in the same way as them. But unlike them, he would never have to stand like that, looking for wrinkles. Gray hair. Signs of slow death.

He looked at her. Ran his finger over her cheek. Traced the crow's feet around her eyes with his claw. "But you don't use them for wrinkles, do you? You're not the type. You use them because they keep you bleeding."

She flushed red. He put a hand on her stomach. She gave a start, but then pressed herself against him. "And as long as you bleed, you can still have children."

She nodded, as if he'd asked for confirmation. He whispered in her ear. "And when you pay people to kill, to rip the teeth out of their lifeless jaws, it's because you're so overflowing with love that all you want is someone to give it to, right?"

"Yes …" she whispered back. A blatant lie.

He wrapped his hand around her throat. Pressed his thumb up against her chin, forcing her head back. "Love, you say? It has nothing to do with your husband? His illness, and his imminent death? I heard a rumor, you see, that his youngest stands to inherit most of his estate. And you've never particularly gotten along with her, have you?"

He let go of her. She stumbled back, gasping for air.

He took a step back and waited until she straightened up again.

"I'm not judging you," he said. "I've heard countless motives, and yours is far from the worst. I don't mind that you buy and sell them. Or that you use them. But tell me, did you think that all you needed to do was find me and then you'd suddenly have eternal life? Did you think this was a gift I bestowed on everyone?"

She shook her head. "I'm willing to earn it. I always have been. I just didn't believe—"

"That I actually existed?"

She didn't need to answer.

"Well, now you know. Now that the smell of my brother fills your home. Now that you've seen us." He could tell it frightened her that he knew.

"Well, Allegra. You're fortunate. You're one of few who is actually in a position to earn the eternal life of a blood slave that you so desperately desire." He lifted a towel from a gold hook. Held it to his nose and breathed in. Thousands of different scents. Natural. Artificial. Human. He let it go again.

"Your hunter, he has something I want. And you're going to help me find it, aren't you?"

Allegra nodded. "Tell me what to do and I'll do it."

"Of course you will. And it's not difficult. All you have to do is talk."

"What do I have to say?"

Graal felt his body tingling. There was so much life in such willingness. It was enough to make you cry. And she wasn't the first. Fear of death was the greatest motivation of all.

"Let me pose a question. Imagine I were to destroy humankind. Every single man and woman. Every single child. Your friends. Your family. Everyone. And you knew that was what I was planning to do. To destroy the world as you know it—or at least that's how it would feel."

He walked around the tub as he talked. Ran his fingers over the smooth enamel. "Under such circumstances, what would it take ... for you to help me?"

The corners of her mouth twitched. She was struggling to maintain control, and he realized that he'd painted far too vivid a picture. He moved back toward her.

"It's purely hypothetical. Neither you nor humankind need be concerned. Use your imagination. What would it take?"

"I suppose ... if I believed there was no hope? And if I ..." She turned away and looked at him in the mirror. "If I hated them. All of them."

He smiled. "Yes. That's what I thought, too."

BLOOD AND SNOW

The stone circle was an island in the sea of people. Every soul in Mannfalla had braved the snow and wind to trudge inside the wall separating Eisvaldr from Mannfalla. The city of the Council from the city of the people. They thronged together, around the stone circle that had been hidden in the walls of the Rite Hall for a thousand years. But the Rite Hall was no more. Only the stones remained under the open sky, the tiled floor between them decorated with faded motifs of mythical creatures and beings.

The wooden floor protecting it had been taken up for the occasion. The layer of ice that had formed on top of it was hardly conducive to fighting.

Rime stood alone in the middle of the circle, waiting for the man who would soon die. He could only hope it wasn't a hapless guardsman or an innocent boy his own age. He had no desire to take a life that had barely begun for a sin committed by Darkdaggar. And everyone knew what that sin was. What he was accused of. Rime's attempted assassination.

The days of doing things behind closed doors were over.

Three councillors were conspicuous in their absence. Miane Fell, Noldhe Saurpassarid, and Leivlugn Taid. They were distancing themselves from the matter by staying away. This was a step too far for them. What made it worse was that Rime knew they believed him. They knew very well what Darkdaggar had done. But for them it was an opportunity to blame Ravnhov. Not to attack their own.

Rime was becoming quite practiced at attacking his own, and he saw little reason to stop now. One more kill. Blood of an innocent. Then it would be done. Darkdaggar would have to admit his guilt and face the consequences. Expulsion from the Council. Room for new blood. Someone who could keep the eleven kingdoms together while Rime did what he now knew had to be done.

Vendors with trays strapped to their chests pushed between befurred ymlings, selling honey cakes and strips of dried fish. One of them had a little girl in tow. She'd cobbled together a black staff with something that was clearly supposed to be a raven sitting on top. Every so often she banged the staff on the ground to shake the snow off the helpless cloth bird. She smiled at him. Who brought children to watch people die?

To the west of the circle, the guardsmen had cleared a space in the crowd for the Council. Jarladin was standing at the front. And Sigra Kleiv, of course. Had it been up to her, the Council would have solved all its conflicts like this.

Darkdaggar stood with his arms folded across his chest. He didn't look nearly as nervous as Rime would have liked.

The sea of people parted to make room for two guardsmen. Between them walked his opponent. Rime's heart started pounding in his chest. It was time. He drew his sword. His opponent did the same, stopping a couple of steps away from him. He took off his fur cloak and threw it out of the circle.

It was Svarteld.

All the blood drained from Rime's face. He suddenly felt chilled to the bone. This couldn't be happening. How could it be? It was impossible! Darkdaggar had hired a brigand to kill him in Ravnhov. Someone who'd barely touched a knife before. And the reason for that was obvious—he could never have asked Kolkagga. Kolkagga were loyal to Rime. That was one of the reasons why the Council hadn't gotten rid of him ages ago. And even if Garm had been stupid enough to ask, none of the shadows would have betrayed him. Not one of them. Not least his own master.

Rime stared at Svarteld, waiting for him to laugh, to reveal that it was all a sick joke. But Svarteld stayed where he was. Black-clad Kolkagga. Bright eyes in a dark face. There was nothing between them now but dancing snow.

Rime's body felt frozen. Weak. Had his blood turned to dust? Sacrificed for the sake of blindcraft? The man before him was his master. Svarteld had supported him when the Seer had fallen and Urd had brought the blind to Bromfjell. He'd stood by him every single day since he had taken the chair. Svarteld was his friend. But he was also more than that. He was also the one person in Ym who could win this fight.

"So this is how we're doing things now?" Svarteld said. "Brother against brother? Councillor against councillor?" His voice was rough.

"Master ..." Rime took a step closer. On the other side of the circle, the drummer lifted his beater, poised to strike. Soon it would be a matter of life and death.

"You can't do this, Svarteld."

Svarteld's face was cold and resolute. The drum sounded and he swept toward Rime, sword raised. Rime only just reacted in time. He parried a blow. Then another. And another. Their blades sang against each other.

The master circled him. Rime followed his movements. It was quiet around them, with hardly a sound to be heard from the crowd. It occurred to Rime that none of them had ever seen anything like it. Ever. A Ravenbearer against Kolkagga's master. Never before. Never again.

Rime bound the Might. He was going to need it. The people were shut out. The stones around him disappeared. It was just him and his master now. The man who had taught him everything he knew. Rime knew he was the weaker of the two. He couldn't find his balance, couldn't find calm. Shock was weighing him down.

"Do you think this is a game?" Svarteld snarled. "You're too stubborn to accept what is, but too weak to build what could be. Do you think Ym is your plaything? That you can take lives and spare them as you see fit?"

Rime swallowed. "I take lives to spare lives. You taught me that."

"And now I'll teach you about duty!" Svarteld threw himself forward. His reach truly was alarming. Rime felt the Might rend asunder, and only just avoided being cut down before the fight had truly begun.

Duty? What did duty mean when no one understood what you were doing? What did duty matter when those closest to you were against you? Despair sullied the Might. Svarteld would never understand. No one would understand. Rime looked around. A sea of gaping faces surrounded the stone circle. Darkdaggar stood amid the other councillors. He gave Rime a crooked smile from under his white hood.

Rime bared his teeth, tightening his grip on the hilt of his sword. Then came the fury. Finally. This was what he knew. This was what he was good at. To Slokna with them all!

He danced around Svarteld. The master knew him well, parrying all his blows before they landed. Rime would have to lower his defenses to get closer. Risk injury. He let his sword fall, exposing his chest.

He felt the sting in his jaw before he saw the blade. The warmth of blood on his cold skin. Nothing serious. Enough to get close. Rime struck. The tip of his sword dragged across Svarteld's thigh. Red dripped down onto the frozen floor. But Svarteld didn't let it stop him. Rime wouldn't stop either. Not until one of them was dead.

"The war isn't being fought here," Rime panted, feeling fatigued far too soon. He remembered the last time he'd tried to reason with men who were out for blood. Kolkagga. His own. In Blindból. They hadn't wanted to know. The master wouldn't want to either. But what else could he do but try?

"Svarteld, what we do here is pointless. The war against the dead-born is happening where she is. Not here."

"But we're here, Rime. *We* are here! Nowhere else!"

The master came at him, unleashing a volley of violent blows. Rime parried, their blades clanging against each other. He could feel a pain deep within, as if every bone in his body were splintering. He parried the final blow too late and felt a stinging in his shoulder. More serious this time. His shirt had a bloodied tear in it. His hair clung to the blood. He gasped for breath.

Training. This is training. We've done this countless times before.

Rime drew on the Might to suppress the pain. He'd have been able to do more had Hirka been there. Had he been able to channel it through her. What he could do on his own seemed woefully inadequate. He swapped sword arm. The other one wasn't cooperating anymore. Willpower was all he had. All that was keeping him going.

He used the momentum of the sword and spun around. Maneuvers he'd practiced thousands of times. He knew himself. He knew his master.

Raudregn.

Svarteld leaped away. He was sweating now, too. Rime knew what was coming. He would lure Rime into coming in low so he could jump over him and attack from behind. He'd fallen for it before.

Svarteld took a couple of steps to the side, lifting his sword with both hands so that it intersected his face. This was it.

Rime lowered his own sword just enough for Svarteld to think he'd succeeded. Then he readied himself and jumped. Ground turned to sky as he rotated. This maneuver often got the better of him, but not this time. There was too much at stake. And now he knew what he was. He was Kolkagga. This was his master's final test.

Blindring. Perfect.

Rime thrust with his sword. It plunged into Svarteld's back and erupted out of his chest. He managed to pull it out again before the master hit the floor with a groan. Grief pulled Rime to his knees. He rolled Svarteld onto his back. The master looked at him. Without hate. Without regret. He opened his mouth.

"Have you ..." Svarteld gasped for breath. "Have you learned your lesson now? Don't start ... what you can't finish." The master was dying, but Rime couldn't remember ever seeing him more alive.

Blood welled forth. Bubbled out of his mouth. Ran down his neck and spread along the cracks in the floor as if through veins. A red tree nourished by death.

But Rime was alive. He should have been dead, but he was alive. What was it his master had said?

The day I lose to you, it'll be out of love.

Rime watched the life leave Svarteld's eyes as Slokna claimed him. Snow settled on his Kolkagga blacks. Rime somehow managed to stand. He could see people celebrating, waving their hands in the air, clapping, jostling each other as if they'd made illicit wagers. But Rime heard nothing. The Might surged through him, shutting everything else out. He was standing in a pocket of silence. Alone. Among thousands.

He'd stood here before. With her. The wind had torn at her red hair, tangling it with his own white hair. He'd loved her. And hated her.

And now he had to risk everything he had. Everything he was.

For her.

BASTARD

Hirka was woken by a searing pain inside her. She gasped for air. Jolted upright in bed and looked down at her stomach. Nothing. It was nothing. She'd just been lying awkwardly and aggravated the wound. It had healed over nicely, but it was still sore.

Where am I?

Stockholm. Stefan's home. At least that was what he'd said. He had keys, but still, something didn't feel right. Stefan wasn't the type to have a two-story bed. Much less one that was full of stuffed animals.

She climbed down to the floor. She had a strange feeling she wasn't alone. Unfamiliar shapes loomed in the darkness. Things she'd never seen before but that still felt familiar. A pointy tent in one corner. Small animals. A pig. A brown horse on its side. She picked it up. It was smooth to the touch. Fake. She hadn't seen a live horse since she'd come here. Were all their animals fake? What had happened to them?

She thought of Vetle, of his wooden horse that had been claimed by the Stryfe back when the tree had fallen. It made her feel sick. Everything she knew was gone.

Hirka put the horse back on the floor and went into the living room. It felt safe there. Different, but safe. The walls were made of stone, not plastic or glass. Thick beams crossed under the ceiling. Even the rug on the floor was more familiar than other rugs she'd seen. Knotted. Real yarn. The kind of rug that was nice to curl up on. Things smelled right.

The room was tidy. That was one of the things that revealed Stefan's lie. He didn't live here. Stefan didn't read books. There were no ashtrays here, and the shoes in the hall belonged to a woman and a child.

Hirka pulled her shirt down over her stomach. It always rode up when she slept. Her underpants used to do that too, but not anymore. Not here. That was one of the few things she actually liked here. Underpants. They fit perfectly, all on their own. And you could get them in light blue, with a bird on them, like the ones she had on. What a world.

A wall of books divided the living room in two. Hirka peeked into the other half, where Naiell was sleeping. He was lying up in an open loft. On his stomach, on the floor. His back rose and fell as he snored.

He wasn't alone.

Stefan was standing beneath the loft, looking at Naiell's arm, which hung over the edge. His claws were dangling in front of Stefan's face, and he was staring at them as if seeing them for the first time. He just stood there, motionless, his white shirt practically glowing in the dark. That and the bandage around his hand. The hand he was holding his gun in.

Hirka bit her lip. Should she hide? Or say something?

Stefan didn't stand a chance against Naiell. And he had to know that. So why try? And why now? Maybe it had all gotten too much for him. Or was it something else?

Blood.

Hirka stepped into view. Stefan turned toward her. He instinctively went to hide the gun, but then seemed to realize the stupidity of it, so didn't bother. Hirka said nothing. Her body was tingling. She knew what it was. Fight or flight. But Svarteld had taught her that was just a feeling. She wasn't going to give in to it.

It was nothing more than her body's response to the realization that she didn't really know Stefan. He belonged to this world, but he was completely at odds with it. He was running, just like her. He owned next to nothing and had gotten on the last nerves of the people he called friends. Hirka had heard him talking with Nils, and on the phone, always saying it was going to pay off. That he was going to make good on all the favors.

Stefan put the gun back in its holster, which was shoved in the waistband of his trousers. She turned away from him. Went and sat on the end of the sofa, in front of the window.

The window stretched from floor to ceiling and looked like a gaping hole in the wall. She felt like she might stumble through it and plummet into the night, toward all the lights below. Streetlights. Cars. Flashing signs. Only the pattering of the rain on the glass made her feel safe, like there was something between her and the outside world. A thin, see-through layer that kept her from falling down among the humans.

She heard a siren somewhere and tried to filter out everything but the sound of the rain. Stefan hovered by the bookcase for a moment. Then he sat down next to her.

"Can't sleep either?" he said.

He smelled of fresh sweat. It annoyed her that she liked it. She leaned forward so she wouldn't have to look at him, but he did the same. Leaning back again would have been stupid, so she stayed like that. Next to him. Her with her arms resting on her bare thighs, him with his elbows on his knees.

"He's not natural. You do know that, right?" he said quietly.

Hirka looked at him. "Are you? Am I?" She sounded angrier than she'd meant to. "I mean ... he exists. He *is*, you know?" she said with a little more warmth. "And if he exists, he's as natural as either of us. If you were going to kill everything that was different, you'd have to start with me. And yourself."

"Am I so different?"

She looked at him again. Stefan Barone. Twice her age. Thirty, maybe. Unshaven. Nervous. And with that little scar that tugged at his lip. But he was handsome. In a way. Warm brown eyes. Short hair with lighter tips and darker roots. He was strong. Even if he was a bit soft around the middle.

He leaned back and crossed his arms over his stomach. She realized that she'd been staring, so she smiled and looked away.

He nudged her. "Do you feel that?" He held out his wounded hand and wiggled his fingers. Hirka put her thumb to the bandage. Pressed down carefully. "Feel what?"

"That. There's a bump, isn't there?"

Hirka didn't feel a bump. She'd picked out the bits of glass and cleaned the wound herself. She put on her gravest expression. "I think it's a piece of glass. It's deep. Near your blood, I think."

Stefan went white. She managed to hold back her smile. "Stefan, I think it's going to reach your heart soon. It might explode."

She giggled. He swatted her nose. "You're fucking hysterical, you are."

Sometimes it didn't feel real, Stefan being a hunter. He stared down at his lap. "Sometimes it's you or them, you know? You think it's so easy, but you don't know what things are like here. It's kill or be killed. That's why I have it. Understand?"

He was talking about the gun. Joking around had set him at ease, so she tried to meet him halfway. "Can I see?" she asked. He gave her a cheeky look, like he was going to say no, but then pulled out the weapon anyway.

"You did say you wanted a longer knife," he said. "That's what this is. If you treat it right."

She didn't answer, deciding to let him take it where he wanted. "This is the dangerous bit," he continued, pretending not to see her make a face. "If you push this button here, it releases the magazine." He pushed it and removed part of the handle. "The bullets are in the magazine, see? When you clean it, you need to check that the magazine is empty before you pull the trigger." His words were as mechanical as the clicks from the gun. He took her hand and wrapped it around the weapon. "You need to have a firm grip. Put your fingers on the top and pull back the slide. When you get it off, like this, you can clean and oil the grooves here." He put his hand over hers. Raised it, so it looked like they were aiming at the window. Warm hand. Cold steel.

He lowered his arm again, loosened her grip, and put the gun on the table. "Let's do this another time," he mumbled. "It's not important."

She caught his eye again. "What are you going to do if you ever get your hands on him?"

"I don't know," Stefan answered. "If you'd asked me a month ago, I'd have said kill him. But it's starting to feel … weird."

"Weird? Killing someone? That's a relief." She rolled her eyes.

"He is your father, isn't he? That changes things."

"No. Father is dead." She pulled her feet up onto the sofa. They were cold. Stefan put a warm hand on one of them, almost covering it.

"Do you have a father, Stefan?"

He pulled her feet onto his lap and started to rub some warmth into them. She wasn't cold, but she let him do it anyway.

"I used to have one. He was from Sweden. Fell in love with my mom. She was from Torino. That's where I grew up."

"Is that far from here?"

"A couple of hours, if Nils is driving."

Hirka smiled. This world seemed much bigger than hers, yet somehow smaller at the same time.

"So where are they now? Your parents?"

He hesitated for a moment.

"My mom took off when I was nine. She was dying. She said she'd been given a chance at a new life. So she took it. Left me with Dad. She might as well have left me on the street. Dad was weak. A fool who chased an Italian diva halfway around the world. He gave her everything and still thought she cared, you know?"

Hirka let him take his time. Let him open up.

"Well, at least it made Dad take on the only project he ever saw through to the end: a slow death. That's something. The worst part is that for years I thought she'd left to spare him having to watch her die. But that was before I saw her again. Years later. Still young. Still alive. A woman who'd only had months to live."

Hirka's hand flew to her mouth. "She's one of them? One of the forgotten?"

Stefan avoided her gaze. "I walked right past my own mother. She didn't recognize me. So I followed her. Saw her with a man who scared the crap out of me."

He laughed. It sounded painful. "I told the other kids that she'd turned into a vampire. One of the living dead. Let's just say that didn't really help my case. I stuck out enough as it was. Half Italian and half Swedish. And with this lip? A teacher told my dad to take me to see a psychologist."

"A psycho-what?"

"A doctor. For your head. The kind you talk to."

"A healer?"

"Whatever you want to call it, it wasn't my dad's thing, you know? A son who was losing his mind. It all got too much for him. The drink got him in the end. Just like so many other poor sods. Pretty sick, right? And I was left high and dry. With nothing. The apartment was rented. I could have moved in with a family that hated me, but who wants to do that at the age of fifteen?"

"I'd have done it when I was fifteen. If I'd had a family."

"When you were fifteen? You mean last year?"

She kicked him. He grabbed her feet and held them still.

"You should be more careful," he said playfully. "Even the hunters knew I wasn't to be messed with. They'd heard what I told people about Mom, so they told me about the sickness. About the rottenness spreading across the world. So then I became one of them. I've been hunting and killing those rotting bastards since I was your age, so you should watch yourself."

Hirka swallowed. Stefan's smile faded as he realized what he'd said. "You're not one of them, Hirka. You may be his, but that doesn't make you one of them. There's nothing rotten about you, girl. Nothing. Me, on the other hand …"

His hand was trembling against her ankle.

"Why do you never say anything, Hirka? You've seen me snap teeth from the jaws of dead men, but you don't say anything."

"What do you want me to say?"

"Say what you said before, that they're as natural as the two of us. Say that it's reprehensible. That they were once people, too. Tell me I'm a bastard."

Hirka shrugged. "You're a bastard."

His eyes glistened. He slumped forward until his head was resting on the back of the sofa. She put her arm around him. Ran her thumb over his shoulder. "You're a bastard, Stefan. They were once people, too. They're as natural as the two of us. It's reprehensible." It was a relief to say it out loud. She made it sound like she was teasing him, but she knew she meant it.

He groaned and buried his face in the sofa. She looked out at the rain hitting the window. It felt like it was raining inside, too. Tickling her body. Tingling.

She was suddenly hyperaware that Stefan was a man. Had he been able to, Father would have whispered from Slokna. Warned her. But Father had been wrong. She wasn't the rot. The rot was passed through the blood of the blind. Not through love. She knew that now.

Stefan lifted his head and looked at her. The despair grew in his eyes. She wanted to tell him that he didn't have to be afraid. That the feeling that something terrible might happen wasn't real. Nothing was going to happen. Nothing bad.

He looked like he was in pain, but he moved closer to her all the same. His nose next to hers. His stubble against her cheek. He closed his eyes. She didn't. His lips found hers. It felt nice, but wrong at the same time. She let him do it. Maybe for the few things he did right. Maybe for all the things he did wrong.

He wasn't Rime. But did it matter? That his eyes were brown, not pale gray like Rime's?

Wolf eyes.

She was about to pull away, but he beat her to it. His head dropped to his chest.

"I am a bastard," he mumbled into his shirt.

She let him sit there like that. A spot of red had appeared on the bandage around his hand, and she realized that the closeness wasn't nearly as harmless as she'd hoped. The rot was spread through blood. Graal's blood. Could she spread it too? Or was she more human than blindling? She had to know. Had to ask the only people who knew.

"I know how you can make up for being a bastard," she said.

Stefan held his breath. Didn't ask, just listened.

"You can take me back to York. To the hospital. I have to see Father Brody," she lied.

BLINDCRAFT

Don't start something you can't finish.

Svarteld's last words, pumped from the depths of his heart. They ought to have been powerful, ought to have meant something to Rime, but they didn't. Svarteld had never understood what Rime was made of, what drove him.

He'd died for nothing.

Knowing the assembly, Darkdaggar would live on in the pits. Disgraced. Broken. But very much alive. A snake of a man. While Svarteld, strong and fearless ...

Rime walked down the Catgut. It was crowded with people, but he paid them no heed. He bumped into someone but didn't stop to apologize. None of them mattered. These were the people who had thronged together to gape at Rime and his master, wolfing down strips of dried fish as Svarteld bled out on the tiled floor.

Wasn't that why Rime had taken the chair? Wasn't this what he'd wanted to put a stop to? Good men dying so that bad people could carry on living? What had the duel achieved other than confirming an injustice that was and would remain the same?

She'll never forgive me.

Thinking about what Hirka had sacrificed to secure his place was unbearable. All he could do now was try to ensure he didn't make any more mistakes. He rubbed the beak in his pocket. His last hope, and the only way to reach her.

No doubt it would come with a price, but no price was too high. Not anymore.

He opened the door and squeezed into the crowd at Damayanti's, pulling his hood up over his head. That was pretty much all he needed to do to avoid being recognized. It was amazing what people didn't see if they weren't looking. But today the risk was greater. They'd only just seen him skewer Kolkagga's master. Svarteld.

The emptiness yawned in his chest. All the congratulations made it worse. He didn't want to see people, much less listen to them. He couldn't stand to be around anyone.

He went up the stairs and pounded on Damayanti's door. It was opened by the same young girl as before, the one with the blond ponytail and blind eye. She let him in.

"Rime-fadri … congratulations on your victory. I've never—"

"Where is she?"

"Take a seat. I'll fetch her."

He went in. The girl looked at the swords on his back, and he could tell she was considering saying something about them, but then she clearly decided it was wiser not to. She left, and only a few seconds later Damayanti appeared through the beaded curtain. The rattling of the beads was like laughter.

He waited for some sort of flirtatious preamble, or a cheeky comment. One of her usual non-invitations. He sincerely hoped she'd try it, so he could have the pleasure of interrupting her. Snapping at her.

Damayanti came toward him. She was wearing a skirt of clinking chainmail rings. Apart from that she was naked, covered only by body paint that transformed her into a walking skeleton. It was probably some warped way of celebrating the duel.

She laid a hand on his chest. "It isn't victory that I see in your eyes," she whispered.

He took her hand and pressed the raven beak into it. "Help me."

She looked troubled. She turned her back on him. It was painted black, like she was hollow inside. "You want to take the beak?"

"I know you can do it. And you will help me. I'm not here to ask nicely, or to discuss it. I need to get to her, and you're going to make it happen. Blindcraft or not."

The curtain rattled again. Two young boys swept past along the corridor, arm in arm.

"Not here," she said. "Wait for me."

She disappeared behind the curtain. Rime stood where he was, concentrating on the weight of his swords. The weight of what he was about to do.

She soon returned wearing more clothes than he could ever remember seeing her in. Trousers, a tunic, and a fur-lined cloak that concealed her figure. "Come. I've told them I won't be dancing this evening."

He followed her out, down the stairs and through the sweaty crowd. Someone shouted her name as they passed, but she nudged him onward, out onto the street, where everything was cold and quiet. The wind played with a thin layer of snow, which collected in the cracks between the cobbles.

"We need somewhere you can rest afterward. Can we go to yours?"

Rime thought about Prete and the rest of the servants. Uncle Dankan and his children. It suddenly occurred to him that he hadn't seen them in weeks. The An-Elderin family home was more theirs than his now. He shook his head. "No, but I know where we can go."

He adjusted his cloak and pulled her after him through the alleyways, past the taverns and the sound of men drinking themselves into a state of exuberance.

Lindri's looked deserted. The river was high, almost covering the poles the teahouse rested on. Rime opened the door and ushered

Damayanti inside. Lindri was the only person there. He was throwing a log on the fire. He looked up. "Rime-fadri ..."

"I need a favor, Lindri. You have a room, right? The one Hirka used?"

Lindri's eyes shifted between him and Damayanti, and Rime suddenly realized how wrong it looked. "I'm asking because I have no other choice. And because I trust you. This isn't what it looks like."

Lindri made no attempt to hide his disappointment. "You should be mindful of the company you keep," he said.

Rime seized on the opportunity to deaden the pain with anger. "Be careful what you accuse me of, Lindri."

Lindri rearranged the logs using a poker. "I was talking to her, Rime-fadri."

Rime felt like he'd been punched. Lindri looked at Damayanti. "The last friend he brought in here died amid the stones this morning." The tea merchant gave a tentative smile. Rime's jaw clenched. Not with all the time in the world would he have been able to explain this. Not to anyone. Not even to himself.

Damayanti gripped his arm. "Really?" she whispered. "Here? You want to do this here?"

Rime shook himself free. "Lindri, listen to me. Hirka's not safe. I'm not here to betray her. I'm here because I need somewhere I can be without anyone knowing."

"For a day or two," Damayanti said. "And I won't be here, if that's any consolation, old man. You needn't worry about me turning this place into a whorehouse."

"It's been called worse," Lindri replied. "The rot house, I've heard. I don't think you could drag it down any farther, young lady."

Rime looked around. Apart from Lindri, they were alone. On a day like this, after a duel like that, the teahouse ought to have been packed. Clearly word had spread that the child of Odin had stayed here.

Lindri waved them into the backroom and led them up a stepladder. "A friend of mine from Himlifall says things will get better. He says they'll forget all about her soon." Lindri opened a door. "But then, he's never met her."

Rime knew all too well what he meant. Forgetting wasn't an option. He'd tried.

Lindri gestured into the room. It was small, with a bench that doubled as a bed and a peephatch looking out across the annex below. Snow had settled on the window ledge. Wooden boxes and burlap sacks were stacked along the walls. There was a smell of tea and spices. "It's just a storeroom, nothing much, certainly not what you're accustomed to, Rime-fadri."

"I'm used to a straw mat on a floor in Blindból, Lindri. I haven't been an An-Elderin since I was fifteen."

Lindri opened his mouth but then closed it again, apparently deciding he was better off not pointing out that only four years had passed since then. The old man stepped aside and let them in. "There are a couple of blankets in that box there. I normally leave them out for patrons, but ..."

Rime understood. There weren't any patrons to use them.

"I'll get you something to eat. I have smoked trout and pickled onions."

"That won't be necessary," Rime replied, but Damayanti cut him off.

"Thank you. That would be wonderful. Do you have any soup?" She sat down on the bed and started untying her shoes. An embarrassing warmth flooded Rime's cheeks. She wasn't exactly making things easier.

But Lindri could think what he wanted. Svarteld was dead, Hirka's life was in danger, the Council was in turmoil, and the blind were making forays into the eleven kingdoms. He couldn't waste time worrying about how things looked.

Lindri nodded. "I have fish stock. I can make a soup." He disappeared back down the ladder.

"So what do you need?" Rime sat down next to Damayanti. She lifted his cloak from his shoulders, folded it, and left it at the foot of the bed.

"I need to be sure that you know what you're asking me to do."

He nodded, unable to say yes, because that would have been a lie.

She continued. "And I need a promise."

"Name it."

"This is your choice. Not mine. Remember that, when you want to kill me for what *you* wanted to do."

"So not an entirely painless process, then?" he said dryly.

She ran her fingers through his hair. There was something in her gaze that was different than before. He was used to her trying to draw him in, to own him, to bend him to her will. Now she hesitated, and it seemed genuine. That was probably what scared him most.

They sat in silence until Lindri came back and set a tray down on one of the boxes of tea. Two bowls of fish soup and a lamp. The glass was cheap, giving everything a greenish tinge.

"Thank you," Damayanti said. "And don't worry if he screams. I promise not to hurt him." Her smile had regained its power. She leaned against Rime and ran her fingers up his thigh. Lindri turned his back and left. He closed the door behind him, the frame groaning.

Rime tore her hand away from his thigh. "That's not why we're here."

"No," she replied. "But it helps if he thinks that. Because you will scream. Lift your arms."

She loosened the lacing at his throat, pulling the cords slowly, as if afraid of what she might find. She pulled his shirt over his head and let it fall to the floor. She looked at him with her mouth half-open, an involuntary reaction that she covered up with a satisfied smile.

"So it's true what they say about Kolkagga," she said. "Lie down, Rime."

He did as he was told, lying back on the bed. She rolled up his cloak and put it under his neck, tipping his head back. Then she dug two containers out of a small bag and put them on the stool. They were small bottles, shaped like spearheads. One made of silver, the other of black glass. She set the beak down next to them. It gaped at him.

Three bizarre objects next to something as commonplace as soup bowls. Damayanti rested her hands on her thighs, steeling herself.

Rime was afraid she might change her mind. He knew what he was doing. He knew there was no other way. She knew that too, but there was still a danger of her backing out. He couldn't let that happen. He had to make sure she went through with it.

"Come on," he said. "I don't want the entire city finding me here with the likes of you."

She gave him a frosty smile, recovering her former resoluteness. "Drink this," she said, giving him the silver bottle. He drank. It was grainy and bitter.

She let a couple of red drops fall from the black bottle onto the beak, which she then rubbed in her hands until it was sticky. The smell of blood filled the room. She lifted the beak up to her face and whispered to it, almost lovingly, as if soothing it. Her hands as red as a butcher's. Though he didn't understand the words, Rime knew it was the language of the blind.

"You speak ..." He stared at her.

"It can only be woken by its mother tongue," she replied. Rime was speechless. All this time he'd longed for knowledge of them, anything that might help him understand, and here she was, speaking the language of the deadborn. A language none of the learned in Mannfalla knew a word of.

What am I doing?

"Find the Might," she said. Her dark hair tumbled down over her chest. She tied it in a knot at the nape of her neck. He did as she said, binding the Might, filling his body.

"What are you waiting for?" he asked.

"For your heart to stop."

Rime jerked, trying to sit up. Damayanti pushed him back down again with one hand, as if he were a powerless child. Pain ripped through his chest and out into his arms. He could hear his heart pounding in his ears. Then slower. Slower. Until it was no longer beating at all.

He could still move, though only just. His body was cold, and he knew he was hovering somewhere between life and death.

Damayanti worked quickly. She let a couple of drops of blood fall into his mouth before pushing his chin up so he wouldn't see what she was doing. But he felt the blade of the knife against his throat, felt her make the incision. His breath stuttered. His body protested. His mind went blank. The Might became frantic with fear. He wanted to throw her off him, to flee. Nothing about what she was doing was natural. This was blindcraft. He was about to sacrifice himself.

This was what you wanted. Take the beak. Take it.

Rime repeated the words in his head. He thanked Svarteld for everything he'd taught him about mind over body. Svarteld. Dead now. They were both dead, in that moment.

She pushed the beak into his throat. It forced its way in as if of its own free will. She pressed the edges of the wound together. Her eyes were steely. Suddenly unfamiliar. She grabbed the bottle and dripped blood over the wound. Rime felt it heal over, a cold draft giving way to warmth as it closed, shutting the beak inside him. He was no longer alone.

Damayanti brought her lips to his throat and whispered in the same strange language as before. Rime wanted to retch but managed not to. He couldn't get air into his lungs. He had a beak in his throat. A raven beak. Bigger than what ought to be possible, but there it was.

Damayanti slammed her fist into his chest. His heart reawakened. His back arched. He gasped for breath. For life. He was alive.

"Drink the rest," Damayanti said, giving him the black bottle. "It's blood of the blind. It might not feel like it, but it will heal you. Faster than anything else you've heard of."

Rime fumbled with the bottle. His fingers were shaking. The Might quivered within him. He managed to steady the bottle, then drank, the blood spreading across his tongue. Sweet. Metallic. Trying to find a way past the foreign body lodged inside him.

Then the beak awoke. Twitching. Gaping. Rime's eyes bulged. He gripped the bed and rolled over onto his side. Pain ripped through his throat. It felt like the beak was taking root, burrowing into him, growing like veins, outward, up toward his jaw, his temples. Into his head. He was being torn apart from the inside. He wanted to scream, but his jaw had locked. His stomach tried to empty itself, but nothing could get past the beak.

Damayanti got up and backed toward the door, keeping her distance from him and the horror unfolding. He reached out to her, fingers grabbing for something, anything. A bowl fell to the floor and smashed. The smell of fish soup mixed with the smell of blood. His throat spasmed and spasmed.

"It'll be over soon," he heard Damayanti say, from what sounded like another world.

The spasms abated, finally easing off. He swallowed again and again. He propped himself up onto his elbow but couldn't lift his head, so he collapsed back onto the bed. He tried to cling to the Might, to bind, but he had nowhere for it to go.

All that existed in that moment was the life in his throat. The roots sending rhythmic jolts up into his head. Pain pulsed through him. Then he went numb.

"Rest now," someone said. And he did.

DAMAYANTI'S FALL

The smell of blood. Tea. Dried fruit.

Rime sat up in the bed. He was sore all over, like after a training session with Svarteld. Then he remembered. He'd clashed swords with his master for the last time.

He found his shirt on the floor and put it on. It felt like someone else was doing it. There was still a bowl of fish soup on the box. Someone had been in to mop up what had ended up on the floor.

Lindri. What has he seen? What does he know?

The pain was still fresh in Rime's mind. It was hard to relax his shoulders, knowing it could come back at any moment. What had she done to him? What did it look like?

He remembered Urd, at Bromfjell, before the deadborn dragged him off. Rotting. Tailless. A wreck of a man.

Rime raised his hand to his throat, expecting to find a gaping wound where the beak was, but he didn't feel anything unusual. Just a raised welt beneath his voice box, barely noticeable to the touch. It hurt to swallow, but he was ravenous. He'd almost forgotten what that felt like. He rested the bowl on his knees and ate. The soup was cold, with a skin on top, but he devoured every last drop.

She knew. That was why she asked for soup.

She'd hesitated. Been close to changing her mind. Even though he was certain that this was what she'd wanted all along. He knew what it meant. And he knew what he'd done.

What would Ilume have said if she could see him now? If she'd witnessed blindcraft? The destruction of all that was right? Perhaps nothing. She would have been more troubled by what he'd done to the Council. And to Svarteld. Augurs removing the mark of the Seer from their robes would have enraged her more than him having blindcraft in his throat.

He got up and his legs wobbled. He found his strength again and flung his cloak over his shoulders. Drew his sword. Checked his reflection in the steel. Distorted and blurred. Bruises under his eyes. A pale line ran down his throat, like an old scar—the only remaining trace of his nightmare. Damayanti must have washed the blood off him.

He sheathed the sword. Left a pile of gold coins on the box. Too many, most would have said, but he was paying for more than food and lodging. He was paying for silence. And he knew Lindri wouldn't accept if he tried to give them to him directly.

Rime strapped his swords to his back and left the room. Climbed down the stepladder to the teahouse. Outside, day was fading into night. People peered inside but continued past. Nevertheless, Lindri had water heating over the hearth, and a row of cast-iron pots on the counter.

"You were here the night she left us," Lindri said, sliding a cup of tea across the counter. "And ever since it's seemed that the Ravenbearer has been ruled by a broken heart, and that was the reason for the chaos in Eisvaldr. But now I don't know what to think, Rime-fadri."

Rime wasn't able to hold back a grimace of pain. "I didn't touch the dancer," he said hoarsely.

Lindri nodded and let the matter drop. Rime wanted to say more, to prove he wasn't crazy, but he knew he wouldn't be able to do it with conviction. Not anymore. He wanted to assure Lindri that Eisvaldr was still standing. That the Council still had a handle on things. That Svarteld had died of his own free will and that there was a reason for everything he was doing. That it was all a part of the fight against the deadborn. But there were no words. Not if he were to preserve what little faith Lindri still had in him.

He took a sip of tea. The heat seared the open wound in his throat. He coughed.

What have I done?

He thanked Lindri, got up, and left the teahouse. He was long overdue for a chat with an ancient blindling who craved freedom. A deadborn who dreamed of being where Rime was now. And now Rime was his slave.

He followed the alleyways in the direction of Damayanti's place. It was said to be the easiest place to find in all of Mannfalla, even though there was no sign outside. All you had to do was follow the crowds of men. This time he heard them before he saw them. A fight?

He rounded the corner and saw a group scattering. The door opened and a broad-shouldered man emerged, dragging a smaller man behind him. He flung him into the gutter. "And stay there!" he grunted, before disappearing back inside.

The man in the gutter started ranting at Rime. "There's no point going in. She ain't dancing tonight. Ain't danced in two days! Don't stop 'em taking your money, though, does it?" He dragged himself up and staggered off down the street.

Rime went inside. The stage at the other end of the room was empty, but there were still plenty of patrons. Drinking was always an option, dancing or no dancing. In any case, the night was still young, and Damayanti wasn't the only dancer, so they were bound to get something.

Rime went upstairs and knocked on Damayanti's door. One of the girls who attended her opened it. "You're early. She didn't expect you till tomorrow." Discreet as ever. The girl had never once used his name or his title.

She showed him in. He waited for her to gesture toward one of the chairs, but she continued through the curtain. "Come."

Rime followed her down the corridor, past a number of doors, the sound of all manner of illicit encounters carrying from within. At the end they came to another staircase, and the girl pointed at a door on the next floor. He thanked her, went up, and knocked.

Damayanti opened the door in a green dress with a laced bodice. For once it wasn't see-through, like her dresses often were. Her hair hung in a dark braid down her back. Her eyes looked naked. No make-up.

"I hadn't expected you for another day or two," she said.

"I've no time to waste." He stepped inside. The room was small and cozy. Candles of various sizes were burning in small niches along the stone walls. An open fire in the middle of the room was surrounded by benches covered in sheepskins. She sat down and stared into the flames. He sat down across from her.

"I expect you've got some sort of act prepared," he said. "That you've planned what's going to happen now and rehearsed what you're going to say. I suggest we skip that and let the beak speak for itself. Just tell me what to do." He could hear the coldness in his own voice. Rougher than usual.

She looked worried. Fearful. She looked nothing like a dancer sitting there like that, with her arms folded across her chest and her shoulders hunched. She looked cold.

He leaned closer to her. "You asked me to remember that you didn't do this. This was my choice, and right now I don't have time for you to find your long-lost morals. I need you to finish what you started. I've learned that the hard way. Now it's your turn. Do what you've been planning since we first met."

"I haven't—"

"Now!"

She jumped. Then she leaned forward and opened a drawer concealed under the table. Pressed a bottle into Rime's hand. The same as the one she'd had before. Black glass with an etched pattern that made it rough to the touch. With a silver cork and an intricate locking mechanism.

"You have to bind," she said. "Draw upon the Might, then take three drops. No more. Then she'll find you."

"She? You mean he, don't you?"

She lowered her eyes, knowing she'd lost. That was what happened when you played games with someone born and raised in Eisvaldr. "Do you think I'm an idiot, Damayanti? That I still expect to find Hirka on the other side of this beak?"

He drew upon the Might, opened the bottle, and let three drops fall down his throat. A moment passed, then his throat started to tingle. The beak was moving. Writhing. He fought to stay calm. He may not have been able to control his body, but at least he could control his reactions. Svarteld had taught him that.

A sound forced its way up from his throat. The voice of a man. Strange. Guttural. Completely at odds with nature. Fear erupted in his chest, but Rime contained it. Forced himself to sit. To listen.

"She said she could bring you to me, Rime An-Elderin. After everything I've heard about you, I admit I had my doubts, but here you are. It's an honor to meet you."

Rime readied himself for pain. A lot of pain. He had something to say and he was going to say it. Regardless of the consequences.

"Graal …" Rime stared into the fire between him and Damayanti. The flames were dancing, taunting him. Daring him to continue. "I only have one thing to say to you. If you touch her … if you so much as lay a hand on her, in any way, it will be the last thing you do. That's not a threat, it's a promise. I'll destroy you."

Damayanti's eyes widened. Her hand flew to her open mouth. He held up his own to keep her from speaking. The silence was suffocating. Then Graal's voice returned.

"You've taken the beak. You are mine. A slave to my blood. I could take your life right now if I wanted to."

"I know," Rime snarled. "I've found the books. I know what I've done. And I know it can't be undone. There is no limit to how much pain you can inflict on me. But I promise you, it won't compare to the pain you'll feel if anything happens to her."

"You knew?" Graal couldn't hide his surprise.

"Yes."

"Yet still you did it?"

"Yes."

Graal sighed, and Rime felt it catch in his throat. "What I wouldn't give to have men like you here, Rime An-Elderin. I have no desire to cause you pain, though I don't blame you for doubting me. We're natural enemies, you and I. You're an ymling, and I'm Dreyri. You call us deadborn. We call you cows. It's been like that for longer than either of us can remember. You with your nineteen years, and me with my two thousand eight hundred. Yet here we are, talking, because we have a common interest."

"Where is she?"

"Well, that's the problem, you see. She's with my brother."

"The Seer …"

"Oh, there are far more suitable names for him than that. But whatever you want to call him, she isn't safe. He's poisoned her with lies. She's afraid of me. And that will only continue as long as she's with him. She has to choose to come to me, and as things stand, that seems highly unlikely. It would take a miracle. Unless, of course, I had something she cares about."

Rime started to laugh, but the burning in his throat stopped him. "You want to use me as bait?"

"Rime An-Elderin, let me assure you that I would not have sunk so low had there been any other way. And she's more important to me than you are. Still, I'd like to ask for your permission."

Rime blinked. Had he heard right? "My permission?"

"Will you help me wrest her from my brother's claws? I was bracing myself to explain, but somehow you've grasped who the real enemy is. She has not. Where does this conviction stem from, Rime An-Elderin?"

Rime remembered Eirik's words in Ravnhov.

"A wise man taught me that the enemy with the most to lose is the one to fear. Not the one who has already lost everything."

It was quiet for a moment. Rime could have sworn he felt Graal smile.

"I can see how you became Ravenbearer. So you'll help me?"

"Send me to the human world, and I promise you'll have his head."

Graal laughed. It vibrated in Rime's throat, but he no longer felt any pain.

"You've got fire, I'll give you that. You think you know what you're asking for, but you'd never understand this place, or survive it. It's like ... well, like another world. And even if you made good on your promise, even if you found him and killed him, you'd still thirst for blood. How much would our agreement be worth then? After my brother, it would be my turn. There's no point denying it. You can't see past what you need right now. Desperation makes it easy to promise such things. No, Rime An-Elderin, having you in Ym is the insurance I need."

Rime couldn't contain his anger. "If you aren't able to keep your word, Graal—if you can't protect her from your brother, then no gateways, no raven rings in the world will hold me back."

"Is it really necessary to sully this agreement with threats?"

"So why do you want her? Because she can help you use the gateways?"

"You know better than that."

Rime remembered what he'd heard and read. "They punished you. You can't use them yourself. You're trapped where you are."

"Nice of him, don't you think? A true brother."

"Then why? What is she to you?"

Another sigh caught in his throat. "She's my daughter, Rime An-Elderin."

Rime looked at Damayanti. Her jaw dropped. Involuntarily revealing that she hadn't known either.

She's one of the blind. Hirka is deadborn. Nábyrn.

It couldn't be true. She looked nothing like them. But Rime felt dangerously uncertain. All the same, he tried to protest. "She's like us! She hasn't … she isn't …"

"She's half-blood. Human on the outside, Dreyri on the inside," Graal said with obvious pride.

"She's a blindling?"

"She is Dreyri. She has blood of the first."

Rime's throat was burning. He swallowed. "So you don't want to hurt her?"

"No more than you do, Rime An-Elderin. Naiell is another story. But he's afraid of me. Hirka is all that stands between us, and he knows it. She's safe as long as he isn't backed into a corner, which means direct confrontation isn't an option. That's why I have to get her to come to me on her own. Without him, and of her own volition. But you should rest now, Rime An-Elderin. This is your first time with the beak, and I don't want to hurt you."

"Wait! The bl—The others that are here. Your people."

"Yes, forgive me, I understand that creates problems. It's the Might. When you haven't had a taste of it in a thousand years, it's easy to get a little … overexcited. But since we have an arrangement now, I'll do my best, Rime An-Elderin. And you have my word that Damayanti won't open the raven rings. No more of our kind will come to your world. Not before our arrangement comes to an end."

The voice disappeared. Not just the sound, but the feeling of someone else's presence. Rime sat looking at his hands. They were shaking. It should have been out of fear, but it wasn't. It was anger. Resolve.

Damayanti got up and moved toward him. Control over the gateways was closer than he'd thought. It had been within his grasp the entire time.

"You took the beak," she whispered. "You knew it would put your life in his hands, but you did it anyway?"

He looked up at her. Hated every word she said, every word she'd ever spoken. Hated that he'd been forced to let her stab him in the back.

The fear in her eyes turned to shame. Her eyes welled up, the tears running down her cheeks and dripping from her chin. She dropped to her knees and rested her hands on his thighs.

He wrapped a hand around her neck. All he wanted was to press down with his thumb and watch her suffocate, but he contented himself with wiping away her tears. Who knew treachery could be so tempting? So bare. So ripe with desire. What drove her? Why would a dancer willingly wake the deadborn and lead them here through the stone doors? Whatever the reason, he knew she'd put it behind her now.

"You're going to tell me everything you know," he said. "Everything you can do. And you're going to break open the raven rings for me."

"He'll kill me if I do what you're asking, Rime."

"Yes, he will. But you're still going to do it."

Equal measures of hope and disbelief filled her eyes. "Do you think you can stop him?"

"I don't know. But that's not why you're going to help me." He could see that she wanted to ask, but she didn't. He explained anyway.

"You came to me like waves crashing on rocks, Damayanti. Fierce. Strong. Intoxicated by your own ability to bend people to your will.

But you've forgotten that now. Because every time I look into your eyes, I see less and less of you, and more and more of me. You will help me now. Because you love me."

"You're just a boy ..." Her mask of contempt shattered as soon as she tried to put it on. She closed her eyes. "You're just a boy," she repeated. It passed her swollen lips as barely a whisper. She buried her face in his lap and sobbed like a child.

SPIDER'S WEB

Hirka sat quietly on a tall stool by the window. She felt trapped, trapped among people, thousands of people, both inside and outside the café. London was a monster. The biggest and most terrifying monster she had ever seen. The buildings were so tall that she was sure they would topple over at any moment. Cars and buses tore past in every direction, rumbling, squealing, and whistling. Music was being pumped out of a box in the corner above her, but even so, people kept chattering. Two big screens showed moving pictures of people on bicycles. She'd never ridden a bicycle.

She tried to make herself as small as she could. She felt an intense urge to run, but she'd promised Stefan she'd stay put, and she knew she'd never get back to York without him. For some reason he thought she would be safer among people, but what did he know?

She sipped the hot chocolate that Stefan had bought her. It was cold. They ought to have been back by now. Both him and Naiell. How long could it take to get another car? They were all over the place. Maybe it was her fault, since she'd asked him not to steal one.

Her bag was wedged between the stool and the window. Her entire life, in one small bag. A bulge revealed where the book was, its soft cover pressed up against the side. It looked like it was trying to push its way out. Like it was reaching out to her. Hirka glanced around before pulling it out. The book none of them had managed to make any sense of. She was the only one still trying.

There was something about it, something strange and familiar all at once. The black leather was faded and scratched. It had no title. No author. Just the symbol stamped into it. Two lines, each the width of a finger, sloping downward. Hirka opened it and flicked through the pale pages. It had to be some sort of joke. So many pages, so little content. Just small circles. Randomly positioned, and with a random number of lines. No coherence. No writing.

Stefan had suggested that it might be some sort of film. That if you flicked rapidly through the pages, the drawings might come to life, but there didn't seem to be any real order to them. Maybe if ...

Hirka glanced up at the window. She felt like she was being watched, like someone she knew was close by.

Outside, people walked past. None of them looked at her. She looked around. A beggar stood on the other side of the street. He held out a paper cup every time someone walked past, but no one gave him anything. No one looked at him. He was young and gaunt. His gloves didn't have fingers.

Hirka put the book back in her bag, shouldered it, and went outside. The street seemed to grow. The cars seemed angrier. She knew she ought to go back inside. Wait for Stefan and Naiell.

You're going to have to get the hang of this world at some point.

Hirka crossed the street. The smell hit her before she was anywhere near him—a faint odor of rot. She stopped. Their eyes met. She waited for a reaction. Recognition. Maybe even for him to attack. He was one of them. One of the forgotten. But he didn't recognize her.

Hirka rummaged in her pockets, found a money note, and put it in his cup. His fingers were chapped and unwashed. He nodded, thanking her profusely. His cheeks were hollow and his eyes seemed distant, as if he wasn't really seeing her.

"How long have you been forgotten?" she asked.

He took the money out of the cup and shoved it in his pocket. "Everyone's forgotten here," he replied. She wasn't sure he knew what she meant. She took a step closer. He looked around and she suddenly realized that he was more scared of her than she was of him. Maybe he thought she was trying to trick him.

"How long were you friends? Before he forgot you?"

His eyes grew sharper. He leaned against the wall. Someone had drawn a skull on it. "You new? You're a young 'un."

She smiled. "I hear that a lot. But I'm not one of you."

He looked around again. Wary. Jittery. "Listen, I don't get involved with kids, and I don't know what you've heard, but you have no idea what you're talking about."

Hirka turned to leave. "Graal," she said over her shoulder. "I'm talking about Graal."

The beggar grabbed her wrist, his eyes suddenly big and wild. Had he realized who she was, what kind of blood ran through her veins? A man walked past and gave the beggar a sharp look. He let go of her as if he'd been burned, reminded of his place at the bottom of the pecking order. He was forgotten, in every way. He wouldn't stand a chance if the situation escalated.

If only he knew. Hirka was just as forgotten, just as small a part of the world they both lived in. Like a ghost, on the outside of everything.

"How many of you are there?" she asked. "Do you ever see him again, after ...?"

The beggar shook his head. He had beautiful eyes. Or at least they had been, once upon a time. "No one knows. I haven't met that many. We're too different. We come from all over, from all times. He's the only thing we have in common. How do you know about this, Red? Do you know him? Could you ...?"

Hirka shook her head. She was in no position to help. If what Stefan said was true, this man was doomed to lose his mind, to descend into madness, to attack people. Stefan would have killed him then and there. Pulled his teeth out and sold them. All without remorse, without feeling he'd done anything wrong. But what gave him the right? How could he condemn people to death for wrongs they were yet to commit?

Hirka found another note in her pocket. One of only two she had left. She tried to put it in his cup, but he put his hand over it. "Don't spend it all on me, Red. We can't help each other."

She moved his hand and stuffed the note inside. "That's not why I'm giving it to you," she said. "Anyway, you don't know that for sure. Maybe you will be able to do something for me someday."

She left him, crossing the street and heading back into the café. She sat down by the window again and looked out. He was gone. Only the skull remained.

"Where've you been?!"

Hirka jumped. Stefan was standing behind her with his phone pressed to his ear, his bag over his shoulder, and a stack of papers in his hand. "Hold on, hold on," he said into the phone, tucking it between his ear and shoulder as he tried to pay for a coffee. He spilled some and swore before taking what was left and heading for the door. He motioned for her to follow.

"Did you go for a walk? Christ, you don't know who might be out there! You were supposed to sit quietly and wait!" He downed his coffee and threw the cup away before tapping his phone and looking at her. "Listen, Allegra's on the phone. She's called three times. I had to answer in the end. Everything's going to hell. She's not stupid. She knows we're up to something. She wants to talk to you. Just make sure it's not about anything other than hair and nails and stuff like that. And say you don't know where we are. Okay?"

He was walking so fast that Hirka was having trouble keeping up. He handed her the phone and she lifted it to her ear. "Hello?" she said, feeling a bit silly.

"Hirka, sweetheart, finally! Lord knows you're not easy to get hold of. Where are you?"

"I … I'm not sure." Hirka jogged after Stefan. Allegra lowered her voice, making it difficult to hear her.

"Can you speak freely? Can Stefan hear what you're saying?"

"I doubt it. He's a bit stressed."

"Well, that's par for the course. Darling, I don't know where to start. I've received a letter from someone claiming to have contacts where you're from. There's news from Mann … Mannfalla. Forgive the pronunciation. I promised I'd pass it along on the condition that Stefan doesn't hear it. I must say, it puts me in something of an awkward position, because I want to keep my promise, but I also want you to hear the news. So what am I to do, my dear?"

Hirka slowed down. All the same, her heart started pounding. She'd never told Allegra where she came from. She said what she knew Allegra wanted to hear.

"I won't tell him anything."

"Oh, that's wonderful! Now, you must excuse me, I don't know who on earth these people are or what this is really about, but …"

Hirka didn't bother pointing out that it wasn't from anyone on Earth. Not if it was news from Ym.

"You know, Hirka, this would be so much easier face-to-face. Shall we say tomorrow?"

"What's the news?" Hirka gritted her teeth. She knew with every fiber of her being that whatever was coming couldn't be good.

"Well, there are three things here, and not a lot of detail, I'm afraid. First of all, two men have had a fight. As men do. Rime and Svarteld. Svarteld is dead, I'm afraid. Rime is going to marry and start a family with a girl from the north. Do you know him? That sounds like much better news. And then finally, there's been a fire at a teahouse. The owner died, but no one else was hurt. The fire was started by someone who disliked a girl who used to stay there.

Dearie me, I have no idea where this came from, but we'll find out together, sweetheart. Let's meet for lunch tomorrow and we'll talk more about it then, okay? Before more people get hurt."

Hirka didn't reply. She couldn't even open her mouth. The phone slipped from her hand and sailed toward the ground. Stefan came running, but he was too late. It hit the asphalt. A bus swept past. The sounds of the city mixed with the pulse throbbing in her ears. A barrage of noise. Stefan was screaming at her, but she couldn't hear him over the roar. He held up the phone. She stared at it. The screen was smashed, white cracks stretching across the black glass like the silken threads of a spider's web.

MAIMED

She's half-blindling. She's deadborn. One of them.

Rime ought to have been disgusted, but they were nothing more than words. He knew who and what she was. She was Hirka. She'd never been anything but Hirka. They could call her what they liked. Menskr. Child of Odin. The rot. Or one of the blind. Deadborn. Nábyrn.

Either way, she was Hirka. The tailless girl.

Six months ago she'd been a piece in the game between Mannfalla and Ravnhov. A thorn in the Council's side. What was she now? A piece in the game for the entire world? Caught between forces no one understood. In a world so different from Ym that Graal didn't think Rime could even survive there.

Well, he'd find out soon enough.

He laced up his bag. Custom-made for Kolkagga, with straps for his scabbards. He wasn't taking much. Knives. Kolkagga blacks. Food. Coins. Healing salve and bandages. Damayanti's bottles. And a drawing of Hirka. The one the Council had used on the posters they'd pasted up all over Mannfalla. A sketch in black ink bearing little resemblance to her, apart from the blood-red hair. He was hardly going to master the language, so that was all he would have to find her.

He strapped on his leather armor. Put on his bag and sheathed his swords at his back. Then he went out into his mother's garden.

Gesa's garden. The pride of the An-Elderin family home. He'd stood here with Ilume the night after the Rite. After he'd watched the guardsmen drag Hirka off to the pits. Blindfolded, her tunic stained with blood.

The garden lay dormant. Only a faint odor of decay betrayed the thaw. Spring would come soon, but the chances of him seeing it were slim. As were the chances of him enjoying the fragile cease-fire between ymlings and blindlings. He'd forged it with blindcraft. With a sacrifice he knew would come at a cost.

Grief seized him. A dark void that threatened to swallow him whole. The void left by Svarteld. By Ilume. The disappointment in Lindri's eyes. That bastard Darkdaggar, who'd sooner see him dead than sit at the Council table. Fellow Kolkagga he'd been forced to kill when he and Hirka were fleeing through Blindból, including Launhug, the man with an inking of Rime on his arm. An icon. What good had it done him, clinging to a survival myth? Idolizing a son of the Council?

New death merged with old. The bare branches started to look like faces.

Don't start something you can't finish.

He had a job to do. Never again would he let the past and his mistakes hold him back. He would fight for as long as Graal saw fit to keep him alive. But there was nothing more he could do here.

Rime followed the path to the square. Pulled his hood up. He already felt like a stranger. A traveler passing through the archways for the very first time. He left Eisvaldr, the city at the end of the city, taking to the streets of Mannfalla. He kept to dark, narrow alleyways until he reached the river. Then he knocked on Damayanti's back door. He could hear men hollering from the entrance around the front.

Damayanti let him in, as arranged. Her clothes were as black as her hair. She looked like an augur. Not at all like the dancer he knew.

She led him into a bedroom and locked the door behind them. He knew without asking that it was hers. It was surprisingly modest, with a bed as the only piece of furniture. It was in the middle of the room, covered in pillows and furs and big enough for three people. It had to have been built where it stood, because it didn't look like it could be moved. The walls had panels decorated with animal bones. She opened one of them, pulling four torches out of the cupboard concealed behind it.

She took his hand and led him to the bed.

"What are you doing?" he asked hoarsely. It was the first time he'd spoken since he got there.

She leaned toward him. Her lips seemed to get even redder. "We're going to bed, Rime An-Elderin. You and I," she whispered in his ear. Then she pulled back the covers and lifted the mattress. Moved some slats aside. There was a trapdoor in the floor below. She turned toward him again. "But we can take our time. There's no rush," she said. Desire and shame flickered across her features.

She was unbelievable. He pointed at his throat. "You can betray me or love me. I'll never let anyone do both. You made your choice a long time ago, Damayanti."

He opened the trapdoor and lit one of the torches. She looked like she was about to respond but then seemed to decide against it. She climbed down through the trapdoor and he followed. He didn't ask where they were going. The trapdoor took them into a cellar. A tunnel with a damp earthen floor. They were near the river. They walked for a while until they came to a wall with a crack in it that they squeezed through. A draft tugged at the torches, drawing out the flames like fiery serpents.

Where is she going? There's only one raven ring in Eisvaldr.

When they reached an opening between two brick walls, he realized where he was.

"Are we ...?"

She nodded. "Inside the city walls. There are several underground sections, but the entrances were bricked up hundreds of years ago."

The wall meandered a little until they reached solid rock. They squeezed through another crack. The air grew thicker until they emerged in a large cave. This was far beneath Eisvaldr, and he suddenly realized what he was looking at: blindling construction. Like what he'd seen under the library. Maybe that was close by.

Damayanti raised the torch, and Rime's eyes widened. The stones were suspended from the ceiling. Huge. Heavy. In a perfect circle.

The raven ring.

He walked into the circle and stared up. "It's the same ring. The same stones ..." His voice bounced between them.

"It's the same one," she affirmed, and lit a new torch with the old one, which was flickering out. He ran his hand across one of the stones. They were hanging at different heights, none of them quite reaching the ground. The ceiling was sloped, he now saw, and black. Completely black. With veins of shinier black running like roots through the rock. It was impossible to say whether these had been created by any living creature or whether they were formed by the Might itself. By a primordial force older than Graal. Older than the world. A hunger took hold of him. A hunger to know. To understand.

To control.

Here, in this place, was where he would leave the world? Here, where the weight of everything forgotten drove stone through earth?

Damayanti pulled a bottle out of a pouch. "Promise not to take too much, Rime. You'll want to, believe me. But it's blood of the blind, and you have to choose whether you want to be master or slave. There's nothing in-between."

"What are *you*?"

She smiled wearily. "Whatever he tells me to be."

"Slave, then," he answered, taking the bottle. Blood of the blind. Blood of the first. Traveler's blood that would open the raven rings for him. Blood that became one with the Might, and that never died or dried up. Lifeblood, from something as terrible as the deadborn. What would he have done had he known that was all he needed to follow her? How far would he have hunted them for their blood?

To Slokna and back.

His anger came in waves. Anger at knowing that he could have left at any time. Without taking the beak. Without becoming Graal's slave. Knowing that Damayanti would suffer for what she was doing was of little comfort.

"And whatever you do, don't give any to the humans," she said. "They can't handle it. That's how they get the rot."

He heard himself laugh. What wouldn't he have given to know the truth she now served him with such ease six months earlier? He'd never believed in the rot, but what did that matter, as long as Hirka believed? Now at least he could keep his promise to her. Find her. Bring her the truth about the rot.

He held out the bottle. "And this heals wounds? Any wound?"

She nodded. "It healed your throat. And Urd's. And one of my girls wouldn't be alive today if it hadn't been for what people call blindcraft. She was torn open when she gave birth to a stillborn daughter. It works."

"Good," Rime answered. He put his bag down on the ground. Took off his armor and pulled off his shirt. "How steady can you hold a sword, Damayanti?" She stared at him while he took off his shoes and trousers as well.

She came closer. He stood naked before her. Her lips parted. She put a hand on his chest. Looked up at him. "What are you doing, Rime? You've made it clear you're not going to give me any of this."

He drew one sword and handed it to her. "My tail," he said.

She staggered back. "You can't! You're going to maim yourself, just to … so no one can …"

"Are you going to help me or do I have to do it myself?"

"Rime, it doesn't matter if you have a tail! It means nothing. They might not be like us, but they're not … they're not animals! They'll understand."

"You think they'll welcome me? Embrace me as one of their own? Like we did with *her*?"

Damayanti shut her eyes. He knew that she understood. People *were* animals. No matter which world you were in. He wouldn't get very far if he showed up in the human world with a tail.

Damayanti gripped the hilt of the sword in both hands. "And when you come back? Do you think people will accept a cripple as Ravenbearer? One who's maimed himself? This is madness!"

Rime had expected her to refuse. And he couldn't force her, which was a shame. It would have been easier with her help. But he was better off doing it himself than risking a half-hearted hack from someone who didn't have the stomach for it.

He took the weapon from her and kneeled on the ground. Gripped the blade of the sword with both hands behind his back and positioned it at the base of his tail.

"Rime …"

He shut her out. Shut everything out. This was simple. He had the strength. The blade was sharp enough to slice a man in half. All he needed to do was push the sword down.

He bound the Might. Clenched his teeth. Tensed his arms. Then he pushed down as hard as he could. He heard his tail thump to the ground behind him. Damayanti stifled a scream with her hand. He didn't move. No pain. Not yet. But it would come.

And come it did. The floor grew sticky, and he directed the Might toward his heart to stop the bleeding. Damayanti fumbled for the bottle on the ground, whispering to herself. "Seer help me …"

Rime tried to fight off the dizziness. She found the bottle, and he felt her cold hands on his back. Then a stinging sensation.

That means it's working.

Hirka had said that once.

Rime steadied himself, jaw locked. The wound was burning where his tail ought to have been. He could see it. Out of the corner of his eye. He couldn't bring himself to look at a part of his own body lying so unnaturally far away.

He was someone else. He was about to leave Ym, through the same stone circle Hirka had used. He was a gaping wound. He was a fight he was bound to lose. He was pain.

He was tailless.

ISAC

They parked in an alleyway a short distance from the hospital, next to two dumpsters. Hirka climbed out of the car. It was early in the morning. Stefan stuck his head out the window. "This is stupid, girl. This is how they get you, you know."

"I have to." She didn't have the energy to say more than that. They'd argued about it all the way there. Stefan couldn't be part of what she was planning to do. He'd never allow it, or forgive her, so he couldn't know.

"Fine, but I'll say it again, any sign of trouble and we're leaving, okay? It doesn't even have to be anything big. If anyone so much as slams a door too hard, we're out of here."

He reached for the back seat and grabbed his beanie. Tossed it to her. "Here. At least try to hide your hair."

Both he and Naiell stayed in the car. They thought she was going to see Father Brody. But that wasn't why she was here.

She was here to see Isac, the man who had tried to kill Father Brody.

If she'd told them that, she'd probably be tied up on the backseat by now—and for good reason. It was reckless. There were a whole load of reasons not to do it. Stefan had rattled off a fair few of them on the way from London to York. Like how the police were keeping an eye on the hospital since two of its patients had been at the scene in the church murders. Even worse, Graal could be watching. Or other Vardar, friends of Isac. Did blood slaves even have friends?

If they were watching, they were watching. She was done hiding. She knew she ought to have been scared, but she just felt numb. Dazed. Crushed by what Allegra had told her.

Lindri and Svarteld were dead, and Rime was going to marry someone. A girl from the north. Sylja, most likely, if she knew Glimmeråsen.

No! It can't be true!

Hope was all she had left. Hope that it was all lies. Venom and hate, meant to torment her. Still … too much of what Allegra had said rang true. The names. The city. That could only mean one thing. There was a way of communicating between worlds. After all, Urd had spoken to her father. He'd said as much himself. This had to have come from somewhere. Who other than Graal could have passed these lies on to Allegra?

Nothing in the world would make Rime kill Svarteld. Nothing. They were more than Kolkagga and master. Svarteld himself had told her how he had dug Rime out of the snow, saving the boy as his parents were smothered by the weight of the avalanche.

And Lindri … She pictured the teahouse in flames by the riverbank. Lindri sleeping on the second floor. Old, wise, and kind. With joints so stiff that he'd never have been able to save himself. Dead? Just because she'd stayed there?

The hate growing in her chest was terrifying. She felt like she was being torn in two. Part of her whispered that no one would do something so heinous. The other part laughed. The dark, strong, violent part. It was beyond certain that there were people who would do such a thing. Graal among them.

And Isac.

She knew nothing about the man Isac had been before Graal had found him, before he'd been infected with the rot. But that didn't matter, because she needed what he was now. One of Graal's slaves. And now she had something he needed. Something she could use to buy the information she needed to find Graal. To find out what the book was for and how to get home. Home to Ym.

A sound made Hirka jump. Birds. Just birds playing in the hedge by the main entrance. It would be spring soon. A new beginning. How many more beginnings would the humans get? How long did they have before the rot took over? The poison that was killing the world so slowly, no one could see it.

She pulled the beanie down farther. Father Brody was in here somewhere, in the same building as the man who had shot him. Had the police made that connection? Stefan seemed to think so.

Hirka went in, making sure not to look at anyone. That was the trick. Pretending you'd been there before. Pretending you belonged, that you knew where you were going.

She followed a round woman in white. The woman disappeared through a door and Hirka continued on alone, looking into the rooms as she passed. It was like walking around in a nightmare. Everything was white or green. Surreal. There was a sharp smell laced with sweat and fear … and soap. It reeked. All the furniture seemed to have machines growing out of it. There were sounds she didn't recognize. Lights flickering in the ceiling. And this was where they brought people who were dying? Why? So their lives would end as quickly as possible?

No, thank you. She wouldn't be dying somewhere like this.

She spotted a pair of feet at the end of a bed. The door was ajar. There was no one else in the room. A familiar odor of rot filled her nostrils, a smell she now knew humans couldn't pick up on. But she wasn't one of them. The blood of the blind flowed through her veins. What she could and couldn't do remained a mystery.

She slipped inside and closed the door behind her.

Isac was lying in a bed that was higher at one end. A broken bed for a broken man. His skin was tinged blue and he was surrounded by machines that she had no interest in understanding. Things that beeped. There was a transparent tube sticking out of his hand. His blond hair was plastered to his temples. Daylight filtered in through the window, bouncing off everything. A dream. This was only a dream.

Was this the kind of nightmare that Graal had planned for her? Strapped to a bed with tubes sticking out everywhere, draining her blood, all so he could use the raven rings and take back Ym, which he had lost a thousand years ago?

"Isac?"

He opened his eyes and gave a start. She could feel the knife in her boot but was surprised to find that she didn't want to draw it. Instead, she put a hand on his arm. "Relax. I'm not here to hurt you."

She could tell he didn't believe her, so she continued. "Not that I'm not tempted, of course. You deserve to be lying here. For what you've done." She let go of his arm again. He gave her a tentative smile.

"Deserve …" His voice was dry and feeble. "You have no idea, missy. I've been punished already. He's abandoned me."

"That's what I was hoping," Hirka said. She braced herself for what she had to do next. She couldn't think about him as an yml—as a human. As a living being. He was what he was. A blood slave.

"It's your fault," he said. "He abandoned me because I couldn't give you to him. God knows what he wants with you, or why you're so important, but you're important enough that he's left me here to rot. And now here you are! Do us a favor, would you? Call him and let him know the job's done? That you're here waiting for him?"

He laughed. It turned into an ugly cough. "No," he wheezed. "Thought not. Do you know what the worst part is? Of being abandoned? The worst part is knowing you mean so little to someone that they can carry on as if you were never there."

Her heart wrenched at his words.

Rime. I abandoned Rime.

It was a mistake she'd never be able to set right, not unless by some miracle she managed to gain the upper hand over Graal.

"He's left me here to die," Isac continued. "Because even if I survive the holes in my chest … the infection … even if I get up and walk out of here, my days will once again be numbered."

"My heart bleeds for you," she replied coolly. "You're just like everyone else. You can die. How unbearable for you."

"He was everything to me," Isac said, looking at her as if he hadn't heard a word she'd said. "Everything. I was as good as nothing to him."

She sat down on a chair by the window. The wooden armrest was cracked. "What do you expect from someone who'll soon need a cake with three thousand candles on it?" she said. Jay had taught her that strange custom. You couldn't eat candles, so they had no business being on cakes. But humans did a lot of strange things. Candles on cakes were the least of it.

He smiled. "I thought you knew nothing. That you were just a random girl. But you know who he is, don't you? The man hunting you?"

"Yes. He's my father."

His smile faded. He looked her up and down as if seeing her for the first time.

He didn't know. That makes it even easier.

Isac laughed. A despondent laugh that quickly died in his throat. His eyes dulled. "That sexless devil has a child. Of course. We were supposed to bring you to him. Unharmed. Of course." Hirka let him believe that. That Graal hadn't intended to hurt her. She had nothing to gain from telling him the truth—that she was a blood bag.

She leaned forward to help him reach the realization she needed him to. "A child, Isac. Blood of his blood."

He looked at her. The life came back into his eyes. A fire amid the pale blue. And she hated herself. Hated what she was going to do. It went against nature. Blindcraft. But what did that matter in a world that was dying? She was half-blindling. An outsider. But it was no longer a weakness. It was a strength.

"Why are you telling me this?" he whispered. His arm twitched. He wanted to touch her but didn't have the strength.

"Graal was looking for a book. What was it for?"

He looked around the room, trying to remember. It seemed the negotiations were underway. "I know! He wasn't looking for it, he owned it. He owned a lot of things. Most of them were kept somewhere safe. In vaults, in collections, in museums, but … I don't know what it is. But I can find out."

"Can it help us open the gateways?"

"Gateways?" He frowned and Hirka felt her hope die. Isac knew nothing. Absolutely nothing.

"You don't know? You can't tell me where he is?"

"Yes, missy, I can." He propped himself up in the bed. His cheeks had regained some of their color. Almost as if he knew the blood was coming. "I can tell you exactly where he is, and how to find him. But you know the price."

She got up. Hesitated. What she was about to do couldn't be undone.

Isac reached for her. "You said something to me, back at the church. Do you remember?" Hirka shook her head. All she remembered from that day was the people who had died. And the man who had murdered them. Mickey. Nervous Mickey.

"When I pulled you out of the car, you said something that stuck with me," Isac continued. "You know how it is. You said one day I'd beg you to spare my life."

She remembered. He didn't need to say more. That day had come.

Hirka pulled the knife out of her boot. She'd hoped it would scare him stiff. It should have. But he didn't have the sense to be scared. His thirst for blood was too strong.

She dug the tip of the knife into her thumb. Blood welled forth. Isac craned his neck toward her. Thirsty. Defiant of death. She brought her thumb to his lips and he started to suckle like a calf. She pulled her thumb back. He opened his mouth for more, his eyes rolling back in his head.

Hirka stared at him. Would something happen? If something did, what would it mean? Or was she more human than blindling?

He reined himself back in and looked at her, cheeks flushed.

"So where do I go to find him?" she asked. She was nervous now. She'd acted without considering the consequences. For all she knew, Isac might jump out of bed and throttle her. She tightened her grip on the knife.

"Go?" he said. "My dear girl, I can give you something better than that." He reached for the phone on his bedside table in a smooth movement she'd have thought impossible only a moment ago. He turned the screen toward her. "You can call him any time you like."

She stared at the symbols on the screen. Her reading was lousy, but the few letters she did recognize matched up with a name she'd heard before. Stefan had come across it while looking into the museum.

Joshua Alexander Cain.

She could call him. Graal was right in front of her. She could talk to him at the touch of a button.

"Write it down for me," she said. Her voice was unsteady.

He found a pen in the drawer of the bedside table and started to scribble on the inside of a chocolate wrapper. He gave it to her. "Here. My number's at the top. So what will you say to him?"

She folded the wrapper and shoved it in her pocket. She didn't have an answer to that. She didn't know.

A sound from the doorway made her drop to the floor. Someone came in. Hirka crawled under the bed and made herself as small as she could. White trousers. Clogs. A woman's voice.

"Good morning, Isac. My goodness—you look amazing! Has the physiotherapist been by? How are you getting on? Do you remember anything more today?"

"Not yet, I'm afraid, Ethel, but I think the fog's starting to lift."

"My word, so talkative! Are you feeling better? You're looking much better!"

"If only you knew, Ethel."

Hirka could almost hear his smile. She didn't move.

"This is most—you know what? I'm going to fetch the doctor, Isac. Just take it easy, now. Don't get too excited." Ethel left the room. Hirka crawled out and jumped to her feet. There were no other doors. She would have to climb out the window. She opened it and leaned out. It was only about twelve feet down to the ground. Easy enough.

"Be careful, missy. They won't be far away. They're keeping an eye on me now that I'm one of them."

"I know," she said.

"Will you come back?"

"Maybe. If I beat Graal."

"So no, then ..."

"Thanks for the show of faith."

"What can I say? He is what he is. He has enough power to make the world come apart at the seams. He's a destroyer. Sublimely beautiful, but a destroyer all the same."

"Then we'll have to hope I have the power to mend it. Because that's what I do. I heal."

She climbed up onto the windowsill. "Look after your teeth, Isac," she said, and jumped.

THE ROT

I have his number. I can call Graal.

It felt like she'd cheated. Found something she wasn't meant to find. A way to reach him. Say something to him. But what would she say?

Hirka pictured him back at the museum. Surrounded by broken glass and screaming people. Everyone rushing past him, making for the exit. But he'd just stood there. A rock in a tempest. He'd watched her go, the hint of a smile on his lips. Just stood there. As if he had all the time in the world. And maybe he did.

The birds in the hedge started up again as she ran past. She looked back. Hoped Father Brody would be all right. Make a full recovery and forget everything that had happened in the church. Forget her. She hoped everyone would forget her. Everyone apart from Rime.

He's already forgotten you. He's marrying Sylja.

Her heart wrenched. Hirka stopped and held a hand to her chest. The weight of everything Allegra had said was bearing down on her again. She stared up at the sky and blinked the tears away.

What had she expected? That they would both grow old alone, each in their own world? There was no way back. He had his life. She had hers.

Life? This is no life!

Maybe she had believed him. Believed that he would come. But Rime was the most powerful man in Ym. Soon to be married to

Sylja. Soon to be a father, even. Happy. And completely unaware that Hirka needed him. Would he realize when the blind returned? When deadborn stormed Mannfalla and helped themselves to all that lived and breathed? Would he make the connection when nábyrn feasted on him? Feasted on his family?

You're one of them. You're deadborn.

Now there was a thought. She was Graal's daughter. That ought to come with some advantages. Maybe they would spare Rime and only feast on Sylja. They could have her. And Lindri's killers. And the Council. And …

Enough. That's enough. You have Graal's number.

She rounded the corner. The sun painted a bright triangle on one wall, which didn't quite stretch all the way down into the alleyway. Naiell sat crouched on one of the dumpsters, staring at Stefan.

"Cigarette. Ci-ga-rette! What do you call them? Don't you have smokes where you're from?" Stefan lit the cigarette. Burned himself and swore. Naiell laughed. It sounded like a magpie. And these two were the only ones she could rely on. A grown man lacking all morals, and a deadborn with a god complex.

Stefan spotted her and dropped the cigarette in a puddle. "So what did the priest say?"

"He was asleep."

"Asleep? Then what took so fucking long? Were you looking for a fix?"

Hirka gave a shrug and opened the car door. The smell of garbage got stronger. More rotten. Naiell cocked his head, nostrils quivering. That was when she realized. Far too late.

An arm pulled her back. Held her in an iron grip. She screamed. The arm pressed down on her throat, cutting it short. Her feet searched for the ground. Naiell jumped down from the dumpster. Stefan reached for his gun. Hirka was dragged backward. A woman and two men came running from the other end of the alleyway.

For a moment she thought they'd come to help, but her hope was short-lived. Naiell launched himself at the woman as she drew a weapon. But it wasn't a gun. Or a knife.

Hirka screamed again, but no sound came out. She tore at the arm around her neck. Naiell slumped to the ground. Stefan fired. The other two moved toward him. *No!* This couldn't be happening.

Svarteld! Remember what Svarteld taught you.

Hirka drove her elbow back. She made contact. Heard a groan. Air. She could breathe. She dropped down onto the ground and the man behind her lost his grip on her. She crawled away. He was young. Blond and handsome. She'd expected a monster. He reached out for her. A newfound determination surged through her. She drew her leg back and kicked him in the knee. He howled. She crawled a little farther away and got to her feet.

Stefan!

He was backed against the wall. One of the men had his gun. They had Naiell, too, and were dragging him away. His head was slumped to one side. Was he dead? Hirka crouched down and sprang up onto the car. Ran across the roof. Enough. She'd had enough. She launched a kick. Caught one man under the chin. His head slammed into the wall. His eyes dimmed. He dropped Stefan's gun as he slumped to the ground.

Hirka dove for the gun. That sent the other two running. Naiell was bleeding from a cut across his shoulder. His cheek was all scraped. He wasn't moving. She shouted to Stefan, but he ignored her. He was too busy chasing the others. Hirka dropped to one knee next to Naiell and shook him.

He opened his eyes and growled. He was alive.

She leaned down to wipe the blood from his cut. He pushed her away and sat up. He sat there looking at his arm, opening and closing his fist. As if he was surprised it still worked. What had they done to him?

She stared at the cut on his shoulder. Something was wrong. Something white oozed from the wound. Then it closed. A gaping wound, and it closed. Slowly. As she looked on. She rubbed her eyes. What had she just seen?

She put her hands on his shoulder and probed with her fingers. All she could see was a red welt. A line. Then even that faded.

In the name of the Seer ...

Then she remembered that he was the Seer. She gasped. The red stains on his shirt were all that told her she hadn't been dreaming. His blood. A trail of red leading to a small pool on the ground a short distance away. She swallowed. Her hands were shaking. She dropped the gun on the ground.

Stefan raced back, gasping for air. "I lost them," he huffed. Hirka shook her head. "No ..."

Behind him, the woman was approaching. Stefan turned. Spotted her. Reached for the gun, but Hirka put her hand over it. Stefan stayed where he was, crouched down, his hand over hers.

Naiell shut his eyes. His head slumped forward. The woman approached them slowly. No one said anything. She got down on all fours. Crawled closer.

The woman was middle-aged. Well-dressed with long, brown hair. A hint of white lace was visible under her blouse, which had opened at the throat. She inched her way closer. Like a nervous cat. Then she bent down over Naiell's blood and licked the ground. She didn't take her eyes off them as she dragged her tongue across the bloody asphalt. Again and again. Hirka felt sick.

Someone wake me up. Now.

The woman started backing away again. Slowly at first. Then faster. Once she was at a safe distance, she got up and ran out onto the street, disappearing into the crowd. Gone.

Stefan grabbed the gun with one hand and pulled Hirka to her feet with the other.

One point to you if you pull me up.

He pulled her close. She could feel the handle of the gun against the back of her head. His heart was pounding.

"Jesus Christ," he whispered.

SYMPHONY OF RAGE

Graal's phone rang the moment he climbed out of the helicopter. It was Matthew. He was a journalist, and a solid connection in England. The call could be important. He answered it.

"Yes?"

Graal let himself in while Matthew described some irrelevant incident. A manhunt in Southern England. A madman with a sword. As if there weren't enough maniacs in the world. He draped his coat over the back of the sofa and sat down next to the raven cadaver.

But Matthew seemed to think it was important. Graal wasn't having a good day, and so far, he hadn't heard anything he was willing to concede might be interesting.

"Matthew, send me a picture and I'll have a look." He hung up and dragged his hands over his face. A moment later, his phone pinged. He looked at the picture.

A young man in a tunic and leather armor that looked convincingly authentic. His hair was white, and he wore two swords on his back. Graal instantly felt uneasy. The man in the picture matched every description he'd heard of Rime An-Elderin.

Graal stared at the phone. It wasn't possible, not by any stretch of the imagination. The Ravenbearer was in his thrall, and he knew it. Coming here would be suicide. Not to mention impossible. Unless Damayanti ...

Instinct took over, his gut taking charge. His three-thousand-year-old heart started pumping as if he were only twenty. Incredulity and fury warred within him.

It wasn't possible. She'd never … she couldn't. She had no reason to. Why would two grown ymlings defy him, knowing what it might cost?

And Damayanti? She had followed him her entire life.

His phone pinged again. Another message from Matthew. A link to an article. Graal read it. Unidentified man. Unknown language.

Blind fury gripped him. Consumed him. He let the phone fall onto the sofa. She'd betrayed him. Damayanti had betrayed him. His most important ally in all of Ym. The temptress. She'd sent Rime An-Elderin through the stones, against Graal's will. Against his clear instructions.

Graal howled. The sound ripped through his body. An unstoppable, primordial force. He grabbed the piano and hurled it at the glass wall, which shattered into a million pieces. The piano sailed through the air, black against gray. Flying. Falling.

It hit the rocks below, reduced to kindling in a chaos of sound. A discordant savagery. A symphony of rage. Keys bounced between the rocks, rolling down the mountainside.

The wind blasted through the broken window, displacing the air and sucking sheet music from shelves, scattering it across the landscape.

Graal gasped for breath. The Might. Had he had it now, no one would have lived to see another day. Not one single human. He hated them. And he hated her. Everything he'd fought for was now balanced on the edge of a knife, because of her.

He pricked his finger with one of his claws, walked over to the raven, and let the blood drip down onto its head. He had to wait a long time for the beak to open. Then he felt her presence, even though she hadn't said a word. Her silence told him everything he needed to know.

He collapsed onto the sofa, not sure where to begin. She didn't say anything either, but he knew she was there. He could smell her fear, her deep despair. Her betrayal.

What pain would he inflict on her first? How long would he torment her before he let her die?

A long time. She would suffer as long as he had. A thousand years. Damayanti's death would span a thousand years. And in those thousand years, she would die a thousand deaths.

He tasted blood. His canines had sunk into his lip. He stared at the raven cadaver, fighting the urge to destroy it. To destroy her.

He could hear her breathing. It was panicked, shaky.

She knew. They both knew.

Her fear and his rage intertwined. He readied himself to scream, to make her scream. One howl and she'd be torn apart.

But something stopped him. He considered what she was. Everything she'd been for him, done for him. He couldn't bring himself to say her name.

He just sat there, with her, for a long time. They couldn't see each other, and not a word passed between them, but she might as well have been sitting right next to him.

He heard her swallow. Afraid she'd ruin the perfect silence, he got up and closed the raven's beak.

HE CAME

Naiell tossed and turned in his sleep. Hirka smoothed his hair back from his forehead. The black tangles spilled down his back and onto the sofa. He was the only one who could sleep. Stefan had gone out to see if he could find a shop that was still open. To buy cigarettes, and some half-rotten fruit for Naiell.

It felt like an eternity had passed since she'd had a break from both of them. Time to herself, somewhere safe. But what did she know about how safe it was here? Maybe it just felt that way because she'd been here before. In the apartment in Stockholm. On Riddargatan, where Stefan claimed to have lived.

He didn't dare stop at hotels, so they'd driven all day and all night, sleeping for a few hours in a parking lot before continuing on their way. But they couldn't keep driving forever. They'd needed somewhere safe, so they'd come back. This time the people who lived there had been home. The woman and Stefan had argued for a long time while Naiell slept in the car and Hirka waited in the hall. They argued like lovers. There was something about the way they spoke to each other. A bitterness. He'd called her Karma. Given her money in the end. Hirka had only glimpsed her as she'd hurried off down the stairs. Beautiful, but angry. Holding a big leather bag in one hand and her daughter's hand in the other.

Hirka leaned against the window. The constant thumping of music came from the street below. People stood in clusters in the dark under a flashing sign. Some of them were drinking. Two were kissing. None of them were steady on their feet.

Hirka sat down again and looked at Naiell. His body looked like it had been carved from stone. Hard. Strong. Pale. Like some sort of strange idol. With back muscles she'd never seen in any ymling. Or any human. Only a couple of days ago he'd had a huge gash in his shoulder. But now there was nothing. Not so much as a scar.

He was a creature built for a life she couldn't imagine. From a world she'd never seen and hoped she never would. Even though she knew she had the same blood. He was Graal's brother. They were family.

Now there was a disturbing thought.

How much did she have in common with him? If she drew her knife right now and sliced into her arm, would it heal before a drop of blood hit the floor?

No. She knew it wouldn't. She'd hurt herself loads of times. Spilled her fair share of blood. True, the wounds had healed quickly, but there was a difference between quickly and … this. No wonder Eirik and Rime had said they were difficult to kill.

Rime … Rime and Sylja. Lindri. Svarteld.

Her heart sank into her stomach, where it lay simmering. Burning anger. Hatred.

She'd done all she could to keep Rime safe, and now he was anything but. Who would help him now? Sylja? *Hah!* She'd like to see him take Sylja out in the forests to fight the deadborn! He'd soon realize what little use she was then. Did he think Sylja would be able to patch him up when death was near? Could Sylja help him channel the Might, so he could keep himself alive? Blackest Blindból, of course she couldn't! Sylja wasn't a child of Odin. Or deadborn. All Sylja could do was dance. Roll her eyes. Smile.

Give him a good life.

Poisonous thoughts. She knew she ought to ignore them, to look at things differently, but knowing that only made it worse. Another burden to bear. Self-loathing on top of pain and grief.

Nothing was as she'd believed anymore. Not even the blind. No one in Ym knew anything about them. They couldn't begin to understand them. She watched Naiell as he slept. He wasn't a monster. He was a friend. And she was one of them. The blind hadn't killed Lindri, or thrown her in the pits in Eisvaldr. *They* had. Ymlings. Ym's kin. Ordinary people.

People mean danger.

An echo from Father, who slumbered in Slokna. Father had known the truth of it. He'd always known. Crones' talk and superstition were the least of her worries. Ordinary people were the real danger.

The loneliness was overwhelming. Everyone she met was either a murderer or doomed to die. But at least now she knew why. Now she knew what the war was about. Blood that could prolong life. Blood of the blind. For just a drop of that blood, people would lick the ground. And because she had the same blood, she was doomed to live a life on the run. Caught between life and death. Between worlds. There was nowhere for her to go. Nowhere she belonged anymore.

But she did have Graal's phone number in her pocket.

Naiell smacked his lips. His mouth dropped open. His canines were like white knives in the dark. According to Stefan, he hadn't been shot. He'd been knocked out by a weapon made of something electric. The same thing that made lights turn on. Phones ring. TVs lie. Everything worked because of this unseen energy. A bit like the Might.

Naiell grabbed her arm. Stared up at her. Confused. She could see it in his eyes. At first it had been like staring into a cup of milk. Impossible to see any emotion. But she could now. She'd started to understand his expressions. Very little could actually be read in people's eyes. It was the small movements around the eyes that gave everything away. The eyelids, the eyebrows ...

"We're back in Stockholm," she said. "You've had a bit of a shock, but you're okay now."

He growled, remembering what had happened. "Where's Stefan?"

"He's out."

He sat up on the sofa. "We're alone?"

She felt her eyes brim with tears. She didn't know why. Alone was just such a horrible word. She didn't want to cry. She wanted to hate. But her heart wouldn't obey. He reached out and lifted her chin, surveying her.

"You trust me."

"Why are you asking me that?"

"I'm not asking, I'm telling. We never shed tears in front of our enemies."

Without stopping to think, she wiped away her tears. She immediately felt anxious.

His hand slid down her throat. "He's useless. The human. We've been with him for weeks and it's still just the three of us."

"How many of us do you think there should be?"

"We need an army, Sulni! Not a halfwit with no knowledge of warfare." He tightened his grip on her shoulder. She could feel his claws through her tunic.

"That's not how it works here, Naiell! We need Stefan. We can't just go out and ... build armies. Or start wars. They have police here. Things are ... I don't know. Everything's connected. It's complicated."

"It was complicated in Ym too, but I still managed a fair bit in one day." He smiled. "And that was on my own." He let go of her and sank back onto the sofa again, closing his eyes. She wished she could make at least some sense of his energy levels. They seemed to go up and down depending on what he ate. He didn't think anything here could be called food. Maybe there were just some things that didn't agree with him.

The front door flew open and Stefan came in with a full shopping bag and a newspaper. He was sweating.

"Wait till you see this," he said.

Stefan tossed the newspaper on the table and started to flip through it. Hirka emptied the groceries out onto the kitchen counter. There were lots of things that Naiell didn't like. But he'd definitely sunk his claws into bananas and cheese before. She went into the living room with them and put them down on the table in front of him. He'd fallen asleep again.

"By all means, dig in ..." Stefan mumbled when she returned.

"He's going to need to eat when he wakes up."

"Where the hell did it go?" Stefan kept flipping through the same pages. "I picked it up in York and forgot about it. Christ, I had no idea ... Here!"

He pointed at some writing in the paper. "The Southampton Ninja! He chopped a cop's leg off. Seriously, chopped it right off! With a sword!"

"I'd have thought you'd seen worse," Hirka said.

"Now listen, I don't know if you've noticed, girl, but there are very few people running around here wearing leather armor and brandishing swords, let me tell you. How many times have I seen that? Let me think ... approximately ... zero!"

"Are you being sarcastic?"

"Congratulations." Stefan found his phone. "Wait, there's more. They think they've got him. At the very least they think they've got him surrounded. Look." He held the phone up for her.

She looked at the photo. It was blurry, and the cracked glass didn't help. That was her fault. She'd dropped his phone when Allegra had called.

All she could see was a fair-haired figure, surrounded by what looked like police. Cars and people. She knew where Stefan was going with this, but he was wrong. Still, her heart started pounding.

"Hirka, he spoke a language nobody understood, and he refused to show ID."

"ID?"

"Identification! Passport. Driver's license. Sound familiar? Christ, I've seen far too much in these last few weeks to think this is a coincidence. This is one of you! They've sent someone after you, haven't they? Let's hope it's the cavalry." He laughed. It sounded a bit manic.

Hirka didn't know what cavalry was, but it didn't matter. "It's not someone from Ym," she said.

"How can you know that? You weren't there!"

"First of all, he has no ..." She searched for the word. She always forgot words when she got upset. "He has no tail."

Stefan stared at her. "Say what?"

It dawned on her that Stefan had never seen anyone with a tail. Or heard about anyone with a tail, for that matter. He was a child of Odin. A human, brought up among humans. Hirka felt dizzy. She sat down at the kitchen table and rested her head in her hands. There were so many things she should have explained. So many things, big and small. She didn't know where to start.

"Wait," Stefan said. "The park was full of people, this *has* to be online somewhere ..." He pulled his computer out of his bag. She couldn't remember ever seeing him like this. He was always agitated, but this was different. He mumbled to himself as he poked the machine and stared at the screen. The light made his skin look blue. He turned the screen toward her.

"Friend of yours?" He grinned and leaned back in his chair.

Hirka stared at the moving picture. People running through a park. Cars screeching. Skidding onto the grass. A man. In the center of the picture. Long white hair. A sword in each hand. Leather straps across his chest.

It had to be. He was tailless, but it had to be him. Without a shadow of a doubt. He walked out of the picture and it stopped moving.

"Rime!" Hirka launched herself at the screen.

Stefan snatched it away from her. "It's a video, girl. Relax."

"RIME!"

She grabbed the computer and shook the screen, but the picture was dead. "What have they done with him?!"

Stefan jumped to his feet and pulled her away from the table. "Hey! Calm down, girl! You heard what I said. They'll get him soon. It's okay."

Okay? What was okay? None of this was okay. Rime was here! And they had him. The police … Graal. He was here, and they'd chopped off his tail.

She tore herself out of Stefan's grasp and reached for the screen. He forced her up against the wall. Pinned her arm against her chest and held her there. "A video. Get it? He's not here, he's in England."

Hirka wanted to fight her way free, but she didn't have the strength. She was powerless. What had they done with Rime? Why was he here? Didn't he know that he couldn't be here? It was dangerous. She couldn't think of a worse place to be.

"We have to get him, Stefan! Now! We have to go now."

Stefan held her tight. He didn't have to say anything. His hesitation spoke volumes. She screamed into his ear. "What are we waiting for!"

He gave her a shake. "Listen, Hirka. He's not going anywhere. We've been driving for days, and we're mixed up in a lot of shit over there. It can wait."

"No, it can't!"

She felt trapped. Penned in. Stefan's arm over her chest. His face right up to hers. He was a stranger. They were never going to understand each other.

She wanted to explain. Had to explain. Rime didn't understand this world. You couldn't just go around chopping people's feet off. Not that you could in Ym, but it definitely wasn't an option here! They'd kill him. Or lock him up and leave him to rot.

This is Graal's handiwork.

Stefan suddenly let go of her. Naiell was standing in the doorway. Broad-shouldered and ready to fight. He was taller and stronger than Stefan. His black hair splayed across his bare shoulders like wings. She'd never seen him look more like Kuro. The raven. Her raven.

"Tell him that we have to get Rime," she said in ymish. "We have to!" Naiell's white eyes slid between her and Stefan. Then he gave a shrug and walked over to the fridge. As if nothing out of the ordinary were going on.

"You wanted your own army!" she screamed at him. "Get Rime and you won't need one!"

She fought to hold back the sobs building in her throat. Then she remembered.

Don't let them see how desperate you are. No one will help you then.

Her own words. She had to rein herself in. Breathe. There was no use fighting. Or begging. That wouldn't save Rime.

He's here. Rime's here.

She slumped down onto the kitchen floor and sat with her head resting against the wall. Stefan crouched down in front of her. He took her hands in his and rubbed them, as if she were cold. "He's not going anywhere, Hirka. They've got him surrounded in the national park. They're going to find him."

She nodded. They'd find him, and they'd die.

"Dammit, girl, we've barely slept in days. None of us are seeing clearly right now. We'll talk about it in the morning." His words were laughable. A confused man's attempt to sound like a grown-up. She nodded again. Wiped her nose on the sleeve of her tunic.

He's here.

She steadied her breathing, clinging to the glimmer of hope amid the black thoughts.

He came.

BLANK PAGES

She waited until the others were asleep. It didn't take long. None of them had had a decent night's sleep in forever. She got up and climbed down from the two-story bed. Pulled on her trousers and her old tunic. Dragged her fingers through her hair. A near impossible task. It would just have to stay tangled. She had no time to lose.

She sat down among the stuffed animals and emptied her bag out onto the floor. She needed to repack it and set aside anything that wasn't necessary. A spare jumper. The half cup she'd been lugging around since leaving the church. She needed to make sure there was room for her waterskin. And the book, which was on the table in the living room—where Naiell was sleeping. That would pose the biggest problem.

That and the fact that she had no idea where she was or where she was going. In York, she had drawn maps of the neighborhood. She didn't have a map of Stockholm.

Hirka finished repacking and shouldered her bag. Then she opened the bedroom door as quietly as she could. It was dark in the living room, apart from the flashing of the sign outside. There was a buzzing every time it flickered out.

She tiptoed past the bookcase dividing the room. Naiell was up in the loft again, lying with one arm over his face. But she couldn't let herself be lulled into a false sense of security. He had good hearing. Better than hers. Her woolly socks muffled her footsteps as she walked. The book was on the table right in front of her. The incredibly important book that had all three of them stumped. What did it matter if Graal got his hands on it? It didn't. Not one bit. But Rime mattered. It was the easiest exchange in the world.

Hirka picked up the book. Naiell rolled onto his side. She stiffened, but he slumbered on. She padded into the kitchen, found the plastic bag from Stefan's trip to the store, and put the book inside. The plastic kept the weather out somehow. She tucked it into her bag, between her clothes.

Now came the hard part.

She found her way to the room where Stefan was sleeping and rested her hand on the door handle. Listened. All was quiet. She pushed the handle down, carefully. It squeaked. She managed to crack the door open. Stefan was in bed with his back to her, still wearing his white, short-sleeved shirt. Not unlike the one she wore to bed. Somehow that made her feel even worse, like she was betraying him. But he wouldn't understand.

His phone was on the table by the bed. She reached for it, not daring to get any closer. Her fingertips made contact with the smooth surface. She pulled it toward her. Then dropped it.

Hirka quickly swooped down and caught it before it hit the floor. She stayed like that for a few moments, her heart in her mouth. She couldn't afford to make such stupid mistakes, not when Rime's life was at stake. She needed to get it together.

She got up again and backed out of the room. She didn't dare close the door behind her.

Her raincoat was hanging on a hook in the hall, next to a dark red coat with fur trim. Where did they get fur in a world without animals? She pulled the coat over her head and put on her yellow boots, shoving her knife down the side of one. Then she carefully opened the door, stepped out, and headed for the stairs, which circled down past the other floors. Soon enough, she was outside.

It had just stopped raining. Her boots splashed against the pavement as she walked. There was hardly anyone around. A couple of cars drove past, their lights dazzling her. One of them whistled. She ran across the road, phone clutched in her hand. Once across, she perched on a window ledge outside a café and dug the chocolate wrapper out of her pocket. Graal's phone number. Now all she had to do was remember.

The phone was like a smooth, black stone in her hand. Cracked screen. Only one button. She pressed it and the screen lit up. She remembered the first time she'd seen that happen. How nervous she'd been about touching it. She'd thought it would be hot, but that wasn't how things worked here. Here light was cold. Dead.

Something moved on the screen, rippling through the text from left to right, and she remembered. Jay had shown her this.

Swipe right.

She touched the screen and dragged her finger across it. A new picture appeared, one crowded with small symbols. Which one was she supposed to tap? She bit her lip. She couldn't afford to get it wrong. She'd done that before and it had ruined everything.

She stared at the symbols. One of them looked familiar. A sort of bow on a green background. That was the one, wasn't it? The one she needed to tap to get the numbers to appear? She had to choose. There was nothing else to be done.

She poked the symbol. The screen filled with numbers. She didn't remember which was which, but it didn't matter. All she needed to do was tap the same number on the screen as on the chocolate wrapper. And then call. What was it Jay had said?

Green to call. Red to end call.

Hirka closed her eyes and took a deep breath. When she opened them again, the screen was black.

No! Please, not now!

She touched the screen again and repeated the steps. Swiping with her finger, tapping the green symbol to make the numbers appear. Then she tapped out the numbers from the chocolate wrapper. Carefully. The final number was hard to make out. A circle with a line attached to it. None of the numbers on the phone looked much like it. The closest was a circle with a curved line underneath. It had to be that one. It couldn't be any of the others. Tap. Done.

Her finger quivered over the green symbol. If she tapped now, she'd get to talk to Graal. Hear his voice.

She pressed her finger to the screen and heard a sound. She lifted the phone to her ear. It sounded like a bird. No voice, just trilling. Maybe he was far away, or maybe the phone had to find him first. Maybe he was asleep. After all, Naiell was always sleeping.

Then a deep voice spoke into her ear. "Yes?"

It's him! Seer preserve me!

Her blood ran cold. All the hairs on her arm stood on end. She opened her mouth but couldn't bring herself to speak. All she could hear was the sound of her own breathing. Then he spoke again.

"Hirka ..."

She jumped. He sounded disconcertingly close. Her name. In his mouth. And it didn't sound like a question. He was certain. He'd known she would contact him.

Because he has Rime.

She nodded—but then she remembered he couldn't see her. She had to speak.

"Let him go," she blurted out in ymish. Every single word she'd learned in the last six months was gone. Out of reach. All she remembered was her mother tongue.

She heard him get up. "I'm working on it. Are you alone?" He replied in the same language.

"No!" she replied, a little too quickly. She heard a door open. Clothes rustle.

"Are the others asleep? Can anyone hear you?"

"I have the book," she said.

There was silence for a moment. "You want to make a trade … for him?"

"If you touch him, I'll kill you!" She squeezed her eyes shut, despairing at how empty the threat sounded. But she meant it. She had something Graal needed, and she had a knife in her boot. If she killed him, it would all be over. She wouldn't have to run anymore. He wouldn't be a threat to Ym. A threat to Rime.

"Funny, he said exactly the same thing about you," Graal said.

Hirka could feel the coldness in her smile. She'd seen Rime kill. "I'd be afraid then, if I were you."

She regretted it the moment it was out of her mouth. She couldn't have him thinking Rime was a danger to him. It could cost Rime his life.

"We can threaten each other to kingdom come when we meet," Graal said. "First things first, you need to get out without anyone seeing you. Now. Understand?"

"I'm not an idiot."

"Where are you?"

"We're in Stockholm."

"Do you have the address?"

She knew the name of the street, but she wasn't sure she should tell him. What if he found the others as well? But Rime's life was at stake. And it was a long street, with a lot of buildings. She decided to risk it.

"Riddargatan."

She heard a tapping noise and realized it was his claws against the phone. The realization made her feel more vulnerable, though she wasn't sure why. It was always the little things that threatened to turn reality on its head. She took a deep breath. Her lungs felt fragile.

"Perfect," he said. "Can you find your way to the sea?"

She got up and sniffed the air. "Yes."

Graal directed her along a side street until she could see the water. She wondered where he was, since clearly he could see her, but she didn't want to ask.

"Do you see a bridge? With statues on both sides?" he asked.

"Yes, I see it."

"Good. Cross the bridge and go straight ahead until you see the zoo."

"The zoo?"

"It's called Skansen. You might not be able to read the signs, but I'm guessing you can smell your way there. Stay close and I'll find you. I'll be there in two hours."

"But—"

"And get rid of the phone."

"It's Stefan's, I can't—"

"Get rid of it."

"No! I want to talk to him!"

There was silence for a moment. Why was Graal hesitating? All she wanted was a word with Rime. A thousand horrible reasons for the silence immediately sprang to mind.

He's dead. He's hurt. He's not actually here. He can't speak.

"It's not that simple," Graal said.

"I want to talk to him! I'm not giving you anything until I've talked to him."

"Give me five minutes and I'll call you back."

Silence.

"Graal?"

Relax, he'll call you. He said so. He'll call. With Rime.

Hirka walked out onto the bridge, putting the city lights behind her, heading toward an unknown darkness. A place where night was allowed to be night. Lamps illuminated the statues. Two on one side of the bridge, and two on the other. They had their backs to her, like they wanted nothing to do with her. She didn't know who they were supposed to be. A man with a horn. Another with a hammer.

She stared at the phone. It would ring, and then she'd get to talk to Rime. A droplet of water landed on the screen. She wiped it off, hoping it wouldn't start raining again. Forgetting to look where she was going, she almost bumped into a sleepy woman in ripped black tights who was dozing against a bin. The woman lifted her head. "This is my spot, girl! Do you want to die?" she slurred.

Hirka backed away. "Not today," she heard herself reply. She started to run. Straight ahead, as Graal had told her. Graal. The man who wanted her dead, and who she'd just arranged to meet. Then the smell hit her. Animals. More than she'd come across in a long time. Trees. Life.

It was dark and she couldn't see a way in, only high fences and locked gates. What had they done? Gathered all the animals in one place? No wonder she never saw them anywhere else.

She needed to find a way in, somewhere to wait, to hide. She followed the fence until an opportunity presented itself. A large birch tree. Hirka threw her bag over the fence and climbed up into the tree. Then she jumped down on the other side. She rolled as she hit the ground, remembering the birch that Father had cut down before he'd told her she was a child of Odin. If only he'd known. It was far worse than that.

Deep down, she knew she wasn't supposed to be there. But then, wild animals weren't supposed to be locked up either, so in a way, they were even. Besides, she was half-animal herself.

The ground was wet from the rain, but her bag had survived. Patches of snow glowed in the darkness. She found a clump of trees, one of which was actually conjoined trees, but someone had cut one of them down, leaving only a stump. She sat on it and stared at the phone.

Still nothing.

He'll call. I have the book. And I have me. That's all he needs.

Hirka pulled the book out of her bag and opened it on her lap. Page after page of circles and lines. Completely random. Not a single word. Perhaps it was some sort of code?

She leaned back against the tree that had been allowed to live, dug her overfilled waterskin out of her bag, and took a sip. Water dripped down onto the open book. She quickly wiped the page with her sleeve, but it had already absorbed every drop. She lifted her arm, almost afraid to look. The ink was bound to have smudged. That was all she needed, to destroy her only bargaining chip.

But the ink was still fine. The paper hadn't even wrinkled. Hirka prodded a transparent patch where one of the drops had landed. It didn't fall apart, as paper tended to do when it got wet. Now that was odd. Very odd.

A spark forced its way through the darkness. Curiosity. Hope. She poured more water into her palm and let it trickle over the book. Hirka focused on one of the circles with lines that looked like a simplistic depiction of a sun. The lines were all different lengths. They had been pointing out into nothing, but not anymore. Now one of the lines joined up with another circle. On one of the pages underneath.

She almost dropped the waterskin in her excitement, accidentally dousing one corner of the book. Water dripped down onto her legs, but the paper was still just as intact, just as strong. The ink wasn't even running.

Now it was sink or swim.

She laid the book on the ground and poured the rest of her water over it. The pages turned transparent, like thin sheets of glass. The drawings were no longer isolated symbols. They were connected. She lifted the book. It was too dark. She couldn't see. She went over to the streetlight by the fence, folding the soft cover aside and holding the pages up toward the light. Lines that had previously pointed out into nothing now pointed at other circles. A network. Connected rings. Hundreds of them. Thousands.

The raven rings.

The realization hit her like lightning. A map. It was a map.

Of course it was. What had she been drawing ever since she'd come to this world? Maps. What made her helpless here? Not having a map, not knowing where she was or where to go. And if there were an unknown number of gateways to an unknown number of worlds, what would be more valuable than anything else?

A map.

Of how many worlds? There had to be hundreds ... Hirka closed the book and hugged it to her chest. Her head was spinning. The light seemed to waver. The fence wasn't standing still anymore.

Madness. This was madness. Graal didn't just want Ym. He wanted everything.

She'd thought she would be trading Rime for a whole world. But it was worse. She would be trading him for every world imaginable.

THE WOLF

Hirka had closed the book. A book of lies. It rested on her lap, deceptively simple. Harmless. A black cover with nothing more than two lines on it. False modesty. It was a weapon in disguise.

She suddenly noticed a familiar smell. Something wild and very much alive. She turned to see two eyes shining at her. White circles in the darkness. A wolf. It stood by a bare tree, staring at her. She knew she ought to get up. Run. But her reflexes had abandoned her. The book in her lap had just shown her eternity. She was being hunted by the rot and waiting for a blindling who wanted to steal her blood. What was a wolf compared to that?

"I'm not scared of you," she whispered. "Eat me and you'd be doing the world a favor. I'd rather you had my blood than Graal."

The wolf growled, baring its teeth. That only served to warm her heart. The world felt real again.

"So what do you think I should do? Should I give him what he needs? My blood and the book? Nice present, right? Here you are, now off you go and destroy a world or two! Or hundreds." She laughed despondently. The wolf took a step closer. Stopped growling. "You're right," she said. "I'm being an idiot."

She was going to bargain for Rime's life. For her own. Not to mention Stefan and Naiell's. But what would she have to bargain with if he already had everything he needed? She had to hide the book.

Hirka put it back into the plastic bag. "Can you keep a secret?" The wolf licked its chops. She started to dig a hole in the ground with her bare hands. The smell of damp earth overwhelmed her. It had been far too long since she'd been surrounded by the smell of nature. A real forest, not those silly park things. She dug down until she was elbow-deep.

Suddenly the phone lit up and started vibrating next to her. She gave a start. Pounced on it. Ran a dirty finger across the screen and held it to her ear.

"Rime?"

"Rime, can you hear her?" Graal asked.

Then she heard the voice that she loved above all else.

"Hirka?"

Her body went limp. She slumped down in front of the hole in the ground, clutching the phone.

"Hirka, do as he says. It's going to be all right. Trust me." His voice sounded like it was coming from somewhere far away. Still it burrowed deep inside of her, consuming what little strength she'd thought she had left. Words jostled for space on her tongue, but she couldn't get any of them out. She wanted to say that she loved him. Hated him. That he was a bloody fool for coming here. He didn't belong here. He was in danger. And he was putting the world in danger.

"Rime, you have to get away from him!"

"I'm not with him. I'm … I don't know where I am."

"Have they given you a phone? Rime?"

"I let him go." Graal's voice again. "Talking is painful for him, and I presume you don't want to hurt him."

Painful?

An image of Urd drove everything else out of her head. Urd. Kneeling on the ground. Dying. The beak eating its way out of his rotting throat. Blindcraft. Urd, who had spoken to her father. To Graal. How?

Rime's voice, deeper and hoarser than before. Rime, who'd never seen a phone. Who was trapped somewhere. Yet she'd still been able to talk to him. The lies from Allegra that had to have come from Ym. But how?

Hirka felt sick. She tried to stop the threads that were coming together in her mind, but it was no use. They were all leading in the same direction. Weaving an ugly certainty. She was being lied to. This was a lie. It had to be.

"Stay where you are. Stay out of sight. I'll be there soon." Graal sounded almost fond. A morbid contrast to what she'd just come to realize. To all that he was, and all that he would do. She wanted to tell him to rot in Slokna, but her tongue felt too big for her mouth. The phone went quiet again. She couldn't hold on to it any longer. It fell to the ground.

Rime has the beak. Urd's beak.

She'd lost. Anything she did now would be meaningless. She could trade the book for Rime, but Graal had already made Rime his slave. How much time did he have? How long before his throat smelled of death?

Hirka hugged her bag, but it was of little comfort. There was nothing to cling to here. She was tumbling through the darkness. A sob forced its way up from her stomach and rippled through her body. Her eyes were stinging and the tears started to flow.

She grabbed the plastic bag and threw the phone inside, along with the book. She knew why Graal wanted her to get rid of it. Stefan could find it. He'd said so himself.

That's how they get you, isn't it?

That was her only hope. Everything had gone to Slokna, but at least Stefan could keep Graal from finding the map of the raven rings. She put the bag in the hole and piled the dirt on top. Patted it down hard with her cold hands. Then she just sat there, the knees of her trousers soaked through.

The wolf came closer. Circled around her, then lay down on the ground. She crawled toward him. Toward the only warmth in this cold place. He let her get closer. Let her curl up next to him.

She breathed in the smell. Closed her eyes. She was home. She was back in Ym. Everything was wild, wet, and wonderful. Rime was safe, she was safe, and there was no such thing as deadborn.

Just for a little while.

While she waited for the end to come.

BLOOD OF MY BLOOD

He's here.

Hirka had nodded off. Before she even opened her eyes, she knew she was no longer alone. The wolf's belly moved up and down under her head as he breathed, but that wasn't what had woken her. It was something else, something more animalistic, and it was close. It was impossible to tell whether it was a smell or just a feeling, but she remembered it from the museum. Graal. Deadborn family.

The wolf woke up and sprang to his feet. He growled at the darkness, hackles raised, fur sticking out like needles around his neck. Hirka tried to get up as well, but she didn't make it farther than her knees. Her body felt weak. Sore. Her eyes puffy.

The map. Rime. The beak. The end of the world.

She felt disconnected from her emotions, as if she simply couldn't face them anymore. Or perhaps they'd frozen. It was colder now.

Graal was here.

A dark outline in the fog, making his way toward her. Tall, with a long coat. He stopped a short distance away, the wind ruffling his short black hair. At first she'd thought his eyes were closed, but now she could see that they were black. He was pale, with high cheekbones.

The blindling raised his hand toward the snarling wolf. The animal whimpered and backed away, head lowered, before disappearing between the trees. Graal reached out to Hirka, and she realized that she was still sitting on the ground. She took his hand without thinking. It closed around hers. Cool. Strong. Claws sharp against her wrist.

She was touching her father. Her father and her enemy. For the first time.

This wasn't how she'd imagined it. She ought to have been standing. Back straight. Wide awake. Not sitting, like this. Not with puffy eyes and rotting leaves in her hair.

He pulled her to her feet. He was nearly as tall as Naiell, but thinner, with an almost boyish appearance. Young and old at the same time. Soft and hard.

She yanked her hand out of his and took a step back, bracing herself for an attack. A blow. A weapon. Anything. It didn't come. He crouched down and locked eyes with her. Fire in black glass. Eyes reflecting worlds. Generations.

"Blood of my blood."

His words confirmed everything she'd feared. What he was doing here. Why she was here. The feelings she'd kept at bay came flooding back, crushing her. An unbearable sea of despair.

Rime was nowhere to be seen. Graal had never intended to make a trade. He wanted everything. She backed away from him. He didn't have everything yet. She still had power. Hirka pulled the knife out of her boot and held it against her wrist, the steel cold against her skin.

"Where's Rime?" She hated that her voice was shaking.

Graal smiled, but his eyes still looked sad. Or perhaps they just seemed that way because they turned down slightly at the corners. It made him beautiful, and she hated that even more.

"You've definitely inherited my penchant for the dramatic," he said. "It gives us good and bad days, I'm afraid. I hope for your sake that you have more of the good ones. Now, I could lie to you. It would make everything so much simpler. I could tell you he's waiting for you. That I'll take you to him. But I don't have him. He's on the run. I have my best people on the case, and I promise you I'll find him. Before the police do."

"Why? What do you want with him? He doesn't belong here!"

"I know you think I brought him here, but I didn't. He had help. From someone I didn't think would help him." Graal was still sitting on his heels, eyes lowered and an air of mournful calm about him. She couldn't help but feel the same. Sad that Rime wasn't here, that this was the end. She'd thought she'd get to see him again. Here. Tonight.

"Rime came here entirely of his own free will," Graal said. "He defied me. Not many people do that. Every day he's here, I lose influence in Mannfalla, and that's hard-won."

Hirka gritted her teeth. "And the raven beak?"

"He took that, too. Once again, entirely of his own free will," Graal replied, showing no sign of surprise that she'd made the connection.

"Liar! He wouldn't take it to escape Slokna itself! Why would he?" It felt good to get it off her chest. He didn't have Rime yet, and that emboldened her. "It's blindcraft! His throat will rot—I've seen it! No one would do something like that of their own free will!"

"You think there are limits to what people would do of their own free will?"

"Not this. Not Rime."

"So maybe we need to reconsider what free will is. Yes, I had everything to gain from him taking it. He's the Ravenbearer. Kolkagga. I couldn't have had a better man on the Council. It's true. But no one forced him. He had his reasons."

Hirka barked out a laugh. She felt like a different person, yet somehow more herself than ever. It scared her. It was like she was watching her own ruin. "Nothing in the world would make him do that."

Graal stood up. "He did it for you. Because he knew you were in danger."

"You're lying!" she shouted, pressing the knife more firmly against her wrist. She could feel her pulse against the steel. "Let Rime go! Get that blindcraft out of his throat or I die now. And you'll never be free. My blood will flow into the ground and feed the worms. Then it'll never be yours!"

She knew she wouldn't be able to follow through on her threat. She could feel the resistance in her entire body. But Graal didn't know that.

"What on earth has he been telling you ..."

It didn't sound like a question, but she was so angry and so scared that she answered anyway. If this was the end, she'd never have a chance to say another word. "They poisoned your blood, I know that much. So you could never use the raven rings. So you could never leave this place."

"That pretty much sums it up," he replied quietly.

"But you can swap your blood! They can do it, the humans. I know they can. At the hospitals. But you can't swap with humans. You need blood from your own kind. You need my blood. So now you get to choose whether you want Rime or your freedom, Graal."

He stared at her, eyes full of doubt. Then he closed them and gave a pained grimace.

Hirka hadn't expected that. She suddenly felt uncertain. She found herself hoping that Naiell had misunderstood, that Stefan had been lying. Maybe she wasn't a blood bag. The knife quivered against her wrist. She could no longer hold it steady.

Then he grabbed her. She didn't have time to react. He stood before her, her knife in his hand. He threw it to the ground. The blade plunged into the earth.

"Hirka, we don't kill each other. Dreyri do not kill Dreyri. He knows that. Yes, I'm trapped here, in the human world. I always will be. He has sealed my fate. An eternity without the Might. I've made my peace with that. I don't need your blood."

Her body betrayed her. Tears started to fall. She was so, so tired. She hoped against hope that everything he was saying was true.

He turned up the collar on his coat and moved closer to her. Strong yet gentle. A movable mountain. "If you don't believe me, then go. My brother will use you, blood of my blood. For all you're worth, until there's nothing left. But I won't force you to stay with me. Go if you want. You're free. I don't need your blood. The only thing that will happen if you die is that I will mourn you until my last breath."

Graal cupped her face in his hands. Plucked a leaf from her hair. Wiped her tears away with his thumb. Careful not to touch her with his claws.

"Hirka, I'm not here to take your life. I'm here to save it."

THE SUCCESSOR

Hirka followed Graal through the trees and out into an open area. There she saw a vessel she'd only seen a few times before. It looked like an enormous insect. Angry and black, and somehow able to fly without proper wings. The fog made it look somber, like a lone funeral carriage. Was this to be her final journey?

Graal opened the door for her. She couldn't bring herself to climb in, not until she knew.

"You can remove it, can't you? The beak? If you didn't force him."

"No."

A small word, yet so painful.

He walked around the insect carriage and climbed in on the other side. "There is someone who can, but no one you'll ever meet. Nor me. They belong to our world. The world of Umpiri."

She shut her eyes. She couldn't think about it. Right now she had to keep a cool head and understand her father. Her enemy. Work out whether she could trust anything Graal said. The blindling who had just turned everything she thought she'd known on its head.

She climbed in and sat down. He handed her a pair of ear cushions, like the ones on Nils's plane. She put them on straight away, not wanting him to think she'd never flown before.

Graal pressed a dizzying number of buttons above them, between them, and in front of them. The carriage started to whine, getting louder and louder as the needles on the panel in front of her quivered. The wings on the roof swished around. Faster and faster, until they melted together. Then they rose off the ground. Climbed up and forward, as if borne by the Might. They soared through the night, above a blanket of lights. Hundreds of thousands of them. The moon appeared above the clouds, and it felt like she was sitting in the hand of Ym. The first, the giant whose body had become the eleven kingdoms. His bones mountains, his blood rivers.

The lights disappeared behind them. They were headed into nothingness, into darkness.

Hirka kept glancing over at her deadborn father. She hated how conflicted she felt. It wasn't supposed to be like that. It was supposed to be simple. Graal was supposed to be like Urd. He was meant to sneer at her. Knock her to the ground. Wrap his hand around her throat and squeeze until she couldn't breathe. He was meant to coerce her, with force. With cruelty. So she'd be able to drive her knife into him. That was the idea.

But Graal coerced her with words, manipulating her with lies she couldn't even begin to understand. He tormented her with insufferable civility. This blindling was to blame for all the misery she'd experienced since birth. She wanted to hate him. She didn't want to go to her death with this suffocating feeling of being drawn to him. But that was what was happening.

He hadn't asked about the book yet, and now it was too late. She'd left it buried with the wolves. A small comfort. Even though she was gone, Stefan and Naiell would find it when they woke up. But sooner or later Graal would realize he'd been deceived. That she didn't have the book he needed. What would he do to her?

I'm not afraid.

She'd imagined all the terrible things that might happen. Over and over again. Now that she was with him, it was nothing like she'd imagined. And that scared her more than anything.

She had no idea how long they'd been flying when the sounds around her changed. The carriage hovered in the air. Then it descended toward an illuminated red circle. They touched down. The sounds faded. The insect died. Graal undid her seat belt and helped her out. They were in the mountains, on the edge of a cliff overlooking snow-covered peaks. There were no lights or signs of life. Just her and Graal. And a cold wind that tugged at her hair.

Part of what she'd thought was mountain was actually a building fused with the black stone. Impossible angles slanting over the abyss.

Graal opened a door and they went inside. Stepped straight into the mountain, with floors and walls of black stone. Unseen light sources in the corridors. Glass and wood. Familiar materials that made her feel at home, even though she'd never seen a home with such distinctive features. She didn't dare think how much a place like this would cost.

They entered a room with windows that angled over the edge of the cliff. A black piano stood in the corner. On the wall behind it hung a picture of a similar instrument, smashed to smithereens. There was a dark sofa that looked hard as stone. A large painting hung on the wall, depicting storm clouds, fire, and a raging mountain.

"*The Great Day of His Wrath*."

She gave a start at the sound of his voice, right behind her. "It's an original. A gift from John Martin. Do you like it?"

She didn't reply. It was nice, in a way, but destruction nonetheless. Graal looked at the picture like he was seeing it for the first time. She got the feeling he did that a lot. He came closer. "And I saw when the lamb broke the sixth seal," he said, as if reading a poem. "And lo, there was a great earthquake, and the sun became black as sackcloth of hair, and the moon became as blood, and the stars of heaven fell unto the earth, even as a fig tree casteth her untimely figs when she is shaken of a mighty wind."

Hirka didn't understand the words, but they sounded horrific. She turned away from him and put her bag down on the sofa. On a glass table in front of her stood the cadaver of a raven. She went to touch it but stopped herself.

"They killed it," Graal said.

"Who?"

"My brother's slaves. Before they sent me here. They didn't call themselves a council back then, but you know who I mean. Everything you believe is based on the story of the twelve warriors."

Hirka remembered. "The twelve who rode into Blindból to stop the bli—to stop you. The first Council." More details came back to her. How it had all ended. How the Seer had saved them all by turning on the blind. His own. She'd never considered that there had been two sides to the war. No one talked about the blind as people. The blind were just the blind. Deadborn. And now one of them was standing here, right behind her.

"No wonder he's scared of you," she whispered.

Graal came to stand next to her. He had an intense presence. "Scared? Blood of my blood, no creature has ever been more driven by fear than my brother is now. And rightly so. He's no longer a god. Powerless without the Might. And he knows he's trapped here. He's not going anywhere without me."

"Then why did he come here?"

"That depends on whether you think him brave or a coward."

"What do you mean?"

"If he's brave, he came of his own free will. The people he betrayed are returning to Ym. We have allies in every region. Even in Mannfalla. If he's brave, he came here to stop me."

"And if he's a coward?"

"Then he spent too much time as a raven. Got lost in his bird brain, with little more than a vague notion of who he was. If he's a coward, it was the raven that brought him here."

Hirka thought about Kuro. The way the raven had been in Ym. Before she'd come here. Before he became Naiell. The raven and the Seer were like night and day.

"He's a coward," she said.

Graal smiled. He walked over to the window and looked out at the dark mountains. "What you need to ask yourself, Hirka, is why my brother would choose to stop a war he helped wage. I know you've heard the story, but I suspect you're too clever to swallow the lies they've force-fed you for centuries. What did he find in the ymling world that made him willing to risk death in order to win? What did Ym have that was worth sacrificing his own people for? That was so powerful that he destroyed the raven rings so he could keep it for himself? So he could live as a god?"

His words pushed their way into her head with explosive force. Twisting everything she knew. It was as if he'd opened a third eye inside her. Made her see anew. And there was no doubt as to what the answer was.

"The Might …"

Graal turned to her and held his arms out demonstratively. "And He saw the beauty of Ym," he quoted from the Book of the Seer, his lip curling into sneer. "Such was the goodness of He who looked upon them that they were all saved by His grace. Such was His sorrow for the fallen that His tears washed away their transgressions. Innocent, they looked upon their seer, and He said unto them: 'All power from the earth has been given unto me.'"

He sat down on the piano stool. "I won't bore you with the details of what they did to me. But you should know that his tree was forged from the blood of the thousands of men and women who fell on the battlefields. From parched earth. From the Might. He drew it through stone. Through worlds. Used ymlings and humans to feed his own might. The flow of the Might diminished. Dried up. And the raven rings died. Not a bad day's work, wouldn't you say?"

Graal leaned forward, rested a finger on one of the keys, and held it there, waiting for a sound that wouldn't come.

Hirka moved closer. "He says it's you. He says you're poisoning the world. That it's dying because of you. But it's because of the Might, isn't it? The world is dying because the Might doesn't exist here. And it doesn't exist here because *he* destroyed it! Because he stopped the flow of the Might? He said it was you, but that's not true."

Graal pressed the key down. A low note slipped out and died quietly between them.

"I so wish I could tell you you're right, Hirka. Win your trust by giving him the dubious honor of being a destroyer of worlds. Yes, I *believe* he doomed everyone but himself to death when he stole the Might. But the truth is I don't know. Maybe things would be different if the Might was still here. Maybe they would have had a chance. But I've lived among humans for a thousand years and gotten to know them all too well. They need no help from my brother to reap their own ruin."

"No one can kill an entire world." She spoke the words even though she had a gnawing suspicion that it wasn't true.

He shrugged. "They say you're a healer, so I understand that it pains you. But you can't heal this world. It's going to die. And I'm going to die with it."

He started to play. Soft. Mournful. Intricate.

"So that's why you hate the humans? So much so that you let them rot?" She wanted to be angry, but the words came out flat. Graal had drained her. Cracked her open. She was leaky as a sieve. Her feelings went straight through her.

"Let them rot? The way I *let* Rime take the beak? Or *let* him come here? Not only do they do it of their own free will, they're willing to step over corpses for it. The few people who know my secret promise me everything they have, and these are people who have everything you could dream of. The only thing they lack is more years to live. Yes, I give it to some of them. Am I to choose loneliness, when they would sacrifice everything to live by my side? You must have seen what they're willing to do."

He stopped playing. Got up. "Hirka, I'm far from innocent. I've done things you would deem horrific. And I'll do more. That's a given. But I don't consider the rot to be one of those things."

She tried to summon the rage she knew she had in her, but it had deserted her. All she had were empty accusations. "But it's not right. It's not natural!"

"It's not sorcery, Hirka. We're more than Umpiri. We're Dreyri, the only surviving descendants of the first. Our blood dominates the human body. Suppresses what's there and takes control. It's not contagious, but it can descend through the ranks. Some of them start to share blood among themselves. They thirst for it the way we thirst for the Might. Some take it by force. Kill each other for it, even though it is diluted with each new generation. Yes, it's poison to them, but not one that kills. It's poison that lets them live. It's the power in our blood. And you're one of us. You are Dreyri. You are blood of my blood."

He held two fingers to his throat. The sign she herself had used to hold back the blind at Bromfjell, without knowing what she'd been doing.

"Not just yours," she said. "I'm half-human, so who was she? I must have had a mother."

"You had two. One who provided the egg, and one who carried you."

"Blindcraft?"

"Science. Had it not been for the humans' need to outdo nature, you'd never have existed."

Hirka swallowed. She was afraid to ask, but she had to. "What happened to them?"

He didn't reply. He just stood there, with one hand on the piano. His silence spoke volumes. What had killed them? Illness? Had they been Vardar? Forgotten? Rotted away, all alone? Or was it him? Would he have been capable of … She thought about everything he'd said. Everything he'd made her believe. Lies. From him. From Allegra, who'd said Lindri was dead. That Rime had killed Svarteld, and that he and Sylja …

"Allegra said that Lindri … and that Rime … you made me believe …" Her voice faltered.

"I had to. Every day you've been here, Naiell has corrupted you with lies. I tried to find you before the raven relinquished control over him, but I failed. So what should I have said, Hirka, when I finally heard your voice? Should I have said that you had to come to me? Should I have said that your life was in danger, and that it was my brother you should fear, not me? What would you have done? Would you have believed me?"

She didn't say anything.

"Exactly," he said, as if she had answered. "I had to make you come to me, a man you were convinced wanted to destroy both you and Ym. So I had to find something worth more to you than either of them."

Rime …

"Think of it as a scale," he continued. "On the one side you had your own life, and the world you grew up in. Those are heavy things. On the other side you had Rime An-Elderin. I helped you choose. I made Ym lighter."

"You don't understand feelings, do you?" she whispered.

He moved toward her.

"Do you thirst for the Might, Hirka?"

The question made her feel inexplicably guilty. Yes, she thirsted for the Might. So much so that she wasn't always sure whether she missed it or Rime more. Graal didn't need to wait for her answer.

"And you've barely been here six months. Imagine living with that thirst for ten years. A hundred years. A thousand."

He started to unbutton his shirt. Stripped it off and dropped it on the floor. His chest was strong and defined, like that of every blindling she'd seen. He loosened his belt. She was starting to feel uneasy, but there was no desire in Graal's black eyes. Her unease was a reflex. A memory of the man in the pits who had tried to take her by force.

Graal pulled off his trousers and stood before her, completely naked. Hirka realized that he wouldn't have been able to take her even if he'd wanted to. He had nothing to take her with. Where his sex should have been, there was a teardrop-shaped scar. A pale hollow that reminded her of her own scar. The one Father had made when he'd found her tailless.

Graal was maimed. Naiell had maimed his own brother to win the battle for the Might. To become the Seer.

The maimed king ...

Graal turned away from her. He had an inking that covered nearly his entire back. She stepped closer. Small, black lines, close together, that started in the middle of his spine and swirled out in a chaotic circle. It looked like a bird's nest. She couldn't think of anything else to compare it to. The effect was almost hypnotic. A spiral pulling her in.

She lifted her hand and rested it on his shoulder blade. Both of them jumped at the touch, but he stayed where he was. She'd never seen anything like it. There was a system in all that wildness. All the lines were the same length and perfectly straight. Still ...

"What is it?" she asked. Her fingers followed the outer edge of the inking, where the lines were darkest, and in toward the spine, where they were older and paler. Maybe she shouldn't have been touching him, but she couldn't help herself. It felt terrifyingly right. He was family. The only family she had. He paused before answering.

"They're days," he said. "Days since I came here. Since I've been imprisoned here with the humans."

Hirka tried to count. It was impossible. "How many are there?"

"As many as there are days in a year. For nine hundred and ninety-nine years."

It was incredible. No wonder they covered almost his entire back. "What happens when you run out of room?"

"That will likely be the day I die," he answered hoarsely.

She felt a sudden sorrow. An intense need to embrace him. She didn't want to feel that way. He was supposed to be her enemy. But it wasn't like that anymore. She believed him. Trusted him.

Seer preserve me ...

But the Seer had no plan to preserve her. Quite the contrary.

He turned around again. "I'll tell you why you were created, Hirka. Because it became possible. They did everything in their power to prevent me from fathering new blood. But here you are. My daughter. The child they feared I would have. You're a miracle. A human with blood of the first. You awakened the gateways."

"You tried to send me to them ..." Hirka remembered Urd's words. "You tried to sacrifice me!"

"Sacrifice? Haven't you heard a word I've said? Had I kept you, you would have been hunted by those who are hunting me. Would that have been better? I know who you're consorting with, and he'd have butchered you like an animal. Wrenched out your teeth and sold them to the highest bidder. And there are plenty more like him. You don't belong here. You're better than them."

"I'm fine being their equal," she muttered.

He lifted her chin.

"They thought my blood was dead, yet here you are. Through you I was going to do all that I was meant to. You were to be sent to Dreyri. Not as a sacrifice, but as a leader. You would have had more power that you can fathom. Power over the Might. Power over flesh and blood. Power to heal or to kill. You would have been raised as one of us. You were to take my place. You were to lead our people to Ym. To the Might."

He let go of her chin. "But that dream died when you disappeared. When the raven rings took you. Now you've grown up with *them*. I can tell you that Umpiri came first. That my brother cut off the flow of the Might, leaving our people to starve. But you'll never believe me. Never understand. You only know us through them. And they don't paint a pretty picture. Fate has put us on opposite sides, and we will always be at odds. I will always fight for the right of our people, and you will always want to stop me."

Hirka's feet gave way. She collapsed onto the sofa. It was wonderfully real. A piece of furniture. Something to hold on to. Something real in what otherwise felt like a dream.

She was half-blindling. Bred to lead the deadborn to Ym. That was the purpose of her existence. She was intended for a completely different life. In a completely different place.

Graal pulled her back to her feet. "I needn't remind you that we're better than them. I needn't remind you of all the lies they tell about us. You know better than most that people always lie about what's different. Anyway, it doesn't matter. You can never become what you were intended to be. But I still love you."

She stared at him. The warmth in his eyes was unbearable.

The pieces started to fall into place in Hirka's mind. The bigger picture. Things she'd been hearing since she was a child, things she'd heard only yesterday. They all came together to form a clearer image. Like the drops of water on the book that had made the pattern emerge, revealing that it was a map.

The map!

Cold flooded her veins. Outside, the sky was getting lighter. Stefan would wake up soon. Him and Naiell. They'd find the phone. And the book.

"Graal …" She swallowed. "What does Sulni mean?"

"Sulni? It's an insect. A sort of mayfly that lives for only one night. Why do you ask?"

"I think I've done something really stupid," she whispered.

SEPARATED

Hirka knew she'd done a lot of stupid things in her life. She'd fallen through the roof of a storehouse down by the quay. She'd fallen from a roof in Ravnhov during a gathering of Eirik's allies. She'd turned up for her Rite day and paid dearly for it. She'd stopped herself from kissing Rime because of the rot, which she now knew couldn't be spread the way people thought. And she'd left Ym. But of all her hare-brained decisions, few compared to this.

The insect carriage flew low and fast as day broke. The world was waking up. Stefan was probably up by now, cursing furiously as he looked for his phone. Or maybe he'd already found it. Maybe they were on their way to the zoo right now. Or even worse, maybe they'd already dug up it and the map.

For all she knew, Naiell had the book in his hands at that very moment. The Seer who had let her believe she was a blood bag. The blindling who had betrayed his own kind, stolen the Might, destroyed the gateways, and perhaps sentenced an unknown number of worlds to death, all without so much as blinking. And she'd given him a map.

The dry grass below flattened out, leaning away from them as they landed. It was still quiet outside. A man was jogging through the park. He looked at them but kept running. She'd seen his type before. People running around but not actually going anywhere.

Hirka took off the ear cushions and waited until the roar had died down. "What'll happen if he finds it?" she asked. Graal hopped down.

"Well, he still doesn't know what it is, does he?"

Hirka hoped not. She supposed Naiell could have been bluffing, but she was pretty sure she was the only one who'd worked it out. But he knew his brother wanted it, and that was perhaps enough.

"Don't despair, blood of my blood. He knows I'm his way out of here. Without me he'll be left here to rot forever. Like I was."

They walked briskly toward the zoo.

"So it's true? You can open the gateways?" What she really wanted to know was whether he could send her home, but she feared she already knew the answer to that. He wasn't going to let her go.

"Not without the Might," he replied. "But I have someone in Mannfalla who can help. If she's still willing."

"Why haven't you brought more Umpiri here? You could have built an army to fight Naiell by now."

He glanced down at her with pride in his sharp features. "Pleading for help won't clear my name. If I'm to be the savior of my people, I can't be seen to beg. I don't need help with my brother. Besides, it's not as simple as you might think. It took me generations to find stones that still had traces of life in them, and generations more to find a beak in Ym. And despite all that, I still haven't found a direct route from here to our people."

"Couldn't you have brought them here through Ym?"

He laughed. The crows alighted from the trees around them. "You make it sound like a travel agency. If only you knew. But right now we have a bigger problem."

They squeezed through a hole in the fence. The one they'd left through before. They picked their way around the outermost edge of the wolf enclosure. It was early. The zoo was still closed. That was something, at least. That meant no one would have let Stefan and Naiell in yet.

"Wait here," she told Graal. She was the one who'd messed up, so it was only fair that she be the one to make things right.

Graal turned up the collar of his coat and stood by the fence while she headed for the trees she'd lain under. She could smell the wolves, but they were nowhere in sight. It was a cool and clear morning. Good visibility. She suddenly felt conspicuous and tried to make herself as small as possible.

Here's the spot.

She crouched down and dug with both hands. The bag was still there, with the book and the phone tucked inside. She was saved. Worlds were saved. She got up and smiled, lifting the bag over her head so Graal could see.

Then she heard voices. Several of them. A dog barking. Someone shouting her name.

Stefan!

Hirka clutched her chest. It felt like her heart had stopped. Then instinct took over. She took out the phone and threw the bag with the book back in the hole, quickly kicking earth over it so no one would see. She turned to see Stefan and Naiell standing on the other side of the fence. Two men were charging toward her. Police? Guards?

She looked back at Graal. The others couldn't see him where he was standing. He couldn't see them either, but he knew what was happening. He gripped the fence. She saw him whisper her name.

She had to choose, and she had to choose quickly. If she ran to Graal, they'd find him and Naiell would realize that the jig was up. That she knew. There would be a clash between the brothers, here at the zoo. And no matter what Graal thought, it wasn't inconceivable that Naiell would emerge the victor. He was bigger and stronger. And then what would happen? Stefan's life would be in danger. Hers, too. Time was running out.

The smaller of the two guards was a few steps away. Hirka clutched the phone to her chest and backed toward them. She looked at Graal. He looked at her.

"Trust me," she whispered, even though he couldn't hear her from where he was. "I am Dreyri." She lifted two fingers to her throat. Understanding crossed his features. He closed his eyes and rested his forehead against the fence. Then he turned and disappeared between the trees.

They don't know anything. They don't know anything.

Hirka repeated the words to herself. The guards reached her. The bigger one, an older man with wispy hair, grabbed her by the nape as if she were a kitten. She only caught snatches of what they were ranting about. Forbidden. Fines. Danger.

They dragged her out through the fence, telling her she'd been lucky.

They don't know anything.

Then she felt Stefan's arms around her. Until he pushed her back and shook her by the shoulders. She was so hungry she could have eaten a horse. She could hear Stefan arguing with the guards. About the fence. Money. Wild animals.

Naiell was standing with his sunglasses on and his hands in his pockets. He was eyeing her, head cocked. He was the most dangerous animal here, but only she knew.

A TRAP

Hirka dreamed she was being torn apart by two ravens. It felt so real that it lingered in her body even after she'd woken up, but she didn't open her eyes. Then the yelling would start up again, and she'd had more than enough of that since they'd collected her from the zoo.

Stefan had laid into her as if she'd gone to Slokna and back. She'd told him she'd gone to meet Graal to trade the book for Rime. Graal had gotten the book, but she hadn't seen Rime. That was what she'd said. And that she'd run away from him.

Caught between two ravens.

If only it were as simple as there being a good raven and a bad raven. That would have made the choice obvious, but it wasn't like that. Graal had won her over. She could no longer pretend otherwise. But he was far from innocent. Frighteningly far. He wanted to let the blind into Ym, and that alone ought to have made her hate him. Turn against him. But she was powerless in the face of his honesty. In the face of his insight into his own nature. He wasn't evil. He just was. What was it he'd said?

I've done things you would deem horrific. And I'll do more. That's a given.

Was she letting his sensitivity get the better of her? His intensity, which mirrored her own?

No, it was more than that. It was the way he carried himself. The way he filled the room with his presence, without even trying.

Without demanding attention, the way Naiell did. The brothers were as different as fire and ice. Naiell considered himself a god. Graal ought to have considered himself a victim, but he didn't. He had a strength that was unshakeable. Even after a thousand years. As if it were in his blood.

Was she supposed to have that same strength? Was that the strength that drove her now? Was she about to give in because he could give her a purpose? A history? Roots? The girl who'd always been nobody. Who'd only known Father. And now she had a heritage that made even Rime's pale in comparison. Had Graal had her the moment he elevated her from being a child of Odin to a leader?

She felt like a different person, and she hated it. She feared he'd managed to change her just by calling her blood of his blood. By saying that he loved her. She didn't need him. She'd never needed anyone. Was she supposed to crawl like a worm just because some immortal called himself her father? It shouldn't change anything.

It changes everything.

Yes, he wanted to conquer Ym. But according to him, Umpiri had been there first. According to him, the Might they thirsted for had been stolen from them. Was it worse to want it back or to take it in the first place? Was it worse to conquer a people or to betray your own people in order to save them?

She didn't know. All she knew was that she was caught between two brothers who hated each other. Only one of them loved her. Only one of them was her father. But she couldn't trust either of them.

If only she could have stopped time. Frozen it, until she'd gotten everything in place. But time had never passed quicker than in the human world. A day was divided into hours. An hour into minutes. Even the minutes were divided up into tiny moments, like grains of sand in an hourglass. And they were running through her fingers.

How was she to do everything she needed to when time passed so quickly?

Rime was a slave to the beak and she couldn't help him. They had to get away from this place, both of them, but Graal would never send her back to Ym. And Naiell had to be stopped. Had she been like Svarteld, she could have killed him without batting an eyelid. Solved the problem, once and for all. But that wasn't her. That wasn't to be. So what was she to do? Arrange for the brothers to meet and let them hash things out? No. Neither of them would accept anything less than the other's death. So much death.

And if that weren't enough, there were people out there with the rot. And a dying world. Or worlds. She needed time to think. She needed a way of making sure Naiell wouldn't touch her. A truce, between everyone. So that the brothers were beyond each other's reach, so that Graal wouldn't hurt Rime, and so that the blind wouldn't ravage Ym. And it had to last long enough for her to find a cure for the beak.

Fragments of a plan began to form in her mind. She wasn't sure how, but she knew what had to happen. It would require her to do things she wasn't sure she could. But she would have to. The question was whether she'd get the chance. Would she be able to fool Naiell? Stay alive long enough to carry out her plan? It didn't seem possible. He'd been watching her like a hawk since they'd found her.

"I know you're awake." Stefan sat down on the floor beside her. His voice was calmer than the day before. Maybe he'd gotten everything out of his system. It had been a lot for him to take in. Not only had he lost her and his phone, the woman whose home they'd been staying in had chucked them out. He hadn't dared stay in Stockholm any longer, so Hirka had had to put up with him yelling at her for three days straight on the way back to York. At least she was back where she'd started, though she didn't know why that was a comfort to her. Maybe he felt the same. Maybe they were just too tired to run any more.

They'd broken into a loft in what Stefan said was an old factory, squashed between two blocks of flats. Dust and dirt had collected in the cracks between the floorboards. Rusted metal pipes ran along the ceiling and the walls. The corners were piled high with all sorts of chains, nails, and pulleys. The symbols painted on the walls told her they weren't the first to break in.

Hirka turned toward Stefan. He was sitting against the wall, hands resting on his knees. "Do you have any idea what it's like, how intense it is, spending a morning with him and not understanding a word he says?" He nodded at Naiell, who was standing at the other end of the room, his claws buried in a tray of raw meat.

She sat up. "Lucky for you he doesn't say much," she said.

"Listen, Hirka … I'm sorry that guy you know is caught up in all this, I really am. I get that you want to find him, I do. I'm not completely clueless. But …"

"Don't ever do that again?"

He was fiddling with a water bottle. Water dripped from the cap and onto the floor. Dark specks grew in the dust. She wondered when he'd last had a cigarette.

"Naiell's right," he said. "You could have been killed. You were lucky."

"Would that have been so bad? Without me, you could go home. Or at least stay at a hotel. Without me you'd have your life back, Stefan."

"Yes, and what a life it was. Fucking spectacular. Really."

She smiled. "So you're saying this is better?"

He bumped his shoulder against hers. "Shut up, girl."

Naiell came over, wearing trousers and nothing else. Hirka felt Stefan tense. He got up and left her with the blindling. She should have trusted his instincts a long time ago.

Naiell looked down at her. It was impossible not to compare him to his brother now. Both had black hair. Graal's was short and wild. Naiell's nearly reached his waist. She remembered thinking that Naiell sounded very clever. But he wasn't really. He just used a lot of words to say very little.

"So did my brother have anything else to say? Did he say anything about what it was?"

"What?"

"The book he was after, which you generously decided to give him."

"I had no choice! I thought he had Rime. And no, he didn't mention what it was."

"He must have said something?" Naiell cocked his head. Studied her. She was sitting in the corner and suddenly realized that was a bad place to be. "We didn't really talk that much, like I said. I was scared out of my mind, and as soon as I heard people, I ran. He didn't have Rime with him, anyway."

Naiell crouched down in front of her. He was uncomfortably close. She looked into his milky eyes. Held his gaze as best she could. She knew she had to give him something. Something he'd believe.

"He said you're a traitor and that I shouldn't trust you."

Naiell threw his head back and laughed. Unleashing the magpie in his throat. "Of course he did. Anything else would be unbelievable."

He looked at her again. She'd have to give him more. "I told him about all the times you saved me. As a raven. Do you remember?"

He looked away without answering.

He doesn't remember. Graal was right. He was more raven than Dreyri.

The window threw squares of pale light across his chest and down to the floor. "So what stroke of genius did he come up with to get you through? I imagine you asked him? The raven rings were dead, and this rotten place has no Might. We have to know how he did it!"

Hirka sighed. "I don't know, he said he had … contacts. On the other side."

"Contacts? How in Slokna could he have contact with …" Naiell suddenly went quiet. Black ink flooded his eyes. Then he got up with a roar. A primal scream from deep within. Stefan glanced over at them. She saw his hand jerk to his hip. Pure reflex.

Naiell started walking in a circle, the dust dancing around him. "The raven. They let him keep the raven."

Hirka fought back a smile.

That's right. The raven you killed.

Naiell's own misdeed had given Graal the means to destroy him.

"Well," Hirka said, "if we kill him, we'll be stuck here. Forever. And I for one have a hard time imagining anything worse."

"So we agree on *something*, Sulni."

Hirka's jaw tensed. She couldn't let him know that she knew what her nickname meant. Then the game would be over. She searched her thoughts for the right words. She had to find a way to use Naiell's weaknesses against him. She had no means of defeating him, or of destroying him. What else could she do but let him destroy himself?

He was a coward, yet vain. That was the key. His pride. That was what she needed to use against him.

"There is something we could do," she said. "We could meet him. Set a trap. Say that we're willing to trade me for Rime. Because it's me he needs, right? My blood?"

Naiell nodded to confirm what she now knew to be a lie. She fought to keep her voice steady. "And when we meet him, we overpower him and force him to send us home."

Naiell folded his arms over his chest. He hesitated. Of course. He'd never dare meet his brother man-to-man. Dreyri-to-Dreyri.

"It's too risky," he said. "Graal has followers here, and no one has managed to find me any."

Hirka stood up. "You're wrong. You have plenty."

He looked at her. She smiled with all the confidence she could muster. "I'm going to give you an army, Naiell. An army of the forgotten. An army of all those he's betrayed."

Naiell held his arms out. "Now we're talking, Sulni!"

He'd taken the bait. Now it was just a matter of keeping her promise. Building an army of the forgotten. Without Stefan finding out, of course. He took a very dim view of the old blood slaves. He wouldn't understand.

But this was bigger than Stefan. Bigger than the forgotten.

This was what she was made for.

SETTING THE BOARD

"I need to borrow your phone," Hirka said, as nonchalantly as she could.

"Couldn't you just steal it? That's what you usually do," Stefan replied as he pulled a rag through the chamber of his gun. It was lying in pieces on the table—a door they'd laid across two stools.

"Can I borrow it or not?"

"Why do *you* need a phone? It's not like you can phone home." He laughed at his own joke and looked at Naiell, before remembering that the blindling couldn't understand a word he said.

"You don't have anyone to call. And I don't have any games on it."

"I want to talk to Allegra. Surely I'm allowed to do that?" It was a lie, but she couldn't exactly tell him she wanted to call the man they'd been running from for the past month.

He put the barrel and the spring back in the slide. "What in God's name do you want to talk to her about?"

Hirka grinned. She'd given that some thought. "Clothes."

Stefan raised an eyebrow. "Clothes?"

"And shoes. Clothes and shoes."

"Do you need to look good to be eaten by the forgotten? New shoes for your own funeral? Women ..." He took his phone out of his back pocket. "Here. Press the green button and you'll get straight through to her. But not a word about where we are, okay?"

Hirka took the phone and went into the next room. She closed the door behind her and pulled the chocolate wrapper out of her pocket. The one with Graal's and Isac's phone numbers on it. She sat on the windowsill. The glass was dirty and divided into small panes. One of them was cracked, held in place by sticky strips. What was that called again? *Tape.* The roll was still on the floor, next to a rusty bucket. All these broken things were depressing. Made her feel sluggish. Everything was catching up with her. All the days on the road. Poisonous food. Too little sleep. Too much death. The forgotten. Graal.

But she couldn't give up now. She could sleep when she got to Slokna. She had to hold out until this was over.

She tapped the phone and Allegra's name disappeared. Then she tapped the green button and the numbers came up. She smiled. She was an expert now. She tapped the numbers in the right order. It rang.

"Yes?" Graal's voice.

"It's me."

"Are you okay? Does anyone know you're calling?"

"No one knows. We left Stockholm. We're back in York now."

"Can you get away from him? I can pick you up wherever."

Hirka lowered her voice. "I haven't been alone since I was with you. He suspects something."

"I expected as much. Hirka, we got the Ravenbearer out of the woods. He's with one of my people. We're going to see whether we can send him home tomorrow."

No! Not yet!

Hirka pressed the phone to her ear, fighting the urge to say she wanted to talk to Rime. Hear his voice. That couldn't happen. Not now. It would tear her apart. The most important thing now was getting Graal to listen.

"I can give you Naiell," she said.

There was silence at the other end. She continued. "I know what you're thinking. The day he dares meet you man-to-man is the day all of Slokna awakes. But I promise I can make him feel bold enough to try. But we need Rime."

"Rime An-Elderin can't be here, Hirka. He loses influence in Mannfalla with every day he's gone."

"Graal, believe me, the next time we meet, you'll be glad you have him."

She thought she could hear him smiling. "What are you planning, blood of my blood?"

"A trade. Me for Rime. And Naiell's freedom. Or that's what I'll let him believe."

"You're playing with fire, Hirka. My brother has killed his own before. He'll never be rid of that taint. He won't hesitate to kill you either, if he's forced to."

"That's what I'm counting on. That's why we need Rime. Give me five days. That's all I'm asking. Five days, then meet us in the burned-out church, in the evening."

She could almost hear the wheels turning. Weighing the risks against the rewards. She was pretty sure he cared about her. After all, she was proof, of sorts, that he'd survived. His heir. Blood of his blood. But he had to care about revenge more. Otherwise he'd refuse.

"Five days," he said at long last.

Hirka felt a stab of disappointment, even though she'd gotten what she wanted. "Good," she said. "But I want to see Rime first."

"That's going to be difficult."

"If anyone can find a way, it's you. I want to see him. And I know you can make it happen," she said. Then she pressed the red button. One down, one to go. She tapped out the other phone number written on the wrapper.

"Yel-low!"

"Hi, Isac," she said.

"Well, I'll be! I was starting to worry I'd never hear from you again, missy. Where are you?" He sounded cheerful, but there was no beating around the bush, she had to give him that.

"I'm back in York. We need to meet."

"How do you know I'm not still in hospital? For all you knew, I could have been dead."

Hirka smiled. "I had a hunch. Can we meet?"

"But of course, little miss. It would be my pleasure. Does this mean you've won?"

"Not yet. How do you feel?"

"Fantastic, since you ask. Haven't felt better in years. I almost feel like buying an electric guitar." Hirka could hear him grinning. She let out a breath. It felt like a weight had been lifted from her shoulders. She had been right. Now she could only hope she hadn't made matters worse.

"And your thirst?" she asked. He was silent for a moment.

"I've cheated death," he replied. "Or was that you?"

"How many of the others can you get hold of by tomorrow?" She assumed she didn't need to explain who she meant.

"Why?"

"How many, Isac?"

"Here in town … six, maybe eight tops."

"That's not enough, we need more."

He laughed. "If you think you can get them to join up and take their revenge on him, you don't know your father as well as you think you do. He's forgotten them, but they'll never forget him. They love him."

"They'll love me more. You know why. Tell them that. I need twelve. At least."

"Listen, missy, if I spread this rumor, more will come than you can handle. There'll be nothing left of you." He was in top form.

Had she not known he'd recently been bedridden with tubes coming out of him, she'd never have believed it.

"Do as I say, Isac. Tell them what I've done for you. What I can give them. When can we meet?"

"Give me two days and I can get you your twelve, but if you want more, you'll have to give them time to fly in."

"I don't have time to wait. Ask them to come and we'll meet in two days, in the alleyway."

"The alleyway? Missy, this is a big city …"

"The alleyway where you dragged me into a car, set fire to the church, and where Stefan almost smashed your skull open. Got it?"

"Thanks for the reminder … What time?"

"Eight o'clock. In the morning."

"Ugh, you are a sadist, missy. I hope you know what you're doing."

"I'm a healer," she replied. "I always know what I'm doing."

It wasn't true, but it felt nice to say, and it soothed her nerves.

She pressed the red button. The two most important pieces were set.

ENOUGH

Hirka left the room and almost walked straight into Stefan. He was waiting for her, arms crossed. Had he been listening?

He held his hand out for his phone. She gave it to him. He tapped the screen and held it up in front of her. "So who will I get through to if I call this number?"

"What number?"

"This number. The last one you called."

Hirka bit her lip. Her blood didn't know whether to run hot or cold. He could see who she'd talked to. She had no explanation. It was over.

"I can tell you one thing," he said. "It won't be Allegra."

Hirka took a couple of steps back and bumped into the wall. Stefan leaned toward her. The number she'd called glowed at her from the screen. She tried to duck around him, but he stopped her with his arm and pressed her up against the wall.

"The last time I checked, Allegra didn't speak your language."

"Stefan …"

"Enough!" He pressed her harder against the wall. His eyes were narrowed. Furious. She lifted her elbow to protect herself, but then he let go. His eyes lost some of their fire. "Enough …" he whispered.

He shoved the phone in his pocket. "I've been hunting him since I was a fucking child, and you go behind my back? What have you done? Sold me out?"

"It's not what you think, Stefan."

"No," he dragged a hand through his hair. "No, it never is."

She looked at him. Brown eyes, brown hair tipped with blond that caught the light shining in through a dirty window. He was just a man. She was surrounded by men. Strong men and weak men. Stefan was human, and there was no way he'd walk away from this unscathed. She had to let him go. It would hurt, but she had no choice.

Hirka craned her neck to look for Naiell, but it was just the two of them. "So you trust Naiell? You believe what he says?" she asked.

"I've never trusted that creature, and I don't trust his brother either. But clearly you do."

"You don't understand, Stefan. I don't trust either of them. But they're going to meet, and it's going to get ugly. If you get your way, they'll end up killing each other. And me. But this isn't your fight."

"Not my fight?! I'm the one who's been tracking him for years! Following his blood slaves. I'm the one who's shown you the world, but this isn't my fight? So what, you're just going to stab me in the back? You gave him the book, girl! In exchange for a boy he didn't even have!"

"That boy is more of a man than you'll ever be! At least he knows he's a murderer. You still think you're a savior. You're a coward, Stefan."

He dragged a hand over his stubble. "A coward who saves you from half-rotten monsters."

"Saves me? You didn't kill me. That doesn't make you a hero."

"I've driven halfway across Europe with you! Every fucking day I fight to—"

"To destroy them, yes. But they're people, Stefan. And I can heal them! Has it ever occurred to you that there might be a cure for the rot? Or would that put you out of a job?"

He raised his fist. She braced herself, but then he let his arm drop again. His anger turned to doubt. She'd hit a nerve he didn't even know he had. Stefan didn't know himself very well.

He lowered his gaze. "So ask him then," he said hoarsely. "Next time you talk. Since you're such good friends. Ask him about his selection criteria. Why my mother? Why not me? If he'd just waited a few years, I'd have been better than her. So why not me? Ask him that. You know, just between friends."

The memory of Stefan standing, gun in hand, beside a sleeping Naiell flashed through her mind. Maybe he hadn't wanted to kill him. Maybe Stefan's hunt was about something that ran much deeper.

It was a bitter realization. She couldn't hide her disgust.

"You hunt them because they have something you don't. You're looking for the same blood. But you've never had the courage to ask for it. Never dared take it."

"They're murderers!"

"There are murderers among them. There are murderers among us all. Don't hunt them again, Stefan. Never again. I'm going to need them."

"For what?"

"To stop a war."

"You're out of your mind, girl! You think you're some kind of fucking superwoman! You think you can change everything, but that's not how the world works, and I can promise you that I understand it better than you."

She couldn't bear to listen to him anymore.

"Stefan, you're no use to anyone. Take your things and get out." She took the three blood stones out of their pouch and threw them on the floor at his feet. "Here. Buy yourself a country or something."

One of the stones rolled toward a gap between the floorboards. Stefan reacted instinctively, bringing his foot down on it. Then he looked at her and quickly lifted it again, as if he had been burned. But it was too late. His greed had revealed itself.

Hirka smiled, and she knew it wasn't pretty. "Now you'll never have to hunt the forgotten again, Stefan. And you won't have to live like this. Wanted by the police, pulling teeth from the mouths of people you've killed. Allegra's slave. Go. Start a new life somewhere. And forget we ever met."

Stefan's eyes darted between her and the stones.

She walked away, leaving him to realize something about himself that she already knew. This evening, when she returned, he'd be gone.

THE FORGOTTEN ARMY

Hirka sat on the floor and flicked through her notebook while she waited for Naiell to wake up. It was strange to see things she'd drawn and written only a few months before. They belonged to a completely different reality. She'd known so little back then, and she'd been so much safer for it.

A child of Odin, sleeping beneath the bells in a church tower with her raven. Struggling with the language and thinking someone might be spying on her from the churchyard. Now what was she? A half-blindling pitting two deadborn against each other in an attempt to stop the rot and save worlds.

She closed the notebook. Her gift from Hlosnian. She'd studied her maps and was pretty sure she knew where they needed to go to find the alleyway. The old compass she'd attached to the leather cover was shaking almost as much as she was. It wouldn't show her the way to anything. She would have to find it herself.

Naiell woke up. He stretched like a cat before dropping down from the rafters. "Where's the other one?"

"Stefan's gone," Hirka replied.

She shoved the notebook in her bag and closed it. "Maybe if you didn't sleep so much, you'd have a better handle on people."

Now wasn't the time to provoke him. She'd soon be standing before forgotten blood slaves, betraying Naiell for all to hear, in a language he fortunately didn't understand. It all depended on him trusting her. On him not ripping her head off before she even got started.

She chucked his clothes at him and opened the door. "Come on. We've got lots to do."

He got dressed and followed her down from the factory loft. It was early. The streets were almost deserted. It was foggy. Everything seemed gray.

"How many of them are there?" Naiell asked. He stayed close to her, seeming bigger than usual.

"Put your glasses on."

She led them away from the main road and in between the houses. She felt nauseous. What worried her most? Someone being there, or no one being there? Both possibilities were just as bad.

"I'm going to tell them they should follow me," Naiell said. "What do you think? Back to Ym? The rot was useful during the war. Humans are better vessels for the Might."

"Yes, so I've heard," she replied, realizing how little of him had been aware while he was Kuro. Otherwise he'd have remembered, known more. As things stood, she could probably have asked him about any moment in the history of Ym from the past thousand years and he wouldn't remember any of them. Not the border dispute between Einneyr and Blossa, not when the ice cracked in Brinnlanda, not when Norrvarje was annexed by Mannfalla in 773. What had he been doing all that time? Building nests? It was a strange thought to grapple with.

She'd asked Graal whether all blindlings could take the form of a raven, but apparently it wasn't that simple. It was a gift reserved for very few Dreyri, a complicated matter she might never understand.

"There," she said, pointing between two tall blocks of flats. They went into the alleyway.

She knew they were there before she saw them. The fog couldn't mask the anticipation in the air. Their presence.

The forgotten came into view between fire escapes and dumpsters. The brick walls were covered in words and symbols she didn't understand. A world unfathomable to most people. A secret language. Wet newspaper clung to the asphalt.

Isac was leaning against the wall by a drainpipe, tossing a coin. He looked at her, straightened up, and smoothed his fair fringe down with one hand. It was strange to see him again, to think that he had been there when Jay died. Still, he hadn't been the one to fire the gun. That had been the mousy man. The one she'd killed. Right here in this alleyway, next to the green dumpster.

She walked into their midst. They were all taller than her, but otherwise all very different. Some of them looked out of place in the alleyway. Others looked like they'd been sleeping there for years.

She recognized some of them, like the woman who had licked Naiell's blood off the ground. She was just as finely dressed as before, in a tight skirt and a pastel blouse. She looked just like anyone else you might see on the street, like the people who would soon be driving and walking around, on their way to work.

Hirka counted fifteen, including Isac. It wasn't a lot, but it would have to be enough to convince Naiell.

"Is this it? Is this what you call an army?" He gave her a reproachful look. It was as if he had read her mind. She was glad none of the others understood ymish.

"These are the people who are going to *build* you an army. These are the people who are going to help us stop Graal. But if you want to start by insulting them, be my guest. Or you can trust me."

Naiell grumbled. Hirka closed the lid of the dumpster. The alleyway now smelled less of garbage, but all the more of the forgotten. It was a cloying scent that seemed to get stronger the longer they'd been forgotten.

She climbed up onto the dumpster and sat down on the edge.

Naiell jumped up after her. The lid gave a metallic clang. He stood behind her with his hands on his hips.

The forgotten gathered around them. They looked exhausted. Some of them had probably lived with the thirst for ages. How would she get through to them?

"Tell them who I am," Naiell said, jutting his chin out.

"I'll tell them what they need to know, and if you interrupt me, you can tell them yourself."

He bared his teeth at her. She was flirting with death, and it would only get worse. But right now, he needed her.

"I'm Hirka," she said. Her voice wavered. She was too nervous. She wiped her clammy hands on her trousers. "I'm Hirka," she said again. "I'm Graal's daughter. Half-Dreyri and half-human. Have you heard that word before? Dreyri?"

Isac raised his hand. The others looked at him. He blushed and lowered it again. Hirka suppressed a smile and continued. "It means blood of the first, and it's the name of our people. You've only met one of us. You know who he is. You might have lived with him. Maybe for a few days, maybe for many years—I don't know. But you've been friends with him. And he's forgotten you."

No one said anything. Men and women stood quietly and listened. To her. She'd always run away from crowds of people. Feared being seen, for obvious reasons. But the time for running was over. She had to talk to them. She had no choice. Even though they were all different and had all found different ways of coping with the loss of Graal's blood. Anger. Grief. Ruin.

They didn't want to hear what Graal had made them. She realized that she would have to appeal to whatever remained of their humanity.

"You've hurt each other. Some of you have hurt innocent people. It's awful. But what was done to you is also awful. Dreyri blood is poison to you. But still you took it. How are your lives now? The long lives you yearned for? How are they, without him? Without Graal? Without his blood?"

"Are you here to tell us how miserable we are?" The speaker was a shapely woman with a glowing complexion. But she had bags under her eyes. Hirka smiled at her.

"I can see why he liked you. You used to be beautiful, before the thirst. I'm guessing you defied him."

The woman's mouth twisted bitterly. Hirka felt a pang in her chest. Her heart ached for them.

"You were all something to him, at some time or other in the last thousand years. But I can help you. I know Isac's told his story. I'm like you. I'm more human than blindling. Just look at me. But all the same, I have blood of the blind in my veins. His blood. Graal's blood. Something in me can tolerate it. I've given it to Isac, and I can give it to you. He no longer thirsts. Isn't that right, Isac?"

Isac shrugged and smiled. "Here, have a feel!" He raised his arms, palms up. The shapely woman rested her fingers against his wrist. Her eyes grew shiny. Isac nodded and reached out toward the others, urging them to get in on the action. "It's beating! I can't remember the last time it beat so much that it could actually be called a pulse. And I no longer thirst. It's like I never met him."

"Does that mean you're going to die?" asked the woman who had challenged Hirka.

"I bloody well hope so," Isac replied. He leaped into the air with an ecstatic howl, grabbing hold of the fire escape above him. He swung back and forth a couple of times before dropping back down onto the asphalt. "I'm alive!" He flung his arms out demonstratively. Hirka didn't know whether to laugh or cry. She'd never imagined anyone being so happy about their own mortality.

"What's he doing?" Naiell asked. "Will he fight for me?"

"Yes, he'll fight for you," she whispered. It made her feel terrible, but it had to be done.

She continued. "Now that you know the truth, you have a choice. You can kill me here and now. Fall on my blood like wolves. But I've asked you here because I know you won't do that. You're done taking. Done suffering. You're here for a fresh start. And you'll have the pleasure of telling Graal that to his face, of showing him that you're not his slaves anymore."

She glanced back at Naiell. "This is Naiell. He's Graal's brother. He's full-blood Dreyri. He doesn't understand a word of what we're saying now. All he understands is his own name."

Naiell smiled and bared his canines.

"He thinks you're here to kneel before him. He thinks you'll fawn over him like you fawned over Graal. And I'm going to let him believe that. You knew and loved Graal. This is Graal's enemy. My enemy. Soon they'll be pitted against each other, brother against brother, and Naiell thinks you'll fight for him. He needs to believe that before he'll dare face Graal. That's how much of a coward he is."

Naiell spread his arms wide and grinned like she'd just told them he was a god. Hirka closed her eyes for a moment before finding the strength to continue. "He's asked me to tell you to fight for him, to help him kill Graal. That's what he thinks I'm doing now. But I'm saying what I know is true. He'll destroy you."

She could see the confusion on all their faces, and that was the last thing she wanted Naiell to see. She quickly explained. "Listen. You're not stupid. You know you have a choice. You can fight for him. But I think you've all experienced more than enough of eternal life, and all it's given you is loneliness. Loneliness and … what's the word?" She rapped her knuckles against her forehead.

I can't forget words. Not now!

The woman in the skirt came to her rescue. "Despair?" Hirka looked up.

"Emptiness," another said.

"Hunger," Isac said.

Darkness. Meaninglessness. Death. The words kept coming. She didn't understand them all, but she knew she'd won. "Yes!" she said. "I think there's something that you long for more than Graal. And that's an escape from what you have now. Will you help me?"

It was suddenly much too quiet. All she could hear was the sound of a city waking up.

A man stepped forward. He'd been standing behind the others, but now she recognized him. It was the beggar from London, the one with the nice eyes and hollow cheeks, wearing the same clothes and the same gloves that left his dirty fingers bare.

"What do you want us to do?"

Hirka suppressed the urge to jump down from the dumpster and hug him. She contented herself with a smile.

"I need as many of you as possible. Send word to everyone who's drunk Graal's poison. All the forgotten. All the Vardar, those who are still his friends, if you can get hold of them. Ask them to come here. Tell them what I can do. In three days, the brothers will meet in that burned-out church. Graal and Naiell. I'll be there, too."

Hirka hesitated. Graal would never set foot in the church if it was full of people. He'd think she'd betrayed him. She'd need time first.

"Come at eight o'clock in the evening. Three evenings from now. With everyone you can find. Unarmed. Please don't spill any blood. If anything, I need you to stop a bloodbath. If you can keep me alive until it's over, I promise to heal you."

They looked at each other. "You'll give us your blood?" the woman in the skirt asked.

"Yes."

"What if lots of people come?"

"Then we'll have to hope I've got lots of blood." Hirka smiled, for all the good it did. "So, if you want to help me, kneel. Let him think he's got his slaves."

One by one they kneeled, fifteen men and women in a narrow alleyway. Surrounded by soggy cardboard boxes and beer cans. Hirka looked up at Naiell.

"You've got your army."

ANGEL

Hirka and Naiell kept to the main streets, trying to blend in. She wasn't sure they were doing a particularly good job of it, but even so, it was their safest bet. The police could still be looking for her after the church murders. Or was that just Stefan's paranoia rubbing off on her?

She pointed at the blackened bell tower and explained to Naiell how the meeting with Graal would play out. She assured him that the forgotten would find more people and hide in the surrounding streets. Graal would think that she and Naiell had come alone.

Naiell was skeptical, but he accepted the plan. He didn't have any other choice. Graal was his only way through the raven rings. His only way to the Might. He was disconcertingly cavalier about the advantage of having the forgotten behind him, about leaving them to kill Graal after he had made the journey home. His new army could deal with his bothersome brother while he sat securely on the throne in Eisvaldr.

The problem was that Naiell would sacrifice Hirka if necessary. She was the leverage he would use to buy his freedom. She knew that. But he didn't know she knew.

So she was walking on eggshells, through streets that had shaken off the last of winter. Always with Naiell by her side, or right behind her. He never let her out of his sight.

The bright spring light had drawn merchants out of their shops.

They stood in rows selling books, bags, and jewelry. Hirka politely declined everything that was held out to her. They didn't have much money left, and they needed food for at least another couple of days. She didn't know what would come afterward. Perhaps nothing.

A beggar stood out from the crowd. She had skin like a dried apple and wore a red kerchief. She was holding out postcards that no one wanted, saying the same words over and over. "Take a postcard. A postcard for you? A postcard for the lady?" Or gentleman, depending on who was walking past.

She approached Hirka. "Take a postcard. A postcard for you, miss?" Hirka knew their money wouldn't stretch that far. She shook her head. The woman thrust the postcard at her. "Free. Just for you, miss."

Hirka glanced down at it. A picture of a mountain erupting. Fire. Destruction. She took it. It was the same picture that had been hanging on Graal's wall. Her instincts told her to hide it from Naiell, but he was distracted by the pigeons on the window ledges above. Food, she supposed.

She turned back to the woman, but she'd already disappeared into the crowd. Hirka stared down at the postcard, hands tingling. There was something stuck to the back. A note. Hirka shoved the postcard into one of the big pockets in her trousers. Naiell didn't seem to notice.

"What do you want?" she asked outside a grocery store.

"Meat," he replied.

"I'm not sure we have enough money for that. If not, I'll get some bananas," she said, hoping he'd wait outside. He did.

Hirka turned down one of the aisles. The light dazzled her. She stopped next to a humming freezer and took out the postcard for a closer look. There were words and numbers on the note. She would have to ask for help. She picked up the only loaf of bread she could find that wasn't wrapped in plastic, a couple of bananas, and a block of cheese. Put it on the counter. Naiell was still standing outside, waiting for her.

Hirka pulled the note off the postcard and showed it to the woman behind the counter. "Excuse me, I got this from a friend, but I'm not very good at reading. Can you tell me what it says?"

The woman leaned forward, her ample bosom getting in the way. She put on her glasses, which had been hanging around her neck. Her hair was fair and curly. Hirka had a strange feeling it wasn't real.

"It's a ticket for a concert this evening," she said finally.

Hirka had been to several concerts, but they'd all been at the church.

"Where?"

"Somewhere called Cave," the woman continued, saying the name as if it tasted foul. She took off her glasses again and looked up at Hirka. "You know, you young people should stop and think about the kind of things you listen to. You don't have to go to these things just because all your friends do."

Hirka wasn't sure how to respond.

"Thanks, I … I'll probably go alone," she said, putting some money on the counter.

"You should talk to your parents about it. The city's not what it used to be. You need to put it there. The money. In the machine." The woman shook her head. Hirka put the money in the right place, bagged her shopping, and went back outside.

Parents? If only she knew. All Hirka had was a deadborn father, and he was probably the one who had bought the ticket. It had to have been him.

Graal had found a way.

She was going to see Rime.

Darkness had fallen outside. The windows in the loft rattled in the wind. Dust danced across the floor, caught in a draft.

Hirka slipped the concert into the conversation as she ate. Naiell was eating in his customary manner, digging his claws into the food until it rotted away. He said it was more efficient that way, because he could take exactly what he needed. Neither more nor less. But finding food that was completely natural wasn't easy.

"Anyway, I found this ticket, so I'm going to head out for a bit, okay?" She had a feeling she sounded like Stefan.

Naiell nodded. "We can do that."

"It's just the one ticket, so I'll have to go alone."

He looked at her and tossed his black hair back. "Too dangerous, Sulni."

Hirka bit her lip. "I'll be quick. I'll just go in for a quick look around. There might be more of the forgotten in there. People we could use. We need everyone we can get, and you can wait right outside."

He shrugged, more amenable now that he'd eaten.

Hirka was growing restless. She only just managed to wait until he'd finished his banana before getting up. Maybe she was hoping for too much. The picture on the postcard didn't guarantee that Graal was involved. And even if he was involved, it could have been a plan to lure her away from Naiell. Not to reunite her with Rime. Maybe it was just a postcard. An ordinary postcard, given out in the hope that people would part with their money.

Then why did she feel so on edge? Why did she feel like she was waiting for lightning to strike? For a storm she couldn't control?

Because a storm is coming. No matter what.

They left the loft and crawled out through a hole in the door where someone had torn away a couple of planks. Then they followed the streetlights onward. Hirka had been worried they wouldn't be able to find their way, but all she had to do was show people the ticket and they were pointed in the right direction.

Young people dressed in black stood in groups along the road and in clusters in front of the doors. A lot of them looked like Naiell. Pale with long, black hair. Others had brightly colored hair. Blue. Green. And painted faces, with black around their eyes. They made her think of Jay. Would Jay be here now if she were still alive?

The smell of smoke and anticipation hung in the air. The crowd of people streamed through the door like a black river. Naiell grabbed her. "Don't be long."

She shook her head and slipped into the crowd before he could change his mind. She immediately regretted it. The crush of bodies at the door was horrendous. Too many people trying to get in all at once. She tried to turn around but was swept inside. It was dark. She couldn't see the ceiling or the walls. Just people.

Hirka started to sweat. Not even during the Rite had there been so many people gathered in one place. She was pushed this way and that. Elbowed in the side. Someone spilled their drink on her. A girl with black around her eyes said she loved her hair. Shouted it to make herself heard over the music being pumped into the room.

People mean danger!

It was hot and smelled of sweat. Perfume. Beer. But it didn't seem to bother anyone else. Hirka put her hands over her ears and fought her way back the way she'd come, trying to get to one of the staircases. It looked a bit quieter upstairs. She managed to squeeze her way up and find some breathing space by the railing.

Take it easy. They're just people.

People unlike any others she'd seen in this world. The girl next to her had lips as black as ink. Her jewelry was like pieces of chainmail. She had her hand tucked into the back pocket of a man with runes on his neck. Another had scars on his arm, as if he'd carved words into it using a knife.

The lights kept flashing and changing color. Hirka was pushed along the railing and up against a wall. Some kind of booth. There were people inside, surrounded by glowing buttons and switches. She had a feeling that they were in charge of this vessel, and that the whole place might take off at any moment. Hirka clung to the railing, trying to rein in her fear. No one else was afraid.

It was just different. That was all. She ought to have been used to that by now.

Focus on what you know.

A woman squeezed past her with a glass in each hand. She was wearing a wide leather belt with lacing that wouldn't have looked out of place down by the river in Mannfalla. A bald man nearby had an inking on his arm that looked like wings. Almost like the mark of the Seer. So not everything was different.

She had to hand it to Graal. In a place like this, no one stood out. No clothes were too strange. No hair too red.

The stage was bathed in smoke and blue light. People jumped up and down below. There were so many of them that they seemed to jump as one. A rippling sea of dancers. They put their hands in the air and made signs with their fingers. Hirka had never seen anything like it.

Her fear faded and she found herself involuntarily spellbound. She stared at the men on the stage, glad Naiell wasn't there. He'd have climbed up there with them, lifted his arms, and bellowed that he was the Seer himself. Commanded the audience to love him. Worship him. Serve him. Maybe that was exactly what those men were bellowing. She didn't know. It was impossible to make out the words. They were incandescent. Wild. Enthralling.

Suddenly the room turned red, as if bathed in blood. Pulsating. Pounding. She was inside a beating heart. In a place that was all emotion. Rage. Desire. Lust. People grabbed at each other. Lost themselves. A place without consequences. Outside of time.

Suddenly she knew he was here.

Rime ...

Hirka leaned over the railing, twisting in the direction her instincts told her to. Then she saw him.

He was standing on the other side of the room, at the top of the stairs. He was as light as the people around him were dark. So familiar. So real amid all this surrealness. An angel, Father Brody might have said—but Father Brody had never known Rime.

The music forced its way inside her as if she'd swallowed it. Throbbing. Growing. It was good that Rime hadn't seen her, because she felt like she might burst, like Kuro had. A cold prickling sensation washed over her. Even so, she felt warmer. Her cheeks were blazing. Was this what it felt like to freeze to death? To get so cold you felt hot?

His long, white hair. The firm set of his lips. The wide leather straps crossing his chest. He was so strong. So real. Ready for battle.

Girls turned to look at him as he made his way along the railing. They nudged each other and stared, drinking him in as she expected Sylja had done on several occasions. A girl with black straps around her thighs stopped him, leaning close and whispering in his ear. Words Rime couldn't possibly understand. Words Hirka couldn't hear. Still, they made her feel powerless.

It couldn't have come at a worse time. She had two deadborn to contend with and needed all the strength she could muster. Rime had ruined everything by coming here. Put worlds at stake. Made her vulnerable. Doomed from the start. Hirka pressed her fist to her chest, but her despair was too strong.

Rime scanned the crowd. Searching. Then he looked up and saw her.

Wolf eyes.

He locked eyes with her as he squeezed through the crowd. He disappeared behind the booth and for a moment she was gripped by panic. She couldn't see the other side. Had he been a dream? A fantasy born of the sorcery around her? But then he rounded the corner and stood before her.

Rime was standing before her.

Hirka swallowed. "What are you doing here?" She could only just hear herself over the music. He didn't reply. He just stood there like one of the stones in the raven ring. Straight-backed and impenetrable.

She tightened her grip on the railing to stop herself from reaching out to him. Because she wanted to. She wanted to so badly that it scared her. "Do you have any idea what you've done, Rime? This is no place for you. For anyone."

"I came to warn you about the Seer. I came to save you," he replied. His voice. That wonderful, husky voice. Saying idiotic things.

"Save me? You came to save me? I'm the one who has to save *you*!" she shouted over the music. "I had everything under control! I had everything under control, and then you arrived! Now everything is … you're going to get both of us killed!" She screamed in competition with the man on the stage, and every word was true. Rime being here rendered her powerless. She was a raw nerve. Exposed and vulnerable.

"Do I look like I need saving? You've left Ym, left your chair. And your tail …" She glanced down. It was just as she'd feared. He was tailless, just like in the pictures Stefan had found. It was as if he'd taken something from her. Something that had never been hers. It unleashed a rage she didn't know she had in her.

"All this," she screamed. "All this, just to come here and tell me something I already know?!"

He nodded, a pained grimace tugging at his lip. His eyes hardened.

Then she spotted the pale mark on his throat. A scar sloping down to the right.

The beak.

He had a beak in his throat. Something vile inside him. Blindcraft. Ruin. He was dead. Already dead. But he smelled so alive. Utterly and exquisitely alive. He smelled of Rime.

She lifted her hand, reaching out toward the scar. He grabbed her hand before she could touch it, his fingers burning around her wrist. He gazed at her. Intense and merciless. "I came to do what I promised," he said. "I came to tell you that the rot's not what you think it is."

Hirka didn't know whether to laugh or cry. "I know that too."

The warmth from his hand seeped beneath her skin and radiated up her arm, making its way to her heart. Would it stop beating? Would it hurt less if she touched him?

He let go of her as if he'd burned himself. She wanted to let her hand drop, but it had a mind of its own. It made its way to his chest, gripping the leather straps. That was all the encouragement he needed.

His lips were on hers before she knew it. He was Rime. He was everything she remembered. Raw. Intense. Demanding. And she had no reason whatsoever to stop him.

He kissed her. It was like being ripped out of Slokna. She felt her eyes stinging and realized she was probably crying, but it didn't matter. Nothing mattered apart from this. This one thing. His lips on hers. The desire. The hunger. They fell back against the wall. He pressed himself against her. Gripped her face in both hands. Their lips parted for a moment and she pulled him toward her again, terrified he'd disappear.

She no longer remembered where she was. Everything had been drowned out by ear-splitting music and the pounding of her heart. She felt like she was drowning in him. Drowning in Rime. Her body quickened, and it knew what it wanted. More than she did herself. All she could do was be swept along by it. She dug her nails into his neck. Pushed her hand under his collar, searching for skin. The smell of him grew sweeter. Heavier. She could feel him losing control. Feel the man he was. The only man. Rime An-Elderin. Son of the Council. Ravenbearer. Kolkagga. And what was she?

Half-blindling. Deadborn.

She tore herself away from him, gasping for breath. He brought his lips to her ear. She could feel the pulse in his temple. He laced his fingers with hers.

"Hirka ..."

It was the most beautiful thing she'd ever heard. Her own name, in Rime's husky voice. It encompassed everything that had happened. Everything that she wanted to happen. Her blood ripped through her veins, warming her in places she'd never thought she'd share. But she wanted to. Oh, how she wanted to.

There was shouting below, down by the entrance. Yelling. Clamoring. She didn't need to look to know why. Naiell. He'd gotten tired of waiting. Perhaps even suspicious. And now he wanted in.

Hirka closed her eyes. She'd lost a lot in her life, but she couldn't lose this. It was too real. Too new. It wasn't fair.

But she knew she'd gotten what she'd asked for. A moment, no more. A brief encounter before the storm. What had she been thinking? Everything hung by a thread. Rime's life. Her life. Entire worlds precariously balanced between two deadborn brothers who would soon come face to face.

"He mustn't know ..." she forced out. There was no way he could have heard her, but Rime understood. They both understood.

Rime slammed his fist into the wall behind her. He growled, standing close as the moments passed, unable to tear himself away. Finally he backed into the crowd, eyes still locked on hers. His lips formed words, drowned out by shouting and music. Still, she knew what he was saying, because she was thinking the same.

He turned away and disappeared.

A bouncer flew through the air from beneath the balcony, toppling a group of people as he landed. Others screeched and threw themselves out of the way.

Hirka leaned her head back against the wall. Exhaled and stared into thin air. Flames shot up from the edge of the stage, as if dragons had awoken. Her lips tingled. Her heart pounded in her ears. She'd never felt warmer.

Nor more crushed.

AN END

Graal headed for the café. He walked among the humans as if he were one of them. Young and old, black and white. Humans with no greater aim than getting through another day and living a peaceful life among family and friends. They would continue in this endeavor no matter their allotted years. Eighteen or eighty. It made no difference.

They walked past him, oblivious. The sun shone in their eyes, and they had to squint to see. But they would never see. The seeing were the blindest of all. They lived as if other places and other realities didn't exist. Not even the far more brutal realities that could be found less than a day away.

But the humans had come a long way. They'd done things he wouldn't have thought possible only a few decades ago. He'd watched them elevate themselves from mere survival to strong civilization. He also knew he'd see the process reverse.

He went into the café. It was pleasantly nostalgic, as they often were. Warm wood, brick, and chalkboards. Three young people were sitting in a corner, all glued to their phones. Two older women were eating cake. The wall behind them was painted black, with drawings of coffee beans. "The Last Ship" by Sting played from the speaker. An interesting man, Graal seemed to remember.

When he reached the counter, a girl with a mop of fair hair smiled at him. He looked at her name tag. "Could I trouble you for a double espresso, Charlotte?"

"Of course. Anything to eat?"

He smiled back. "Maybe later."

He paid, sat down on a tall stool by the window, and looked out at the church. As expected, the area was cordoned off. Not only had it been condemned after the fire, but it was also a murder scene. Soon to be doubly so.

This was the place she'd chosen. In two days, he would meet Naiell there. Brother. Seer. Betrayer.

She'd chosen well, Hirka had. Blood of his blood.

Charlotte appeared with his espresso. Perfectly creamy. She'd made an effort. He smiled at her, careful not to expose too much canine. "Are you religious, Charlotte?"

"Me? No. I'm not Bible material," she laughed. Then she looked at the church. "Is that ...? Did you used to go there?"

He shook his head. "I'm not one of God's favorites, either," he replied. She laughed again, tucking her hair behind her ear. He could tell she wanted to linger, but she returned to her work all the same.

He pulled off his gloves and dipped a claw in the coffee to check how pure it was. He sifted through the thousand different chemicals he knew he'd find. Oils, heterocyclic compounds, sulfur ... Surprisingly little contamination from pesticides and detergents. He indulged himself with a sip and glanced down at the newspaper lying open next to him.

The reality of the human world screamed at him from its pages. Conflicts over borders and resources. A photo of dead birds on a motorway caught his eye. Over a hundred of them, apparently. They'd rained down on the roads of Northampton, like in a scene from a film, according to eyewitnesses.

He closed the paper. He knew how the story would end without reading on. With researchers claiming that all the noise must have scared or confused the birds and caused them to fly into power lines.

He remembered how his own raven had been killed. They'd wrung its neck. He could still hear it like it had happened yesterday. A sudden snap. A smothered screech.

He'd been powerless. Shackled. Maimed. Castrated. On the orders of his own brother. A brother with whom he'd fought side by side.

The images hit him like a tidal wave. Kneeling in his own blood. The pain in his groin. His manhood, given to the ravens. They'd fought over it, tearing at it with their beaks, digging their talons into his back. The poison in his veins. The Might that had torn him apart from the inside. The scorching of his blood. If he tried to go through the raven rings now, he'd end his days as dust, caught in a void. That was how the Seer had been born. That was how his brother had become a god.

Neither of them had thought they'd ever meet again. Least of all Naiell. And that's how it would have remained, had they not made one fatal error. They'd let him keep the dead bird. Their stupidity had been his salvation.

They'd laughed at him, not understanding why he wanted to keep a carcass. A mangy bag of feathers. A companion that would rot. Laughed but allowed it. Perhaps because it had seemed pathetic.

And with that they'd brought about their own ruin. They'd given him a weapon. Something he could use, even if they killed the raven rings. He had the beak.

It had taken him a thousand long years. A thousand. Just to find someone who could reach him. Who could help him find raven rings that still held traces of the Might. He'd never forgotten. Never given up. And now the day was upon him. Naiell was here, in the city. He could smell him. It was the smell of fear. Of the end.

The church stood there like a burned-out promise, one of its walls tagged with red spray paint. *We are all blind.*

BETRAYAL

Hirka sat on the roof and looked out across the city. It felt treacherously alive. Cars zipped around, people walked, big cranes moved blocks of stone to build more houses. Bigger houses. Death was invisible to those who weren't looking for it. It rested in asphalt. Crawled in gray grass. Gnawed at bare trees that couldn't find enough sustenance to grow leaves.

But it was also cunning. Death gleamed in the apples that never rotted. The rot was here, and it always would be. It was as Graal had said. She couldn't save this world. She might be able to save some people, a life or two, but time was running out. Its days were numbered.

It felt wrong to abandon it for a place where the Might still existed. Surely everyone here deserved the same chance? Were they all doomed to die for something Naiell had done a thousand years ago? It just wasn't right.

She fiddled with the roll of tape she'd found next to the broken window.

Was there a way of getting humans through the raven rings? How many of them was there room for in Ym? Could the eleven kingdoms accommodate the inhabitants of this world? A chill ran down her spine. She remembered Allegra's hungry look when she'd seen the stones.

And they're common where you come from?

And if it were possible … If Mannfalla could accommodate as many humans as ymlings, what would they do there? The same as they'd done here?

The thought was more unbearable than letting them die.

So she'd choose plants over humans? Animals that couldn't speak over animals that could? What did that say about her?

She'd probably find out that evening.

She glanced over at the church. She could only see the spire from here. It was idyllically situated, surrounded by trees that would soon be in leaf, but beneath them, humans lay rotting. And everything would only continue to rot. She didn't know what would happen, but she knew that evening would in all likelihood be her last.

She and Naiell each had their own plan. He thought she didn't know what he was willing to do. He thought she'd built him an army. What would he do when he realized? And what would Graal say when he saw the forgotten? If they came, that was. And would Rime be there?

The sky blazed behind tall buildings, the sun turning the river red. Soon evening would be upon them. Soon everything would be uncertain. If she survived the evening, she would leave this world. For another she didn't know. Last time she'd cried. Struggled to come to terms with it.

This time everything was different. There was no council to overthrow. No halls to tear down. And she wouldn't be sad to leave.

She'd wanted out of this world ever since she'd arrived. Nothing could be worse than this place, which was slowly dying in a whirl of flashing lights and screeching cars. She wasn't human. She was Dreyri. She was half-blindling. It terrified her that she'd embraced it so wholeheartedly. Maybe it had something to do with Graal's promises. Vague words about power over life and death. About power over the Might. Was she even more stupid than the ymlings? Had she simply found another seer to follow?

She tugged at the shells hanging from the end of the ties on her bag. They were indistinguishable from the ones found here. What else did all worlds have in common? Where were the roots of everything that was the same? Of all the hundreds of worlds she'd seen on the map? Was there anything there?

The red faded in the sky. It was time.

She found the end of the tape and tore off two strips. They stuck to her fingers, impossible to put down, so she attached them to her arm. She pulled her knife out of her boot and laid it against her forearm. Lengthwise, so the tip stuck out from her elbow when she bent her arm. It wasn't protruding quite far enough, so she pushed it up a bit and bent her elbow again.

Better. Enough to wound, but not so much that it could be seen.

She wrapped the tape around the hilt and attached it to her arm. Tested it. It held. The two strips of gray tape kept the knife in place. They'd have to. She pulled her sleeve back down. Put the rest of the tape in her bag, got up, and climbed back through the roof hatch. She dropped down onto the floor and went to find Naiell.

"Time to go," she said.

He was standing at the window, surrounded by half-spoiled food. He'd eaten. A lot. He was still wearing Stefan's clothes, but he'd never seemed less familiar.

He cocked his head and looked at her. Eyes white as blank paper. Without words. Without meaning.

"Bring what you need," she said. "We won't be coming back here."

"I don't have anything here that I need."

"Me neither."

She looked around the dusty loft that they'd been living in for the last few days. Dirty. Moldering. Rusted metal parts strewn everywhere. She found herself wondering whether the parts would make something if she put them together. Could she repair it?

She'd never know.

She walked out and heard Naiell follow. She wanted to implore the Seer to make sure the knife wouldn't be seen, but there was no point. The Seer was right behind her. He was the one she needed protection from.

She had only herself to rely on.

The church was more desolate than she remembered. A burned-out ruin. Someone had tried to cover the roof with plastic, but it had blown off in several places. The gate was locked with a chain, and tall metal fences with yellow signs and striped tape stood in front of it. Not much of an obstacle considering the stone wall surrounding the churchyard wasn't any taller than Hirka. She climbed up.

"Where are they?" Naiell asked. "Where's my army?"

"We've talked about this, Naiell. I told them to wait until Graal was inside. They're out here. Hidden in the streets." She looked around, hoping she was right.

She could see the outline of a man under a streetlight nearby. It looked like he was tossing a coin. She nudged Naiell and nodded toward the figure. "There's Isac. They're here."

Naiell grinned and jumped over the fence. He paused on the other side, studying every detail. Every gravestone. Every corner. He was anxious, keeping his guard up. She knew he'd never have come had there been any other option.

There was no way out of the human world without Graal. Without his allies in Ym, who had the Might and the knowledge to open the stone way. All the same, Naiell hesitated, and she couldn't blame him. The humiliation he'd let his brother suffer had been festering for a thousand years. Unforgivable cruelty, committed in the belief that they would never see each other again.

The church door was locked, but that didn't matter. There were plenty of ways in. Hirka walked around the side. There was a strange smell. She thought back to when she'd set fire to the cabin before traveling to Ravnhov, but this was something else. Burnt wood mixed with something artificial she couldn't place. Something sharp. That was one of the reasons she'd chosen this place. It was abandoned yet familiar, and the fire would mask the smell of the forgotten from Graal.

Many of the tall windows were broken and covered with plastic. She pulled herself up onto the nearest ledge, peeled back the plastic, and climbed in.

It was dark inside. The air felt close. Water dripped down from the plastic on the roof. Where it had been blown back, she could see right up at the clouds.

Wet leaves clung to the pews. The front rows were nothing more than charred kindling. Soot stained the walls. Shards of colored glass were strewn across the floor. The windows must have shattered. One of the chandeliers had fallen down and lay broken over the back of a pew, arms pointing every which way.

The area around the altar was the worst. The door she'd used to access the tower was gone. All that remained was the hole in the wall, barred by fallen beams. The altar was bare. A book lay open on the floor, its pages black. Wordless. Hirka crouched down and turned a page. It disintegrated between her fingers.

She looked up at the altarpiece. It had melted. She saw no god. No faces. Nothing at all.

It was here that everything would end.

She walked along the aisle toward the door. Jay had lain here. Her mum and little sister over there. All dead now. Someone had tried to clean up the blood, but traces of it still remained between the stones.

Hirka unlocked the door and let Naiell in. He walked to the front of the church and sat on the altar where Father Brody had lain. "This was your house?"

"No. I just stayed here."

It seemed so long ago. There was so much she hadn't known back then. Everything was different now. She was a different person. No longer unaware of what was hunting her. No longer the girl hiding in the bell tower, afraid of being tailless. Of being a child of Odin. She was much stronger now—but somehow more vulnerable than ever.

"Come," Naiell said.

Hirka steeled herself. She knew what was coming. The show for Graal. The pretense of exchanging her for Rime, and for Naiell's freedom. But pretense or not, it would be fraught with peril. Naiell wanted her dead. She was the progeny he'd done his utmost to prevent. She'd have been dead already, had she not been what he assumed was an ignorant hostage.

That said, there was still a tiny chance she was wrong. She couldn't know for sure that Naiell was as bloodthirsty as she suspected. She wouldn't know the truth until the brothers came face to face.

She smiled. Father Brody had always said that people found their true selves in the church. Showed their true nature.

Hirka walked over to Naiell and sat down next to him. The difference in size between them chased her heart even farther up her throat. She carefully bent her arm, feeling the knife taped there. She hoped she wouldn't have to use it.

She gazed up at the ceiling. The arches were broken and sticking up into the sky like claws. She could see stars, far above. Were they holding their breath, just like her?

Couldn't they just come already? Graal and Rime? Couldn't this just be over? She looked at Naiell. "Are you scared?" she asked.

"Would you be?" he hissed.

"I don't know. Depends what had happened, and I don't know much about that," she lied.

"He lost. That's what happened."

That pretty much sums it up.

Wasn't that what Graal had said?

Naiell got up and pulled off his shirt. He threw it on the floor and beat his palms against his chest. A strange, ritualistic act. Affirming that he was strong and ready for anything. He walked over to the burned-out corner and started tearing away the boards covering the hole in the wall. An escape route, in case something went wrong.

"Maybe a mountaintop would've been better." Hirka was unable to hide the contempt in her voice.

Naiell came toward her. She forced herself to stay where she was. He jabbed a claw at her. "You know nothing about my brother. It's called being sensible, Sulni."

"If I know nothing, it's because you haven't told me anything," she said.

"I've told you enough that you ought to fear him."

"You've told me enough about him that I ought to fear *you*." As soon as it was out of her mouth, she bit her lip. His eyes gleamed. White amid all the charred black.

"You're right," he said. "If you had any sense, you'd fear me more than you do."

"You must have done something awful to be this scared," she muttered.

"I'm not scared!" He swept toward her. She leaped to her feet and backed against the wall.

"I used to tell myself that, too."

She couldn't keep her mouth shut. She had too much on her mind. But now wasn't the time. She knew that. She was about to destroy everything she'd planned. But still it came out. "If you're so scared of facing the consequences, you should never have done what you did!"

Naiell bared his canines but didn't reply.

"She's right, brother."

Hirka looked at the door. It was Graal, standing in the opening between the church hall and the vestibule. She recognized the outline of his long coat. His wild hair.

He came closer. Took off his glasses and stuck them in his jacket pocket. She heard a hiss from Naiell. Catlike.

Another figure appeared behind Graal.

Rime.

Hirka clutched her chest. Her lips started to tingle. Her body remembered. His swords stuck up behind him. His white hair had been tied back. Some of it hung loose, framing his face. It was all so familiar that she wanted to scream.

He looked at her. Inside her. She could hear him thinking her name. She forgot all the plans she'd made. Only one thing mattered.

Hirka started to move toward him, but then she was pulled back. Naiell had a firm hand on her shoulder. "Now, now. We're here to make an exchange, remember?" His claws stuck through her tunic. Sharp against her skin.

Rime drew one of his swords, but Graal raised a hand to stop him. "Wait. She's smarter than that."

Her deadborn father started to make his way along the wall on the outside of the pews. He walked slowly, up toward the altar. His eyes fixed on Naiell, just behind her.

Hirka was pulled back. Naiell wanted her farther away. He moved in the opposite direction of Graal. Toward the door. Even with her in his claws, he didn't feel like he had enough of an upper hand to stay put.

Rime swung his sword through the air, adjusting his grip. "Have you ever known pain, Seer?" His voice was sharp as his steel.

"In almost three millennia? I'd say so," Naiell replied derisively. He was holding her so close that she could feel his breath on the back of her head.

“Not like this,” Rime said. “Not like you’ll feel if you lay a hand on her.”

Hirka dragged a hand over her face. Dear, sweet Rime. Her hero. Her idiot. He still thought he was here to save her, when in reality, it was the other way around.

Naiell laughed and moved his claws up toward her throat. Hirka swallowed and tried to shut out the images of food she’d seen rotting in his hands.

“Look at yourself, Graal. You look like *them*!” he said. “You’ve changed. How could you?”

Graal reached the altar and stopped. “After a thousand years, the question is rather how you’re still the same.”

Naiell snorted. “You *sound* like them, too.”

Hirka caught a whiff of something under the charred smell. Sweet. Half-rotten.

“They’re here,” she whispered to Naiell. He loosened his grip.

Two humans came through the door. And another three, right behind them. Then even more. Hirka wanted to cry with relief. The forgotten were here. Salvation. Scores of them. Familiar and unfamiliar faces, all affected to varying degrees by the rot. Some emaciated and wearing worn clothes. Others still healthy. They spread out along the walls. Between the pews. Twenty. Thirty. More entered through the gap in the wall where Naiell had removed the boards.

Isac came through the broken window, dropping down onto the floor a short distance away.

Graal met her gaze. She could see coal-black doubt in his eyes. An unspoken question.

Have you betrayed me?

She held his gaze and shook her head, hoping he would understand.

Rime drew his second sword. She knew him so well. Saw him reading the room. Planning his moves. He had no way of knowing who was friend and who was foe. She could only hope he didn't act rashly.

The forgotten filled the church, one by one. Pale in the dark. A nightmarish mass. Even more were coming through the gap in the wall. A steady stream between the gravestones. The dead walking over the dead. There had to be almost a hundred of them.

Naiell grinned at her. As if they were allies now. He had his army. He was no longer afraid. He was surrounded by those he thought would protect him.

Hirka tried to move away from him, but he gripped her arm. Wanted her close. That was what she'd feared. He pulled her out into the aisle. They had to be the most morbid couple that had ever stood there.

"So, brother," he spat. "Shall we talk about getting me home?"

He was so proud. So overinflated. He was the Seer. Accustomed to unconditional adoration. "I'll be merciful and have them kill you as soon as you get me back to Ym."

"You never were the brightest spark, Naiell. Who's going to force me? You?" Graal smiled. He'd longed for this moment longer than anyone could know. Hirka remembered all the lines on his back. Each a reminder of injustice.

Naiell raised his arms out to the sides and slowly spun in the aisle. Displaying himself. Muscles rippled across his bare chest. He looked like the altarpiece Hirka knew was still there somewhere. Behind the ashes. "Have your eyes failed you? Me and my army!" he shouted.

"*My* army," Hirka said.

Naiell turned toward her. She pulled away from him, took a deep breath, and repeated herself. "My army, Naiell. Not yours. Mine."

The forgotten crowded around them. Moved toward them between the pews. It took a moment for Naiell's confusion to turn to disbelief.

"No?" he uttered doubtfully. He looked at her.

Then he screamed. An unnatural sound from the depths of his being. His canines gleamed in his open jaws.

"YOU BETRAYED ME?!"

Over by the altar, Graal started to laugh. "How does it feel, brother? How does it feel to be betrayed?"

Naiell's eyes darted around the hall. He was surrounded. His rage turned to fear. It was starting to dawn on him what was happening.

"You betrayed me," he repeated hoarsely.

"No," Hirka replied. "You betrayed me. And in return, I'm saving your skin."

The forgotten closed in around him. He swung his arms around to keep them at bay. "I can give them eternal life! In *my* service! Tell them that! Eternal life! You have nothing!"

"I can give them something better than eternal life," Hirka said. "I can give them freedom. And a chance to forgive."

Naiell's eyes darkened. His lips quivered. He threw himself at her. She saw it coming and pulled away. She stumbled into a pew. He grabbed her, his claws digging into her throat. The forgotten crowded around them. Hirka raised a hand to stop them. Naiell needed her alive. For a little longer. Luckily Graal and Rime knew that, too.

Naiell hissed in her ear. "You thought you could beat me? You're nothing, Sulni. Nothing!" He was pressed against her back. Hirka could taste the fear. Like steel in her mouth. Too much was at stake. But she knew what she had to do. It was now or never.

She flung her elbow back, into his body. He groaned, his grip on her throat loosening. She tore herself free, skin stinging under the tape holding the knife in place. Naiell stooped forward with his hands pressed to his stomach. She'd hit her mark. But she knew he would heal quickly. It wouldn't be nearly enough to stop him.

He got up again.

"Nothing?" she said. She was scared and stretched to breaking point, but she'd had more than enough of being nobody.

"I'm no mayfly. I'm Hirka!" she screamed. "I destroyed you in Ym. I can destroy you here, too." He grabbed her. She swiped her elbow across his chest with all the strength she could muster. The tip of the knife sliced into him. Red blood sprayed across the faces of the closest forgotten.

Everything would happen at once. She knew that. Could see it in the faces of the old blood slaves. Some of them had a wild look in their eyes. Some of them had already lost the fight.

No! You're strong!

But the sticky red fluid had roused their thirst. Their craving. They threw themselves on the floor. Over the precious drops seeping between the stones. Farther back, others started climbing over each other to get closer. Jumping over the pews. Naiell howled in pain and made a grab for her, but she pressed herself into the throng of forgotten. Between …

Stefan?

Stefan was standing in the opening in the wall, gaping at the teeming sea of forgotten. For a moment he seemed frozen. Unable to understand or react. Then he drew his gun.

No! This is not how it's supposed to end!

Despair gripped her heart. Squeezed it into pieces. She heard Graal shout. Heard the forgotten fighting their way toward Naiell. She turned to look at him, but he had disappeared beneath them. Drowned under his own army.

Stefan grabbed her and pulled her close. He shouted something, but she didn't hear a word. Chaos reigned. Rime came running toward them. Stefan raised the gun and Hirka threw herself at his arm, sinking her teeth into it. Biting down until he yowled. She wrestled the gun away from him. Clutched it in her hand.

No one dies today.

She aimed at one of the few windows that were still intact and pulled the trigger. There was a bang. Her arm jerked. She pulled the trigger again. More bangs. The sound of tinkling glass. She felt like she'd been hit as well. As if she were breaking, just like the glass. Shattering into pieces. Raining down on the floor. She was destruction. She was destroyed. Everything she touched went to pieces.

Her forgotten army recovered their composure and scrambled back, away from the falling glass and ruined idols. Naiell was left behind, crawling in the aisle. Hirka threw the gun at the wall.

Everything fell silent. Silent as Slokna. She could feel a wetness in her hair. Something dripped down onto her face. She looked up at the gaping hole in the roof. It had started to rain.

BROTHERS

Graal walked down the aisle toward his fallen brother. Glass crunched beneath his feet. His leather coat glistened in the rain, like the leaves on the ground. Naiell grabbed a pew and tried to pull himself up, but then he fell to the floor again and started crawling back instead.

"What have you done?" Stefan whispered behind her.

"It had to happen sooner or later," she replied. "And considering a thousand years have passed, this is later."

Pain shot through her arm. The knife. It had cut into her. She reached under her tunic and tore it loose. The tape was wet with rain and blood.

The forgotten were silent. Some of them were staring at Stefan. They knew who he was. The hunter.

"So have you got enough sense to be afraid, or are you too busy counting teeth?" Hirka asked.

Stefan pulled her close and laughed into her hair. He shoved his hand in her pocket and dropped something inside. "I think these belong to you," he said. Her stones. He'd made a choice, and he wanted her to know. She kept her back to him, his arm across her chest. He needed her more than she needed him.

Rime's eyes were boring into her, but she couldn't bring herself to look at him. She didn't have the strength, and she wouldn't until all this was over.

Graal stopped in front of Naiell. "*Koy, waiad kwainsair, umkhadari!*"

Strange words without meaning. But her body recognized them.

Naiell's hair was plastered to his face. Fanned across his shoulders like wet raven wings. The gash in his chest had closed, only a line of raised skin indicating where she'd cut him. He bared his teeth like a wolf. But Hirka had seen Graal tame wolves before.

It was an incredible sight. A half-naked, sinewy beast, wearing Stefan's old trousers. He crawled across the floor before his finely dressed, much slimmer brother.

Hirka's throat was stinging from Naiell's claws, but it still pained her to see him that way.

"I'd have faced you wherever and whenever," Graal said. "Unarmed and alone. Yet you come here with an army? With a hundred men and women? How many did you have last time, brother? A hundred thousand thrice over?"

"Are you blaming me for what men do at war?" Naiell replied.

Graal tipped his head back and closed his eyes. Then he looked down at his brother again.

"You misunderstand me. This is not a discussion. This is not an opportunity to explain or defend yourself. I'm not wondering why." His voice grew louder and louder. "I—know—why!"

Hirka feared he was losing his temper.

"You were given all the power under the sun!" he shouted, the echo bouncing between the walls. Then he leaned over Naiell. "Weren't you, brother?" he asked quietly. "All the power. Yours alone. You and the Might. You're desperate for it now, aren't you? Thirsting for it. But you'll never find it. The earth is barren here. Had you only let the Might live, brother, you could have bound it now. Drawn on it. Poetic, don't you think? You orchestrated your own ruin when you sentenced everything outside of Ym to death."

Graal crouched down, cocked his head, and gazed at Naiell. They looked more like each other now. So much anger. So much hate. It was poison, and Hirka could feel it spreading under her skin. She'd done everything in her power to save lives. This had to stop. Now.

Naiell didn't dare look his brother in the eye. His breath came in short gasps. Graal reached out, as if to touch him, but he stopped himself. He straightened up again. More glass crunched beneath his feet.

"Hirka was of the impression I wanted to use her. That I needed her blood to replace what you scorched. Who could have given her such an idea, brother? What kind of monster would paint such a grisly picture? I'm almost tempted to try. After all, I have you here. Wouldn't it be glorious if I traveled home with your blood in my veins? A poor substitute for what you destroyed. What do you think, brother?"

Hirka tore herself out of Stefan's grasp and approached the altar. "That's enough, Graal. It's over."

Graal turned to her. "Blood of my blood, this has barely even begun. Our people will always fight for the Might. For the right to Ym. You know what we are."

"So who will you be once you've succeeded?" she asked.

He gave her a wondering look. The forgotten stared at her. Beggars, leaders, women and men alike. Rime. Stefan. Isac.

She needed to strike while the iron was hot.

"Do you want to be the one to lead them to the Might? Or do you want to remain the loser in exile? You have that choice now. Naiell betrayed them. Took what they wanted and kept it for himself. They hate him. You hate him. But he's your brother. We're both blood of your blood. And Dreyri don't kill Dreyri. Isn't that right, Father?"

Hirka saw Rime lower his gaze out of the corner of her eye. Perhaps he had only just realized who she was. That she was half-blindling. The truth drove a wedge between them, and it pained her.

She took a step toward Graal. "This is the moment. Not a thousand years ago. Not a thousand years in the future. Now. You choose your fate here and now. If you kill your own brother, they'll never follow you."

"I was sentenced to die here. They'd never follow me anyway."

"You're wrong." Hirka went over to him. "They don't need to follow you. They can follow me."

The silence was charged, like when Graal had been sitting at the piano, fingers hovering over the keys. The sound of everything that was yet to come. The smell of ash mixed with the smell of fear. Of blood.

She looked up at Graal. At the deadborn who had begotten her. "You can do something better than kill him. You can give him to them. Give them the one who betrayed them. Send him to them, along with me, and they'll forever know it was your blood that brought him back. That he was your gift to them."

She could tell he hadn't considered that. She had a chance. A tiny chance. "You said it yourself, Graal. What has Ym done for me? They threw me in the pits. Humiliated me. Hunted and despised me. You created me to live among Dreyri. To take your place. To be the one who would lead them to the Might. Graal—whether you like it or not, I'm your only hope."

His features had softened. He understood, but he was still hesitant. "You didn't grow up there. You don't know them. They'll eat you alive."

"Let them try! I've brought Ym to its knees before and I can do it again. Just ask Rime. I'm blood of your blood." She pointed at the forgotten. "You see them? They're not here for you. They're not here for Naiell. They're here for *me*. I swear I can do this. I can deliver the Might to our people."

Rime came toward her. He was frowning. "You'd sacrifice Ym? For him?!"

She looked at him. "No. For you."

Graal laughed. "She's right, Rime An-Elderin. She knows you've taken the beak. Dreyri possess the knowledge she needs to remove it. I know what she's thinking, and she's thinking further ahead than you. I look forward to seeing her in your chair."

Hirka rested a hand on her father's chest. "I'm not promising you a world, Graal. I'm not promising you annihilation, or the ruin of all ymlings. That won't happen. But I promise you'll get what you want. You'll get to go home. You'll get to feel the Might again."

Graal turned to Naiell and beamed. "Hear that, brother? This is my daughter. Blood of my blood. See what she's become!"

Naiell stared at her, eyes black with fear. "It's a death sentence! They'll kill me!"

Hirka snarled at him. "Then you'd best pray to whatever gods you might have that I'm able to lead them. That they'll listen to me and spare your life. Because without me, you're a dead man."

Graal put his hands on her shoulders. "Blood of my blood, you're greater than I'd ever dared hope. We'll do it your way."

Hirka felt a tingling in her chest. A peculiar warmth mixed with the pain. Was it weariness? No, it was something else. Something she couldn't remember ever feeling before. Pride. She was proud of who she was.

She lowered her eyes. "Yes. We'll do it my way. If I survive the night."

"Why wouldn't you survive?" Graal asked.

Isac took a step forward from the ranks of the forgotten.

"She's going to pay your debt."

THE DEBT

Hirka sat down heavily on the altar. Soot clung to her yellow boots. The forgotten stood in silence around her, waiting. For salvation. What if she couldn't help them after all? She was too tired to pursue the thought any further. She had to try. She'd promised.

They were all so different. Slaves to the thirst. Graal's followers. Some were well-dressed. Beautiful. Perhaps they hadn't thirsted long. Others looked exhausted. Young men with blue circles under their eyes and cracked fingers. The type she'd seen sitting in the streets. The type people looked right through. Desperation had many faces.

She rolled up the sleeve of her tunic. Then she drew her knife and made a cut in her forearm. Blood started trickling down toward her wrist.

Stefan shouted and pushed between the forgotten. Over toward her.

"This! This is your cure?" He stared at her like she'd lost her mind. "For all of them? Can't you count, girl?!"

"They don't need much, hunter." Isac spat the last word. Stefan looked around as if he'd only just realized who he was surrounded by. His hand moved instinctively to his chest, hiding the small container of teeth he wore around his neck. Teeth from the forgotten.

He backed away. "Haven't you people heard of hygiene? Surely there's a more civilized way of doing this? At a hospital? What the actual fuck."

Deep down she knew that Stefan was more worried about himself than her. This was all he knew. The forgotten. The hunt for Graal. If she cured the rot, life as he knew it would be over.

Hirka smiled at him. She wanted to explain but was too tired. And the solution was so simple. It would soon be over. "A hospital, Stefan?"

His gaze faltered. He remembered. In this world she was nameless. Numberless. She didn't exist. And even if she had, they both knew that none of the forgotten would let her go before they got what they'd been promised.

Stefan turned to Graal. "And you … You're going to let her do this? Clean up your mess? She's just a girl!"

Graal walked toward Stefan, who stayed where he was despite every instinct. They stood face to face. The hunter and his Graal.

Hirka found herself wondering whether her father knew who was standing before him. Did he know that Stefan was more forgotten than the forgotten themselves? That he'd been abandoned by a woman who had chosen Graal over her own son? Maybe that didn't matter to Graal. Maybe that sort of thing meant little to someone who would never die.

Stefan was shaking.

Graal rested his white gaze on him. "Forgive me," he said.

Stefan's face twisted in pain. He looked like he wanted to reply, but nothing came out of his mouth. Graal caught his eye again. "My blood is yours, Stefan, if you want it."

Hirka hardly dared breathe. Many of the forgotten standing before her would have accepted. Even now. Even though they knew the pain it would bring in time, when they were no longer close to Graal.

Stefan shook his head and fell to his knees. Then he started to cry, in deep, gasping sobs. Hirka felt for him. She knew what he'd said no to. Understood the strength it had taken. He looked broken, kneeling on the floor. But he'd never been stronger.

His sobs prompted the forgotten to throng together before the altar, his strength infecting the very people he'd always hunted. They were ready for her.

The first to approach was the beggar from London. The man with the nice eyes and hollow cheeks. He looked at her arm and then at the others, confused about what he was supposed to do.

Hirka offered him her arm. He took it in his hands. His chapped hands in their fingerless gloves. He clamped his mouth over the cut. It was cool against her skin. Isac said something to him, but she didn't hear what. It was as if all sound were muffled. All she could hear was the rain drumming against the church floor. The plastic on the roof flapping in the wind.

The beggar moved aside to make way for a woman she'd never seen before. Dark hair. Anxious. She lifted Hirka's arm to her mouth, drinking what would finally give her back her death. Drinking before moving aside for the next person.

Hirka's arm started to tingle. She gazed up at the sky. She'd won. Won the ceasefire she needed. Rime would return home. Graal wouldn't hurt him. Not for now. Naiell was alive. Graal was alive. She was alive.

For the time being.

But at what cost? Would it cost Ym? She tried not to think about it, about how she didn't know where she was going. About how she had to leave Rime again after a kiss that had torn her from the clutches of Slokna.

And the next time they met, they would be enemies.

An ymling and a blindling. Dreyri. Each on their own side of the war she knew would come.

She felt numb. Darkness was closing in on her. Was this what it had been like for Rime as a child? Sitting on a pedestal, blessing hordes of ymlings in Eisvaldr? She smiled. Her blood roared in her ears. Wet, pale faces came and went, drinking from her as if she were a holy grail.

The wind blew in through the hole in the wall, sweeping ash along the aisle. The pages of the burnt book started to flutter on the floor, coming loose and sailing in black flakes through the air before gradually crumbling into dust.

She felt dizzy. Blood ran down her arm, collecting in her palm and dripping onto the floor.

Soon. Enough soon.

She tried to get up but fell. Fell among the humans.

Faces hovered over her. Rime. Rime was there. He reached out to her as she fell. Everything seemed so interminably slow. He grabbed hold of her. Turned and called out to someone. Soundlessly.

His white hair whipped in the wind as he shouted. She smiled.

One point to me if you pull me up.

AN ACCOMPLISHED LIAR

"Why here?" Rime asked.

Graal leaned against the wall and looked at him. The Ravenbearer was standing with his hand against the window, staring at the mountaintops. The composure he exhibited was impressive, given the circumstances. The shock had to have been tremendous, encountering a culture he lacked all the prerequisites to understand.

"Few places are more beautiful than the Norwegian mountains. It's quiet here. I can hear myself play," Graal replied, nodding in the direction of the piano. "If I'm interrupted, it's by ravens. Nothing else. You get tired of all the noise. Eventually."

He was young, Rime An-Elderin. The eleven kingdoms had never had a younger ravenbearer. Graal felt a kinship with him. They were more alike than Rime thought. Graal had also been the youngest. The prodigy. Destined to lead the first to victory. Together with his brother. He hoped Rime had better allies. He wanted a better fate for him than his own.

Graal filled two glasses with wine and handed one to Rime.

"We're enemies," Rime said without looking at him.

"Not today." Graal set his glass down on the piano.

Rime was remarkably stubborn. So full of fire. Full of life. He had the same blood in his veins as the first warriors. The twelve who had sealed Graal's fate and sent him here. He was a true child of Ym. The question was whether that would make things simpler or more difficult. Graal needed to bend him to his will. Make him do what he couldn't do himself.

"Enemies don't want the same thing," Graal said. "We do. She's in there recovering her strength. Making new blood after a sacrifice neither you nor I would have made. We both want her to survive. Both you and I want what's best for her. That makes us allies. Today."

Rime turned toward him. The leather straps creaked across his chest. A heavenly sound Graal hadn't heard in centuries. The sound of passion. Conviction. Strength. It was a whisper from a place where survival still depended on how much sweat you were willing to offer.

He felt a stab of shame. He'd been like Rime, once. Balanced between ice and fire. He'd taken what was rightfully his with his own hands. Young and arrogant. Now he moved money around. Meaningless figures, to places with imagined value. Survival was free here. All the same, his hands were dirtier now than they'd ever been before.

It's just one of those days.

Graal was used to the mood swings, but it wasn't always easy to know when they were coming. They had a tendency to make things foggy. He had to fight to remember what he really thought. Dig through layers of false information to find his true self. Melancholy was an accomplished liar.

Rime's face was close. "I'm being civilized because I have no other choice," he said through clenched teeth. "Not for any other reason. Because you have power over her, and power over me. The day you lose that power will be the day you realize we're enemies."

Graal smiled, suppressing a shiver. He'd wondered what kind of power could compel Damayanti to betray him. The answer was standing right in front of him. Hair and eyes as white as snow. Wearing linen and leather, with twin promises of death strapped to his back.

In another life, Graal would have taken him. Kept him for himself. Given him life in return, and never forgotten him. It was unexpectedly painful to know it couldn't be that way.

He swirled the wine in his glass but didn't drink. Wine had a tendency to make matters worse.

"Would you feel better if you could kill me, Rime? Would you feel you'd achieved something important if you shed more blood? Is that still how they measure victory in Mannfalla? Is it really that difficult to sit at a table with people you disagree with?"

Rime's gaze faltered. Graal had struck a nerve. "Disagree? You want to conquer the eleven kingdoms! Crush my people!"

Graal sighed and sat down on the sofa next to the raven cadaver. "What is it you call us, Rime? Blind? Deadborn? Nábyrn? Our people have a name. Umpiri. Blood of the first. In our stories, the world was created by the first raven. By Um. Over the years, Um became Ym. If you doubt my claim, you needn't look further than what you call your world. Ym is named after us."

Rime walked around the edge of the room and stopped in front of the painting, just like Hirka had done. "And what of it? I bet there are myths in your world that come from ymlings."

"Certainly. And there are myths here in the human world that come from us. That's the problem with humans and ymlings. Your lives are too short. You mix up your stories and have poor memories. Before even a century has passed, their origin is forgotten. I've been here for almost a thousand years, and I've seen my story twisted into something unrecognizable. I've been a wounded king, a holy grail, and a bloodsucking zombie. As if I'd ever drink human blood. What am I, a barbarian?"

"You let them drink yours, so that sounds about right to me."

Graal took a sip of his wine. It was tart. He hadn't drunk wine in a long time. He set his glass down on the table, next to the raven cadaver.

"Where I come from, there's nothing purer than blood. Your kind understood that once as well. But nobody understands it anymore. Maybe she'll change that. If she lives long enough. And both of us want her to live."

Graal knew Rime would take the bait. But would he go far enough? Could he make him do what he wanted?

He could hear the Ravenbearer approaching. Part of him enjoyed the danger he represented. An armed Kolkagga, who in his ardent simplicity believed in sacrificing himself to kill him. No matter the consequences. But Rime An-Elderin wasn't to be underestimated.

"So why are you letting him go with her? It's madness! You know that as well as I do. He'll kill her as soon as the opportunity presents itself."

"Undoubtedly," Graal replied. "I have to trust they'll kill him first."

"Trust? You see what she's done. If anyone can prevent a bloodbath, it's her. They'll let him live if she asks them to. Your trust is misplaced, and she'll suffer for it."

"Possibly. After all, Dreyri don't kill Dreyri. But I suspect they'll soon dispense with that rule when presented with my brother."

Rime walked around the sofa and met his gaze. "He'll live. And work against her. Find ways to destroy her. Every single day!"

"Every single hour."

"So why?! What's the point of her taking the enemy of the people with her if she won't let them punish him? Why are you letting him go with her?"

Graal struggled to suppress a smile. This was almost too easy. "Because she'd never forgive me if I killed him."

Rime gaped at him. "You care more about what she thinks of you than her safety." It wasn't a question. His lip curled in distaste.

Graal got up. "Don't you?"

"No."

"Well, you're welcome to try negotiating with him. He's locked in the cellar. He's not going anywhere. He'll have no choice but to listen to you. But I think he'd prefer death to what awaits him. We don't kill each other, but we can inflict pain. It's an art our people have mastered so well that most who die choose that fate."

Graal could tell that Rime was hesitating, so he gave him a moment to come to the right conclusion. Graal had waited for a thousand years, and he wasn't going to let his brother leave this world. At least not with his daughter. Blood of his blood.

If Rime didn't kill Naiell, he would do it himself. There was no doubt about that. It would give him more pleasure than he cared to admit, but killing one's own brother couldn't be swept under the rug, and it couldn't be done without losing Hirka's trust—something he was willing to do almost anything to keep.

Rime had to be the executioner. It would also weaken the only tie Hirka had to Ym. The bond between her and Rime.

"So let me talk to him," Rime said.

"Of course," Graal replied. "Follow me."

THE PRICE

Rime stared at the cellar door. It was made of solid steel. Smooth as a sword. Its surface was flawless. But someone had to have made it.

Behind this door was the Seer. Naiell. The blindling who had turned on his own people to save Ym. That was what the Book of the Seer said. That was what Rime had been hearing since the day he was born.

Even his own existence was a blessing from the Seer. A birth that could have ended in tragedy. It had almost killed both him and his mother before he'd taken his first breath. But then Ilume had arrived at her daughter's childbed with a gaggle of healers, announcing that the Seer had decreed the child would live.

That was how he had been born. The child everyone had been waiting for. Rime An-Elderin. Blessed by a god he'd dedicated his life to. Worshipped. Served with blood. Raged against. Until the final end. Until he'd broken in to see the Raven, only to discover that He didn't exist.

But the Seer had committed a greater sin than not existing. He'd forgotten them all.

Rime put his hand on the door. It was cold against his palm. He let the coldness fill him, affirm what he had to do. Hirka would never understand. Or forgive him. But it was better that she lived as his enemy than didn't live at all. And was it such a sin to give a man death rather than an eternity of torment?

Don't start something you can't finish.

He pressed the button next to the door. Heard the sound of bolts sliding back. A click. Then the door cracked open and Rime went in. The Seer leaped to his feet. He was still naked apart from the trousers belonging to that human. The one who'd put his arm around Hirka.

A light on the wall came on without Rime touching it. The light hit the blindling's chest. Bare. Strong. Unmarred by its encounter with Hirka's knife. No wonder fear of the nábyrn ran so deep among ymlings. No wonder one of them had risen to a position of absolute power. As a god.

My god. The Seer I followed.

Naiell gave him a derisive smile. "He sends *you* to do a job he doesn't dare do himself?"

"I begged to do it," Rime replied. "Since I've already killed you in Ym."

"You flatter yourself. I'm alive and well, Rime."

"So you know who I am?"

"I lived in the raven for a long time, but I still picked up on some things." Naiell looked down at his claws.

"Lived in the raven? While a whole world followed you? I dedicated my entire life to your words. Your false ideas."

Naiell laughed. A croaking that bounced off smooth walls. "Says the boy who's barely seen twenty winters. Forgive me if I don't cry, mayfly, but your entire life is over in a breath. You haven't lived long enough to understand that you can't blame others for your own idolatry. You bent the knee for someone who wasn't there. Which of us has sinned? You or I?"

Rime realized he was right. Naiell had seized power because he could. People had followed him because they wanted to. As they now followed Rime. Like the forgotten followed Graal.

"I forgive you," Rime said. "I forgive you for seizing power. But I don't forgive you for your theft of the Might. For stopping the flow and closing the gateways. I don't forgive you for all those who gave their lives so you could have absolute power. And I don't forgive you for what you're planning to do. To her. The first chance you get, you'll stab her in the back. To save your own skin."

Naiell winked, as if they shared a secret. "Not straight away. That's much too simple for my tastes. She'll suffer first, you can count on that."

Rime reached over his shoulder and drew a sword.

Naiell's upper lip pulled back to bare his canines. "You're proving how little you know about Umpiri. It doesn't matter what you do. Or what I do. She'll suffer regardless."

Rime lowered his sword. "You're right."

Hirka wanted to save lives. Not take them.

So what torment was he to inflict on her? That which would come from being destroyed by Naiell, or that which would come from knowing that Rime had killed him? He was trapped between his own conviction and hers. He'd already lost.

But he'd known that before he'd come down to the cellar, so why was he hesitating? The choice was simple. Did he want her love, or her safety?

Rime looked at the Seer. For him, death was undoubtedly preferable to meeting his own people again. He longed for the easiest way out. The coward's way out.

Rime turned his back on him.

He heard the Seer come closer. "No one turns their back on me, An-Elderin."

"You turned your back on all of us," Rime replied without looking around.

"And I'll do it again. After Umpiri have burned. After she's drawn her last breath. I promise you, boy, she's going to wish she'd never been born. You asked whether I've known true pain. None of us have, compared to what she'll experience. My brother's cursed progeny is going to lose her virginity to a sword."

Rime closed his eyes. His choice was made. He was Kolkagga. He didn't start anything he couldn't finish.

He felt the Seer approaching. Rime whirled around, his sword an extension of his arm. Weightless. Fluid. Then it met resistance. Slowed as it hit flesh. Then sped up again. He knew the maneuver better than the back of his hand.

Ravnringr. Perfect.

He'd spun all the way around and now stood with his back to what he knew to be a dead Seer. Blood dripped from his sword. He stared at the door.

Hirka ...

She was standing in the doorway, wearing only a white shirt. Hair wild and red around wide eyes. Blood had sprayed across her bare legs.

He heard the Seer fall to the floor behind him.

Hirka went pale. Her eyes brimmed with grief. Grief that kept coming until there was nothing but emptiness.

She turned her back on him and ran up the stairs. He didn't go after her. There was nothing he could say. Nothing he could do. He pulled a rag out of his pocket and dragged it along the blade. Wiped away the Seer's blood.

He'd made his choice. He knew who he was. What he was willing to do.

Now he was paying the price.

ARMOR

Hirka followed the black stone walls around the room, looking at Graal's collection. Bowls, cups, and sculptures. Various items in various sizes. The only thing they had in common was that they were all broken. They'd been glued back together, but not so the breaks couldn't be seen, like most people would have done. These had been repaired with pure gold. As if calling attention to the flaws were the whole point.

An art form, Graal had said, with a name she no longer remembered, from a country she'd never heard of. The point was to demonstrate that something could be more beautiful because it had been broken.

Hirka rested her fingers on the rough surface of a black bowl. Gold spread from the edge like blood vessels. A golden tree. It was certainly beautiful, but the bowl would never be the same again. It was also one of few that it had been possible to repair. For every bowl in this room there were ten thousand that would never be put back together again. That had been broken beyond recognition. Obliterated.

Like the flow of the Might between worlds.

It was about acceptance, Graal had said. About seeing beauty in that which was fleeting. In the traces of what had happened. Graal said a lot of strange things.

She left the bowls and went into the living room. It felt odd to be there alone. Her only company was the raven cadaver by the sofa.

Hirka went over to the window. It was getting dark. The mountaintops were turning gray, becoming one with the sky. It made her feel dizzy, though that might just have been the blood loss. Images flashed through her mind. The beggar with the chapped hands. The plastic on the church roof flapping in the wind. The blood running between her fingers.

Graal said she'd been seen by a good doctor. A woman he trusted, who had taken samples of her blood to find out why she was able to cure the rot. She had mixed blood that gave her resistance, he'd said. It didn't feel that way.

She could sense him coming. He stepped into the room.

"Is he gone?" Hirka asked without turning around.

Graal came closer. "He's gone."

Hirka leaned against the glass. It reflected them both.

Rime was back in Ym. To prevent the Council from falling apart, and undoubtedly to serve Graal in secret. He didn't have a choice, now that he had the beak in his throat.

Hirka clenched her teeth. "Good," she whispered. "And Stefan's mother? Did you find her?"

"I found her. She can be saved."

Hirka took a deep breath, relieved. She had to be pleased about what she could fix. Not despair over what was lost.

"And the book?"

Graal put the bag on the floor and pulled out the book. He gave it to her and she hugged it to her chest. The map of the worlds. Power no one could be allowed to have. It remained to be seen whether he would let her take it with her.

He lingered behind her. They looked at each other in the window. No one would have guessed they were father and daughter. The tall, dark-haired blindling with the red-haired girl standing before him.

"Not a day passed when I didn't think of you," Graal said. "About whether you were alive. Whether you'd actually grown up somewhere, against all odds. Who you'd become, and how much of our kind there was in you. You were human to look at. Their eyes. Their fingers. No claws. I wondered what would happen when you cut your first teeth. Would they be like ours? And the Might ... I thought about what you would be able to do with it. Use it like us, or amplify it, like a human. And most important of all, would you die, like them? Or live, like us?"

Hirka felt queasy. She couldn't heal herself like the blind, that much was for certain. And nothing seemed to indicate that she would live longer than a human. Even with the more keenly developed senses. Abilities she'd used her entire life without thinking about them. That was how she always knew whether someone was going to die, whether they had a mortal wound. The smell.

Graal put his hands on her shoulders, his claws pointing at her chest from each side. Like decorative pauldrons. Armor. He was her armor. His blood. Hers.

Dreyri.

SOPPY

The hospital was bathed in sunshine. Nature outshone everything she'd experienced, continuing its cycle, changing slowly from winter to spring. But what about when this world died? Would the light die, too? And when would that happen? Not overnight, she'd realized that. Even the Might didn't move that quickly.

She walked up the steps and inside. The corridors seemed bigger than before. Less scary. She was still an outsider, but she wasn't worried about anyone stopping her or asking what she was doing there. It didn't matter anymore. Human rules didn't apply to her.

Father Brody was lying alone in a room with two beds. He was awake. The curtains were drawn. The sunlight hit his pillow, shining in his thin hair. His face wasn't as round as it used to be.

She walked over to the bed. His face lit up when he spotted her. It was the first time she'd seen him smile without looking like he needed a wee.

"My dear girl, I thought the Lord had taken you," he said, his voice thick with emotion. He didn't have any tubes going into his hands, like Isac had had. There was fruit and chocolate on his bedside table. He was okay. She could smell it.

She took his hand. "He certainly tried."

It was strange to see him in such a way. White shirt and bare arms. More man than priest. He squeezed her hand in both of his. "I don't know where to start. Everything keeps slipping away from me."

"You don't need to start anywhere, Father Brody. I know what happened."

"They've asked me to tell them if you come. Are you in trouble? Is it them? The ones who ..." He couldn't bring himself to finish the sentence. His eyes were still just as kind, but she could also see a shadow of pain in them that she knew would be there for a long time. Maybe forever.

Hirka shook her head. "Not anymore, Father Brody. I'm okay now."

"What happened?"

"I found the devil."

He stroked her hand, not saying anything for a few moments. Then the color returned to his face. "Where's your bird? The raven that got sick. Did it recover?"

Hirka lowered her gaze. "No, he died."

"I'm sorry to hear that."

"Yes. He ... I met an old friend. He did something awful, but he's gone back home now. I might never see him again."

"That's a shame, Hirka. But you're strong. Strong enough to forgive. Do you know him well?"

Hirka remembered pumping music. Rime glowing in a dark sea of people. The kiss. Frantic and intense. The mere memory made her heart start pounding.

"Yes. Too well."

"Anger won't help you, Hirka."

"I know, Father Brody."

They looked at each other for a moment. Hirka was waiting for the regret to kick in, regret that she had to leave, but it didn't. This world had never been for her.

"Father Brody, I have to go home. And we probably won't see each other again."

He looked out the window and nodded. She had a feeling he understood a lot more than he was letting on.

"But I have something for you," she said, rummaging in her pocket. She found one of the blood stones and put it on the bedside table. "It's small but very valuable. I promise it's not stolen." She found the piece of paper with Allegra's phone number and left that next to it, putting his glass on top so it wouldn't be lost. "And here's a number you can call to get a good price. Don't let her fool you. She's got lots of money. You can use it to fix the church. Or give it to the poor. Whatever you think's best."

Father Brody opened his mouth, but she warded off his protests by taking his chocolate. "I'll take this, so we're ... what's the word?"

"Even?"

"Even." She put the chocolate in her bag. He gave a croaky laugh, eyes full of wonder, as if he'd forgotten how laughter was supposed to sound.

"Hirka, you have no idea how many times I've asked the Almighty why you came into my life. And why He wanted to put me in here. Burn his house. But I haven't been given any answers."

Hirka shouldered her bag again. "Stefan says some men just want to see the world burn. They don't even know why." She leaned over and kissed his forehead. "Thank you for everything, Father Brody."

She left feeling better than she'd thought she would. Outside, birds chattered in the hedge. The trees had started to come into leaf, and the smell of spring hung in the air.

Stefan was waiting for her in the car park. He was leaning against a car he'd rented but straightened up as soon as he spotted her. He would drive her to the hotel and Graal would collect her from there. Then she would travel to the world of the blind. What would happen after that was anyone's guess.

Stefan ran his fingers through his hair. "Was he okay?"

"He will be."

"Good."

"I gave him one of the stones."

"Brilliant use of resources. It'll be wasted on religious propaganda."

She handed him the two other stones. "Here. Get yourself a life."

"Hirka …"

"None of that, Stefan. You need a life. Pay your debt to Nils. Get him to fly you somewhere."

He stroked the stones with his thumb. "You promised them to Allegra."

"No, I promised she'd get them if I sold them. Now I'm giving them away. That's different. Sell them to her, if you like."

He shook the black stones in his fist. They clacked against each other. "You know I'd do anything for you, right?"

"Yes, I know. You're a real … what's it you always say?"

"Hero?"

"Bastard."

Hirka shoved her hand in her pocket, found the piece of paper, and gave it to him. "I have something else for you. It's a phone number."

"I already have one, but cheers." He grinned and put the stones in his pocket.

"It belongs to someone you know."

He looked at her. His smile faltered, as if he knew something serious was coming. "Who?"

"Your mum."

Stefan's face turned ashen. Hirka was quick to reassure him. "She's doing fine. She's been away from Graal for eight years and managed well. Graal has some of my blood and says she can be saved. If you want."

He leaned back and gripped the roof of the car. Exhaled. His stomach was flatter now.

"She can't be saved, Hirka. Even if the rot is stopped, she's terminally ill. She was ill before she met him. She's going to die, okay?"

"Everyone dies. We're already dead," Hirka replied, stepping closer to him. He immediately let go of the car and put his arms around her. She could no longer feel the chain around his neck. Nowhere to keep teeth.

"Are you sure you know what you're doing?" he asked.

"No, but I have to go anyway."

"Just so you know, that sucks. Are there any magical spells or things I can use? Run naked around the church three times under a full moon or something? I have to be able to visit you somehow, right?"

"You're too old for me," she said with a smile.

He laughed. "So what happened to the ninja? The boy, I mean?"

Hirka didn't reply. She'd thought that Stefan would be the one to fall, and Rime the one to rise. Everything was turned on its head. She felt dizzy. Had she remembered to take her iron tablets?

Hirka pulled away from Stefan and they both got into the car. He reached into the back and grabbed a plastic bag. "I have something for you, too," he said, dropping the bag in her lap.

"A present?"

"No, Jesus, not a fucking present, just a … something I found." He drummed his fingers against the steering wheel.

"I didn't think you were …" She tried to remember the word. It was one of the first he'd taught her. It was in her notebook. "Soppy."

"Soppy?"

"Sentimental. Romantic. Soppy."

"Do you want it or not?" He went to take the bag back, but she tore it away from him and opened it. There was a shirt inside. She held it up against herself. It had short sleeves and was a nice soft green color, with a red cross and white letters on the chest.

"What does it say?"

"I survived the zombie apocalypse," he grinned, as if it were self-explanatory. Then he realized she didn't understand. "The apocalypse, yeah?" He looked at her. "The end of the world? And zombies are kind of like … oh, forget it. It's funny. I considered one of those 'I'm flying solo' things, but …"

She leaned toward him and kissed him on his unshaven jaw. His cheeks flushed.

"You just seem older. Sometimes. That's all," he muttered, starting the car.

THE GATEWAYS

"Are you allowed to land here?" Hirka asked. The question seemed to amuse Graal. He pulled handles and pressed buttons. The insect carriage touched down. The wings slowed on the roof, the noise diminishing to small sighs.

"Yes, you just need permission from the landowner. That was easy enough. Finding out where you came through was more difficult. Had Rime not ended up with the police on his back in Southampton, it could have taken a lot longer to find the right stone circle."

"I see," she said, as if she knew what he was talking about.

"But we'd better get a move on," he said. "Those clouds look heavy, and there's going to be a lot of wind."

They left the carriage and continued on foot across the barren upland. The sky was gray and the wind was picking up already.

Graal was carrying a black box. She was carrying her bag. It was heavier now, because of the box containing the Seer's heart. Proof that the enemy of the people had been defeated. But she hadn't wanted him dead. And Graal had been willing to let her travel with him. Rime's bloodthirst was to blame for Naiell not walking by her side right now.

They reached the crest of one of the rolling hills and saw the stone circle. Around thirty stones, with more lying on the ground. Half consumed by moss and heath. Nothing compared to the raven ring in Mannfalla, but there was something nice about the stones being a bit smaller. And so roughly hewn.

This was where she'd come through. She'd expected to feel the same panic as last time, but she didn't. Maybe because there were no signs of life. Just open countryside. It was as if the city didn't even exist. Here everything was silent. She felt closer to the Might.

They stopped in the middle of the circle. Graal put down the box and undid a catch by the handle. Then he lifted out the glass cage with the raven cadaver. Though it was more skeleton than cadaver, really. Very little remained in the way of flesh and feathers.

Graal looked at her. A few moments passed before he spoke. "It won't be easy."

"So you keep saying," she replied. It was difficult to leave it at that. She wished she could be furious with him. Say that if he was so worried about her, he could let her travel back to Ym and stay there. To Slokna with getting the blind through the gateways. Forget the Might and die among the humans as any respectable person would.

But she couldn't say anything. He had to believe in her. Believe she could help him. Otherwise he would keep her here and not let her fix what needed fixing. Like the beak in Rime's throat.

He'd said there was nothing he could do, but she was fairly sure he was lying. She'd seen the beak crawl out of Urd. Not a pretty sight, and he couldn't have survived. She supposed she'd find out soon enough. The thought made her hair stand on end. If Urd was still alive, he was in the world of the blind, too.

"There are so many things I should have told you," Graal said. "About us. About the people you'll meet."

Hirka shrugged. "Nothing you can say will help prepare me."

She knew that now. She'd been frantic when she'd had to leave Ym. She'd wanted to know more about the humans, to understand where she was going. But the shock would have been just as great regardless of what she'd learned in advance.

She was balanced between worlds. Between various forces and convictions. Everything was far too intertwined. Graal would fight for the blind to enter Ym, where the Might was. Rime would fight to make sure they never set foot there. But there was little he could do now that he was Graal's slave.

And what about her? What would she do?

She'd promised Graal she would lead them to the Might. What she feared most was that she would want it too, in the end. Far too much damage had been done. Damage that couldn't be healed.

"Damayanti will meet you," he said.

"I know, I know. Underground in Ym, and then straight on to your world. I've traveled alone before."

He smiled. Then he jabbed one of his claws into his finger and dripped blood onto the raven. It started to move as if it were coming to life. Jerking. Convulsing. It was a sight she'd never forget.

"Damayanti?" Graal enquired.

"I'm in position now," the raven said in a soft female voice. "Do you see anything?"

Hirka stared between the stones. The grass leaned toward the opening as if the wind were tugging at it from the other side.

"We see it," Graal replied.

Hirka looked at him. His sorrowful gaze was fixed on the stones. A black longing that made her feel sorry for him. She didn't know whether she loved him or hated him. Her father. Her deadborn father. Who had created her to command an army. To bring about the destruction of Ym.

But maybe it didn't matter whether you loved or hated.

The clouds rolled darkly behind him. A storm was coming. He caressed her cheek with a claw. "Good luck, blood of my blood."

She nodded and hugged her notebook to her chest. Memories from the human world. She would need it again. New things to learn. Things she would wish she'd never learned. The needle of the compass on the cover swung this way and that. As if there were no north or south anymore.

Hirka looked down at her yellow boots. Then she looked up and walked between the stones.

The space between worlds enveloped her.

ACKNOWLEDGMENTS

First and foremost, my most heartfelt thanks to everyone who made *Odin's Child* a success by reading, recommending, reviewing, and sharing. Particularly to all my superfans who follow me on Facebook, Twitter, and Instagram. You're out of your minds, and you know who you are. I see you, I promise. And thank you to Fabelprosaens Venner, who awarded *Odin's Child* the Fabel Prize, and to everyone who nominated it for the Booksellers' Prize, the Book Bloggers' Prize, and the Ministry of Culture's First Book Prize. I'm touched and deeply grateful.

Living with someone who is always in two universes takes superhuman patience. Thank you so much for yours, dearest Kim. The same can be said to Mom, and to the rest of my family, friends, and colleagues. I promise to call you soon …

No woman is an island. Thank you so much dear Tone Almhjell (*The Twistrose Key*) and Tonje Tornes (*Nymph*), my magnificent fellow authors and sounding boards at Write Away. Tonje said it best on Facebook when she said: "I never needed the heart emoticon until I met you." <3 And of course, thank you to my other amazing writer friends at Fabelprosalauget.

I'd have collapsed by page three without coffee. Thank you to the lovely ladies at Camillo Bastrup. Sorry for monopolizing the back table for over a year. And to Mean Bean, where I also spend a lot of time. Similarly, thank you to Supreme Roastworks, Fuglen, and Java for my caffeine fixes in Oslo.

The launch party for *Odin's Child* was unforgettable! Thank you to every single person who attended, particularly those who helped me arrange it: Maja Selmer Medgård, my right hand for the evening; Frederik Kolderup and Jørgen Ljøstad at Non Dos; Jon Marius Sletten, the inked chef; Anders Braathen, the hipster chef; Ragni Hansen, who baked tail cake; and Halvor and Robin at Fuglen, who provided the setting.

There is something very special about Gyldendal Norsk Forlag. Thank you so much to all you lovely, clever people. Particularly my wonderful editor Espen Dahl, and my former editor Marianne Koch Knudsen, who took *The Rot* with her into retirement. And an extra thank you to Eva C. Thesen, a real rock.

Thank you to Anne Cathrine and Henrik at Gyldendal Agency, The Raven Rings' outward face; to Pasi Loman, the agent who took the series to Brazil; to Maja Lindqvist, who took it to Sweden; to Erich Kruse Nielsen, an exceptionally dedicated narrator at Lydbokforlaget; and to translators Ina Steinman and Ylva Klempe.

Then to the experts who have contributed to *The Rot* with their research. Thank you to:

Alexander K. Lykke, linguistic consultant who developed the language of the blind

Nils Chaboud, who knows about flying

Rolv Bruun, who knows about churches and church bells

Doctor Yngvar Hansen-Tangen, who knows how blood works
Sidsel Yndestad, who knows about nursing

Special thanks to Lise Myhre, the marvelous creator of Nemi, the character who proudly flies the flag for otherness. She also loves the Raven Rings.

GLOSSARY

CHARACTERS IN THIS WORLD

Allegra Sanuto	a wealthy woman
Father Brody	a priest who gives Hirka shelter
Graal	one of the blind
Hirka	the tailless girl
Isac	a blood slave
Jay	Hirka's friend
Naiell	one of the blind
Nils	an associate of Stefan's
Silvio Sanuto	Allegra's ailing husband
Stefan Barone	a hunter

CHARACTERS IN YM

Damayanti	a dancer
Eirik Viljarsón	chieftain of Ravnhov
Hlosnian	a stone carver and stone whisperer
Ilume An-Elderin	Rime's grandmother; a deceased councillor
Kuro	a raven
Lindri	a teahouse owner
Northree	a shepherd in the library
Svarteld	master of Kolkagga
Sylja Glimmeråsen	the wealthiest girl in Elveroa

Tein	son of Eirik of Ravnhov
Urd Vanfarinn	a former councillor
Vetle	a simple boy; Ramoja's son

COUNCILLORS

Rime An-Elderin

Sigra Kleiv	**Jarladin An-Sarin**
Leivlugn Taid	**Miane Fell**
Noldhe Saurpassarid	**Freid Vangard**
Eir Kobb	**Garm Darkdaggar**
Saulhe Jakinnin	**Tyrme Jekense**

PLACES IN YM

the Alldjup	a gorge with the River Stryfe running through it
Blindból	a forbidden mountain range
Bromfjell	a mountain near Ravnhov, home to the stone circle where Urd opened the gateway for the blind
Eisvaldr	a walled city within Mannfalla; the home of the Council
Elveroa	a small village where Hirka and Rime spent some of their childhoods
Mannfalla	the biggest city in Ym
the Ora	a river running through Mannfalla
Ravnhov	an independent settlement in the region of Foggard
the Rite Hall	a large ceremonial hall built around an old stone circle where the Rite occurred each year

CONCEPTS

binding	the act of using or drawing upon the Might
blindcraft	the feared and forbidden way in which the blind use the Might
the Book of the Seer	the official history of Ym

the blind	an ancient people feared throughout Ym. Synonymous with deadborn, nábyrn, and Umpiri
child of Odin	someone from a world beyond Ym, born without a tail, who cannot bind the Might. Synonymous with embling and menskr
the Council	the twelve individuals who interpret the word of the Seer and govern all of Ym
Dreyri	high-born Umpiri
the forgotten	blood slaves abandoned by their master
Kolkagga	the Council's assassins
the Might	a powerful current of energy that can be drawn upon for strength
the Rite	a coming-of-age ceremony during which young people were given the Seer's blessing and protection
the rot	a disease believed by ymlings to be carried by children of Odin. Also a derogatory term used to refer to them
Slokna	where the dead go to rest
the Seer's tree	a tree of glass and stone where the Seer was believed to live, destroyed by Rime
twalif	a low-ranking military commander
the Twelve	the warriors who—with the help of the Seer—once defended Ym against the blind
Vardar	blood slaves still in their master's favor
ymlings	people from the land of Ym; those born with tails and the ability to bind the Might

THE LANGUAGE OF THE BLIND

Headwords unless otherwise noted are:
For nouns nom. sing., for verbs present infinitive (see *Abbreviations* below glossary). Nouns are listed with grammatical gender after the headword (m., f., or n.). Verbs are listed with inflectional class (v1, v2, or v3).

Entry	Explanation
dósem v3	to be, copular verb; to exist
esse acc. sing.	you (implying that the object is of lower social status): acc. sing. of *iss*
koy interj. indec.	see! (corresponds to Latin *ecce*!, English *lo*!)
koyem v1	to sense, to perceive with the senses
kroyo loc. sing.	where (referring to place): locative singular of *krai*
kwainsair n.	cruel imprisonment; prison cell, prison
óz	I
ozá	I (implying that the speaker is of higher social status)
sulni m.	mayfly, small harmless insect
umkhadari m.	brother (formal)
umǫni m.	the Language, the Tongue (mostly when referring to the language of the First; other languages are called *umþéles*); i. e. "something closely related to the tongue"
waiad n.	my, n. sing. of *wai* my, m. sing.

Abbreviations

acc.	accusative
f.	feminine
ind.	indeclinable
interj.	interjection
loc.	locative
m.	masculine
n.	neuter
nom.	nominative
pl.	plural
sing.	singular
v1–v3	verb, inflectional class 1–3

The list is just a taste of the language of the blind, which was developed in collaboration with linguist Alexander K. Lykke.

Siri Pettersen made her sensational debut in 2013 with the Norwegian publication of *Odin's Child*, the first book in The Raven Rings trilogy, which has earned numerous awards and nominations at home and abroad. Siri has a background as a designer and comics creator. Her roots are in Finnsnes and Trondheim, but she now lives in Oslo, where you're likely to find her in a coffee shop. According to fellow writers, her superpower is "mega motivation"—the ability to inspire other creative souls. Visit her at SiriPettersen.com, or follow her on Twitter or Instagram @SiriPettersen.

Siân Mackie is a translator of Scandinavian literature into English. They were born in Scotland and have an MA in Scandinavian Studies and an MSc in Literary Translation as a Creative Practice from the University of Edinburgh. They have translated a wide range of works, from young adult and children's literature—including Ingunn Thon's *A Postcard for Ollis*, which was nominated for the 2021 Carnegie Medal—to thrillers and nonfiction. They live in Southampton on the south coast of England.

Paul Russell Garrett translates from Norwegian and Danish, with drama holding a particular interest for him. He has translated a dozen plays and has a further ten published translations to his name, including Lars Mytting's *The Sixteen Trees of the Somme*, long-listed for the International Dublin Literary Award, and a pair of novels by Christina Hesselholdt, *Companions* and *Vivian*. Originally from Vancouver, Paul is based in east London.

Siân and Paul have previously collaborated on a translation of *A Doll's House* by Henrik Ibsen, which was commissioned by Foreign Affairs theater company and performed in 2015 in east London. They hope their shared passion for bringing Norwegian literature to English-speaking audiences will continue in future collaborations, and they are currently translating the next book in the Raven Rings series.

WELCOME TO THE UNIVERSE OF SIRI PETTERSEN,

Re-read the book that started it all.

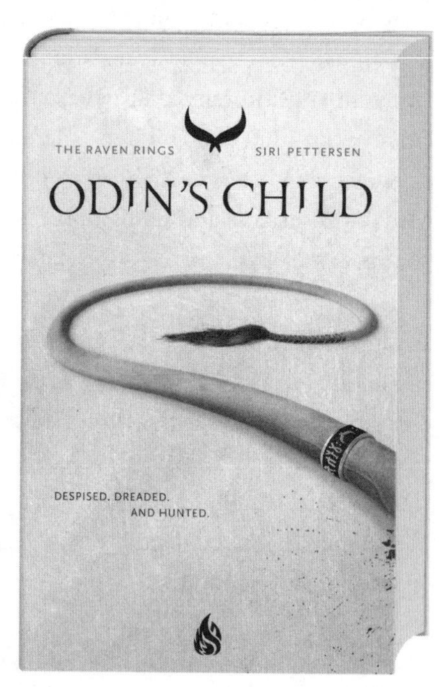

The Raven Rings – Odin's Child (1)
Available now!
ISBN 978-1-64690-000-8

"AN INTRICATE, ENGAGING NOVEL."
—*KIRKUS REVIEWS*

Brinnlanda
Ende
Norrvarje
Ulvheim
Nöttland
Vestvarjin
Varjin
Norr
Fross
Eiksbana
Frossabu
Gardfjella
Vestymsjo
Elversa
Hrafnfell
Foggard
Ravnhov
Blindbol
Kolskaug
Mannfalla
and Eisvalde
Brekka
Teygge
Brott
Kleiva
Hjalt
Kleiv
Insbrott
Eldrin
Ora
Nådvellir
Orakana
Himlifall
Småle
Seule
Jåltnes
Kettli
Saurpassa
Angbrō
Kaupe
Mara
Jonnav
Ko